Wha [illegible] about
CASSANDRA and the COWBOY

...a breathtaking Western novel filled with suspense and rock-solid truths based on the Word of God.

Karen Seelenbinder, author of
Dear Caregiver: Take a Moment and Walk with Me

Janine Mick Wills has crafted an exceptional historical romance set in Texas. The dialogue captures the tension of the period as well as the dynamic interactions between the characters—excellent!

Grant P. Ferguson, author of the ***Cliftopolis*** *series*

...a brilliant combination of faith, hope, and young love set in the southwestern part of 19th century Texas.

SG Myers, author of the ***Amazing Grace*** *series*

...has all the elements of a delightful read and will stay with you long after you finish the last page.

Carolina Judy, book reviewer

CASSANDRA AND THE COWBOY

JANINE MICK WILLS

Journey Fiction

Published by Journey Fiction
Las Vegas, Nevada
www.journeyfiction.com

Scripture quotations taken from the King James Version of the Bible.

Cover design by Jennifer L. Farey

ISBN 978-1-946892-24-9

Acknowledgements

First and foremost, to my Lord and Savior Jesus Christ,
may my writing always honor and glorify You.

To my dearest hubby Jeff,
thank you for introducing me to the Lord
and for giving me the freedom to spread my writing wings.

To the best three "kids" in the world, Jason, Jennifer, and Jared,
you three are my greatest accomplishment and biggest blessing.

To Mary Helen Peterfy Mick, who's now in heaven with the Lord,
I did it, Mommy! Thank you for believing in my abilities.
I wish you were here to read this book.

To my publisher and editor Jennifer Farey of Journey Fiction,
thank you for taking a chance on me and answering my "thousands"
of questions.

To the greatest Launch Team ever,
thank you for loving Cassandra almost as much as me, for finding
those last minute boo-boos, and for helping me
tell the "world" about Cass and company.

And to Sandy Pickett,
thank you for holding my hand while I wrote Cass.
I couldn't have done this without you, Pal.

And we know that all things work together for good to them that love God, to them who are the called according to his purpose.

Romans 8:28

One

Goose Neck Ridge, Texas
August 1887

Cassandra Pickett began pacing her bedroom floor as the morning sun first marked the horizon. Now, the sun topped the roof of the barn and still she paced, counting the reasons she did not want to marry Phillip Brigham. But with each pass of the room and each swish of her emerald gown, her resolve weakened. She had to marry her neighbor or risk losing the Triple P.

She dug her fingernails into the palms of her hands, finding the pain easier to bear than the confusion in her heart. She bowed her head in prayer.

"Lord, Mama and I have been praying the same thing for weeks now. Since it seems you only hear the prayers of preachers and righteous people, I can understand why you don't answer my prayers, but why won't you answer Mama's? She's more righteous than any ten people I know."

Cassandra cast her gaze upward to the peaked ceiling of her bedroom. Did her prayers even make it that far? Or did they fly out the window and disappear into the clear Texas sky? She wasn't sure, but she continued praying, just in case God was listening.

"Phillip will be here soon, Lord, and he'll want my answer. Should I marry him or not? If you'd give me a sign, I sure would appreciate it. Oh… and if you're not too busy, please send some rain."

She cocked her head and waited for God's reply. The clock's pendulum not only marked the futility of her heavenly father answering her prayer, but it also bore witness to Phillip's arrival in half an hour. The thought twisted Cassandra's stomach into a knot.

She breathed in the calming scent of her mother's roses wafting through the bedroom window. *Breathe in 1, 2, 3, 4. Breathe out 1, 2, 3—*

"God doesn't care, God doesn't care," two blackbirds seemed to taunt from outside the window.

The pair perched in the oak tree Cassandra's father planted twenty years ago when he carved the Triple P Ranch from the dry Texas soil. Lightning had struck the tree, leaving a jagged rift in its bark. But the great oak bore the scar and refused to succumb to outside forces that might attack its weakened state.

"If it's true you don't care, Lord, you've left me no other choice." Cassandra crossed the room and shut the window with a bang. The glass panes rattled, scattering the ebony doomsayers into a cloudless sky, which hadn't seen rain in two weeks.

"I'll marry Phillip, but I won't be a trophy upon his arm." She yanked the comb from her chignon, releasing auburn waves that fell in riotous confusion to her waist. Deeming her appearance still too fitting, she crumpled and tugged her gown until it, like her disheveled hair, mocked its former beauty.

"Cassandra Jane. Whatever are you doing?"

Cassandra cringed at her mother's voice. Helen Pickett had crossed the pinewood floor with only a whisper of sound, but the dismay in her dove-gray eyes spoke volumes. "Phillip will be arriving soon. What will he think when he sees you in such disarray?"

Cassandra's words tumbled out like Goose Neck Creek after a good, hard rain. "I don't give a fig what Phillip thinks about me. In fact, the less he thinks about me, the better."

"The two of you were once good friends. Will you ever tell me what happened?"

Cassandra reined in a sigh. Only her father had known of Phillip's betrayal three years ago. She would not ask her mother to bear that burden as well. "I don't love him. That's all."

"If it is providence for you to marry Phillip, you will learn to love him. God helped me love your father when he—"

"Of course, you loved Papa. He was kind as well as handsome, and he fell in love with you the moment you met. Phillip doesn't appeal to me like that at all. Well, I suppose he is handsome." Cassandra lifted her chin. "As for God, if he hadn't allowed Papa to die in the first place, we wouldn't be in this predicament."

"How many times must I tell you? God is not to blame for your father's death nor for our financial dilemma. Your father was the one who…" Helen patted the gaily-colored quilt covering the bed. "Please, darling, sit down. I have something long overdue to tell you."

Cassandra rejected the invitation. "You've told me time and time again God answers prayers, but right now he and I are on different sides of the same fence. When I get to heaven, I'm gonna march right up and ask him why he allowed all this to happen."

Helen raised a pale hand to her throat. "Cassandra, how can you talk in such a manner?" She smoothed a wrinkle from her black dress of mourning as if the gesture would help maintain her calm demeanor.

Cassandra bit her knuckle. *Lord, I've done it again. I've upset Mama. Why can't I be like her and trust you in the midst of turmoil?* She silently quoted a Bible verse about bridling the tongue. Her mother insisted she memorize Scripture to aid in times of need, but Cassandra found she remembered the verses after she needed them, not beforehand.

"Mama, you can stop worrying about the Triple P. I've decided to marry Phillip. He has more than enough money to repay our loan."

"Are you sure? I do not want you to marry him because of the ranch. Ever since we spoke with Mr. Higgins, I have prayed for another way. But it appears for the first time, God has not answered my prayers." Her gaze left Cassandra to stare out the bedroom window.

"I'm afraid he has answered them. Our salvation is in the form of Phillip Brigham." Cassandra trudged to the armoire to pick out a new gown. "Don't worry. I'll do as you say and learn to–to care for him."

Even for her mother's sake, Cassandra refused to say the word *love*. Though one day her heart might forgive Phillip, the two of them would never share the same kind of love as her parents had.

Without waiting for a reply, she opened the armoire door and slid her navy gown off its hanger. The subtle folds of material gathered in the back and trickled to the floor, but the gown weighed heavy in Cassandra's hands. As heavy as the lie she'd just told her mother.

☆☆☆

Helen descended the staircase with a heavy heart. Halfway down the stairs, she stopped and caressed a framed picture hanging on the wall. If she had known the photograph was to be the last one taken of her husband, she would have insisted she and Cassandra join him in another.

"Why did you do it, Samuel?" she asked his smiling face, knowing full well the reason. She gripped the banister and prayed. "Oh, Lord, I should have told Cassandra the truth, but she loved her father so. The knowledge of what he did would only bring her more grief."

At the foot of the stairs, she called for the housekeeper. "Maria, *¿dónde está?* I need you, please."

A Mexican woman wearing a black dress smudged with flour, waddled through the dining room doors. The aroma of a freshly-baked apple pie trailed after her. The heat from the kitchen had caused wisps of coal-black hair to escape the bun on the back of her head.

"Did you call, Señora Pickett?" Maria Martinez wiped her hands on an apron circling a rounded waist that could no longer hide the baby growing within.

"Would you please help Cassandra change into another gown?"

Maria's dark-chocolate eyes widened. "What is wrong with the one she had on? It was beautiful and matched her eyes *muy perfecto*."

Helen was about to agree when the sound of knocking peppered the hallway. Maria aimed for the front door.

"Señor Brigham has arrived." Maria's announcement did little to hide her displeasure. "I saw him ride up on his big yellow horse. Do you want me to run him off?"

"Certainly not," Helen scolded. "I will let him in. Quickly. Go help Cassandra."

Maria clambered up the stairs, muttering all the way in Spanish. When her footsteps had receded, Helen assumed a pleasant face and opened the door. She craned her neck to look up at Phillip. His charcoal-gray suit and brocade waistcoat were more fitting for an eastern gentleman than a Texas rancher.

"Good morning, Mrs. Pickett." Phillip's voice held the promise of an accomplished baritone.

Good manners kept Helen from saying that the black top hat he tucked under his arm was a bit pretentious for a mid-morning call. "Hello, Phillip. Will you please come in?"

Phillip's smile almost reached eyes a shade lighter than his suit. "I would be delighted. And how are you this fine morning?" He ran a hand through hair the same color as his hat.

"I am well, thank you. We were not expecting you for another half-hour. Cassandra is not quite ready. If you would be so kind as to wait in the study, I will tell her you have arrived."

☆☆☆

Cassandra fiddled with the lace neckline of her chemise and toyed with the idea of feigning a headache. She could crawl back into bed, throw the quilt over her head, and—

Maria bustled into the bedroom and scowled at the crumpled emerald gown laying on the floor. Cassandra braced against the forthcoming reprimand. Maria did not disappoint.

"Now I see why your mamá asked me to help you. Just look at your beautiful dress. And after I spent all that time ironing it." She picked up the garment and laid it over the footboard of the bed. "Sometimes I do not understand what goes on inside that head of yours, young lady."

Maria helped Cassandra slip back into her petticoat. "It is good your figure does not need a corset. There is no time to lace it up now. Señor Brigham has arrived early." She smacked her lips as though the mere mention of Phillip's name had put a bad taste in her mouth. She snatched the navy gown off the bed, gave it a shake, and raised her chin. Cassandra meekly stretched up her arms for Maria to slide the garment over her head.

Maria deftly fastened the cloth-covered buttons on the back of the gown. "Does your behavior have anything to do with Señor Brigham's visit?"

"Oh, Maria. I've got to marry him."

"And this is what you want?"

"What else can I do? We don't have the money to repay Papa's loan." Cassandra frowned as she skimmed her hair with a silver-plated brush. "Mama thinks I can learn to love him after we're married."

"That is because your dear mamá chooses to think the best of everything."

Though Maria's tone had lightened, Cassandra knew she'd struggled to do it. Her opinion of Phillip was less than stellar, probably based on the gossip she shared with Bella, the Lazy Acres cook. Bella had been in the Brigham employ since before Phillip's birth and took great pride in knowing everything that happened around Goose Neck Ridge.

Helen hurried into the room. "Cassandra, you must finish getting ready. Phillip is waiting."

Maria rummaged through the vanity drawer and pulled out a navy ribbon. She gathered Cassandra's hair at the base of her neck and tied the ribbon into a bow. "That will do. Now scoot. Your mamá and I will stay here and pray while you talk to Señor Brigham."

Cassandra complied, knowing life proceeded more smoothly when she followed Maria's orders. But as she trudged downstairs, she dreaded her forthcoming answer to the man whose purse strings held the fate of the Triple P Ranch.

Two

Phillip waited for Helen to climb the stairs before he entered the study. The room was tastefully decorated and smelled of lemon and beeswax. Surely a testament to that busybody housekeeper.

Striding to the window, he skirted a pair of Chippendale chairs facing an inlaid writing table with carved legs. He squinted against the glare of the sun that was beating a path across the never-ending prairie. How could anyone endure Texas with its days of oppressive heat and nights that chilled the bones?

Grandfather, may you rest in peace, why in heaven's name did you leave Boston and come here in the first place? You may have built a ranch that surpassed every other in the territory, but Lazy Acres or not, this land drains the life out of a man and destroys his soul.

Phillip's consternation turned into a satisfied smile. The plans he'd set into play months ago were about to reach fruition. Grandfather would be proud. Like him, Phillip had multiplied the hand he'd been dealt, but unlike the Brigham patriarch, he planned to take the family's fortune back to Boston, not away from it.

Boston. Ever since he and his father visited his maternal grandparents last year, Phillip had longed to return to the city of elegant mansions, intellectual pursuits, and high society soirees. The McAllister influence may have opened every elite door in the city, but Phillip's good looks and intellect had kept them that way. He was determined to move to Boston and purchase an estate to rival the grandeur of the one his grandparents owned. Nothing could make him happier than to leave Texas and never look back, but first, he had to convince Cassandra to marry him.

Phillip crossed to the oak bookcase dominating the far end of the room. Its shelves bore the weight of a hundred tomes lined up like stiff-backed soldiers. The books ranged from classic literature to fictional works by little-known authors. He removed a copy of *A Tale of Two Cities* and read the first page before sandwiching the book back between *Silas Marner* and *Little Women.*

"Samuel Pickett," he said to the empty room, "your taste in furnishings was impeccable, but why did you bring all these books to this God-forsaken land? They only put more ideas into that headstrong daughter of yours."

The swish of material interrupted Phillip's soliloquy. Even with his back to the door, he knew Cassandra had entered the room. It was the smell of her rose-scented perfume. His breath caught in his throat at the sight of her. Could any woman be more beautiful?

His gaze started at her slippered feet, stayed an extra moment where her gown hugged her slim waist, then bypassed the high neckline to stop at her exquisite jade-colored eyes. The heightened color of her cheeks and the loose tendrils at her temples led him to believe she'd run down the stairs to greet him. He rather fancied that idea.

Taking care to keep from rushing to her side, Phillip closed the gap between them with measured tread. "Angels themselves must envy you this morning, Cassandra. For even heaven itself cannot be as beautiful as you."

"Did I hear you say Papa's name? Something about books and God? I know you enjoyed reading, but it's been years since I've heard you mention the Lord's name. Other than the time Smokey stomped on your foot." Her full lips turned up into a smile.

"Uh, yes. You're right. I told the Lord your father amassed quite the collection." He clasped her hands in his. "We have an important matter to discuss. Our betrothal. Have you made up your mind?"

Cassandra's expression turned serious as she wiggled her hands free. "Please, Phillip. Couldn't you loan us the money instead? I promise we'll repay you."

Phillip checked his impatience. Not only had Samuel passed his love of learning onto Cassandra but also his dismal financial acumen. Everyone but she knew money had slipped through his fingers like warm butter in July.

He lowered his voice and talked slowly, hoping she would understand this time. "I've told you, it's not good business to lend money to friends. When we marry, I'll repay your loan and restore your ranch. It's a shame your father didn't leave it in better condition."

"Papa did everything he could to save the Triple P. How unfortunate his pockets weren't as deep as yours."

Ignoring the lift of Cassandra's chin, Phillip continued the speech he'd practiced on the ride over. "You're right. Your father did try. I meant to say, the ranch needs work, which takes money. My money will be yours the moment we marry. After our honeymoon, we'll rebuild your ranch. Then we can leave Texas and move to Boston, where people are civilized." There, he'd said it.

"Boston? What about the Triple P?"

"You know I plan to sell my ranch after the period of mourning for my father passes. Our marriage will restore the land your father took from me and increase the value of Lazy Acres. Between the sale of it and the Triple P, I–I mean we–will be rich." Phillip regretted his ill-chosen words as soon as he spoke them, but why couldn't she realize his design would benefit them both?

Cassandra's eyes glittered the color of an emerald necklace he'd once seen her mother wear. "Mama and I would never sell the Triple P. And we both know my father obtained your land fair and square."

"With your father's passing, it's too late to worry about what he did or didn't do. But with my help, the bank won't foreclose on the Triple P and leave you and your mother destitute. And in the process we can make a handsome profit from it."

"Is money all you think about?"

Though his conscience warned otherwise, Phillip leaned closer and whispered in her ear. "I also dream of the day you become my wife."

Phillip correctly guessed her intent and blocked the door to keep her from fleeing the room. "Please, Cassandra. Remember the time we rode to White Top Mountains and carved our initials on the side of the cave? You said you loved me, and we would marry when you turned eighteen. You're twenty now."

"I know how old I am, and you can't hold me accountable for words I spoke six years ago. Yes, I did say I loved you. You were my best friend, but what does a fourteen-year-old know about love? And the love you want from me now is far different."

She elbowed him aside. "I need some fresh air. Out of my way, please." She picked up the sides of her dress and sashayed out of the study. The screen door squeaked open and then banged shut behind her.

Phillip closed his eyes and blew through pursed lips. Why did he always allow that woman to get under his skin? He followed Cassandra into the heat of the day and caught up to her at the end of the veranda, but not before she turned her back to him.

"Cassandra, you will love Boston, and my grandparents can provide us an introduction into polite society."

"I have no desire to live in society, polite or otherwise. I'm perfectly happy here. And what about Mama and Maria? And Rafael, Carlos, and Roberto?"

"Your mother would come with us, of course. And as far as your Mexicans, I'm sure they could find work somewhere in Goose Neck Ridge."

"Those four are like family and with Maria expecting…" She waved her hands in frustration. "How could you think I would leave them or the Triple P?"

Phillip lifted a silken strand of hair from Cassandra's cheek. "Please. I can make you forget this ranch if you'd let me." Hoping to kiss her sweet lips, he drew her into his arms, all the while silencing the rationale to use caution.

Out of the corner of his eye, he saw her hand rise to slap him. He caught her wrist and pinned it to her side. "Is that any way to treat your future husband?" His lips came down on hers.

"If ya know what's good for ya," a deep voice rumbled across the yard, "you'll unhand the young lady."

Phillip spun on his heels. A sandy-haired cowboy stood no more than thirty feet away. Where had he come from?

The man's stormy-blue eyes locked onto Phillip's. "Looks to me like the little missy's not interested in ya."

"Who are you?" Phillip demanded.

The cowboy's strides ate the distance between the two men. "It doesn't matter who I am, but I suggest you apologize to her lest I forget my momma's good manners and send you packin'."

Phillip took a step toward the stranger. "Why, you—"

The cowboy whipped out his six-shooter and brought it within a hair's breadth of Phillip's forehead. He could smell the cold steel.

"I said apologize and be on your way."

Clenching his hands, Phillip clicked his heels together and bowed to Cassandra. "Miss Pickett." He straightened to his nearly six-foot height, which left him several inches shorter than the stranger. "You better watch your back. The next time we meet, I'll be holding a gun."

He swung onto the back of his palomino stallion and dug his heels into the animal's sides. The horse whinnied and shot forward, sending a cloud of dust into the air. A few minutes later, Phillip looked back over his shoulder. The Triple P appeared no more than a speck on the southern horizon.

Three

Cassandra sagged against the porch railing, begging her knees not to buckle. Memories from three years ago flooded her soul. She'd only been seventeen when Phillip—She stopped her mind from visiting that dark place.

The cowboy slid his gun back into its holster. "Ma'am, when I rode up here, I didn't know what kind of welcome I'd get, but I sure wasn't expectin' this one." The heels of his boots scuffed the floorboards as he angled across the porch toward her.

Cassandra peeked up at the cowboy through veiled lashes. He was tall like Phillip and their tanned complexions were similar, though Phillip never would have appeared in public without shaving first. And those eyes–a Texas sky right before twilight.

She scolded her silly, fluttering heart. *What is wrong with me? This man just chased off the Triple P's only hope, and here I stand like a lovesick calf.*

Planting her hands on her hips, she looked up into the cowboy's amused eyes. "Do you have any idea what you just did?"

"Beggin' your pardon, ma'am, I thought I chased off an unwanted varmint. Aren't ya glad I arrived when I did?"

Cassandra caught the word *yes* before it slipped from her lips.

The cowboy stepped closer. "In my opinion, that fellow needed his plow cleaned."

"I did not ask for your opinion nor did I ask you to barge up here and interfere."

"Well, I didn't exactly barge, ma'am. My horse just trotted here. And I didn't think savin' a damsel in distress was interferin'." He thrust a hand under her chin. "Let's try again. My name's Matthew Atkins, but my friends call me Matt."

When Cassandra eyed his outstretched hand, he chuckled. "Ma'am, your name?"

"Stop calling me ma'am. My name is Cassandra Jane Pickett, and I am not a damsel in distress."

"Plum nice to meet ya, Cassandra Jane." Matt's eyes twinkled a merry blue. "I meant no harm callin' you a damsel, but you did look a wee bit in distress."

Cassandra tried to flounce past the cowboy, but he sidestepped and blocked her path. She pulled a wry face and tried again, but this time, she tripped on the hem of her dress. Matt's arms snaked out and caught her, his calloused thumbs brushing the inside of her wrists. Cassandra fought the quiver edging up her back.

"Would you kindly unhand me?" she asked, breaking free from his hold.

"Whoa there. Would you mind tellin' me why you're as upset as a prairie hen dunked sideways in the river? Where I come from, a man who doesn't protect a woman's honor isn't worth spittin' on."

"My honor was fully under control, thank you, and I did not need your help, and I certainly don't want your spit."

"I don't mean to feed your fire, ma'am, but things looked different from where I stood."

"Maybe you should stand someplace else."

Matt shuffled a step to his left and presented a maddening grin. "How about over here? Better?"

"That's not what I meant, and you know it." She stomped a foot. "Are all men so aggravating?"

"I'll be the first to admit we men have our moments. But the one I chased off didn't deserve a moment or the time of day." He scanned the field and pointed to the three vaqueros working a herd of cattle. "I'm surprised those hands didn't run that scalawag off."

"Those men know I can take care of myself. And it's their job to watch the cattle while my father and th–thirty of the men are rounding up strays. They'll be back any moment."

Matt's lips quirked into a smile. "Thirty men to round up some strays, huh? You must have quite the spread here." He looped his thumbs under his worn belt and rocked back on his heels. "If you don't mind, I'll stick around until your father gets back. I'd like to ask him if he's hirin'."

"I do mind, and Papa is not hiring."

The screen door squeaked open. Helen stepped onto the porch with a curious expression. Cassandra's pride kept her from running over and hugging her mother. Mama would know how to get rid of the stranger.

Helen crossed the porch to Cassandra's side. "Did Phillip leave already?"

"This cowboy chased him off."

Helen reached out to touch Cassandra's arm. "Is everything all right?"

"The name's Matt Atkins, ma'am." He removed his Stetson and raked fingers through his thick hair. "Your daughter's fine. I'm sorry if I stuck my nose where it didn't belong, but a rascal like that needed runnin' off."

Helen tried to speak. "Mr. Atkins—"

"Call me, Matt. See, Cassandra Jane here—"

"I can speak for myself, thank you."

"Cassandra, please." The brief look from her mother silenced Cassandra. Helen searched Matt's face. "Why would Phillip act in an unbecoming manner?"

"I think he was a mite bit too charmed by your daughter. Can't say I blame him. She's purty like her mama."

Helen's cheeks colored pink. Cassandra's mouth dropped open. How could Mama fall for such a blatant attempt at flattery? Couldn't she see right through this cowboy?

Helen's uplifted hand kept Cassandra from calling out Matt's effusive compliment. "If Phillip was not behaving like a gentleman, I am grateful for your arrival."

"I was glad to help the little lady out." His gaze took in the barn and surrounding fields. "If you don't mind my sayin' so, ya got a nice spread here."

Helen's face brightened. She settled on one of the wrought iron chairs scattered the length of the porch. A loose floorboard creaked but held steady.

Cassandra suppressed a groan. Her mother loved nothing better than talking about the Lord and the Triple P. Like most of the neighboring ranches, the Triple P saw few visitors. Anyone who stopped by before noon received an invitation to sup and often enjoyed fellowship until the afternoon shadows touched the porch. Cassandra sent up a fervent prayer God would help her mother speak quickly and get rid of Matt before the noonday meal.

"After the war ended and before we married, my husband w–worked—" Helen cleared her throat. "He worked his way back here from Colorado. He planned to farm, but when he saw all the maverick cattle roaming free and the cow towns popping up across the plains, he thought ranching might be easier than pushing a plow. With only three thousand acres, he never became a Texas cattle baron, but God was good. He gave us all we needed. At least for the first nineteen years of our marriage."

An orphaned calf, with problems of its own, lowed from the barn. "Mama," Cassandra said, "Buddy's calling for his dinner. I'm sure he needs tending to, and we've taken up enough of Mr. Atkins's time."

"Rafael fed Buddy before breakfast," Helen replied. "You can give him his bottle after we eat."

"Well, maybe we should let Mr. Atkins get going anyway."

"I've got no place to rush off to. I'd like to hear the rest of the story. And, Cassandra *Jane*, I said my friends call me Matt."

"I just met you. I would hardly call us friends."

"Cassandra." Helen's eyes showed a hint of annoyance.

"Go, on, Mrs. Pickett," Matt encouraged. "What happened after those nineteen years?"

"Last summer we suffered the worst drought since we settled here."

Matt nodded in understanding. "Yep. The Great Drought of '86. You're lucky you're so far south. You missed the bad winter before it. Many of the spreads up north lost most of their livestock. When cattle prices dropped, they had to sell out."

"True, but we lost over half our cattle and fifty of our horses. God uses trials to strengthen his children, but after the drought he chose the greatest of all…"

She stared off into the distance. Cassandra assumed her mother had returned to the past before Papa died and they had labored side-by-side, building a life for themselves and then later for her, their only child.

"Ma'am, I didn't mean to remind ya of unpleasant memories. If you'd point me in the direction of your husband, I'd like to see if he's hirin'."

A puzzled expression crossed Helen's face. "I thought Cassandra had told you. My husband passed away nine months ago."

Matt's side-long glance gave Cassandra a sudden urge to study the floorboard under her feet.

"I'm sorry, Mrs. Pickett. I didn't know."

"If Samuel was alive, Phillip Brigham would not have been here in the first pla—"

"That was Phillip Brigham?"

Why had the cowboy's eyes turned stormy? "Do you know our neighbor?" Cassandra voiced her suspicion.

Matt rubbed his stubbled chin. "No. I heard he owns a big spread around here."

Helen pointed toward the range of hills to the north. "He owns the Lazy Acres on the other side of White Top Mountains. His ranch also extends east toward Goose Neck Ridge and is the closest one to ours. I believe in his own way, he wants to help us."

"Help? What do you mean?"

"That's our business," Cassandra said. This stranger had no privilege to their affairs. She threw her mother a desperate look. "Isn't it, Mama?"

"It is a long story, but I am afraid we can only afford to pay the few men we have. You could try the Diamond D Ranch three miles south of here or the Fairfax spread on our western border. I would not suggest Lazy Acres. I doubt Phillip would be pleased to see you again." She smiled up at Matt.

"If you don't mind my sayin', ma'am, I like the looks of this place. My needs are few, and I'm willin' to exchange an honest day's work for a dry roof over my head and food in my belly."

"We're not hiring," Cassandra said. "Besides your penchant for interfering, it appears you don't hear well, either."

"Cassandra Jane," Helen admonished.

Cassandra shrank back against the side of the house, feeling like a fool.

"Penchant?" A puzzled look crossed Matt's face. "I don't know what that means, but if you'd give me a chance, you'll be happy with my work. And if you're not, I'll pack up my saddlebag and bedroll and be gone faster than a Texas twister."

Helen studied Matt. Cassandra knew her mother to be a good judge of character, but there was something about this cowboy she didn't trust.

"All right," Helen said. "We have plenty of room in the bunkhouse, and as far as food is concerned, Maria is the best cook in the territory. You have got yourself a job." She shook Matt's hand and with one look, stifled the protest rising in Cassandra's throat. "Cassandra, please tell Maria to set another place. I will have one of the men show Matt the grounds before we eat."

She rang an iron dinner bell hanging from the porch. One of the vaqueros waved his hat and sent his horse toward the house. Cassandra wished Carlos would unloose his lariat, swing the lope over Matt's broad shoulders, and haul him back in the direction he'd come, whatever direction that had been.

Behind her mother's back, she inched over to him. "You might fool Mama," she whispered, "but you don't fool me. What are you up to?"

"I need food and a place to sleep. That's all."

"You better be telling the truth. If you try to hurt Mama or anything on this ranch, you'll have me to contend with." She fled inside and slammed the door.

Cassandra leaned against the doorframe and took several deep breaths. After she regained her composure, she called out, "Maria, come here, please."

Maria emerged from the kitchen with a potato clutched in one hand and a knife in the other.

"Please set an extra plate," Cassandra said. "Mama's hired a new man."

"A new man? I would say from the rosy color on your cheeks you think him most handsome." Laughing, Maria scuttled back to the kitchen.

Cassandra frowned at the retreating back of the woman who'd loved and cared for her since she was five years old. True, Matt's looks might cause a woman's head to turn, but right now she wished a hundred plagues on his handsome face and uninvited interference.

Guilt washed over her less than charitable thoughts, but she chased it away. The Bible did warn of wolves in sheep's clothing, didn't it? She would not concede the warning was against men teaching false doctrine and not cowboys looking for work.

The smell of roast beef drifted in from the kitchen. One thing was certain, the noonday meal would not disappoint Mr. Matt Atkins. At the notion of partaking food with the new hand, Cassandra dashed upstairs. That cowboy might think her lacking in manners, but she'd give him no cause to fault her appearance.

Call me a damsel, will you? I'll show you what a real damsel looks like.

FOUR

Matt gauged the vaquero guiding his Paint horse toward the porch. Short of stature, his faded shirt hung loosely over a lean-muscled frame, and the lines around his eyes showed evidence of long hours spent in the unforgiving Texas sun. The man settled back in his saddle and looked expectantly at Mrs. Pickett.

"Matt," Helen said, "meet Carlos Maldonado. Carlos, this is Matt Atkins. He is going to work here. Please help get his horse settled and then show him the bunkhouse and grounds."

"Sí, Señora Pickett." A smile creased the vaquero's face.

He reached down from the saddle and exchanged a firm handshake with Matt. "I am happy to meet you, Señor Matt. Me, Rafael, and Roberto could use the help. Do you know much about cattle?

"I do."

"And horses?"

"I know my way around a horse."

"That is very good. We have a few yearlings to gentle and a mare that still needs work."

"Carlos," Helen said, "you need to speak to Cassandra first. You know she oversees the training of the horses."

Carlos's eyes darted to the house. "You are right, Señora Pickett. I am sorry."

"You did not tell me which ranch you worked at before coming here," Helen said to Matt.

"The Circle T outside of Fort Worth."

"I know of it. That is George Thompson's ranch."

"Yep, but everyone in those parts calls him Big George."

"Several years back, Samuel joined some of Mr. Thompson's men. They drove a herd up the Chisholm Trail to Kansas."

"I never met your husband, so that must have been before I worked at the Circle T. But I've made that trip a couple of times since then. Nowadays, a lot of ranchers use the Great Western Trail. I imagine in a few more years the Chisholm will be a thing of the past."

"Times are changing, but the ranchers around Fort Worth still need the Chisholm Trail to drive their herds north to catch trains for eastern and western markets." Helen cracked open the screen door. "If you will excuse me." Matt tipped his hat before she reentered the house.

Carlos motioned Matt to follow him toward a solidly-built barn and a sturdy corral. Beyond it, an open dogtrot connected Matt's new sleeping quarters to a deserted cookhouse. A substantial cottage and an assortment of other storage and outbuildings of lesser build completed the ranch's ensemble. As the two men passed a smokehouse, the smell of salted meat made Matt's mouth water. He hadn't eaten since he passed through Brownwood the day before.

Matt gave a shrill whistle. A dark bay horse that had been eating grass by the barn trotted up, dispersing a flock of chickens. The birds squawked and scattered but quickly regrouped and resumed scratching for dinner.

"That is a fine horse," Carlos said.

"This is King's Ransom or King for short." Matt stroked the white blaze running the length of the horse's face. King returned the affection by nibbling Matt's shirt with velvet lips.

"I have never seen such a stallion. What kind is he?"

"He's a Morgan. I aim to breed him to the local cowponies."

"The Picketts still own a few nice mares. They would make good wives for your grand horse, eh?"

Matt joined Carlos's laughter and thanked the lucky stars for his good fortune. Things had worked out better than he'd expected. Now, he could snoop around and get what he came for, and while he was at it, he could help the Pickett women get their ranch back on its feet. If that spitfire Cassandra Jane would let him. Her haughty spirit was a sight to behold, but she sure pleased the eye with those sparkling green eyes and all that wavy, red hair.

Matt nodded in satisfaction. Yes. Everything was going to work out just fine.

★★★

A warm, rose-scented breeze fluttered the lace curtain of Cassandra's bedroom window. She stood on her tiptoes and leaned against the window frame. From her vantage point, she could see Matt and Carlos but couldn't hear their conversation.

She tapped a finger on her cheek as questions tumbled through her mind. Who was this Matt Atkins, and why was he so bent on working at the Triple P? Was he running from the law?

If he were on the lam, a small town like Goose Neck Ridge would be a perfect place to hole up. Everyone knew Marshal Jeffers had only arrested eleven people in the last year. Five of them needed to sleep off their whiskey, two had left the mercantile without paying for their purchases, and four had disturbed the peace. That didn't include Carl Ellison, who'd been ticketed for a reckless buggy drive through town, trying to impress his new girlfriend.

When Carlos turned his head toward the house, Cassandra jerked away from the window. If he suspected she was watching Matt, the vaquero would tease her endlessly. He and Rafael took great delight in ribbing her, more like older brothers than hired hands.

Cassandra sat at her vanity dresser and twisted her hair into a chignon. After securing the knot with a silver filigree comb, she preened in front of the mirror.

Pride goeth before destruction, and a haughty spirit before a fall, the Holy Spirit convicted her.

"That may be true," she said out loud in reply, "but Matt Atkins is the only proud person on this ranch."

And why behold the mote in your brother's eye, but do not see the beam in your own?

"Matt, my brother? Ha. He will never be part of this family," she argued, trying to quench the Holy Spirit's rebuttal.

The sound of the front door opening brought her to her feet. She bounded down the stairs, and seeing her mother was alone, rushed over and demanded, "Mama, you can't be serious about hiring that cowboy."

"I am."

"But you don't know the first thing about him. He could be a cattle rustler or a murderer." Cassandra regretted the words as soon as they left her mouth.

"Young lady, I would suggest you restrain that tongue of yours."

"I'm sorry. I shouldn't have said that."

Helen placed her hands on Cassandra's shoulders, the tone of her voice easing. "I cannot explain it, but I believe this stranger, and not Phillip, is the answer to our prayers."

"That blue-eyed scoundrel is not the answer to any of my prayers."

"I would hardly call him that after he came to your aid. Whatever possessed Phillip to act in such an unbecoming manner?"

"I'm not worried about Phillip. It's Matt Atkins who worries me. Are you sure we should hire him?"

"Why are you so concerned? Cowboys have come and gone around this ranch for years. And please, you must mind your manners. Your father and I did not raise you to be so impolite."

"Yes, but—"

"Cassandra." Helen's eyes turned the color of slate.

Cassandra bit back her doubtful reply and fixed her eyes on the floor. "Yes, Mama. If you say so."

"Good. I am glad we agree." Helen nudged her toward the kitchen. "Now, let us take a chance and ask Maria if she could use our help. She really should get off her feet."

Cassandra consented, but her mind still reeled with questions about the new hand. She didn't have any answers yet, but she would keep an eye on Matt Atkins until she did–all the while denying it might be enjoyable.

⭑⭑⭑

Matt lifted the saddle and pad from King's back. When he'd arrived out west, he paid a handsome price for the saddle. It took a few days for King to grow accustomed to the extra weight and large wooden stirrups, but the investment had been a good one. He soon learned a reliable mount, a good saddle, and a leak-proof bedroll were a cowboy's most prized possessions.

He ran a hand down King's legs. After two years of chasing ornery steers over half of Texas, he was thankful his horse showed no signs of ill effects. "We almost made it home, didn't we, boy?" he whispered. King swished his long, black tail at a buzzing fly. "Sorry, I don't have a treat. Maybe I can get you one later."

"We can ask Maria," Carlos said, lugging over a bucket of fresh water and an armload of hay for King. "She grows many apples and keeps them in the cellar behind the house. Señorita Cassie sneaks them for the horses, though Maria pretends she does not see it."

Matt's mind didn't travel far for that image. He could see Cassandra tiptoeing down into the cellar and sneaking out with a couple of apples.

Carlos pointed to a wooden rack near the stall. "You can put your tack over there." He slid a hand down King's neck. "You say he is a Morgan?"

"King's a descendant of Figure, the first Morgan horse. Figure's owner wanted to sell him as a colt, but no one would buy him. People said he was too little."

"This horse cannot come from such a small animal." Carlos gave the horse an expert eye. "He is over sixteen hands at his withers. Much bigger than our cowponies."

"He's taller than the average Morgan, but he carries the other traits of his forefather. Straight legs, thick muscles, and a nice head. He can work all day, then race home like a colt. He can also haul a heavy wagon or trot in style while pullin' a rig. I'm hopin' folks 'round here might breed their mares to him."

"If your horse can do all that, you will soon become a rich man. Señorita Cassie is in charge of the livestock. We will talk to her. She knows much about cattle and horses. She can even outride and out rope me and Rafael. Though Roberto, Rafael's son, comes very close."

Matt couldn't imagine anyone as prissy as Cassandra being a bonafide cowgirl. He scratched his head. Did she suspect him? He thought his story had sounded plausible, and Mrs. Pickett believed it. But why did the two women need Phillip Brigham's help? His jaw twitched as the answers eluded him.

"What can you tell me about your neighbor Phillip Brigham?" he asked.

Carlos smacked his lips and twirled a length of hay between his fingers. His eyes shone, and Matt thanked heaven the vaquero was like most hands, eager to share ranch gossip.

"Señor Brigham comes from a long line of rich men. His papá made much money from shipping many cattle across the country. It was a sad day when his boot caught in the stirrup and his horse dragged him to death."

Matt winced. "Ranchin' can be tough work. I take it Cassandra doesn't care for Phillip?"

"You are right. I saw Señor Brigham's stallion take off faster than old Bullet over there running after a rabbit."

At the mention of his name, a tan dog of unknown breeding lifted his head from his nap. His black-tipped tail beat the ground in steady rhythm, causing puffs of dust to dance skyward.

"Did you have anything to do with Señor Brigham leaving so quickly?" Carlos asked.

"Someone needed to ride him out on a rail. He's not a pleasant man."

"He has been unhappy since he lost some land to Señor Pickett."

"How did that happen?"

"Señor Brigham has never cared for cattle or his family ranch. He would rather be a big city gentleman than a Texas rancher. For a long time he has talked about selling Lazy Acres."

Matt gripped the top rail of the stall. "Go on."

"Several years ago he rode into town and stopped at a saloon. He drank too much whiskey and got too friendly with the Señoritas working there. Señor Pickett rode by and heard Señor Brigham's loud voice. He knew big trouble would come soon, so he asked Señor Brigham to go home. When he said no, Señor Pickett offered him one hundred acres for a bet to leave the saloon."

"That's some wager."

Carlos gave a quick nod. "Señor Brigham thought himself a grand card player. He put up one hundred acres including Cedar Ridge. If he had been sober, he would not have offered that land. Goose Neck Creek runs through it. The Lazy Acres vaqueros sometimes used its deep waterhole to water the cattle."

"And?"

"Señor Brigham was outmatched. His straight hand of cards lost to Señor Pickett's full house."

Carlos motioned Matt to follow him outside. Matt shielded his eyes from the sun that was pushing noon and got another good look at the Picketts' home.

The two-story structure was built of white-painted lumber and roofed with wooden shingles. Two peaked gables accented the front while smoke curled from a chimney hidden at the back, where Matt assumed the kitchen lay. White lace curtains peeked out from behind cheery, green-trimmed window frames. He envisioned Cassandra adding the touch of color with her red hair pulled back in a scarf and that cute nose of hers stuck high in the air.

She sure was a feisty thing, all horns and rattles. If a woman back East ever showed that kind of pluck, her father or husband would have turned her over his knee.

He shook his head. *No way, buddy. You've already crossed that troubled river. You're not going over it again.*

"Is there more to the story?" he asked Carlos.

"Sí. Señor Brigham did not want to honor his wager, but a roomful of people heard him make it. He said he would get back his land one way or another. I think he plans to wed Señorita Cassie to do so."

"That man is a ruffian. Why would she think about marryin' him?"

Carlos lifted his slim shoulders. "Things were much different when they were children. They were good friends. Everyone thought they would marry one day. But something very bad must have happened several years ago. Señor Brigham stopped coming to visit, and Señorita Cassie stopped talking about him."

"Do you know what it was?"

"No. But one day I asked Señor Pickett why he did not come to visit anymore. It was the only time *el jefe* raised his voice at me. He apologized afterward, but I never brought it up again."

"Do you think Cassandra might marry Phillip?"

"If I were a betting man, I would take that wager. Maria shares all that goes on in the big house. She said Señorita Cassie would marry him to save the Triple P. The ranch is most important to her."

The idea of Cassandra as Phillip's bride disturbed Matt more than he cared to admit. Why? He didn't know. He'd just met her, and she sure didn't care for him.

He dragged his attention back to Carlos. "From talkin' to Mrs. Pickett, I gather the ranch is on hard times. Is there anything I can do to help?"

"The fate of the Triple P is now in the hands of the good Lord. So, unless you have much money in your saddlebag, there is nothing you can do." Carlos tugged the frayed collar of Matt's shirt. "And I can tell, Señor Matt, you are not a rich man."

The dinner bell rang out, interrupting the two men. Mrs. Pickett waved from the porch and went back inside.

Carlos patted his stomach. "You must drop off your things in the bunkhouse before we head to the big house and enjoy Maria's fine cooking."

"The hands eat in the main house?"

"There is only me, Rafael, and Roberto now. We are like family. Soon you will be family too. No? Maria baked an apple pie for our noon meal. Her pies could tame the devil himself. But we must hurry. She does not like dinner to get cold."

As they hurried to the bunkhouse, Matt couldn't think of anything better than a good meal and another chance to spar with the saucy mistress of the Triple P.

FIVE

As soon as Phillip entered the Lazy Acres compound, he reined in his lathered horse. His mind tumbled with thoughts of his forced dismissal from the Triple P. He had half a mind to go back and—

"*Buenos dias,* Señor Brigham," a voice called out from behind one of the five posts supporting the red-tiled roof of the veranda.

Phillip steadied his nerves before addressing the one who had wished him a good day. "I know you are hiding, my little Juanita. You can come out now."

"You were not gone long." The voice piped up again, but this time paired with the happy face of a little girl with skin the color of warm caramel. Her dusty feet peeped out from under the hem of a scooped-neck dress of muslin tied with a turquoise sash. She skipped across the U-shaped courtyard, which was dotted with sweet-smelling orange and lemon trees. A thick, eight-foot wall closed the courtyard off from the outside world, but Juanita wiggled easily through its wrought iron gate.

She took one look at Phillip's tired horse and balled her small fists on her hips. "You should not ride Sunny so hard. He is a good horse."

Phillip squatted to the girl's eye level and patted her head, his frustration fleeing as fast as his ride back from the Triple P. "I'm sorry. We were in a hurry."

Juanita López rewarded the apology with a sweet smile before patting the horse's neck. The horse lipped the young girl's arm. Juanita giggled. "I remember when Sunny was just a small colt, and you let me name him. You took much care in his training." She shook a finger at Phillip. "So, I insist you must treat him better."

"You're right. You can help Antonio rub him down." He reached into his saddlebag and retrieved something before pitching the reins to a nearby vaquero and saying, "Take care of him."

The man touched the brim of his hat and trotted the winded animal toward the barn. Juanita turned to follow the pair.

"Wait," Phillip said. "I have something to give you first." When he handed Juanita the picture book he'd purchased at the mercantile, her near-black eyes filled with joy and gratitude. "But I insist you practice your English when you read it," he instructed. "*Sé que entiendo español.*"

"I know you understand Spanish," Juanita parroted his words back in perfect English.

Phillip tweaked the young girl's nose. "You little imp."

Though he doubted it possible, Juanita's smile brightened even more. "I pretend not to understand, so you will spend more time teaching me."

She studied the book's cover of a little girl and her older brother playing with a brown-spotted dog. "*Muchas gracias,* Señor Brigham. Can I read it to you now?"

"Maybe later. I have business to attend." He shooed her away. "Go on. Sunny is waiting, and don't let Antonio give the beast water until he cools off."

With a shy wave and clutching her new treasure, Juanita scampered to the barn, her blue-black braids flying out like raven's wings. She called back, "Do not worry. I will make sure Antonio takes good care of your Sunny. *Hasta luego.*"

"I will see you later as well," Phillip replied.

Why couldn't Cassandra be as sweet and compliant as Juanita? Her refusal to accept his marriage proposal had proved disappointing. He knew he'd gain control of the Triple P one way or the other, by marriage or upon foreclosure, but thinking of Cassandra as his wife had kept him awake many a night.

Phillip stroked his chin, his thoughts returning to the two-bit cowboy who'd humiliated him in front of her. Who was he, and what was he doing at the Triple P? For some reason he looked familiar. Phillip chided himself. What was he thinking? All cowboys looked the same.

"I need answers," he said as he bounded up the porch steps. The cypress trees framing the thick adobe walls offered a reprieve from the Texas heat but did little to temper Phillip's mood.

A short man, who barely came to Phillip's shoulder, waited in the hallway. Sweat dotted William Higgins's forehead and upper lip. This malady occurred to the Goose Neck Ridge banker whenever Phillip was around, no matter what the temperature. Higgins pulled a handkerchief from the pocket of his tweed suit and mopped his face.

"G–Good day, Mr. Brigham."

Phillip swept by the man and entered his study. "Tell Jack Dalton I want to speak with him the minute we're through."

"Yes, sir. Right away, sir." The banker scurried down the hall.

Phillip slammed the door after Higgins. The vibration sent an oil painting of a herd of Longhorns crashing to the floor. He replaced his father's favorite piece of art and began ticking off every detail of his plans for Lazy Acres and the Triple P. Five minutes later a tentative knock sounded at the door. Higgins's balding head peeked into the room. Phillip motioned for him to enter.

He steepled his fingers and peered down his nose at Higgins. "What did they want?"

"Uh, what did who want?"

"Cassandra and Helen Pickett."

"W–What makes you think I know anything about them?"

"Jack Dalton spotted them outside the bank two days ago. He said there weren't any supplies in the back of their buggy. And since you're looking as nervous as a jackrabbit in a coyote's mouth, they must have stopped in to see you."

The words whooshed out of Higgins. "They handed me fifty-five dollars. Miss Pickett said it was all they had. She begged me for more time. I talked to the board of directors, and they're willing to extend the loan. Your father would have if he were still alive."

"But he isn't, is he?"

Higgins puffed out his chest as though mustering his last trace of courage. "No, he isn't, but since he sold the bank before he died, you no longer have a say in the matter."

Phillip set his lips in a hard line and looked down his nose at Higgins. The banker's mettle disappeared like a child's balloon released from its mooring. His frame melted to the floor.

"I'm not the saint my father was," Phillip said. "And though the Brigham name no longer graces the bank's door, I have more money deposited in it than all the residents of Goose Neck Ridge put together. The board will bow to my bidding. So tuck that nonsense to bed and let me see the ledger Jack told you to bring me. I need to verify the figures away from the board members' prying eyes."

Higgins pushed his spectacles up the bridge of his nose and meekly handed over a leather-bound ledger. Phillip riffled through its pages until he found the one he wanted. *Samuel Pickett – The Triple P – August 1886*. After skimming the page to reaffirm the figures, he dropped the ledger onto his desk.

"In the improbable event my marriage to Cassandra does not take place," he waved a dismissive hand, "you will sell me the Triple P for twenty-five cents on the dollar. Right?" His expression dared contradiction.

Higgins blinked his pale eyes in agreement but asked, "What if the Picketts do come up with the money?"

"You take care of your part, and I'll take care of mine." Phillip wagged a finger in Higgins's face. "Don't disappoint me. I've too much invested in this for it to go awry." He crossed his arms and turned his back on the banker. "On your way out, tell Dalton to get in here."

Higgins plucked up the ledger and fled the study. A moment later a rawboned cowboy swaggered in and stopped an arm's length from Phillip. Phillip hid his distaste for the man who'd do anything for money, though their association had started because of it.

The first time he had hired Jack Dalton was to take care of cattle rustlers on the western border of Lazy Acres. The men were crafty, swooping down under cover of night and only taking a few head at a time so not to be noticed.

Phillip's neighbor and fellow rancher, E.J. Fairfax, said if a problem needed solving, Jack Dalton was the one to solve it. The bodies of the cattle rustlers were never found, and Phillip hadn't inquired into what happened to them.

"Whatcha needin', boss?" Jack asked. His hair fell in greasy ropes around a face bearing scars of childhood smallpox. His buckskins were dirty and torn, and Phillip stepped back from breath that reeked of tobacco, liquor, and poor dental hygiene. He motioned to a recently-purchased gentleman's chair across from his desk. Jack draped a leg over the chair's velvet arm and leaned forward to spit into a brass spittoon.

Phillip managed to keep his voice calm. "The Triple P's hired a new hand. I need you to find out who he is, where he's from, and what he's doing there."

"I don't work for free, ya know."

Phillip plucked a key from his vest pocket, bypassed the false drawer on the left side of his desk, and unlocked a drawer on the right. He freed two bills from a stack of money and pushed them across the desk. When Jack grabbed the cash, his elbow knocked over an inkwell whose hinged lid, unfortunately, was open. Black liquid raced across the top of the desk and dripped onto the Oriental rug underneath it. Phillip leapt back to protect his clothing as the ink seeped into the cream and navy, hand-knotted carpet.

Jack showed no regret for what he'd done. He eyed the bills before folding them in two. "A couple of five-spots don't go too far."

"If you fail me, money will be the least of your worries."

"Don't aim on failin' ya anytime soon. Why ya interested in this man?"

"That's my business. Now get going and do your job."

"Whatever you say, boss." Jack stuffed the bills into his shirt pocket and ambled out of the study.

Phillip strode across the room and called down the hallway for one of the housemaids. "Rosa, come here, please."

A short Mexican woman appeared almost instantly. She wore a black dress encircled by a white-starched apron. Though fine lines marked the edges of her eyes and the corners of her mouth, the beauty of her youth was still apparent.

"Sí, Señor Brigham?"

"Would you please clean up this mess?" He pointed to the rug.

"Sí. I will do it right away."

Phillip watched the woman hasten to the kitchen for what he assumed were cleaning supplies. He favored Rosa López and her eight-year-old daughter Juanita above his other servants. Juanita had been one year old when her father succumbed to pneumonia. In pity, Harold Brigham, Phillip's father, allowed Rosa to bring the baby to the hacienda while she worked. When Juanita became a toddler, she followed

Phillip like a young pup, and through the years filled the void of the little sister he'd always wanted but never had.

Phillip frowned at the mess Jack had made on the expensive wool rug. He hoped Rosa could remove the stain. Cassandra had once commented on the carpet's beauty and said one day she would like to visit the Orient where it had been fashioned. He licked his lips. Maybe he would take her there for their honeymoon.

SIX

Matt waited while Carlos swung open the bunkhouse door. The rusty hinges creaked in protest, and a musty smell escaped from the depth of the room. Carlos swiped at the cobwebs dangling from the top of the doorframe.

"I am sorry. No one has stayed here for many months. Not since Señora Pickett let the other vaqueros go."

Though sunlight pierced the dirt-streaked windows, Matt had to blink until his eyes adjusted to the room's dark interior. His new living quarters were small but adequate with a planked floor, whitewashed walls, and a crude fireplace. A hand-hewn table was shoved next to a row of rope beds, and he assumed either Cassandra or her mother had stitched the simple patchwork quilts covering the straw mattresses.

Carlos cast a worried look at the main house. "A pump is outside on the left. You must hurry and wash up."

Matt appreciated Carlos's concern. If the Triple P housekeeper was anything like Zeke Owens, the chuck wagon cook at the Circle T, it would be a mistake to keep her waiting.

When Matt started working for Big George a year ago, he learned that only fools argue with a skunk, a mule, or a cook. Zeke brandished his position like his big wooden spoon and wouldn't think twice about denying a meal to a hungry cowboy. He once poured an entire pot of stew on the ground just to prove a point.

Matt heard water sloshing outside and figured Carlos was washing his hands. He dropped his gear on the bed with a thump, sending swirls of dust into the air. His parents would have been shocked at the meager belongings stowed in his bedroll–two flannel shirts, three pairs of woolen socks, and an extra pair of jeans he should have replaced months ago.

He pulled two pieces of paper out of his shirt pocket. The first was a letter that bore the marks of having been read countless times. Its contents had shattered his world, but he hoped the other piece of paper would put it back together again.

A gust of wind sneaked into the room and rustled the papers. Matt refolded the letter and tucked it back into his pocket. He shoved the other paper under the mattress, making sure it was hidden from view.

He sent up a quick prayer. *Lord, I don't know why you dealt me this hand, but I'm gonna make the best of it one way or another.* Matt gritted his teeth. It was time to let go of the past. It was time to move on.

☆☆☆

Cassandra pressed an ear to the double dining room doors and listened to the muted conversation coming from the other side. She heard Matt's voice first.

"This meal sure looks and smells great."

Cassandra knew Maria would beam at the compliment. Her chief joy and concern were the smooth running of the Pickett household and the feeding of its occupants.

"You will not be disappointed." Cassandra strained to hear her mother's soft voice. "I wonder what is taking Cassandra so long?"

The voice of Rafael Martinez, the other Triple P vaquero and Maria's husband, boomed out. "She is probably upstairs getting pretty for Señor Matt here."

"I'm not sure Cassandra Jane cares what I think," Matt replied. "Besides, I doubt she could make herself any prettier than she already is."

Cassandra's face grew hot, but she pressed her ear even closer to the door.

"I will find out what is keeping her," Helen said, opening the doors before Cassandra could jump back. She tumbled into the dining room and landed at her startled mother's feet.

Helen bent over and whispered, "Cassandra, your petticoat."

Cassandra yanked her dress over the lace-edged undergarment and prayed for the earth to open up and swallow her. Roberto, Rafael and Maria's twelve-year-old son, nudged Matt aside and extended his hand to her.

With flaming cheeks, she accepted his offer and leapt to her feet. "Thank you, Roberto."

The boy admired her with eyes the same shape and color as his mother's. "You are welcome, Miss Cassie. And might I say, you look very pretty?"

Helen's voice held a hint of teasing. "Were you eavesdropping, dear?"

"N–No. You just opened the door as I was coming in."

Maria hid a giggle behind plump hands, and Rafael chortled so hard, he started coughing. Carlos gleefully whacked him on the back.

"I appreciate a dramatic entrance," Matt said, "but I'm kinda on the side of believin' her." His lips twitched as if he was trying to keep from smiling.

"I can defend myself, thank you," Cassandra replied.

With a flourish Matt pulled out the high back armchair at the head of the table for her. She stepped past it. "That one is Mama's."

She stopped at the engraved side chair to the immediate right and said in a sweet voice, "Rafael, would you be so kind?" Rafael offered his quick and easy smile and whipped the chair out in a comical imitation of Matt.

"*Gracias.*" Cassandra dropped daintily onto the chair.

"*De nada.*" Rafael winked at Matt, then seated Maria across from Cassandra.

Matt offered Helen the chair Cassandra had declined. "May I?"

"Why, thank you, Matt."

Rafael squeezed his husky frame between Carlos and Maria. When Matt filled the seat next to Cassandra, Roberto's eyes darkened. He slumped into the only vacant chair left, the one on the other side of Matt.

Matt leaned toward Cassandra and whispered, "I like what you did to your hair."

Her hands flew to her chignon. She avoided Carlos and Rafael's grins and pretended to admire the painted roses circling her china plate.

Helen reached for Cassandra and Carlos's hand. "Let us ask the Lord's blessing on the food."

Cassandra gulped. Did Mama really expect her to join hands with Matt in prayer? Roberto must have felt the same way. His expression turned dour, and he thrust his left hand under his leg.

"Mama," Cassandra said, "Mr. Atkins might not be a praying man."

"I–I send up a prayer now and again."

Why had Matt hesitated? Had he lied about praying and was only putting on airs for Mama?

Fearful of causing another scene, Cassandra placed two fingers into Matt's upturned palm. He circled them in a warm grasp. Goosebumps pricked her arm, but she kept still. Her mother took prayer time seriously.

It wasn't that Cassandra minded prayer. At an early age, her parents had taught her to talk to God and read the Scriptures. She enjoyed reading the Bible, but prayer had remained a mystery to her. Did God really listen to impetuous young ladies like herself, or did he only hear the petitions of good people like Mama and Reverend Doyle? Cassandra wasn't sure, but since Mama believed so highly in talking to God, she figured she should keep on trying. Especially now that the Triple P was in financial trouble.

When Helen began her prayer of grace, Matt squeezed Cassandra's fingers.

"Dear Lord," Helen said, "we thank you for this meal and for sending Mr. Atkins our way. I pray for the Triple P. May your will be done, and may we always trust in your care and provision. Amen."

A chorus of *amen*s circled the table.

"Come on," Rafael insisted. "We will insult my Maria if we do not eat."

Seven pairs of hands reached for the laden dishes sitting on a brightly embroidered tablecloth. Cassandra was glad Carlos's plate hid the bird she had stitched. It resembled an ugly owl instead of a regal blue jay.

She wrung her hands under the table. *Please, Carlos. Please, don't lift your plate.* But to her dismay, Carlos couldn't resist. He raised his plate high above his head. "Señor Matt, our Señorita Cassie helped sew this tablecloth."

Matt cocked his head as if to get a better look. "That's pretty good. Did you sew the quilts in the bunkhouse?"

Cassandra wished she had, but the three sitting across the table would expose her if she dared to take the credit. "No. Mama made them."

"They're mite purty. All I can sew is a button, and it usually ends up crooked." He pointed to the two mismatched and uneven buttons on his shirt.

"Miss Cassie does not need to sew," Roberto said. "Her job is to take care of the ranch." He jabbed a piece of roast beef off the serving dish and glared at Matt.

"Now, Roberto," Helen gently admonished, "there is nothing wrong with Cassandra doing both of them." She turned her attention to Matt. "Samuel taught Cassandra the skills she would need to take over the ranch one day, but I made sure she also learned the gentle arts of cooking and sewing. Under Maria's tutelage, she took to the kitchen like a duck to a pond, but I stopped trying to teach her to sew." She patted Cassandra's hand and smiled. "I told her she must marry a wealthy man and hire someone to do her sewing."

Cassandra forgot her less than perfect needlework as she watched Matt tuck into the food. He piled a mountain of mashed potatoes next to three slices of roast beef, and two heaping spoonfuls of fresh green beans. Then he pushed the beans aside to make room for two of Mama's fluffy biscuits. Could one man possibly eat so much? But Matt not only accomplished the impossible, he asked for seconds.

After Helen told him Cassandra had churned the butter, he slapped a glob on a biscuit and said over a mouthful, "This tastes great."

"Thanks," Cassandra mumbled. She chased a green bean around her plate with a fork until she accidentally pushed it off onto the table. She scooped it up, hoping no one had noticed.

"Señorita Cassie," Carlos said, "I am glad you caught the bean before it ran off the table."

Cassandra squirmed under Matt's grin. He jostled her elbow with his next bite. Had he done that on purpose? She scooted her chair away from him. Her mother kept silent much to Cassandra's relief. She folded and refolded the napkin in her lap certain she could not eat another bite.

When Helen offered Matt the biscuits for the third time, he held up a hand. "No, thank you, ma'am."

She set the biscuits back on the table. "Where do you hail from originally? I did not ask you earlier."

Matt wiped a dab of gravy off his lower lip. "I was born outside of Boston. My father owns–owned a horse farm."

"What brought you here?"

He shifted in his chair. "Highway robbers killed my parents as they came home from the theater one evening."

Cassandra's heart softened. The loss of her father had been great, but Matt had lost both of his parents. She touched his arm and said to her mother, "Mama, maybe we shouldn't pry."

"You are right. I am sorry."

"I don't mind talking about my parents," Matt said. "I loved them. They gave me a good life. Though my father's farm was successful, he still owed money to the bank when he died. I sold the farm, paid off his debts, and headed out west. Like all men, I wanted fame, fortune, and a place to call home. I've not had much luck finding them yet, but I'll keep looking 'til I do."

The similarities of Matt's life to hers amazed Cassandra. She relaxed against the back of her chair.

"Rafael," Matt said, finishing off his mashed potatoes with the last piece of a biscuit. "I see why you married Maria. She is not only a handsome woman but also a great cook."

Rafael used his napkin to wipe the neatly trimmed mustache of which he took great pride. He patted his wife's back. "My Maria is a fine-looking woman, is she not? I have had fifteen happy years with her by my side and her baby brother. And almost thirteen with our Roberto." He tousled Carlos's hair and winked across the table at his son.

"You two are brother and sister?" Matt asked Carlos.

"Sí. We were born in a little town called Ojinaga."

Matt laid his napkin next to his empty plate. "I've never heard of Ojinaga. Is it in Texas?"

"Oh, no. Ojinaga is a tiny village south of the border. The good Lord led Señor Pickett there. He was picking up a herd of longhorns and paid Maria a grand price to cook dinner for his hired hands. He called Rafael a fool for not catching her eye."

Rafael interrupted. "She was the most beautiful woman in all the territory. And with a fine figure to match." The sparkle in his eyes matched the love he carried for his wife. "But I was too scared of her father to show my interest. He had a big voice and a body to match."

Maria elbowed Rafael, and Carlos picked the story back up. "Señor Pickett invited me and Maria to come live here at the Triple P. Our parents were not so happy, but they knew he offered us a better life. After they gave their blessing, Maria hurried to pack our few belongings. The next morning, we waited by the chuck wagon in case Señor Pickett forgot his invitation. When Rafael saw us leaving, he threw his clothes in a saddlebag, kissed his parents, brother, and three sisters adios, and galloped after Señor Pickett."

The edges of Maria's mouth curled up in fond memory. "Rafael is a most proud man, but that day he begged Señor Pickett to let him come too. After we came to the Triple P, Rafael asked me to be his wife. He, Carlos, and Señor Pickett built us the little house on the other side of the barn. Three years later our Roberto was born." She sniffed and dabbed her eyes with her napkin. "Señor Pickett was a big man in many ways. God rest his soul." She made a sign of the cross.

Rafael kissed Maria's hand. "I am most thankful for my Maria and Roberto and for the little one we soon will have." He patted her belly.

Color crept up Maria's cheeks. She swatted him with the back of her hand, but her words were heartfelt. "I am most blessed. I could not ask for a better husband than my Rafael."

Maria shot Cassandra a knowing look. *"Tal vez dices Señor Brigham, 'no' y piense en casarse con un buen hombre como Señor Matt."*

Cassandra stifled a gasp. True, she wanted to refuse Phillip's marriage proposal, but to consider Matt instead? What was Maria thinking? And for pity's sake, why did she mention the possibility right in front of him?

She cast a sideways glance at Matt who just shrugged at Maria. Thank goodness, he didn't understand Spanish. Cassandra made a mental note to scold her later.

Matt met Rafael's gaze. "You're a lucky man to have such a wife."

Cassandra longed to ask if he wished for the same but at her mother's knowing look and uplifted brow, she bit the inside of her cheek and kept silent.

Rafael cleared his throat. "And now, my dear wife, how about a piece of that apple pie?"

Maria jumped up. "One moment. I will be right back."

Cassandra stared at her untouched plate and rested a hand on her stomach. On any given day, she enjoyed Maria's cooking, but this time the food tasted like sawdust. "For some reason, I'm not hungry." She bit back a groan. The last thing she needed was to give Rafael and Carlos more ammunition to use against her.

Thankfully, Carlos only leaned over the table and whispered, "Señorita Cassie, if you do not eat a piece of Maria's pie, she will make us all pay. After you finish, you can show Señor Matt the rest of the ranch. We did not get far before we came inside."

"That is an excellent idea," Helen said. "Cassandra, you look like you could use some fresh air." Her determined expression silenced any argument Cassandra wanted to give.

"Yes, Mama."

"Señora Pickett," Roberto spoke up, "I can show Mr. Matt the ranch. I am sure Miss Cassie has more important things to do."

Rafael gave Roberto a stern look. "Your job this afternoon is to clean the horses' stalls. Remember?"

Roberto crossed his arms and sank into his chair. "Yes, Papá."

Maria strutted back into the room, carrying a golden-brown pie.

"Good," Helen said as she passed out the dessert plates. "It is settled. Now, let us all have a big piece of pie."

SEVEN

For the third time that day, Cassandra changed her clothes. This time she donned a mustard-colored blouse and a pair of dungarees that hugged her slim legs. She studied herself from all angles in the mirror. Would Matt be as tolerant of a woman wearing pants as her papa had been?

No one had ever called her father conventional. He stood against slavery during the Civil War even when Texas joined the Confederacy. He also believed the Women's Christian Temperance Union was a noble organization to support the social reform of women and to fight the evil effects of alcohol.

Her father had been the one to encourage Cassandra to throw out her sidesaddle and ride astride. Helen, who believed the only stand a woman should take was beside her husband, opposed the idea. "It is indecent, Samuel. What will people think?"

Samuel said he didn't give a hoot what people thought. It was high time Cassandra learned how to ride, rope, and herd cattle, all of which were accomplished from the back of a horse. He won the day with a compromise. Helen agreed

Cassandra could ride astride but insisted she wear a riding skirt.

A skilled seamstress, Helen set about sewing the billowy garment. The bulky material bunched up around Cassandra's legs and scared the horses when it blew in the wind. Helen stitched a shorter version but insisted Cassandra wear knickers underneath it. Before long, Samuel cajoled Helen into letting Cassandra try on a pair of Carlos's work pants.

Carlos handed the pair over with nary a word much to Cassandra's surprise and great relief. She grabbed the pants, ran upstairs, and slipped into what her mother would call *shameful attire*. For a glorious moment, she reveled in her newfound freedom.

Rafael crowed at the sight. Cassandra stood five inches taller than Carlos, and the pants rode high above her ankles. She quickly tucked the hems of the pants into her boots. From that day on, no one had commented about her manly attire, though Cassandra still sensed her mother's disapproval.

Cassandra hooked her fingers in the waist of her jeans like she'd seen Matt do and swaggered in front of the mirror. She dissolved into a fit of giggles. "Mama would be shocked," she told her merry reflection.

She plaited her hair and tied off the thick braid with a yellow ribbon. After one more glance in the mirror, she hurried down the stairs and tiptoed up the hallway, hoping to avoid her mother.

Maria clucked from the kitchen. "Your mamá would not like you wearing those pants in front of the new hand. You know what she would say, 'One cannot act like a lady and wear the clothes of a man'."

"Mama won't mind. Well, not a lot. And I don't care what Matt Atkins thinks. I'm not about to change my manner of dress for any man."

"Oh, no? Just you wait. One day the right one will come along. Your heart will beat fast, and you will find it hard to breathe. You will see things in a different light."

Cassandra ignored Maria's smug expression, refusing to admit she'd already suffered those chronic symptoms around Matt. Knowing Maria would be watching through the dining room window, Cassandra made her way to the corral with graceful, ladylike steps.

The effort was not lost on Matt. He circled her with a low whistle. "Well, if that don't beat all." He scratched the back of his head, causing his hat to tilt at a rakish angle.

Cassandra took her horse's lead rope from him. "Is there something wrong?"

"Your mother lets you wear those things?"

"She does. Haven't you seen a woman wearing pants before?"

"Well, the view's certainly nice, but I've only seen a couple of rancher's wives wearin' pants, and they considered their britches an extension of their husbands. Back East, ladies leave the pants-wearin' to the men."

"If that's the case, I'm glad I live in Texas. And I am not an extension of anyone."

"I don't doubt that for a minute."

He reached for her saddle, but Cassandra grabbed it first and settled it on Smokey's back. "Thank you, but I can tack up my own horse."

"I was just tryin' to help."

"I don't—"

"I know." Matt threw his hands up in surrender. "You don't need my help." He pointed to a chestnut horse tacked up and tied outside the corral. "Carlos said I could ride Ben and give King a rest. Is that all right with you?" At the sound of his name, Ben whickered. Smokey answered with a high-pitched whinny of his own. Cassandra grudgingly mumbled an agreement to Matt's request.

Matt patted Smokey's dark gray neck. "Smokey's a nice-lookin' animal. Almost as nice as my Morgan."

"Smokey can run circles around your horse."

"You think so?"

"Yes, I do. Papa brought him home as a yearling for my fifteenth birthday. He could run like the wind. Last April we beat fifteen other horses at the Spring Festival."

Cassandra would never forget that race. The wind had sung in her ears as she and Smokey passed one horse after another to gain on the leaders. The crowd cheered as the horses galloped the last leg of the race down the middle of Main Street. Smokey beat E.J. Fairfax's black stallion by two lengths. Her father hugged her tight and said how proud he was. His words had meant more than the first-place ribbon she and Smokey won that day.

Cassandra caressed the butter-soft leather of the saddle. "Papa let me use the purse to buy Smokey this saddle. It was only fair since he'd done most of the work to win it."

Smokey lifted his head and blew into Matt's nostrils. When Matt returned the puff of air, the horse nibbled his chin.

"What are you doing?" Cassandra asked.

"I'm gettin' acquainted with your horse. When horses meet, they blow in each other's noses. Same as people shakin' hands." He nudged her closer. "You try."

She gave him a quizzical look but blew lightly into her horse's flared nostrils. Smokey returned the greeting, his warm breath tickling her face. "I think you're plumb loco, but Smokey believes you."

Matt showed his dimples, causing Cassandra to grab the stirrup and steady her legs that had suddenly gone weak. How could one man be both annoying and compelling at the same time?

"Did you learn that trick on your horse farm?" she asked, tightening the saddle's cinch.

"Sure did."

"Your expertise might prove useful around here." She took stock of him over her horse's back. "Why'd you leave a big operation like the Circle T to finagle a job here? Why didn't you try Lazy Acres? It's a hundred times bigger than our ranch."

"I didn't finagle this job. Your mother hired me, remember? You sure do ask a lot of questions, young lady."

"I can ask a hired hand anything I want, and I am not young. I'm twenty years old."

"A whole twenty, huh?"

Cassandra longed to wipe the smile off Matt's unshaven face. Instead, she tapped her foot–hard. "I'm waiting."

"If you insist. You already know why I left Boston..."

He paused as though waiting for her to make a comment. When she didn't, he continued. "I didn't know what to do after I sold the family farm. Relatives were slim and few, so I figured I'd leave Boston and start over."

Cassandra adjusted the throat latch on Smokey's bridle. It was strange Matt had wanted to leave Boston, and Phillip wanted to move there. Would she ever understand men?

"Go on," she urged.

"The *Boston Herald* had posted a classified ad about a big ranch near Fort Worth needin' help. Said it shipped cattle all the way to New England."

"The Circle T?"

"Yep. I didn't end up there until later, but since I was a fair horseman, the idea of cowboyin' did draw my interest. The Wild West and all."

"Like in a western novel?"

"I've read a few."

"And you believed all that's written in them?"

"I admit. I found out their take on the West was greatly exaggerated."

"That's because city slickers write that stuff. They don't know the difference between a heifer and a bull."

"You're probably right. Anyhow, King and I rode the rails all the way to Texas. He hated bein' cooped up in the livestock car, so I spent most of the trip back there keepin' him company. We landed at a small outfit near Texarkana called the Risin' Sun."

"I've never heard of it."

"It's a couple hundred miles east of Fort Worth. Willard Tate was as desperate for cheap help as I was for a job. He taught a chuck-eater like me everything I needed to know about bein' a cowboy. How to rope, drive a herd, brand cattle, and fire a six-shooter. Before I moved on, he said I could pass as a bone-seasoned cowboy, but it took some time before I could talk like one.

"I learned to hide my accent and picked up cowboy slang along the way, so people couldn't tell I was from Boston. You Texans don't hanker too kindly to us Yankees."

Cassandra's chin jutted out in pride. "You're right, considering we seceded from the Union during the War."

Matt raised both of his hands. "I didn't mean to ruffle your feathers."

Even though the War had ended over twenty years ago, Cassandra still defended the Confederate cause, all except for one group of men enslaving another. But the North had been the adversary, not Matt. She willed her shoulders to relax. "Where'd you go after the Rising Sun?"

"I cowboyed here and there as I headed toward Fort Worth. My story gets long and borin' after that, but the short of it is, I finally ended up at the Circle T."

He handed her the reins. "That's enough for now. If you'd show me the ranch, maybe I can think of a way to help."

"What makes you think we need help?" She snapped her fingers. "Carlos. He told you."

"He mentioned the Triple P's sufferin' hard times, but I figured that from talkin' with your mother. But Carlos did tell me—"

"He told you about the loan."

Matt's forehead wrinkled. "He didn't say anything about a loan, but you just did. You want to tell me about it?"

Cassandra rolled her eyes in admission and quoted a verse from Proverbs under her breath. *Whoso keepeth his mouth and tongue keepeth his soul from troubles.* If King Solomon could do it, why couldn't she?

"I should have kept that to myself. Mama will not be happy I told you."

"I doubt she'll be mad, 'specially if I can help."

"What can you do?"

"I might surprise you but only if you tell what's up."

"We can talk about it later." Cassandra squeezed her eyes shut and asked God to forgive her lie. It would be a freezing snowstorm on a hot, Texas day before she revealed another thing to Matt Atkins.

EIGHT

"Would you like to see the ranch now?" Cassandra asked Matt as she swung up in the saddle and gathered the reins.

Matt tipped his hat. "Sure. Lead the way."

Their horses splashed across Goose Neck Creek, the wide stream that coursed down from the north and then twisted around the house. A branch of it broke off eastward and headed toward town, giving Goose Neck Ridge its name.

Cassandra and Matt approached a herd of cattle varying in size, shape, and color from speckles and tawny brindles to solid colors and splotchy patches of white on red. Several of the animals raised their heads and watched the riders draw near.

"That's an interesting lot," Matt observed.

"Before the drought, our cattle covered this entire area."

"That creek didn't help?"

"It did in the beginning, but eventually the water dried up."

Even now, Cassandra could hear the desperate cries of thirsty cattle and picture the mournful animals as they dropped to their knees and died. For months the air smelled of dead flesh as vultures and other scavengers picked the carcasses clean. The merciless sun, which began the death knell, finished the job, leaving a graveyard of bleached bones.

The morbid thoughts made Cassandra shudder. Glad for a distraction, she watched Bullet lope by, half-heartedly chasing one of the barn cats. The orange and white cat scurried up a tree and hissed at the dog. "Bullet," she hollered, "leave Max alone."

Across the creek, Rafael and Carlos were trying to mend a break in the fence line, but every time they turned their backs, three of the younger bulls breached by them trying to get to greener pastures. Rafael waved his wide-brimmed sombrero and yelled at the animals in Spanish. Cassandra was glad Maria hadn't taught her those words.

"Those are two hardworkin' men," Matt commented.

"We all work hard."

"Sorry. Didn't mean to imply otherwise."

"I'm responsible for all the livestock."

"You don't say?"

"You doubt me?"

Matt raised his hands in mock protest. "Not I, fair maiden. You're dressed like a cowboy. A cowboy you must be."

Cassandra's lips tightened. *Just you wait, Matt Atkins. I'll show you.* And as if on cue, a rust-speckled calf broke from the herd and trotted upstream. She urged Smokey after the runaway creature. "Watch this," she yelled back at Matt.

As Smokey's long strides gained ground, Cassandra swung her lariat overhead and cast the loop to land neatly around the calf's neck. Smokey skidded to a stop, and she jumped off his back, then captured the calf's legs with a short piece of rope. The helpless animal mooed forlornly.

Matt cantered up and reined in his horse. "That was pretty good."

Cassandra's prowess may have impressed Matt, but her performance did not fool Carlos and Rafael. The two men, who had closed the gap in the fence, jogged over.

Rafael flashed his bigger-than-Texas grin. "Señorita Cassie, would it not have been easier to herd the little one back to his mother?"

Carlos batted his eyes. "But Rafael, then she could not have shown Señor Matt what a fine cowgirl she is."

"I–I wanted to check the brand." Cassandra made a quick trace of the 3P brand on the calf's hindquarter. "You did a good job."

She loosened the rope, and the animal bolted back to the herd. Its mother first nuzzled and then butted the wayward calf with her broad head.

"Mama cow is teaching her baby a lesson," Carlos commented.

As the four watched the cattle pulling up swathes of grass, Bullet sprinted by again, but this time chasing the yip of a nearby prairie dog. A chorus of urgent chirps warned the others to disappear down their holes. Bullet zig-zagged back and forth with his tail held high, sniffing the ground in a futile attempt to find his prey.

"I see you still have a few nice head of cattle," Matt said to Rafael and Carlos. "I wouldn't let all the bulls run with the herd though."

Rafael removed his huge sombrero and wiped the sweat from his forehead with a shirt sleeve. Cassandra had teased him about the hat, saying one day a strong wind might pick up both it and him and carry them all the way back to Mexico.

"I do not understand," Rafael said as he shoved the sombrero back on his head and adjusted the bonnet strings. "We always let the bulls choose the ladies that most interest them." He elbowed Carlos.

Matt laughed and pointed to a red bull with a bald white face and a white underbelly. "That big one? He's a Hereford, isn't he?"

"Sí. His name is Old Bull. Señor Pickett paid much money for him."

"He doesn't look old. What's his age?"

"This is only his second summer."

"He can father a whole herd of calves before his breedin' days are over. If you bred your best cows to him, the calves would be bigger and of a better quality."

Rafael exchanged a look with Carlos. "That is a good idea. In a few generations, we would have a strong herd again."

"That will help in the future," Matt said, "but to help your financial situation right now, you could sell the lesser cattle, though they won't bring the money they could have a few years back."

Cassandra stepped between the men. "Mr. Atkins, I'm in charge of the livestock. If you have any ideas, you can discuss them with me first."

"Sorry, boss lady. And how many times have I told you to call me Matt?"

Cassandra swung back onto Smokey. "If you refuse to acknowledge me, I'll call you whatever I please."

"Good luck, Señor Matt. You are going to need it," Carlos said before he and Rafael beat a path back to work.

Matt waved at the two men and grinned at Cassandra. "If you aren't somethin'. But you're right. I should have addressed you as well." He tugged the brim of his hat. "Please accept my humble apology."

"Don't let it happen again. Understand?"

"Yes, ma'am. I'll try to remember."

"You better."

"I said I would. Why don't you believe me?"

"Oh, that's rich. You sneak a job out from under my mother, tell me the best way to raise my cattle, and then ask why I doubt you? It's as plain as the sky is blue."

He shrugged. "Well, maybe I made a mistake coming here. Since you don't want me around, I'll be on my way." Matt wheeled his horse in the direction of the barn.

For a long moment, Cassandra watched the muscles of Matt's back play against his shirt. "Don't go," she called out, afraid she'd overreacted.

Matt reined in his horse and waited for her to draw alongside him.

"I just can't figure out why you're so anxious to help," Cassandra said. "I keep telling you we don't need it."

Leather creaked as Matt relaxed in the saddle. "Needin' help isn't a sign of weakness. It can be a sign of strength if you ask for it. And you, Cassandra Jane, are a strong woman." He leaned over and nudged her arm. "I accept your apology, and

I'm sorry I didn't include you in my conversation with Rafael and Carlos. My father uses that method of breedin'—"

"Uses? Didn't you say your father had died?"

"I meant to say he used that method. My father and I were so close, I sometimes feel like he's still alive."

"I understand. I feel Papa's presence every day."

Matt cleared his throat. "Can I see the rest of the ranch, or am I gonna have to beg?"

Cassandra ignored his teasing expression and urged Smokey to a ground-covering trot.

"Hey, hold up," Matt called after her. "Where's the fire?"

Instead of waiting for him, Cassandra touched Smokey's sides with her heels, and the horse shot forward. "Catch us if you can," she yelled back.

The wind freed Cassandra's braid, whipping auburn tresses around her shoulders like a cape. As Smokey's stride increased, the ground rushed by in a blur. A glance behind her showed Matt leaning over Ben's neck, struggling to hold on to his hat. Within minutes she and Smokey had left them far behind. She circled back and allowed Matt to catch up.

"If you aren't something burnin' the breeze," he said. "But if I'd been on King, you and Smokey would have been eatin' our dust."

"In your dreams at night." No horse from Boston could outrun her horse.

"If I weren't worried you'd fire me, I'd head back to the barn, saddle King, and show you who's got the fastest horse."

"Who says I won't fire you anyway?"

"And we were starting to get along so nicely, too." Matt's eyes twinkled in a maddening way.

The pair continued their trek with Cassandra pointing out landmarks as familiar to her as the inside of her bedroom. Since the day she could sit a horse, she had traversed this land either side-by-side with her father or by dogging the vaqueros and cowhands who often complained when she got in the way. But as she grew older, her riding and roping skills made her an integral part of the ranch, much to father's pride and her joy.

A pair of tumbleweeds made a feeble effort to roll by. An errant gust of wind rewarded their effort and sent the plants whirling past Smokey. The horse snorted and tossed his head. Cassandra patted his neck in reassurance.

She searched the sky for clouds, but the air was hot and thick and smelled dusty with no hint of rain. Ever since last year's drought, she worried about the weather. For now, the grass was holding steady, though here and there burnt-sienna touched some of its ends.

Cassandra loved this part of the ranch. The distant hills fought for prominence against the closer flat-top mesas. Not to be outdone, crooked mesquite and cacti vied with lavender dots of verbena. Cassandra longed to dismount and gather a bouquet of the delicate flowers. She and Papa had picked them for Mama, who proclaimed them almost as beautiful as her beloved roses.

Cassandra and Matt rode past a butte crumbling under its stony weight. Ripples of heat swirled off the sunbaked rocks that cluttered its base.

"I'll say this about Texas summers," Matt commented, "they're hotter than a firecracker on the fourth of July."

"December and January make up for it. Breaking ice for a bunch of thirsty horses and cattle is my least favorite job."

"You should see winters in Boston. The snowfall's pretty, but horses have a hard time pushin' through the drifts, and other means of transportation come to a halt. Most people just hunker down and wait it out 'til spring."

"That's another good reason not to—" Cassandra caught herself before she could say *marry Phillip and move to Boston*. She silently thanked the Lord for at least one modicum of restraint.

"What's that?" Matt asked.

"Uh, nothing. Do you miss Boston?"

"Well, it's home. I'd planned to go back there until..."

"Until what?"

"Uh, nothing." Matt aped back her words, and Cassandra conceded if she didn't want him to know her thoughts, she better not push him for his. At least not now.

"I do like Texas," he said, "with its wind-swept prairies, rushin' rivers, tall mountains, and areas like that one." He pointed to the trees stretching out before them. "Look at 'em. More than a man could use in a lifetime."

"Papa loved this state too. He said if a man didn't live and die in Texas, he'd never lived at all. Even years after it was admitted to the Union, he claimed Texas had enough wealth and resources to stand on its own."

"Can I ask what happened to your father?"

"I'll show you." She gave Smokey a loose rein, and the horse quickened his pace. Ben followed Smokey's lead.

The thick grass muffled the two-beat trot of the horses' hooves. Cassandra and Matt evaded stray cacti, tangled thickets, and underbrush before working the horses through a stand of live oak, juniper, and sumac trees. After they cleared the woods, Cassandra brought Smokey to a halt.

Straight ahead, blue-green cedars wrinkled the base of a canyon like a quilt on an unmade bed. On a ridge above the steep walls, an abandoned cabin was hemmed in on three sides by more cedars. Only the dovetailed joints showed evidence of the care Cassandra's father had put into building it. The dried mud and leaves that had once kept out drafts and moisture had flaked off, and a piece of deerskin flapped against a broken windowpane.

Cassandra breathed in the tangy scent of the trees.

"Cedar Ridge?" Matt asked.

"Yes, but there's plenty more trees here than cedars."

She pointed to the head of the canyon formed by two limestone walls. Craggy lines marred their surface, and patches of green showed the vigilant effort of native plants as they dug in and secured a foothold. The water in its center reflected the cloudless sky.

"Papa didn't die from natural causes. Cattle rustlers shot him. Rafael found him right over there." Cassandra's finger shook as she pointed to the spot.

"I'm sorry, Cassandra."

"Did Carlos tell you how Papa got this land?"

"Yes."

"He didn't necessarily want more property, but the waterhole did help after Goose Neck Creek dried up. It's deeper than it looks. All the cattle couldn't drink here at one time, so Carlos and I would wait at the ranch with half the herd while Papa and Rafael brought the other half. The day Papa died, Rafael's horse had pulled up lame. Papa insisted he walk the horse back and get another mount."

Cassandra couldn't stop her lips from quivering. "W–When Rafael returned, the cattle were gone, and Papa was dead. Rafael brought his body back to the house before he and Carlos raced to town to round up a posse."

"Did they catch whoever did it?"

"No, the rustlers had driven the cattle south down the North Concho River to cover their tracks. Unfortunately, the marshal and the men traveled north. By the time they circled back, the sun had set. The next morning the rustlers were long gone."

Tears slipped down Cassandra's face. Matt leaned over and brushed them away with his thumb. "I'm sorry."

"You must have felt the same when your parents died."

"About my parents—"

"Please. I don't want to talk about it anymore. Can we go?"

"Sure. You can show me the rest of the ranch another time, but when we get back, I'd like to talk to your mother about those ideas I've already shared and these trees on your property."

They dismounted and let the horses drink from the waterhole. Cassandra fiddled with her reins and winged a hollow prayer heavenward. *Lord, no matter how many times I try, I speak out of turn. Please don't let Mama be upset when she finds out I told Matt about the loan.*

The fight left Cassandra. What was the use? God was probably busy and not listening to her prayer anyway.

⋆⋆⋆

From the deep shadows of a stand of cedars, a lone cowboy studied the riders. He fished a match from his shirt pocket and stooped down to strike it against the stony ground. The flame flickered and lit his face as he started a long brown cheroot. After Cassandra and Matt vanished from the ridgeline, the cowboy stamped out his cigar. He sprang onto his horse's back and galloped straight for the Lazy Acres Ranch.

Nine

Cassandra fretted the entire ride back to the ranch. Would God answer her prayer and keep Matt from asking her mother about the loan? Afraid she couldn't trust the Lord or Matt, she prepared her only defense. Confession.

She asked Carlos to take care of Smokey and then sped inside the house to find her mother arranging a vase of roses in the dining room. Cassandra ignored the scent that usually calmed her.

"Oh, Mama. I told Matt what happened to Papa and about the loan. I assumed Carlos had already told him. I tried to cover it up, but now Matt wants to help. I'm sorry..." Her voice trailed off in misery.

To her astonishment, her mother said, "That is wonderful news."

"It is?"

"Matt's willingness to help might be the answer to our prayers."

Before Cassandra could voice a contradiction, Matt entered the room. She bit her knuckle and stared at her feet.

"Mrs. Pickett," Matt said, "while Cassandra Jane was showing me around, I came up with a couple of ideas that might help the ranch."

He pulled out a chair for Helen, but before he could do the same for Cassandra, she whipped out a chair from under the table and sat on its edge. Matt shrugged and straddled the chair across from her.

"First," he said, "you need to cull the lesser cattle from your herd for some immediate cash. The men and I can build a fence on the far side of the creek to hold Old Bull. Then you can breed him to your better cows to build a stronger herd. You can also spread the word he'd make a good cross with the thinner Texas longhorn. Though the Beef Bonanza has died down, some ranches are still gettin' fifteen dollars a head for good stock, which he could produce."

"But the loan is due next month," Helen replied. "Even if we sold the inferior cattle, there would not be enough money to repay the bank."

"I have another idea. I met two men in Fort Worth who work for the S & R Railroad. They're plannin' on layin' line from Sweetwater almost into Mexico just north of Goose Neck Ridge."

"How does that affect us?"

Matt laced his fingers behind his head "I noticed all the trees growin' by Cedar Ridge. Straight as arrows, reachin' for the sky. Since the railroad's gonna need timber for ties, you could offer yours. With a contract under your belt, the bank is sure to extend your loan. Tomorrow I'd like to help Rafael and Carlos cull the herd and start buildin' the fence for Old Bull, but the day after that I can wire Big George and see if he's interested in your timber."

"Mr. Thompson?" Helen questioned.

"Cattle's his main business, but after the Union and Central Pacific met east and west at Promontory, he figured the future held rails runnin' north and south. He invested in the S and R Railroad. Didn't take long for him to make a profit. He branched out, bought a couple hotels, a bank, a stop on the stagecoach line, a paper mill, and the *Fort Worth Daily Gazette* until he sold it a few years ago. Now, he's one of the richest men in Fort Worth."

Cassandra tapped her fingers on the table. Life was unfair. Here, she and Mama were struggling to keep their home, and men like George Thompson and Phillip Brigham had more than enough money to spare. "Too bad Papa didn't invest in the railroad. Huh, Mama?"

"I am sure Mr. Thompson is resourceful, but God is the one who gives certain men wealth." Helen's voice quickened in excitement, "But Matt's ideas are good ones."

Something akin to guilt swept Matt's chiseled features. "Don't get your hopes up yet. These plans may not work."

"God is in control. We must trust him." Helen's eyes shone a crystal gray. "I cannot wait for the others to hear about this."

⭑⭑⭑

Helen let Cassandra share the good news that evening. Tears wet Maria's eyes. She thanked the good Lord and threatened to give Matt a big hug. He stumbled away from her and said, "Thanks, but that won't be necessary."

The moment Rafael, Carlos, and Roberto came into the house, Maria jabbered the news so rapidly in Spanish, Cassandra had a hard time following her.

"Would you mind if we all spoke English?" Matt asked. "My Spanish is a bit rusty."

Cassandra's mouth dropped open. Had he understood Maria's comment about her marrying him? "I thought you didn't understand Spanish, Señor Atkins."

"You never asked. I've picked up a few words since I came out west. Enough to agree with Maria," his voice lowered to a whisper, "you shouldn't marry Phillip Brigham."

"That doesn't concern you."

"Just voicin' my opinion."

"If I want your opinion—"

He tapped the end of her nose. "I know. You'll ask me for it."

"Señor Matt," Rafael spoke up, "will the railroad be here soon?"

"It's hard to say. On a good day, a crew can lay two to five miles of track. If they keep that up..." Cassandra held her breath while he calculated the numbers on his fingers. "Near as I can tell, come October."

"Would they not already have timber lined up?" Rafael smoothed his mustache as he pondered the possibility.

"Yes, Mr. Matt, what makes you think your idea will work?" Roberto asked from the corner of the dining room, suspicion stamping his face.

"I'm gonna send a telegram to Big George and find out."

"I sure hope he doesn't say no," Cassandra said, daring her heart to hope for the first time.

Maria hugged Cassandra's neck. "It is no time to hang out your wash-day face. You must have faith in the Lord and believe he will use Señor Matt's idea to save our ranch."

"How can I have a wash-day face, Maria? I don't even know what that is."

"That is when the corners of your mouth turn down like wet sheets hanging on the line."

Cassandra laughed and threw up her palms in surrender. Right now, the possibility of saving the Triple P filled her with such happiness, she couldn't be aggravated with Maria or Matt.

⭑⭑⭑

The meal that evening reminded Cassandra of those shared with her father. Everyone but her mother and Roberto prattled merrily as the others interrupted each other in their desire to be heard. Her mother did interject a remark now and again, but Roberto sat sullen, staring at his half-eaten plate. Cassandra chalked up his reticence to being made to clean the stalls that afternoon.

To celebrate the occasion, Maria had prepared a cottage pie. Matt dug into the steaming chunks of savory beef layered with fresh corn and smothered in creamy mashed potatoes. Each time he emptied his plate, Maria filled it back up. After the third helping, he held up a hand in protest.

"If I keep eating like this, King won't be able to carry me into town to send that telegram."

Rafael and Carlos broke into whoops of laughter. "You are a funny man, Señor Matt," Rafael said, wiping his tears with a handkerchief.

Matt continued to entertain with tales of growing up and playing pranks on the family butler. Cassandra giggled at the image of him putting itching powder in Randolph's socks and tying the poor man's shoelaces together. Even Roberto seemed amused by the antics, though he was quick to turn his head whenever Matt glanced his way.

"And Randolph didn't get mad and tell your parents what you did?" Cassandra asked.

"He loved me, though after pulling all those tricks, I'm not sure how. As far as I know, he kept all my secrets."

Cassandra couldn't imagine a big eastern estate with a butler and a full-time staff, but she did understand Randolph's fierce loyalty to his young charge. Maria had done the same for her–covering for an incomplete chore, giving bear hugs instead of a scolding, and sneaking her sweet bits before supper.

"What happened to Randolph when you sold your family home?" Cassandra asked.

"An equally nice place hired him." Matt reached out for a bowl of creamy custard pudding flecked with cinnamon. "Anyone ready for dessert?"

After supper Matt insisted on helping Maria clear the table, much to her delight and to considerable ribbing from Carlos and Rafael. Each time he crossed the dining room with a stack of dishes, the two men bowed in a grand gesture.

"Señor Matt," Carlos said. "Do all men from Boston help the womenfolk in the kitchen?"

"No," he chuckled. "Only real men help with kitchen work." He elbowed Rafael in the ribs. "It wouldn't hurt you to learn your way around the kitchen."

The big man flashed Matt a grin. "I do not ask Maria to help brand the new calves, and she does not ask me to help bake her pies."

Maria flicked her husband with a dish towel. "The last thing I want, *mi amor*, is for you to step foot into my kitchen."

"It's true," Cassandra agreed. "Maria tolerates me and Mama's help, but only because she's having a baby in a few months and sometimes gets tired." She turned toward Matt and Carlos. "Why don't you boys go to the study and do whatever eastern gentlemen do after supper?"

"I'll pass," Matt replied. "Gentlemen in Boston usually drink a glass of port and smoke a cigar. I don't cotton to either one."

Cassandra shooed the men toward the door. "We don't have any liquor in the house or those nasty-smelling cigars. You work out the details for saving the Triple P, and we ladies will finish up in here. But," she warned, "I expect you to tell me what you discuss later on."

Matt saluted Cassandra. "Will do, boss lady. My work here is done." He marched through the dining room doors and then stopped to ask, "Which way is the study?"

Carlos grabbed Matt's arm and pulled him to the left. "This way, Señor Matt." Rafael followed the pair, still praising Maria in Spanish for the fine meal she'd prepared. Roberto slouched behind his father with his hands jammed deep in his pants pockets.

Maria wrapped an arm around Cassandra's shoulders as they followed Helen into the kitchen. "I think my Roberto is jealous of Señor Matt."

"Why?" Cassandra asked, tying an apron around her waist.

"Do you not notice how he keeps a special eye on you? Helping you with chores and giving compliments when you wear a pretty dress at supper?"

Cassandra considered Maria's words. True, Roberto was a pleasant shadow, but did he think of her as more than a big sister? "He never seemed jealous of Phillip."

"Roberto is a good judge of character like you, Señora Pickett." Maria nodded at Helen, who was pouring water warmed on the stove into a dish basin. "He can tell Señor Brigham does not hold your heart. I think he senses an attraction between you and Señor Matt."

Cassandra wrinkled her nose. "Well, he's wrong. I don't have any feelings for Matt other than gratitude for his ideas to help save the ranch. And besides, Roberto is a child."

"He is nearly thirteen and almost a man." Maria handed a dishcloth to Cassandra and a towel to Helen. "The two of you can wash and dry," she instructed.

Cassandra dipped her hands into the warm, sudsy water. "I don't want to mislead Roberto."

"Life is not always kind to boys as they become men. Hard times will help his heart learn to care, so one day he will fall in love with the one God chooses for him."

"I'll find the right time and talk to him." Cassandra handed her mother a plate to rinse and dry. Excitement heightened her voice. "Mama, we're going to save the ranch."

"There is still much to do and much that needs to fall into place," Helen reminded her.

"But now, there's a chance I won't have to marry Phillip."

"Darling, why would you consider marrying him if he wants to sell the Triple P and move to Boston?"

"I didn't know his plans until he told me, but I could talk him out of them."

Cassandra had no idea if she could convince Phillip to stay in Texas, but she would ride that pony to death if need be. She wrenched a cast iron skillet from Maria. "Stop that. You must not work so hard in your condition."

"And what condition is that?" Maria harrumphed. "Women have been having babies since Eve got kicked out of the Garden."

"We worry about you," Helen added. "Especially since you had such a difficult time with Roberto."

Cassandra had been eight years old when Roberto was born. Her mother had brought Maria, pale and shaking, into the house while Carlos galloped his horse to Goose Neck Ridge for the doctor. Her father hustled Cassandra out to the barn where they passed the time by grooming the horses and cleaning all of the tack. Evening shadows filled the barn before Roberto arrived into the world, healthy and squalling at the top of his lungs.

But the doctor ordered Maria to bed for the next several weeks with the grim news she could never bear another child. Though she and Rafael had longed for a home full of children, they accepted God's will. Twelve years later, the Lord had chosen to bless them with the baby she now carried.

"I will be fine," Maria said. She handed Cassandra another dirty pan. "Maybe the good Lord has sent Señor Matt at just the right time."

"God's timing is perfect," Helen said as she stacked the last of the clean plates. "He is never too early, and he is never too late."

"Mama, how do you keep trusting God? I can trust him when things are good, but it's difficult when they aren't."

"He has always taken care of us. Though I admit, I spent extra time this afternoon praying about the timber for the railroad ties." She repressed a yawn. "It has been a busy day. I am going to retire for the night. Are you coming?"

"I'm too excited to sleep," Cassandra said. "After I finish in here, I'm going to sit on the porch for a while. I'll be up in a bit."

Cassandra and Maria chatted about the day's events while Cassandra finished washing the pots and pans. She was dumping the dirty water out the back door when Maria said, "Go on. You have done enough. I will finish tidying up."

"All right, but you must promise not to overdo."

"If you and your mamá had your way, I would not be doing anything." Maria bumped Cassandra aside with a swing of a hip. "You go now and see if Señor Matt has come up with any more ideas to save the ranch."

The heels of Cassandra's shoes struck a rhythmic path across the dining room floor. As she walked up the hall, she heard the muffled voices of the men coming from the study. She wanted to press her ear to the door and listen, but a mental picture of her unladylike entrance at the noon meal kept her moving toward the porch.

"Señor Matt," Carlos said as the study door opened behind her, "I am not sure those ideas will work. But you can tell the ladies about them in the morning. Unless you want to tell Señorita Cassie right now. It looks like she is about to go outside. Maybe she needs more fresh air."

Cassandra refrained from giving Carlos a snappy retort, and instead, gave Matt a hopeful look. "I'm going to sit on the porch. Would you care to join me?" She crossed her fingers behind her back and pretended not to notice the sour look Roberto sent in Matt's direction.

"I'd love to, Cassandra Jane. Lead the way."

Rafael called out to Maria. "*Mi amor,* are you about finished?"

"Sí, my Rafael." Maria crossed the dining room floor and said, "*Hasta mañana,* Miss Cassie. Señor Matt. Do not stay up too late. We have a full day ahead of us tomorrow."

She put her hand into the crook of Rafael's arm and motioned for Roberto and Carlos to follow. The four strolled home, their voices fading into the star-flecked night.

Ten

Cassandra lifted her mint-colored shawl off a peg by the door. She smiled, remembering how her father had surprised her with the silk wrap and matching dinner dress. At the time, her mother insisted the dress was too formal for ranch life, but her father pshawed the complaint and bought Cassandra two more just like it in different colors.

Maria told Cassandra, "You must tell your papá to stop buying you so many dresses. You can barely close your armoire's door, and I am the one who must do all the ironing." She had been teasing. Everyone in the household loved Cassandra's father and enjoyed the things he bought.

Matt took the shawl from Cassandra. "Here. Let me help." His fingers brushed her arms as he settled the soft material around her shoulders. Cassandra shivered more from the gesture than the cool breeze that was chasing away the heat of the day. She gathered the shawl under her chin and managed a weak thank you.

The oil lamps, glowing from inside the house, helped create comfortable shadows on the porch. Cassandra relaxed onto one of the chairs. "It's a beautiful night."

"I agree." Matt closed his eyes and leaned against the porch railing.

Cassandra snatched the opportunity to admire his profile–thick lashes, the kind any woman would envy, offset a slight Roman nose above a full mouth and strong jawline. For a fanciful moment she envisioned him as Chiron, the centaur in the book of Greek mythology her father had read to her. She wondered what her mother would think of her brazen scrutiny. She knew what Roberto's reaction would be. Her face set in a frown at the young boy's jealousy.

"Matt?"

"Hmm?"

"Do you think Roberto is jealous of you?"

"Oh, you noticed?"

"I didn't until Maria mentioned it. I can't for the life of me figure out why."

"He's not had to share your friendship until I rode up. He sees me as competition. Not that I am," he was quick to add.

"I plan to talk to him."

"I don't know. It's enough the young man feels someone's movin' in on his territory without you pointin' it out."

"What would you suggest?" Cassandra couldn't believe she was asking Matt for advice on matters of the heart.

"It might be better if I talk to him. Man to man. Let him know he'll have a crush on several pretty girls," he winked at Cassandra, "before he finds the right one."

Cassandra pursed her lips, not sure if she agreed with Matt's suggestion. She decided if the opportunity presented itself, she would also talk to Roberto.

"Those roses sure smell sweet," Matt said. "Your perfume smells just like 'em."

Cassandra's cheeks tingled. He had noticed. "Mama works hard to grow the roses in the dry soil. She learned how to make perfume from a book Papa bought her. She extracts the oil from the petals."

"Did you ever try sellin' it? Women in Boston would line up ten-deep to buy perfume that smelled so nice."

"It never crossed our minds. How do you come up with all these ideas?"

"After I sold White Oak Manor, I learned to be resourceful."

"White Oak Manor? That's a strange name."

"For your information, huge white oak trees surrounded my home and shaded the horse pastures. Now, as I was tellin' ya this afternoon... about a year ago, I met Big George Thompson. I was droppin' off a herd in Dallas, and he was pickin' out some breedin' stock. We talked a spell and he hired me, right there on the spot."

"You do have a knack for convincing people to hire you."

"Why, Cassandra Jane, that's only one of my many talents. Are you interested in the others?" He sidled up beside her chair.

Cassandra jumped to her feet and backed away. Why had he said that? "T–Tell me about the cattle drives you worked for Mr. Thompson," she said, fiddling with the collar of her dress.

Matt crossed his arms and settled against the porch railing again. "Last year we took five-thousand head up the Chisholm

Trail to Ellsworth. From there the cattle boarded the old Kansas Pacific Railroad to Denver."

"I wanted to go on a cattle drive, but Papa wouldn't let me. He said it was too dangerous."

"And right he was. I almost lost my life crossin' the South Platte River. We were comin' off a hard rain, and the river was flowin' fast. King and I got tangled up with a big ol' heifer, and she about pulled us both under."

He rubbed his temples as though blotting out the memory. "On top of that, we worried about the weather and stampedes."

"I think riding all day and sleeping under a star-studded sky would be fun."

"I wouldn't call sleepin' on the hard ground with nothin' but a saddle for a pillow fun. Nor is workin' sun-up to sun-down with nary a break in between." He gazed up at the night sky. "But I did learn to tell time and direction by the stars."

"Papa knew the constellations. He gave up trying to show me. I never could find them."

"Come here. I'll show you a couple."

Cassandra's heart beat wildly in her throat.

"C'mon. I won't bite. At least not hard."

After she dragged her feet to his side, he pointed to the brightest star. "There's the North Star."

He was standing so close, his wool shirt brushed her arm. "I–I can find that one," she said.

"Good. Above and to the left are the Great and Little Bears. Their backs, hindquarters, and tails are shaped like ladles standin' on end."

"All I see are pinpoints of light hanging from a black velvet sky."

"That's mighty poetic, but those fancy words won't help you find them."

"Then show me."

He made a fist of her hand, then guided a finger upward. "Go up and to the left of the North Star. See their long tails?" He traced the outline of the bears with her finger.

Cassandra quivered at his touch before realizing she could make out the shape of the constellations. "I can see them. They're facing each other."

"Notice the Great Bear's position? It's eight o'clock. When it dips under the North Star, one cowboy's shift ends and the next one begins. If we were out on the range, it'd be time for the second watch."

He tightened his warm fingers over hers. Cassandra looked down at her feet and traced her shadow with the toe of her slipper.

"You did that earlier today," Matt said.

"Did what?"

"Looked down 'cause you were uncomfortable."

"I did not."

"Look at me." He lifted her chin, so she had to meet his eyes. "You don't have to be scared. I won't hurt you."

Cassandra wiggled her hand from his grasp. "You were kind of vague this afternoon when I asked why you left the Circle T. Care to elaborate?"

He paused as though measuring his words. "Let's say it was time to move on. I'm glad I did, or I wouldn't have met you. And your mother and the others."

She turned her head to keep Matt from seeing how pleased his comment had made her. "Did you men discuss plans for the ranch?" she asked to change the subject.

"A few. But—"

"You need to share them with me. I am in charge around here."

"I know, boss lady. You told me that on more than one occasion today."

"It's the truth. Mama and Papa didn't have a son, and as the only child, the responsibility of the ranch falls on me."

"I understand. My father wanted me to take over White Oak Manor when the time came."

"Would he have been disappointed you sold it and moved on?"

"I'm sure he would have." Matt slapped his hands against the side of his legs. "But I can't do anything about that now. How about we enjoy this nice evening and save Triple P business for the morning?"

Cassandra had to agree. The night was lovely. But first thing tomorrow she'd remind him to share any plans he had for her ranch.

The two sat in pleasant silence and listened to the gentle voices of the night. The steady hum of crickets accompanied the stirring of cattle and an occasional grunt from the pigs. A great horned owl winged its way over the barn, its outline darker than the night. Matt mimicked the owl's hoot and then a coyote's howl as it defended its territory.

"Did you know coyotes mate for life?" Cassandra asked. "They set up a den, and the male brings food to the female until the pups are born."

"Who'd ever thought those critters had any redeemin' qualities?"

"They can be quite family-like. If a female doesn't find a mate, she'll help raise her mother and sisters' litters. This way the pups are never on their own."

Silence filled the space between them until Matt said, "That's better than bein' an unwanted pup."

"You don't care for coyotes?"

"They have their purpose in God's design."

She latched onto the opportunity to ask, "Matt, are you religious?"

"That's kind of personal, don't you think?"

"Papa said if a man confesses the Lord before men, the Lord will confess him in heaven."

"I can't say I've done much confessing as of late."

"Is there a reason?"

"I'd rather not say."

"As far as the Lord goes, I'm not sure about a few things myself. I feel foolish talking about them to Mama. She makes the Christian life seem so easy. Even after Papa died, she kept trusting the Lord. I wish I could—"

"You don't have to tell me this."

"I don't mind talking about religion."

"I can take it or leave it."

"You don't put religion on and off like a hat."

"I'm not, Miss High-and-Mighty. I'm just rethinkin' my position."

Cassandra battled a frown. Why was he getting so upset? She braved on. "I was seven when I became a Christian, and I haven't changed my mind about it, but I'm not as strong in the

Lord as I'd like to be." Matt's next words were so low, Cassandra had to lean closer to hear them.

"The Christian walk is one of growth. You begin like a baby and grow as your faith increases. Unless you wander off God's path."

Cassandra contemplated his comment. She hadn't wandered away, but was she still a baby in Christ?

"I know I'm on the right path," she said, "but I don't think I've traveled very far up it. How about you?"

"Can we drop the subject? I don't want to talk about it."

The set of Matt's jaw shut down the conversation as sure as Cassandra wanted to keep it open. She made a silent vow to find out what had darkened his view of God.

She breathed in the night air, a mix of the cool breeze, the prairie settling at night, and her mother's roses. "I love this place."

"I can't believe you're thinkin' about marryin' Phillip Brigham to save it."

"Carlos told you?"

"Yes, but there's got to be a better way to get the money you need. No matter what, it'd be a terrible mistake to marry a man you don't love." The floorboards creaked under his chair as he shifted his weight.

"Phillip wasn't always bad."

"Are you kiddin'?"

Cassandra argued her point. "Though he's five years older than me, we used to be best friends. We rode horses and read novels together. We also read Christian literature and acted out Bible stories. Mrs. Brigham didn't like us doing either of those for some reason. If she caught us, she made Phillip go inside the house and sent me home."

"I can't imagine Phillip havin' anything to do with God." Matt was silent for a moment. "Why didn't his mother like you actin' out Bible stories? Seems harmless enough to me."

"I'm not sure. Bella, the Lazy Acres cook, swore Mrs. Brigham was a Christian, but she didn't show many Christ-like qualities. She wasn't a loving person. Bella told Maria she wasn't even sure Mrs. Brigham loved her husband." Cassandra bit her knuckle, not sure she should continue sharing Lazy Acres gossip.

"If that's true, how'd she and Mr. Brigham get together?"

"They met when he was visiting his older brother in Boston." She tapped her cheek with one finger. "Hmm, you're from Boston, and you seemed surprised when you heard Phillip's name this morning. Did you know his aunt and uncle? I can't remember his aunt's name, but his uncle's name is Walter."

Matt rose to his feet and then disappeared into the dark recesses of the porch. "I might have heard of them. But Boston's a big city, and Brigham's a common name."

"Well, Bella said Mrs. Brigham, who was Miss McAllister at the time, never walked on the traditional side. She was intrigued with Mr. Brigham being a big Texas rancher and insisted her parents host a dinner party and invite him and Walter. They barely left each other's side the remainder of his stay in Boston. After he returned home, she found out she was in–in the family way."

"It's all right, Cassandra Jane. I know where babies come from."

Cassandra hoped the shadows of the porch covered her burning cheeks.

"The McAllisters wouldn't allow their good name to be tarnished," she continued. "so they sent Margaret to her aunt's house in Philadelphia until after the baby was born. She threatened to go to Texas and find Harold, but her parents forbade her to leave."

"What happened to the baby?"

"It died at birth. Margaret was heart-broken and made good on her threat. She fled to Texas, married Mr. Brigham, and not once returned to Boston. Bella said she never got over the death of her child. Even when Phillip came along, she didn't seem happy, but at least she was content being *La Patrona* of Lazy Acres. She used to ride her big black horse and keep an eye on the vaqueros to make sure they did their job."

"Is she still alive?" Matt's words were tight.

"No. When Phillip was fifteen, she died giving birth to a stillborn baby girl. He didn't cry when they buried his mother, but he did when they lowered his sister's tiny coffin into the ground. He always wanted to be a big brother. I understand his desire for a sibling. Mama had a riding accident right after I was born and couldn't have any more children."

She made a small gesture with her hands. "Then when Phillip's father died... Well, he's not been the same." Pity for Phillip washed over Cassandra despite herself. Matt must have felt the same thing for he pulled a handkerchief out of his pocket and ran it over his eyes.

"I'm sorry," Cassandra said. "I shouldn't have shared that. It's probably just gossip."

"I'm tired. That's all."

"My story upset you, didn't it?"

"I said I'm tired. Can you leave it at that?" The tone of his voice was hard.

"My story affected you, didn't it? Matt Atkins, I think underneath that rugged hide of yours, beats a kind and gentle heart."

Her words failed to ease the tension that had come between them. She rose to her feet in resignation. "Saving ranches is hard work. I'm calling it a night. Tomorrow's another day."

Cassandra trudged inside leaving Matt staring stone-faced into the night with his thoughts. *Whatever did I say wrong this time?*

Eleven

At the breakfast table the next morning, Matt still seemed pensive. At least toward Cassandra. He perked up when Rafael, Carlos, and Roberto stepped into the dining room. The four men shoveled down scrambled eggs, slabs of smoked ham, leftover biscuits, and steaming cups of coffee. But to Cassandra's chagrin, every time she spoke to Matt, he steered the conversation back to the vaqueros.

After breakfast the men headed out to build the fence for Old Bull. Matt asked Rafael, Carlos, and Roberto to carry the equipment and insisted Cassandra sit under the big oak tree and watch them work. His patronizing smile when she protested did nothing to improve her mood, nor did the sweat trickling down her neck from a stiff southern breeze. She aimed a defiant look at Matt before yanking on her leather work gloves and picking up a posthole digger.

"Young lady, I told you I don't need your help," he scolded.

"And I said I'm not young."

"I forgot. Twenty and still single, huh? I bet ya haven't even been kissed yet. Am I right?"

Cassandra wasn't about to admit that, other than her father kissing her forehead or cheek, she'd only been kissed by Billy Dunlap, and that was behind the schoolhouse in third grade. Unfortunately, their teacher, Miss Richardson, caught the juvenile attempt and made them sit in opposite corners of the room for an hour. And there had been Phillip in the— She chased the sordid image away.

She grimaced at Matt. "I will not dignify that ribald question with an answer."

"Ribald? I've heard of the horse color piebald." He pointed to Carlos's horse grazing in the field to his left. "But I've never heard of the word ribald. You sure use some high-falootin' words."

Cassandra clenched her teeth to keep from zinging him with a hundred more. His jabs were stretching the thread of her patience to a breaking point.

He reached out a palm for the digger. "I said I don't need your help."

Cassandra swung the implement away from him. "I'm not helping you, I'm helping Carlos, Rafael, and Roberto."

"They're fine. Right, men?" Carlos and Rafael bobbed their heads and continued unrolling barbed wire. Roberto frowned from where he worked, lining up the fence posts.

Matt seized the post hole digger from Cassandra. "I would not consider myself a gentleman if I let you do a man's work." He held her off at arm's length while she grabbed for the digger.

"You're anything but a gentleman. I could do this if you'd stop being bull-headed and give me that thing."

“Me? You win the blue ribbon for being bull-headed.” He handed over the digger. “All right. Hey, Carlos. Rafael. You too, Roberto. Cassandra Jane’s gonna show us how to dig a hole.” The men looked up with uncertainty from their work.

Cassandra narrowed her eyes at Matt. “That wasn’t necessary.”

“I know.” He flashed a perfect set of teeth. “It would help if you wet the ground first.”

She avoided the truth of his statement. “I don’t need to.”

“As you wish.”

Cassandra pushed up her shirtsleeves, blew out a breath, and dropped the post hole digger onto the hard-packed ground. The claws barely nicked the soil.

“Maybe, Señorita Cassie, you should lift it a bit higher,” Carlos suggested. She ignored his and Rafael’s grin. Her next effort only drove the digger two inches farther.

“Miss Cassie, you can do it,” Roberto encouraged, though his face showed his own misgiving.

Matt pried the tool from her fingers. “You stubborn redhead. I said soak the ground first. But, no, you’ve gotta do things your way. Goodness, back East—”

“Back East,” Cassandra mimicked Matt, “women let the men do the pants-wearin’ and the post hole diggin’.”

“You’re right. Back East, men are men and women are women.”

“And what do those women do all day? Wait for rich men to sweep them off their feet, get married, and have a passel of children?”

A muscle in Matt’s jaw tensed. “A few do.”

He rammed the post hole digger into the ground with such force a claw broke. With a stifled curse he grabbed a bucket and stormed off toward the creek. Carlos and Rafael exchanged a surprised glance with Cassandra.

What's wrong with him? He makes sweeping accusations against me, and I make one comment about eastern women, and he gets upset?

Rafael mouthed, "Blessed are the peacemakers."

Cassandra shook her head so hard her hat shifted over one eye. Why did she have to offer the olive branch? Matt had been the one to run off. Rafael kept making a scat-motion with his hands.

"Oh, all right," Cassandra said. Rafael would keep pestering her until she did as he suggested. He and Maria shared that same knack.

She straightened her hat and lengthened her strides to catch up to Matt. "Wait. I didn't mean to upset you. I'm sure there are many fine ladies back East, but I wasn't reared to sit and drink tea and eat crumpets all day." She mumbled, "And I should have soaked the ground first."

"What was that?"

"You heard me. I should have soaked the ground first." But not willing to let a dead horse lie, she asked, "Did a pretty little eastern woman try to get all your money?" She giggled at the silly idea. Matt, a wealthy man? Other than his horse and tack, everything he possessed was either in his bedroll or his saddlebag.

"I don't have any money, but a woman with silver-colored hair and eyes the color of violets jilted a rich friend of mine.

When she met a wealthier man, she dropped Ethan faster than that mama cow over there dropped her calf last night."

Cassandra's gaze followed his to the newest addition of the Triple P. The brown and white calf bumped its mother's underbelly as it nursed. "Was your friend angry?"

"What do you think?"

Cassandra flinched at the harsh tone of Matt's voice. "I don't know."

"He still loved her, so he begged her to stay. She laughed in his face. Told him to come back when he had more to offer."

Cassandra couldn't fathom any woman being so heartless, but other than Phillip's mother, she'd never met anyone from back East. Eastern women must be different. "What happened to him?"

"He left Boston to prove himself."

"And?"

"Last I heard he's still trying." He pointed back to the broken post hole digger. "I'm sorry about that, and I'm sorry I raised my voice. But I can't get over your wantin' to dress and act like a man."

"Matt Atkins, I'll have you know that underneath these pants I'm all woman." Her cheeks flamed hot as soon as the words left her mouth. Matt's lips twitched into a smile, and she rushed on.

"I meant, Papa not only taught me how to run the ranch, but he also insisted I receive an education. When I outgrew the schoolhouse, he hired a tutor from New Orleans to teach me French, Latin, literature, grammar, and numbers. I even taught school for a year until Papa had to let the vaqueros go and needed my help back here."

"You were a teacher?"

"I received high scores on the exam for my teaching certificate. At the time, Papa said he could sell one steer and clear more profit than I made in a month, but I loved those children and would have taught them even if I hadn't received a dime."

"How did you manage a roomful of kids? Oh. I know." He stopped to face her. "You used the same endearing voice you use on me, right?"

Cassandra refused to be ensnared by Matt's twinkling eyes. "On rare occasions I needed to raise my voice, but many of the children had hard lives at home. I wanted the schoolhouse to be a place where they could learn to better themselves."

"The West hasn't been easy to tame. Many people lost their lives blazin' trails and buildin' towns that benefited those who came later."

"Papa's mother and father almost died coming here from Virginia. Papa proclaimed Grandfather the most stubborn man in the county. After he arrived here from Ireland—"

"I should have known you had Irish blood. With all the fiery red hair to match the grit of yours."

"Would you, please, let me finish?"

"Do continue, me fair Irish maiden." Matt raised an arm above his head and sashayed a circle around Cassandra. She couldn't help but laugh at his imitation of an Irish jig.

"My grandparents lived in Richmond until the day Grandfather upped and told Grandmother to pack their necessities. They were heading to Texas. The trip wasn't easy, but even after getting caught in a snowstorm and a flood, they arrived at Goose Neck Ridge when it was only a fledgling town."

"So, you got your pluck from them?"

Cassandra was about to protest again, but Matt lifted a hand and said, "Go on."

"They built a respectable cabin, and a year later Papa arrived. Three years after that my Uncle Richard was born. Grandmother poured herself into the boys. Since she'd come from southern gentry, she taught them to read and write, plus the genteel manners she'd practiced in Richmond. Those lessons stuck. Papa taught them to me, though he wouldn't admit to Mama they were as important to learn as ranch work. He even taught me to waltz."

"You can waltz?"

"Yes, Mr. Only-women-back-East-are-ladies, I can waltz. Can you?"

"Most definitely. As can all eastern men of good breeding."

The image of Matt waltzing across a ballroom in his work-worn clothes, Stetson, and mule-ear boots made Cassandra giggle.

"What's so funny?"

"I can picture men from Boston dancing at a fancy ball, but not a cowboy."

"I can't remember the last time I dressed up and shook a boot on the dancefloor. Since I left home, King's been my sole partner. He may sidestep now and again, but not once has he waltzed."

Cassandra should have cared less that Matt had led a solitary life since he left Boston. She'd only met him yesterday, and after all, he was a hired hand. But the news he'd not had any female companionship the past several years still gave her a certain amount of satisfaction.

"What happened to your grandparents?" Matt asked.

"After struggling for years, Grandfather admitted the Wild West wasn't for him. He, Grandmother, and Uncle Richard moved back to Richmond. Papa didn't go with them. He'd heard about gold in Colorado, so he headed up that way."

"Yep. They found deposits up there ten years after the California gold rush. Did your father find any?"

"He never talked much about his days in Colorado, but Mama said he made enough to get by. I'm glad he didn't stay there, or he never would have met Mama, and there'd be no Triple P."

"If ya don't mind my askin', does your mother have any family who could help with your loan?"

Cassandra gave a sad shake of her head. "Mama was only seventeen when she met Papa. The spring after they married, her baby sister contracted smallpox and passed away. A health officer quarantined their home, but it was too late. Both of her parents fell sick, and they, plus her two younger brothers died."

"I'm sorry. It must have been hard on her."

"It was. Up until then, she'd been carefree. What you easterners call the belle of the ball. She used to love to dance, but Papa said after her family died, she changed. She lost her mischievous spirit and started taking things more seriously. Now, with Papa gone and the ranch in trouble," Cassandra raised her hands in a helpless gesture, "I don't know how she keeps trusting God."

"Your mother's strong and a woman of faith. And from what my parents taught me, faith can sustain a person through any trial." His eyes left her face, and Cassandra wondered why he suddenly looked uncomfortable.

"Well, how about your father's family?" he asked. "The ones back east. Are they in a position to help?"

"Mama would never ask. Uncle Richard is a cobbler with a wife and five children, and he took on the responsibility of caring for Grandmother after Grandfather died. We couldn't ask them to take us on as well."

"Sometimes people have enough problems of their own." Matt removed his hat, then raked fingers through his damp hair. "It sure is a hot one."

Phillip smooths his hair back just like that, Cassandra thought. She shook her head. The heat must be getting to her.

Matt shoved his hat back on and continued toward the creek. He called over his shoulder, "I'm gonna cool off while I fill this bucket. You comin'?"

"Only if I can go first."

She jogged by Matt and led the way through tangled reeds that lined the loamy bank of the creek. A ground squirrel scurried through the undergrowth, and birds chirped and trilled from the tops of the mesquite trees. After Cassandra and Matt wended their way downstream, they reached a chain of rocks that snaked across the creek. As the water rippled across the formation, it made a pleasant gurgling sound.

The two plopped down at the water's edge and peeled off their boots and socks. "Did you and the men come up with any other ideas to save the Triple P?" she asked, pushing her socks deep inside her boots. The last time she'd waded in the creek, one of her socks fell into the water, and she had to chase it downstream before she caught up to it.

"I tossed around a few like sellin' some of your other livestock. But Rafael said you need all of it for either breedin' purposes or for food. Then I mentioned sellin' some of your land."

Cassandra gave an emphatic shake of her head. "Mama and I wouldn't sell one acre, especially to Mr. Fairfax or Phillip. They're the only ones who would benefit from it anyway. Papa and Mr. Fairfax clashed over their border for years, and though Phillip is anxious to get his hands on the Triple P, he doesn't need one more inch of Texas soil."

"Rafael did say you wouldn't sell your land. So, right now all we've got is the possibility of a timber contract and breedin' Old Bull, once we cull the herd."

"You and Roberto can do that. If the two of you spend some time together, he might see things differently and come around."

"Good idea," Matt said. He surveyed the area around the creek.

"Whatcha looking for? Snakes?"

"Yeah, you can't be too careful 'round those water moccasins. They can get ya both on land or under the water." Satisfied the water bore no danger, he splashed his face. "On the way here from Goose Neck Ridge, I met a fellow who thinks this creek brings good luck."

"That must have been Gus Lawson. He worked for Papa now and again. A couple summers ago, he was helping string fence line and drank from the creek. He swears it's how he got his wife. He met her the very next day, and she accepted his proposal two weeks later."

"He could be right. He introduced me to Mrs. Lawson. She's a comely woman at that."

At the mention of pretty Alicia Lawson, Cassandra frowned at the smattering of freckles on her arms and unfavorably compared them to the dark skin and black hair Alicia inherited from her Mexican father and Cherokee mother. Did Matt prefer that kind of a woman?

☆☆☆

Cassandra waded into the creek. The cool water sent goosebumps racing up her legs. Shiny black minnows skittered past her wiggling toes, while a silvery-blue bream tried his best to hide in a submerged tree stump. She lifted a foot out of the water. *At least my ankles are trimmer than Alicia Lawson's.*

Matt gulped a handful of water and closed his eyes. "Lucky creek, if you're granting wishes today, I wish good fortune on the Triple P."

Cassandra seized the opportunity. She slapped the surface of the creek and sent a sheet of diamond droplets right at Matt's face.

"You little vixen." He blinked water from his eyes before scooping his Stetson into the creek and lunging for Cassandra. She struggled to reach the bank, but he caught up to her and dumped the water on her head.

"Matt Atkins. Why you–" She pushed against his chest. He tumbled backward but not before he snagged her wrist and took her under the water with him. Cassandra sputtered in protest as her head bobbed back to the surface. She tried to stand, but her feet kept slipping on the mossy rocks.

Matt helped her to regain her balance. "Are you all right?"

"Just peachy." Cassandra wrung the water from her braid and the tails of her shirt. Matt brushed a drop of water from the tip of her nose. The warm touch on her wet skin sent a shiver up her spine, followed by a rush of embarrassment. She shouldn't let him get to her like that.

"You know," she said to ward off the feeling, "a hired hand shouldn't throw his boss into a creek."

She'd meant for her words to tease him, but Matt's expression turned serious as he fished his soggy hat from the creek and heaved himself out of the water. "You're right, Miss Pickett. I do need to learn my place. I've just never worked for a woman before. I'm used to men being in charge."

Cassandra's eyes burned from the water dripping in them and Matt's insinuation she couldn't run her ranch. She snatched up her boots and sprinted past him, hoping to distance herself from the man, who since his arrival, had affected her in ways she wasn't ready to admit.

"Ouch," she called out, hopping on one foot. She'd stepped on a sharp stone embedded in the ground.

"Here, boss lady." Matt scooped her into his arms. "Let me lend you a hand or in this case, two good, strong arms."

"Please. Put me down."

"Quit squirming, or I'll dump you back in the water." He turned toward the creek

"Matt, don't. I'll be still." With no place to put her arms other than around his shoulders, she closed her eyes against his warm, wet scent and her rising emotions.

He gave her a little squeeze. "You thought calling me a hired hand would bother me, huh?"

"It didn't?"

"No way. My hide's tougher than a buffalo's. I just wanted to tease you too." His breath tickled her brow.

"Well, my hide's just as tough."

"There's no doubt about that."

Matt carried her past a grinning Carlos and Rafael and a very put-out Roberto before setting her down under the oak tree, where he'd told her to sit in the first place. "Now, if you wanna help out, how about bringin' us men some nice, tall glasses of lemonade?"

"I am your boss, not your servant," Cassandra fumed before limping toward the house.

Matt Atkins, the last thing I'll do is get you something to drink. And one way or another, I'll show you I can run a ranch and still be a perfect lady.

TWELVE

Matt saw neither a glass of lemonade nor Cassandra the rest of the afternoon. At supper she evaded his attempts at conversation, leaving uncomfortable gaps of silence around the dinner table. He wasn't sure Helen knew what had happened, but Maria surely did. Her icy glare could have peeled the paper off the dining room walls.

As for Rafael and Carlos, the two men talked a loud, brave front about the progress made on Old Bull's fence. But when Carlos said his arms were sore from digging post holes, Cassandra's lips thinned, and her eyes narrowed. Rafael harrumphed, causing the color to rise in Carlos's face, and he remained quiet for the rest of the meal. Matt was grateful Roberto's animosity seemed kept in check by Maria and Mrs. Pickett's presence, or the boy might have challenged him to a duel at sunrise.

Matt's chair creaked in protest as he leaned back and risked a sideways glance at Cassandra. She kept her eyes pinned on her plate while she jabbed a piece of beef with her fork. He almost joked that the meat was already dead, but common sense prevailed. It made no sense to antagonize her any further. Instead, he forced down his food and excused himself. The silence of the bunkhouse would be easier to bear than the silence coming from her.

A chill had settled over the heat of the day, and a full moon tried to hide behind a strip of gauzy clouds that couldn't hold enough moisture to wet a handkerchief.

Lord, we sure could use some rain.

The screen door banged shut behind Matt. Had Cassandra followed him? He turned to the crunching sound of footsteps.

"Mr. Matt, I need a word with you." Roberto advanced toward him, a scowl drawing his brows together. "I do not know what you did, but you have made Miss Cassie most unhappy." He straightened to his full height, which left him a hand's span shorter than Matt.

Matt rubbed the back of his neck. "You're right, Roberto. I don't always think before I speak. You ever done that?" He noted a flicker of agreement in the boy's dark eyes. "And it's not easy to understand women. You'll find that out soon enough when you fall in love."

Roberto's eyes darted toward the house.

He's already in love–with Cassandra Jane.

"I remember when I first fell in love," Matt said. "I was about your age. Maybe a little older. Her name was Mary Jo Callahan. We went to school together, and she was the purtiest thing I'd ever seen."

"Like Miss Cassie?"

"Yep. Just like Miss Cassie. Mary Jo wasn't interested in me though. She held a candle for a boy named Fred Wiggington.

But I kept following her around, leavin' flowers and small gifts on her desk."

"And did Miss Mary Jo accept your affection?"

"No, she didn't. Hurt like crazy, but when I became a man, I accepted the rejection as part of growin' up. You feel the same way about Miss Cassie as I did Mary Jo, don't you?"

Roberto tugged on the collar of his shirt. "I am most fond of Miss Cassie."

"I don't blame ya. Cassandra Jane is a fine woman. But remember, you're still young. There's plenty of time for the good Lord to bring a charmin' señorita your way."

Matt cast his eyes upward. Why in the world was he giving Roberto advice about God and women? He'd trusted the Lord to send him the right woman and look how that ended up. He wagged his head. Advice was easier given than received.

"I am not so young," Roberto argued. "I am twelve. I will be thirteen next month and only seven years younger than Miss Cassie. Do you think I am too young for her?"

"It's not my place to say."

Roberto kicked a loose rock and sent it skittering toward the barn. "What happened to Miss Mary Jo?"

"Oh, she married a man a heck of a lot better than me. And I'm glad. Love's kinda like that. You want the best for the person you care about."

"I will think about what you said. But I warn you. Do not make Miss Cassie unhappy again. I will be watching." Roberto turned on his heel and headed for his family's cottage.

Watching the boy walk away, Matt shook his head and smiled. *Roberto, I've got news for you. This isn't the last time your straw's gonna get wet over a beautiful woman.*

⁂

The next morning at the breakfast table Matt fared no better with Cassandra. He wished she'd speak to him, even call him a hired hand again. Though having no appetite, he threw back a breakfast of crisp bacon and fluffy flapjacks so he could escape to the barn and think of a way to make up with her.

The chickens ran up to him, expecting handfuls of corn, but when he bypassed them to grain the horses and feed Buddy, they resumed pecking the ground, Matt quickly forgotten. He pumped water into the stock tanks, slopped the pigs, then doubled back to throw the corn to the chickens. He backed away from the rooster, who puffed up his feathers, cocked his head, and with unblinking eyes challenged him to take a step closer.

The milk cow greeted him with a low and drawn out moo. "Sorry, Daisy. Maria should be along soon to take care of you."

Worried about his uncertain status with the housekeeper, Matt hustled over to King. He'd best saddle up and head to Goose Neck Ridge before she showed up to milk the cow. He stroked King's velvet nose as the animal lipped an apple from his hand. At least she hadn't caught him taking the apple from the cellar.

Matt worked quickly but not quick enough. He heard the screen door bang shut and saw Cassandra coming toward the barn carrying a basket to collect the eggs. Maria followed in her wake, swinging a metal bucket and wearing a less than cordial expression. Cassandra's orange shirt clashed with her hair, but Matt would have walked on nails before he told her that. When she swept by him without a word, he felt the cold breeze. Maria halted in front of him, and he had the good sense to tuck his chin to his chest.

"I am not happy you have upset Miss Cassie." Maria punctuated each word with a jab of the bucket. "I hope you have not done the same thing to Daisy. I do not want curdled milk."

Matt raised his hands in the air. "I didn't touch her. Daisy that is, not Cassandra Jane. Well, I did touch Cassandra... but only because she hurt her foot."

"It sounds like you do not know what you mean." Maria pushed him out of her way.

Matt hurried to finish saddling his horse. He was about to mount up when Cassandra brushed by him, leading a chestnut mare toward the corral. Maybe if he made the first move, she'd follow his lead. He exhaled a deep breath.

"How's your foot?" he asked. "You were still limping at breakfast."

"I'm fine," came the curt reply.

Against his better judgment, Matt pushed up his sleeves and followed her into the corral. "Can I give you a few pointers?"

"What makes you think I'd want them?"

"I'm not askin' for the deed to the Triple P. I'd just like to show you how we trained our horses back at White Oak Manor."

To his surprise, Cassandra relinquished the lead rope. Matt blew into Ginny's nostrils and scratched her neck and withers to help her relax. He exchanged the lead rope for a long line and attached it to the bridle ring.

"Whoa," he said and tightened his fingers on the line to get the horse's attention.

"She's already at a whoa."

"I know that."

"I can't tell from where I'm standing." She moved a step to the right. "How about over here. Better?"

Matt chose not to take Cassandra's bait. Instead, he circled Ginny around the corral, alternating her gaits and calling out "walk," "trot," and "lope" to teach her voice commands. He repeated the process in the other direction before cooling the horse off and handing the long line back to Cassandra.

"See," he said. "Ginny's smart. If you work her this way, she'll learn to obey your voice, and it'll give her a soft mouth." He nudged her toward the mare. "Go ahead. You try."

"I'd rather not."

"Aw, come on, Cassandra Jane. What's it gonna hurt?"

She shot him a mutinous look before loosening the line and asking Ginny to walk. The mare stepped forward and circled the coral. Cassandra's face lit up but quickly sobered when Matt praised her effort.

"I don't need your approval, thank you." Her voice matched her less-than-appreciative expression.

That little imp. If she isn't the most prideful woman I've ever met.

Though her lack of gratitude grated his pride, Matt figured the best recourse was to leave before she told him to. He swung into the saddle, and said, "Jog," loud enough for her to hear. King broke into a fast trot and left the Triple P in a haze of dust.

The mid-morning sun beat down on the pair and spread ripples of heat over the endless prairie. Tall grass waved and presented a friendly backdrop against cedars that struggled to support their scraggly limbs. Closer by, warped mesquite with thin, shimmery leaves huddled together against the fierce sun. Unfazed by the heat, splashes of yellow prickly pears bore promise of the crimson fruit to come.

"It's goin' to be another Texas scorcher, King." The horse snorted and tossed his thick, black mane.

The land possessed a raw beauty no man could tame but would gladly die trying. Harold Brigham and Samuel Pickett had paid that price, but while the former's death had made Phillip a rich man, the demise of the latter had pushed the Triple P to the verge of bankruptcy.

He patted his horse's neck. "King, I've got to find a way to help the ladies save the Triple P, so that head-strong Cassandra Jane won't have to marry Phillip Brigham."

Matt swore under his breath. He was letting his heart get mixed up with his head again. Cassandra's involvement with Phillip should be no concern of his, but his treacherous mind returned to their evening on the porch. He closed his eyes and recalled the outline of her face and the smell of her rose-scented perfume.

King tugged at the bit, and Matt allowed the stallion to break into a gallop. But no matter how fast they raced toward Goose Neck Ridge, Matt couldn't outrun his thoughts of Cassandra Jane Pickett.

THIRTEEN

After Matt had left Cassandra and the Triple P far behind, he reined King to a walk and guided the horse over land where vast herds of buffalo once roamed. The ever-encroaching railroad had needed meat to feed its crews, and the U.S. army had killed the primary food source of the Plains Indians to force them onto reservations so the government could confiscate their land. Matt shook his head at man's tendency to take, destroy, or kill whatever got in his way.

The sun was pushing its way toward noon when the hodge-podge of buildings making up Goose Neck Ridge popped into view. Matt raised a hand to a couple of cowboys holding a herd of longhorns together. More than likely, they were waiting their turn into town for a shave and a bath before making the long drive up the Great Western Trail. Dust tinged the air as the cattle shuffled and lowed, their horns clacking against each other.

Matt reined his horse up the wide, pitted street leading into town and stepped down at the first building on his right. The word SALOON adorned the plate-glass windows flanking the double doors. Before he finished tying up King, the horse thrust his nose into the water trough next to the hitching rail.

Matt didn't fancy the idea of entering an establishment that catered to professional gamblers, entertainers, and ladies of ill repute. His friends in Boston had ribbed him about his lack of vices, including drinking alcohol, but he found the idea of allowing liquor to impair one's faculties as foolish. A saloon, though, would allow him to blend in and obtain information.

As soon as he swept through the bat-wing doors, the stench of cigar smoke, stale beer, and sweaty bodies assaulted him. Loud voices clamoring for service vied with the tinkling notes of a piano. Matt wended his way through the room, avoiding the under-dressed and over-rouged women who hovered near tables and lounged on the laps of men playing cards. After stepping over a man who was passed out on the floor, he reached the bar that stretched the length of the room.

A crusty old barkeep blew on a glass before wiping the fog off with a towel. "Never seen ya 'round here before, stranger. Who ya be? And whatcha need?"

Matt raised his voice above the din, ignoring the first question but answering the second. "I could use a glass of water and directions to the nearest lawyer and the telegraph office."

The wizened man poured water into the glass and handed it to Matt. "Mr. Harvey's place is up..." He counted out loud. "Uh, seven doors on the right and the telegraph office is past it on the left. Ya owe me a nickel for the water." He whispered in a raspy voice. "I don't charge none for the directions."

"Thanks, mister. Could you tell me anything about—"

"Hey, Otis. Looks like we got one of those fellars from back East. Ain't that sweet?"

In his haste to get the answers he needed, Matt had forgotten to hide his eastern accent. A craggy-faced cowboy in a dirty shirt and scarred boots sauntered up and spread his fingers on the bar. Another cowboy, uglier and dirtier than the first, rubbed his whiskered face before stumbling up to Matt.

"Yeah, Jed. He talks like one of them eastern deb-u-tantes."

Otis snatched Matt's glass and dumped the contents on the floor. "If ya come in here, ya drink whiskey."

Matt tossed a dime on the counter for the barkeep. "Thanks for the directions." He brushed Otis aside and headed for the saloon doors. The cowboy named Jed blocked the way, his broken-toothed grin inches from Matt's face.

"Where ya goin'? Me and Otis ain't done talkin' to ya."

"If you gentlemen would excuse me."

Jed threw back his head and guffawed. Matt flinched at the man's breath.

"This guy ain't too smart. Called us gentlemen, he did." He performed a curtsy, then slid closer to Matt and sneered. "We ain't no gentlemen."

Matt let a deliberate moment of silence pass. "All right. Would you men excuse me?"

Jed shoved Matt's shoulder and knocked him into the bar. "No, we ain't excusin' you. And what in tarnation are ya gonna do about it?"

"If you touch me again, you'll find out." Matt's fingers grazed the gun resting on his right hip.

"Oooh. Let's find out." Jed shoved him again, and Matt's .45 cleared leather. He planted the barrel in the cowboy's soft midsection. Otis went for his weapon, but Matt hit the man's hand and sent the gun spinning across the floor. Chairs crashed to the floor as the saloon patrons sprang to their feet. Men faded into the walls, but not so far away as to miss a good fight. The saloon girls screamed and fled to a hidden room underneath the stairs.

"I said, 'If you men would excuse me'." Matt nudged Jed with his gun and warned Otis with his eyes as he backed out of the doors. He freed King's reins, then mounted in a fluid motion before easing away from the saloon. Excited voices rose up behind him.

"Hey, who's that?"

"I dunno. He's new to these parts. Pulled his gun faster than a coyote catchin' a one-legged chicken."

"I bet even Wild Bill couldn't draw that fast."

Matt kept watch for the two cowboys as he passed a livery stable and blacksmith shop set a long stone's throw from the street. A forge filled the air with its acrid black smoke. Through the haze, he made out the face of a bear of a man shoeing a dapple-gray horse. The man raised his chin in greeting.

Up from the livery, two bawdy men loafed against the side of a whitewashed building and beckoned to a scantily dressed woman leaning out an upstairs window. She answered the men's comments with a randy one of her own. Two doors past that, a pleasant-faced woman exited the mercantile, her arms laden with packages.

Matt tipped his hat. "Ma'am."

"Morning, sir," came the reply.

A blonde-haired boy of about six or seven tugged the woman's dress. "Mama, Mama. You forgot my lemon drops."

Matt urged King past a café, a dressmaker's shop, a meat market, a drugstore that also housed a doctor's office, another saloon, and the marshal's office before stopping in front of a two-story building overshadowed by the Goose Neck Ridge Bank. The false front added height to the building, while its roofed portico and slate-gray shutters lent a business-like air. A sign, painted in perfect white letters, declared the entrance to Winston Harvey's law office.

Matt sprang up the steps, ducked under the awning, and entered the office. The smell of lingering tobacco and ancient law books filled the cozy interior, coaxing him back to winter days spent in his father's library, curled up by a crackling fire with a good book.

A Roman-nosed woman with frizzy, orange hair stopped sweeping and acknowledged Matt. She leaned an enormous broom against a desk straining under a burden of paper and files.

"How can I be helpin' ya, sir?" she asked in a thick Irish brogue.

This time Matt was careful not to use his eastern accent. "I'd like to speak with Mr. Harvey, ma'am."

"Now, don'tcha be callin' me 'ma'am'. Me name's Fiona, but ye won't be talkin' to Uncle Winnie today. Nor the next day nor the next." She cracked a smile shy of two teeth. "He and Auntie Allison be gone to San Francisco. Poor Uncle Winnie's not had a day's rest since he moved here and started this practice. Doc Wilson said his heart might stop tickin' if he didn't get away. Auntie Allison had their bags packed 'fore ol' Doc left the house."

"He did what?" Frustration hardened Matt's voice.

Fiona picked up the broom and took a fixed stand. "Can't ya make out good English? He and Auntie Allison be gone to California."

"When will they be back?"

"A mere fortnight-and-a-half."

"I have important business that can't wait. A courier was supposed to deliver two documents to Mr. Harvey. They'd have my name on them. My name's—"

" 'Fraid I can't be doin' no lawyerin' for ya." Fiona wrinkled her nose, which was no easy feat. "Uncle Winnie'd have me hide if I did that. I only promised I'd keep an eye on the place and tidy up while he was gone."

Matt reached into his shirt pocket for his last pay from Big George Thompson. Maybe he could bribe the woman with a couple of bills, but before he could make an offer, she shooed him toward the door with her broom. "Get on now. Come back in three weeks."

Matt battled the disappointing setback by acknowledging another three weeks wouldn't make that much of a difference. Since he was barking at a knot with Mr. Harvey's niece, he left without bidding her goodbye and headed up the street, hoping for better success at the telegraph and post office.

He maneuvered around a loose board on the steps and entered the modest, clapboard building. The smell of paper and dusty mailbags permeated the room. A quick survey revealed cubbyholes awaiting the day's mail on his right, and a smattering of chairs on the left. The rickety seats faced each other, daring townsfolk to wander in and sit at their own peril. Matt headed to the back where a telegraph machine rested on a long counter. A hand-lettered sign leaned next to it, posting the rates.

A tall, thin woman with a friendly smile dotted with dimples, stood behind the counter. Wrinkles and gray wisps of hair framed her periwinkle eyes. "Hello, sir. I'm Irene Skinner. May I help you?"

"Yes, ma'am. I'd like to send two telegrams."

The woman hollered with a voice that rivaled her height. "Arthur!"

A curtain in the back of the room parted, and a man with thinning white hair shuffled across the floorboards. He was dressed in a gray, cotton shirt and a pair of baggy pants that were doing their best to slide down despite his suspenders. He looked up at his wife.

"Yes, Irene?"

"This cowboy wants to send a couple of telegrams." The woman looked back at Matt. "If I can do anything else for ya, have my husband give me a holler."

"Thanks, ma'am. I will."

Arthur Skinner hobbled behind the counter and pulled out two pieces of paper from a cubbyhole and a pencil from a rusty tin can. "Write your messages and where they're goin'. I'll do the rest." He watched from across the counter as Matt scribbled his first message. "Boston? Ya got family up that-a-way?"

"I know some people back there."

"Why ya in Goose Neck Ridge?"

"Let's say I needed a change of scenery. How long have you been a telegraph operator, Mr. Skinner?"

"I've been mannin' this office since it first set up. Let's see… be nine years come next March. Thought I'd never learn that Morse system. The first few months I heard tappin' noises even in my sleep. It'd cost ya seven-fifty to send ten words on the first telegraph machine. We've come a long way since then. Abe Lincoln hisself didn't want those lines snakin' across the plains. Said men couldn't get 'nough poles and equipment out there and feared the Injuns would just tear 'em down."

Arthur chuckled. "Mr. Lincoln shouldn't have worried 'bout it none. Those Injuns thought evil spirits flowed through them wires. They threw their arms overhead and raced their ponies under 'em fast as lightnin'."

Matt shoved the paper across the counter. "Progress isn't always easy."

Arthur settled a pair of spectacles on his leathered face. "Let's see. This goes to Walter Brigham in Boston. He any kin to Phillip Brigham at Lazy Acres? I heard he had a few relatives back east."

"Must be a coincidence. Brigham's a common name in Boston."

"Ya don't say?" He continued reading Matt's message. "'Sorry. Going to get it. E.' Is that right?"

"Yes, sir. And speakin' of Phillip Brigham, I heard his operation is the biggest and most prominent one 'round these parts. You know anything about it?"

"Yup, Lazy Acres is the king o' ranches. Phillip's granddaddy started it. He was known for takin' whatever he wanted. Must have passed a generation 'cause ol' Harold was never like his pa. Then along came Phillip, and he filled up his grandaddy's shoes."

“What else can you tell me about Phillip?” Matt leaned forward, hoping Arthur would continue his friendly banter.

“He’s the only man of real influence ‘round here. Well, there’s Mr. Brewer. But ol’ man Brewer’s holdin’s are here in town.” Arthur named them off on his fingers. “He owns the mercantile, the town hotel, and the newspaper. And he works as a land agent and owns this telegraph office. Though the Western Union ain’t none too happy about the competition.”

Arthur scratched the thinning hair on the top of his head. “He wanted to open a playhouse, but Rev’rend Doyle shut down that idea in a hurry. Him thinkin’ actors and actresses can’t fit through them pearly gates. The old codger.”

“You were talking about Phillip Brigham?”

“Oh, yeah. Mr. Brewer’s a small turnip compared to Mr. Brigham.”

“Is Phillip buyin’ area ranches to increase his borders?”

“Where’d ya go hearin’ that? The only ranch he’s interested in is the Pickett place. That’s what Irene told me, and she heard it from Charlie Brewer’s wife, Mabel. Not sure who she heard it from. Maybe Mildred Higgins.”

Arthur leaned across the counter. “But between you and me, Irene said he’s more interested in that Pickett woman than the ranch. The daughter–not the mother.” His pleased look asked Matt to appreciate the humor. When it was not received, he drummed his fingers on the counter. “Rumor is the bank’s ‘bout ready to foreclose on it. It’s a shame, too. I liked Sam Pickett.”

While he tapped out the telegram to Boston, Matt scribbled a message to George Thompson.

S & R coming to GNR. Can get local timber for ties. Let me know. M. Atkins.

Arthur snatched the paper from Matt. "George Thompson of Fort Worth? Now, he's what ya'd call a man of influence. Cattle and money comin' out his ears. Heard he hooked up with the Bar K boys last summer in Jacksboro. Went that-a-way toward Oklahoma with five-thousand head of cattle. People saw the dust 'fore the cows came through."

"I heard about it." Matt didn't share he'd been part of the drive. And Arthur was right. The cattle's hooves had sent up a blanket of dust that covered everything for miles around, especially the unfortunate drag riders at the back of the herd.

Arthur tapped out the second message. "Ya owe me two bucks." When Matt placed the bills on Arthur's outstretched palm, he chortled and pocketed the money.

Matt dropped the pencil into the tin can. "I need to get back to the ranch."

"Gotta poke some cows, eh? You being a cowpoke and all." Arthur slapped his thigh at his joke.

"The cattle don't get poked until they arrive at the stockyard. Then they use the sticks to drive them into the railcars."

Arthur's grin dissolved. "Some people wouldn't know a good joke if it walked up and shook their hand." He sniffed. "By the way, what ranch ya at?"

"The Pickett place."

"Well, I'll be. Is that why you was askin' about Phillip Brigham? You 'fraid he's gonna buy the Pickett place, and you'd be out of a job?"

"Something like that. Thanks for your help. It's been nice talkin' to ya." Matt cut Arthur off. Anything else said would be town fodder before sundown.

"Humph. Don't need to get so huffy." He picked up the slips of paper and studied Matt's messages. "Ya didn't tell me your name, cowboy."

"Atkins. Matt Atkins."

"Why'd ya sign this telegram with an E?"

"My middle name's Earl."

"If that ain't peculiar. Usin' two different names." Arthur peered over the top of his spectacles. "Well, Mr. Matt Earl Atkins, come back, and we'll talk some more. Though doubt it'll be about the Pickett place. They won't be ownin' it much longer."

"You never can tell." Matt touched the brim of his hat and opened the door to leave. As he headed down the steps, an unkempt cowboy bumped into him. The man yanked his hat over his brow without a word of apology and disappeared into the building.

Matt ignored the man's rudeness, choosing to let it pass and not call him out. He'd already courted enough trouble for one day. He didn't need any more. What he needed to do was get to the mercantile and buy something for Cassandra Jane before he talked himself out of it.

FOURTEEN

Matt led his horse back down the street to the mercantile. A hand-painted sign with tall white letters hung from the eaves of the veranda and bragged of the store's importance. *C.L. Brewer Emporium, Groceries, Hardware, Dry Goods, Clothing, and Other Necessities.* A smaller sign underneath touted *C.L. Brewer, Land Agent.*

Like Mr. Harvey's office, a storefront built onto the second story heightened the mercantile's appearance. Matt circumvented the wares spilling onto the boardwalk that ran the length of the store. He opened the door but stepped back to allow a farmer and his wife to enter first. A bell tied to the doorknob announced their arrival.

Matt removed his hat and breathed in the pleasant mixture of tanned leather, spices, smoked meat, and coffee. Wooden shelves held everything from soap and lanterns to clocks and bins of nails. He acknowledged a middle-aged woman measuring material behind the yard-goods counter. Bolts of fabric in shades of blue, goldenrod, and russet lounged in neat rows behind her. A gray-headed couple with their backs to him appeared to be picking out dry goods. Across the aisle two children pressed their noses against a glass case full of peppermints, creamy caramels, chocolate squares, lemon drops, and sour balls of every color. Their matching red hair and freckles suggested they were brother and sister. Would Cassandra have children with that color hair one day? He hoped their father would not be Phillip Brigham.

A man with a neat salt and pepper mustache and pewter-colored hair waited on the children. He exuded a friendly but assured air. He called to Matt in a loud voice. "Howdy. I'm Charlie Brewer." He pointed to a dark-haired, energetic woman stacking boxes of shoes at the back of the store. "That's my wife, Mabel. One of us will be right with you."

"Take your time. I'm just lookin'."

Halfway to Goose Neck Ridge, Matt had decided to regain Cassandra's favor with a gift from the mercantile. To hide his subterfuge, he planned to buy a present for the other members of the Pickett household as well. His conscience pricked his heart for not only trying to buy Cassandra's affection but also for wanting to see her enchanting eyes light up in appreciation.

He flicked an ostrich feather sticking out of the band of a blue felt bonnet. "I can't see Cassandra Jane wearing anything as silly as that."

"I beg your pardon?" a soprano voice behind him asked.

A short, attractive woman eyed him curiously. A hat, identical to the one he held, perched atop hair the color of freshly-ground coffee. Her matching indigo dress gathered in the back over a generous bustle. It puzzled Matt why women insisted upon expanding their backsides with those contraptions. He preferred dresses that fell in folds to the floor like the ones Cassandra wore.

His hands fumbled as he set the bonnet back on the rack. "Sorry, ma'am. I was talkin' to myself."

"Are you thinking about buying that hat?"

"Uh, no. But I am looking for a gift for my—"

"Your wife?"

"No, my–my sister."

"Your sister?" Her blue-gray eyes brightened. "I can help. I do know a thing or two about what young women like." She slipped to within inches of Matt, extended a gloved hand, and wiggled her fingers under his nose. "My name is Elizabeth Anne Baxter. What's yours?"

Matt stepped back from the overeager woman, but as he did, he knocked over the rack holding the bonnets. Hats of cranberry red, green, amethyst, and cornflower rolled across the floor like wagon wheels. Elizabeth tittered and bent over to help pick them up.

Matt turned away to hide his burning cheeks. "Sorry. Clumsy of me."

Elizabeth replaced the last hat and extended her hand again. "Your name?"

"I'm Matt Atkins." His large hand engulfed her small one.

"Matt Atkins. Sounds rugged and handsome. It suits you well. So, what is this sister of yours like?"

"Well, she's tall." He brought his fingers up to the level of his nose, which put Elizabeth under it with a good six inches to spare. "And she has shiny hair–like a chestnut's coat in the afternoon sun."

"Good thing she's not your sweetheart. She'd not like you comparing her to a smelly horse."

Matt fought back a frown. He'd never found buying a gift for a woman easy, and Miss Baxter's meddling was making it worse. His eyes darted around the store, searching for a means of escape.

Elizabeth rapped his shoulder with her fan. "Are you listening to me?"

"Y–Yes. What were you saying?"

Elizabeth hid a giggle behind the fan. "My, my, you are the nervous type, aren't you?" The store's bell jingled, and she pointed to the retreating backs of the elderly couple Matt had noticed when he entered the mercantile. "Those are my grandparents. I must be going. Maybe I'll see you the next time I'm in town."

"Sure. That'd be nice," he lied. "Good day." Her giggles followed his flight to the back of the store.

"Good day, sir." Another woman's voice startled Matt. "I'm sorry." Mrs. Brewer's brown eyes confirmed her words. "I didn't mean to scare you."

Matt checked to make sure Elizabeth had indeed left the store. "That's all right. I'm buying a few things for my–my family."

"Can I be of assistance?"

"No." Matt spoke louder than he intended. He lowered his voice. "I'm fine. Thank you."

He chose three pocketknives, one for Carlos, Rafael, and Roberto, and a packet of flower seeds for Mrs. Pickett. He questioned his wisdom in picking out a rolling pin for Maria. There was a good chance she might want to use it on him.

He lingered over a row of hair combs nestled on a length of ebony velvet in a display case. An ivory comb carved with birds and flowers caught his eye.

"I changed my mind, ma'am. Can I see that one?" he asked Mrs. Brewer.

She reached in the case and handed the comb to Matt. "That's the prettiest one. It came in yesterday."

The comb was cool and smooth between Matt's fingers, and he imagined placing it in Cassandra's hair. Not caring for where his thoughts were leading, he clutched the comb, snatched his other purchases, and marched to the front of the store. He found little room at the counter to set down his gifts. The cash register, a set of scales, a spool of wrapping paper, and bottles of perfume filled up much of the space.

"Did you find what you needed?" Mr. Brewer asked.

Matt maneuvered the items across the counter. "Yes, sir. Would you wrap the comb by itself?"

Mr. Brewer tucked the comb in a separate piece of tan paper. "I know everyone in Goose Neck Ridge. You passing through?"

Matt wanted to lie to the man. He was tired of people asking who he was and his reason for being there, but if Arthur Skinner was right, Mr. Brewer's influence might prove beneficial in the future. It wouldn't do a lick of good to alienate him now.

"Nope. I just got into town. I'm thinkin' about hangin' around, though."

"If you need a job, the *Goose Neck Ridge Gazette* is looking for a part-time typesetter, but you look like a man who'd be more comfortable in a saddle." Mr. Brewer wrapped the other purchases and tied them together with a piece of string. "Did you try Lazy Acres? Phillip Brigham's got the largest cattle outfit in the territory. I assume he could use the help."

"Thanks. I might get out there."

Mr. Brewer shoved Matt's purchases back across the counter. "That will be two dollars and sixty cents."

Matt handed over the twenty-dollar bill Big George had given as a bonus before he left the Circle T. Mr. Brewer eyed the twenty-spot in appreciation. Matt took that as a good sign.

"About ranches. Rumor has it, Mr. Brigham is buying up area ranches to increase his holdings. Do you know anything about that?"

Mr. Brewer leaned over the counter and let his gaze sweep Matt from head to scuffed boots. "Why are you asking... cowboy?"

"I know some people back east who are thinkin' about buyin' land out here. They might be interested in a smaller spread. Maybe one like the Triple P."

"If the Triple P comes up for sale, those people can contact me personally. Thank you, sir. Come again." He turned his back to Matt, closing their conversation.

"You're welcome. I will." Disappointed, Matt trudged out of the store.

He slipped his purchases into his saddlebag, swung up onto King, and then settled grimly in the saddle. Mr. Brewer hadn't confirmed Phillip's plan to get the Triple P by either marrying Cassandra or buying the ranch upon foreclosure. But Matt couldn't shake the feeling that was precisely what the cad planned to do.

"Yoo-hoo, Mr. Atkins. See you later." Elizabeth stood in the back of a horse-drawn wagon, waving furiously at him. The wagon lurched forward, sending her back onto the seat with a thump. To keep from being pitched over the side, she braced herself with one hand but kept right on waving with the other.

Matt muzzled a grin. Afraid the animated woman might say more, he gave King his head. The horse broke into a gallop, and Matt didn't slow the pace until Goose Neck Ridge lay far behind.

He reined King to a walk and patted the horse's damp neck. "Sorry, boy. Had to leave in a hurry. We still have a few ranches to stop at, but after that, we'll go easy the rest of the way home."

Home. He hadn't called any place that since he'd left Boston. Before the fiasco there, he'd planned to settle down and father a handful or two of children. But after he left White Oak Manor, he resigned himself to bachelorhood and the life of a cowboy. Until he received that letter. Then he'd met Cassandra Jane Pickett and revisited all those dreams.

"Listen to me, King. I'm ridin' the same old pony. You'd think I'd learn by now not to trust women. Besides, I've got a job to do, and no one, especially a red-haired minx, is going to keep me from it." King nickered and tossed his head, jangling the bit.

Matt set his teeth, determined to concentrate on the business at hand, but his mind kept drifting to how beautiful the ivory comb would look in Cassandra's hair.

☆☆☆

When Matt rode off, it had taken no small effort for Cassandra not to chase after him and make a face. She acknowledged the idea as silly. Ginny nuzzled her arm. "You did well, girl. I have to admit it, Matt was right."

Rafael intercepted Cassandra as she led the horse back toward the barn. "How did Ginny do?"

"She's learning fast. Thanks to—" She bit her bottom lip, not wanting to give due credit.

"Señor Matt? He knows much about horses. He said we could breed his big stallion to some of the mares. I think it is a very good idea."

Once again, Cassandra had to admit Matt was right. "I know, but we don't have many left. I'm even training Ginny to be a saddle horse now."

Rafael patted the horse's nose. "This mare has given the Triple P many fine colts. What about the little bay and the gray mare? Could we not breed them?"

"They are the only ones. I remember when we had more horses than we needed. Now, look." Sorrow made its way into her voice.

"I am sorry for what has happened. Do you think we can save the ranch?" Concern marked the older man's near-black eyes.

Cassandra forced a positive tone back into her voice. "Everything will work out. If worse comes to worst, I can marry Phillip and convince him not to move to Boston."

"I would rather go back to Mexico than see you marry Señor Brigham." Rafael bowed his head. "I am sorry. That was not Christian of me to say."

"There's still almost a month before the loan is due."

"We will be like your mamá and have faith. Maybe the Lord will give us the timber contract Señor Matt talked about."

"We can always hope."

"No, Señorita Cassie. We can pray." Rafael's mood lightened, and he whistled as he returned to work.

Cassandra closed her eyes and shook her head. Was she the only person on the Triple P who doubted prayer? "Come on, Ginny." She shelved her thoughts as she untacked the mare.

"Miss Cassie," Maria's voice carried out from the porch. "I need you. Now."

Cassandra sighed. Maria had extracted a promise to help shell beans that morning. Cassandra didn't mind the tedious chore, but she had wanted to help Carlos work one of the colts first.

She located the vaquero and explained the reason for Maria's summon. His eyes crinkled at the corners. "It is wise to obey my sister. She believes kitchen work is the most important part of running a ranch. Rafael, Roberto, and I still have much to do on the fence. We can work the little one later this afternoon."

Cassandra made her way inside the house, but one glimpse of the overflowing baskets of field beans made her want to turn tail and flee the kitchen. Maria sat at the table, already shelling the pods. The beans dropped into a metal pan with a plink, plink sound.

The aroma of stewed chicken seasoned with rosemary drew Cassandra to a pot cooking on the cast-iron stove. She removed the lid, releasing ribbons of steam into the already warm kitchen.

"That chicken can cook by itself," Maria said. She motioned for Cassandra to sit opposite her and slid another pan across the table. "So, Señor Matt has made you unhappy two times in two days?"

"I have no idea what you're talking about."

"Do you think because I stay inside most of the time, I do not know what goes on outside this house?" She tilted her chin toward the dining room window. "I see much that happens on this ranch. Like Señor Matt showing you a new way to trot your horse in little circles."

"Since Papa died. I'm responsible for this ranch, but Matt doesn't think I can run it."

"He has told you this?"

"Not in so many words, but every time he's around, he shows me another way to do things."

"That is the way of men. They cannot help it. God has put in them a desire to lead. Though I would not tell him so, I believe he wants to help you and the Triple P."

Cassandra stopped shelling beans. "But this isn't his ranch. I don't need his help."

"You do not see my point. I am trying to explain why you and Señor Matt bump heads like two stubborn goats. What would happen if you, your mamá, Carlos, Rafael, Roberto, and I all took care of the livestock?"

"It would be confusing. We'd all have different ideas of what to do."

Maria's eyes twinkled. "Like what happens if I let you and your mamá help fix dinner?"

"Yes, but I know more about the livestock than anyone else on the ranch."

"This is true. So, you think the others should listen to you, right?"

Cassandra leaned back with satisfaction. *See. Maria agrees with me. Matt doesn't need to tell me how to run things.* Her smugness flew out the open window at Maria's next words.

"But because you are in charge, you should listen to those who are under you. No? Let me ask you something. Who in this house makes the best biscuits?"

"Mama does. We all know that."

"But who runs the kitchen?"

"Maria, that's a silly question. You do."

"But when biscuits are to be made, I let your mamá make them. As the one in charge, I step aside and let another do what is best. Do you know what your problem is, little one?"

Cassandra slumped in her chair. "I suppose you're going to tell me."

"Pride. You want to run things all by yourself and do not like Señor Matt's help. But you may hurt the ranch because you do not take the advice he gives."

"But he's so doggone aggravating. He goes around saying, 'Back East we do this,' or, 'Eastern women don't wear pants'."

Maria leaned across the table and laid a hand on Cassandra's arm. "I see you have many feelings for this cowboy, eh?"

"Not that kind."

"Sparks of affection often shoot high and become flames of love."

"Love? Matt Atkins, love, and I do not belong in the same sentence."

"When I met my Rafael, I thought the same thing."

"You never told me that."

"And ruin his reputation? He likes people to think the first moment I saw him, my heart went boom-boom." Maria dumped her beans and the few Cassandra had shelled into a pot of boiling water. She heaved herself back into the chair and grabbed another handful of beans.

"The day Carlos and I came to the Triple P, we were dirty, tired, and scared. But your papá offered us a new life, and I tried to be brave. Once we arrived here, Rafael did his best to impress me. He was as handsome as he is now, but not so big. I have taken good care of *mi esposo.*" She winked at Cassandra.

"He also had the same big voice," Maria continued. "Every day he said as loud as he could, 'Señorita, you are the most beautiful thing I have seen all day'."

"That is so romantic."

Maria snorted. "I saw only cattle, horses, and other cowboys. I did not take his compliment in the light he intended. For many weeks he worked to win my favor, but like you and Señor Matt, my fire and his water did not mix. My new position as cook and housekeeper was above a vaquero."

"I know this story has a happy ending."

"And it does. I admitted my pride was making my heart very sad and allowed Rafael to court me. Three months later, he asked your papá if he might have my hand in marriage. We became man and wife right here on the ranch. With a preacher, lemonade, and even a cake."

"I still think it sounds romantic."

"Maybe the same thing will happen to you and Señor Matt. You two are starting out much like me and Rafael."

Maria, I love you with all my heart, but you are plumb loco. I could never love Matt Atkins. Could I?

Unbidden, Cassandra tossed her handful of beans back into the basket. Maria narrowed her eyes, and Cassandra snatched the beans back up again.

"Just because that happened to you and Rafael, doesn't mean it will happen to me and Matt."

"You cannot tell what future the Lord holds. Recite to me Romans eight and verse twenty-eight."

"Maria. There are times you're as bad as Mama."

"Recite, please."

"And we know all things work together for good to them that love God, to them who are the called according to his purpose," Cassandra said with little enthusiasm.

"You did not say that with much meaning. Again, please."

In a stronger voice, Cassandra repeated the verse, but the words were no more heartfelt.

Helen entered the kitchen with her hands clasped to her breast. "Darling, I heard you quote Scripture." She hugged Cassandra's neck. "I am glad you are starting to believe God's word."

Cassandra exchanged a glance with Maria. Neither corrected the misconception.

Helen sat down on the empty chair across from Cassandra. "It looks like the two of you need help." She scooped up a fistful of beans. "Now, what were you talking about?"

FIFTEEN

By the time Cassandra saw Matt returning to the Triple P, the rays of the afternoon sun had dipped into the kitchen window and were reflecting off the jars of canned beans on the counter. She dashed over to the window to get a closer look, almost dropping the plates she'd been putting away in the sideboard.

Maria took the plates from her. "Ah, Señor Matt is back." She bullied Cassandra to the door. "Go. You will feel better if you two make up."

Cassandra rushed out the front door, but then slowed her pace and dawdled down the porch steps. No sense appearing overeager. In the shadow of the barn, she saw Matt handing items to Carlos, Rafael, and Roberto. She picked her pace back up.

"*Muchas gracias,* Señor Matt," said Carlos. Cassandra stood on her tip toes to see beyond Matt's broad shoulders.

Carlos showed her a new pocketknife "Señorita Cassie, Señor Matt got all of us a present."

Rafael held up his knife for Cassandra to examine, while Roberto murmured thanks for the one Matt insisted he take. "Is it not a beauty?" Rafael questioned. "And look," he held up the rolling pin. "Señor Matt got a wooden thing for Maria and a pack of seeds for your mamá."

Cassandra clasped her hands in front of her in anticipation.

"I picked up a few things at the mercantile," Matt said. He pulled on the reins and led King into the barn.

Hadn't he gotten anything for her? Cassandra trailed him to King's stall, trying her best to act nonchalant. "Did you send the telegram to Mr. Thompson?"

"Yep. Hopefully, we'll hear back from him in a few days."

"He has to say yes." She hung up the bridle Matt handed her. "Did anything interesting happen while you were in town?"

"Nope. Just an ordinary visit. I did talk to a few ranchers on the way back and asked if they wanted to breed their cattle to Old Bull."

"And?"

"Jim Sexton at the Diamond D said he'd think about it. The others weren't sure, but I'll keep askin' around." He flopped his saddle on the rack with a thump and stuffed a small package inside his shirt.

"What do you have there?" Cassandra asked, her hope and curiosity aroused for the second time.

"Nothin'." He jammed his Stetson over his forehead. "If you'll excuse me, I need to see your mother and Maria." He fled the barn and left Cassandra staring at his back and wondering why he hadn't gotten her a gift.

At supper that evening Cassandra ignored Matt, prompting quick looks from her mother. Rafael and Carlos chattered on and on about the knives Matt had given them. Even her mother mentioned his generosity.

"Thank you for the seeds, Matt. After the next rain, I'll plant them among the rose bushes."

"Miss Cassie," Maria spoke up. "What did Señor Matt get you?"

"Here, Maria." Matt rolled up his shirtsleeves. "Let me help you clear the dishes."

Rafael nudged Matt aside and picked up the unfinished platter of chicken. "No, Señor Matt. Tonight I plan to learn my way around the kitchen."

Cassandra trudged to the dining room door. "I'm calling it a day. Good night."

Matt captured her hand. "It's still early. Come with me." He gave Helen a knowing nod, which she returned.

Cassandra allowed Matt to lead the way into the parlor, all the while trying to ignore his hand holding hers. He indicated she sit down and then reached behind the divan.

"What are you doing?" she asked.

He held up a finger and retrieved the small package she'd seen at the barn. "I bought you a gift today."

"You did?"

"Don't get any ideas. I bought one for the others too."

"I hoped you'd gotten me one."

"I noticed."

She took the package from him and peeled off the first layer of paper.

"You don't have to be so careful. It won't break."

Cassandra ripped off the rest of the paper to reveal the comb. "Oh, Matt. It's lovely. How did you know I would like an ivory comb?"

"I didn't. I just thought it'd look pretty in all that wavy hair of yours."

Impulsively, she jumped to her feet and kissed his cheek. He smelled clean like soap, and his day's growth of beard tickled her lips. Had his cheeks colored? In the flickering candlelight, she couldn't be sure.

She swept up a section of hair and secured it with the comb. "How does it look?"

"You look beautiful." Matt's voice was thick with emotion as he drew closer to her.

She backed away from him and yanked the comb from her hair. "Th–Thanks. I'll wear it another time."

"Why did you do that?"

"Do what?"

"I told you not to be scared of me."

"I'm not," she said, looking down at the comb and twiddling it in her fingers.

"Cassandra Jane, you're the most perplexin' thing. One minute you act like I might have a chance with you, and the next minute, you're puttin' on airs."

Have a chance with him? Cassandra's mind chased the possibility down a quick hole but came up empty. She couldn't consider a future with Matt until she was certain the Triple P was safe. And that might mean marrying Phillip if the timber bid fell through.

"I'm tired," she said. "Thanks again for the gift. I'll see you in the morning." Before he could say another word, she clutched the comb and made a dash for the door.

Cassandra bounded up the stairs to her bedroom. *Matt Atkins, you're the one who's perplexing. Even when you're being pleasant, you manage to unnerve me.*

⭑⭑⭑

"Maria, I don't need your help," Cassandra scolded. "I can finish getting ready myself. I'll be downstairs in a few minutes."

Maria's face was dubious at best. "The past couple of days you have acted *muy* loco. Señor Matt is behind all this, isn't he? I see you stare at him when he is not looking. One moment you shoot arrows at him with your eyes, the next moment your cheeks are all aglow. Like they are this minute."

Cassandra hid her stinging cheeks by hunting for her brush in the vanity drawer. She never could hide anything from Maria. "I'm not sure what to think about Matt. I doubt we could have a future together. If Mama and I can't convince the bank to extend Papa's loan, I'll have no other choice than to apologize to Phillip and beg him to marry me."

"Marry for money or for love?" Maria grabbed the brush and arranged Cassandra's hair into loose curls that fell almost to her waist. She tucked a shorter piece of hair behind Cassandra's ear.

"Me and Rafael do not have much, but I would pick his love over money any day." She patted Cassandra's arm. "Little one, the good Lord will work everything out. Maybe you and your mamá will pay off the bank, and you can fall in love with Señor Matt. Then you can have the Triple P and love."

"Don't be silly. The last thing I would do is marry Matt Atkins. He's–He's..."

Maria chuckled. "He has moved into your heart? No? Now, let me help with your gown."

"Maria, you are the one who is loco. My heart is all my own. No man will ever own it." She sniffed the air. "Is that dinner burning?"

Maria glanced nervously toward the door. "I will go, but if you cannot fasten those buttons, do not call for me." She grumbled all the way downstairs.

Cassandra closed the bedroom door and lifted the silk dinner dress over her head. The honey-amber folds slipped past her shoulders to land at her bare feet. As she labored with the buttons, she wished she'd not tricked Maria into leaving.

Her father had given her the dress a year ago, the day he'd returned from driving a small herd of longhorns to Abilene. Little did they know it would be his last cattle drive.

When she hugged his neck, she heard paper crinkle behind his back. "Papa, what do you have there?"

Samuel's hazel eyes twinkled. "Cassie, my love, I saw this in a shop window and had to buy it for you. Close your eyes and hold out your hands."

Cassandra obeyed, but her eyes flew open the moment the package touched her fingertips. She yanked off the string and ripped off the paper. The dress shimmered in the afternoon sun.

She pressed the silky material against her cheek. "Oh, Papa. It's beautiful."

"I knew the color would match your hair. But that's not all." He dug in his coat pocket. "I have another gift for you."

"You shouldn't have. This dress is more than enough."

"I can get my darling daughter anything I want." He thrust a slender velvet box into her hands.

Cassandra lifted the lid. Her breath caught at the sight of a pearl necklace and earrings. The sunlight picked up the sheen of each matching pearl. "I'm speechless."

Samuel hugged her close. "First time for that."

She pinched his rust-colored beard. "I'll forgive you those words, especially since you are home and have brought me such wonderful gifts. I'll wear them at supper this evening. Maria is fixing a special meal to welcome you back."

The dinner had been a joyous occasion, filled with love and laughter. Three months later her father had been killed, and Cassandra had not worn the gown or the necklace since.

Her throat tightened. "Oh, Papa. I don't want to marry Phillip, but time is running out."

A gentle breeze riffled the curtain, bringing with it the scent of roses. Was Papa sending a sign from heaven? Cassandra hurried to the window and flipped back the curtain.

The sun was melding into the horizon and setting the mountain range ablaze in burnt orange and flaming red. The same fiery scene her father had compared to a place called hell when Cassandra was only seven years old. She couldn't believe her beloved hills could look like a place created for the devil and his angels, but she had bowed her head and asked God to save her soul and keep her from going there.

Could she still pray to God with that kind of faith?

Cassandra folded her hands and bowed her head. "Lord, you answered my prayers back then, can you do it now? Mama says you can. She even thinks Matt Atkins is the answer to our prayers. If he is, could you let us know for sure? And Lord, you know we still need a good hard rain. That last shower barely made a difference. Please send some soon. Thank you for listening to me. At least I think you're listening. Amen."

She crossed to her vanity and picked up the ivory comb Matt had given her. Her face flushed at the brashness she showed in kissing his cheek. What had she been thinking? That was the problem. She'd been thinking too much lately and all about that handsome cowboy.

She slid on a pair of slippers a shade darker than her dress and tucked the comb in her hair. At the last minute, she decided to wear the pearl necklace. When she fastened its clasp, the necklace nestled in the hollow of her throat. She dabbed perfume behind her ears before clipping the earrings in place. Hopefully, Matt would appreciate her effort. After a final look in the mirror, she descended the stairs.

Carlos's mouth gaped open when he saw her. "It was worth the wait, Señorita Cassie." Rafael bobbed his head in agreement, and Roberto exclaimed, "You are beautiful, Miss Cassie."

Helen rushed across the room and embraced Cassandra. "Darling, you are wearing the dress and the pearls." She inclined her head toward Matt. "Her father said she looked like an angel in this dress."

"I agree. You're lovely." He offered her the crook of his arm. "May I?"

Cassandra remembered little of the meal save Matt's gaze upon her face. Each time their eyes met, he either grinned or winked. Rafael and Carlos enjoyed the interchange, elbowing one another and speaking agreeably in Spanish. Though Roberto did not seem pleased, he did eat a generous helping of roast pork and glazed sweet potatoes and on occasion, contributed to the conversation. Her mother appeared to contemplate the pink stains dotting Cassandra's cheeks but thankfully withheld her comments.

Whenever Matt's eyes lingered on Cassandra, Maria piled more food onto his plate. "Señor Matt, you need to spend more time eating and less time looking at Miss Cassie."

"You're right, Maria." Matt winked at Cassandra and tucked into another slice of pork swimming in gravy.

After dinner Rafael and Carlos excused themselves to check on the animals. Roberto volunteered to clean up, insisting his mother rest. Maria protested and bustled after him into the kitchen. Cassandra knew she would instruct Roberto with every dish he washed.

"Matt," Helen said, "maybe we can talk Cassandra into playing the pianoforte."

Matt took Cassandra's hand and followed Helen into the parlor. Candlelight seeped into the corners of the room, chasing away the darkness and creating a warm glow on the rosewood pianoforte. The scent of beeswax gave evidence Maria had recently polished the instrument.

After seating Cassandra on the piano's padded stool, Matt eased himself onto the chair beside her. Cassandra's fingers trembled as she began to play, and she hit several wrong notes before regaining her composure. As her confidence increased, she lost herself in the beautiful, haunting strains of Beethoven's "Moonlight Sonata."

At the song's conclusion, Matt hollered, "Bravo."

Helen clapped in approval. "That was one of Samuel's favorite songs. When he discovered Cassandra had an ear for music, he had the pianoforte shipped here from England. He never denied his sweet daughter anything."

"Mama, Papa spoiled you as well. The house is full of things he bought with you in mind."

Helen's face turned serious. "Yes, your father was good to me. Now that he is gone, I am grateful for the reminders of his love" Her expression brightened when she said to Matt, "On occasion, the pianoforte does my bidding. May I play while you and Cassandra try your hand at dancing? Samuel believed young ladies should learn to waltz, so he taught her himself."

"It would be my honor. Cassandra Jane? He presented his hand to her and whispered, "So, you *can* waltz."

Cassandra shyly averted her gaze and allowed Matt to lead her to the center of the room. He gathered her into his arms and placed a hand on the small of her back, drawing her close. She placed her free hand on his shoulder, swallowed hard, and told her heart to stop its wild raging.

The one, two, three beat of the "Blue Danube Waltz" carried them around and around the room. Cassandra followed Matt's lead with ease, molding into his embrace. The music and the billowy folds of her dress surrounded them. She turned her head from his tender but intense gaze.

"Look at me," he whispered in her ear, and she kept her eyes on his until, all too soon, the song ended. His expression mirrored her desire to continue dancing.

Helen closed the lid of the pianoforte. "It's good to hear music and laughter in our home again. We owe much of that to you, Matt."

Matt bowed his head at Helen. "You must promise me the first dance next time."

A rosy blush tinted Helen's cheeks. Cassandra thrilled to see her mother's happiness. Since Matt's arrival and his suggestion of a timber contract, the mood of the entire household had changed.

"It has been a long day," Helen said. "I will bid the two of you a good evening."

"Good night, Mama."

"Mrs. Pickett."

Cassandra remained motionless until her mother's footsteps ascended the stairs. "Thank you, Matt. Thank you for bringing joy back into Mama's life. She misses Papa so."

"Your mother is a wonderful woman. You favor her." He drew her back into his arms. "You red-headed vixen. You sure have bewitched me."

His lips brushed her forehead, warm as honey on a summer's day. She quivered in his embrace. "I told you not to be afraid of me," he whispered as he traced the outline of her mouth with a finger.

She clung to him and closed her eyes. He was going to kiss her. But instead of the touch of his lips, he let out a sigh and released his hold on her.

"I better head to the bunkhouse. We need to finish that fence tomorrow." He tweaked her nose. "I might even let you help with the postholes this time."

Cassandra gripped the pianoforte to steady her weak knees. With an effort she kept her voice light and replied, "I might surprise you and dig one."

"Nothing you do would surprise me, darlin'." Matt touched the ivory comb, his eyes changing to smoky blue. "I knew it would look beautiful on you." He pulled away from her. "Good night, Cassandra."

A moment later the front door closed with a soft click. Cassandra touched her brow, still warm from his lips. She climbed the stairs to her bedroom, knowing full well sleep would not come easy that night.

SIXTEEN

Phillip's black pants and shirt matched his mood. He banged his fist on the desk, taking care not to hit the inkwell. Where was Jack Dalton? He was supposed to have been there at one o'clock. Jack's insolence and the Oriental rug bearing the reminder of his crass behavior did nothing to improve Phillip's disposition. He used the toe of his boot to slide the spittoon over the ink stain Rosa had not been able to remove.

Each hollow tick of the grandfather clock made it more difficult for Phillip to keep his temper in check. He poured a snifter of brandy from a cut-glass decanter and threw the golden-brown liquid down his throat, grateful for the distraction of the burning sensation.

Ten minutes and another snifter of brandy later, the door to the study swung open. Jack sauntered in as though the world had stopped and was waiting for him.

Phillip set his glass on the desk. "Nice of you to finally show up. Where have you been?"

"I've got a few other pots in the fire. You're not the only one who needs my special way of doin' things. I'm just makin' some money on the side. Can't fault a man for that, can ya?"

"I've half a mind to fire you."

"Come on, Mr. Brigham," Jack's spurs jangling as he ambled across the room. "We need each other. I need all that money of yours, and you need me to do the things you won't do. I'd say we make a good pair."

"We are not a pair. I'm your boss. You should have been here a half an hour ago."

"Had to make a certain woman happy 'fore I left town." Jack's yellow teeth showed through a lecherous grin. "You get the idea?"

Phillip did get the idea, and he didn't like it. He hated being on the same level as the man standing in front of him.

"Did you learn anything about that cowboy at the Triple P?"

Jack scratched his chin, which hadn't seen a razor in a week. "His name's Matt Earl Atkins. Worked at the Circle T for 'bout a year."

"George Thompson's place. Go on."

"Before that, he worked at a couple other ranches. Some small outfit in Texarkana. Think it was the Risin' Sun, and one in Waco called the Runnin' H. Not sure where he come from 'fore that."

Jack leaned over and snatched an imported cigar from an inlaid box sitting on the desk. He struck a match on the bottom of his boot, touched the flame to the tip of the cigar, and puffed until it glowed. He tilted his head back and exhaled two smoke circles that floated aimlessly toward the ceiling.

Phillip hated the bitter smell of cigars. He kept them only for important guests, which Jack was not. He leaned back in his chair to avoid a smoke ring Jack blew his way. "What else can you tell me about him?"

"I'm gettin' there. A man needs to slow down and enjoy life. Like this here." He waved the cigar.

"I'm waiting."

"That cowboy's been askin' about Lazy Acres and you buyin' up more land. First, I thought he found out how poor those Pickett women are and was gonna ask you for a better payin' job. But then I heard him askin' if there was any ranches for sale. Maybe he's thinkin' about stickin' around and buyin' a place. Maybe even the Triple P after the bank closes on it."

Phillip considered Jack's words. Matt Atkins knew better than to ask for a job at Lazy Acres, and there was no way a cowhand could afford even a small spread like the Triple P.

"And?"

"He's also been askin' ranchers to breed their cattle to the Picketts' bull. Says it could improve their stock. Most of 'em said no, but a few been thinkin' about it. They'd rather breed their mares to that big ol' hoss of his."

Phillip ran a hand through his hair. The Pickett's could never make enough money from breeding their bull to repay their loan, and who cared if the local ranchers bred their mares to Matt's stallion?

"He turned 'em down flat. Said he didn't care nothing about breedin' his hoss." Jack stubbed out his cigar in the ashtray on Phillip's desk. "And yesterday he popped in and out of Mr. Harvey's office and sent a couple telegrams. One was to George

Thompson about timber for the railroad fixin' to come this way."

Phillip drummed his fingers on the desk. Why hadn't he anticipated the approaching railroad? Surely, that cowboy was acting on behalf of the Pickett women. If Cassandra and her mother got a timber contract, they could possibly use the prospect of future revenue against their loan.

"And the second telegram?"

"Give me a chance. Wouldn't hurt ya none to work on your patience." Jack stretched his arms above his head and raised scraggly eyebrows.

Phillip checked the impulse to grab Jack by the shoulders and throw him out of the study. "Answer my question. What about the second telegram?"

"That one went to Walter Brigham of Boston. He some kin of yours?"

How does Matt know my uncle? Phillip's mind sought for an answer.

Jack shrugged. "Said he was gonna get somethin'. Don't know what. Telegraphs are only so long." He cackled at his joke. "I bumped into him comin' out of the telegraph office, but he don't know who I am."

If Jack had been any brighter, he would have noticed the silence filling the room and the blood draining from Phillip's face.

What was Matt getting? Did it have anything to do with his seeing Mr. Harvey and possibly wanting to buy a ranch? Maybe he has more money than I thought.

"I want you to double your efforts," Phillip said. "This time don't let Atkins see you and find out what he wants with Mr.

Harvey. While you're at it, keep an eye on Cassandra and her mother and let me know if they come up with any more money to put on their loan."

"It's gonna cost ya."

Phillip whipped out the key from his vest pocket, unlocked the desk drawer, and peeled off a handful of bills. "The cost is the least of my concerns. Just do it."

Jack grabbed the money and held it to his nose. "Nothin' smells sweeter than this. Not even those painted ladies in town." His lips moved as he counted the bills. "This is better than last time but still ain't enough."

A muscle in Phillip's jaw flicked. "Bring me back something I can use, and I'll give you three times that much."

"Sounds fair, but even if you can't use what I bring, you're still gonna owe me. I don't work for nothin'."

He heaved himself to his feet, pocketed the money, and called back over his shoulder, "Oh, this might interest ya too. That cowboy's getting mighty chummy with the Triple P clan. 'Specially with that pretty little redhead. Seen 'em takin' cozy rides 'round the ranch the past few days. He's movin' in on your territory."

Phillip collapsed into his chair. In a week's time, his plans had started to unravel. Now, he had to count on Jack Dalton to help tie them back together. He needed an ace in the hole just in case that imbecile didn't come through.

Ace in the hole. Phillip frowned at the irony. It was an ace of hearts that had completed Samuel Pickett's full house and set all of this in motion. For the hundredth time he wished he'd never gotten drunk and played that game of poker. If he had kept his head, he'd be established in Boston by now.

His mind grappled with what he should do. The clattering of pots and pans in the kitchen rose over the din of his thoughts. Bella had mentioned making a pot of vegetable soup for the noon meal, but Phillip knew he wouldn't eat a bite until he salvaged his plans and put them back on track.

He arranged and rearranged the papers on his desk as he contemplated his situation. That Triple P cowboy was proving to be more of a problem than he'd anticipated. And how had the Pickett women come up with the idea to bid on a timber contract in the first place? Had that cowboy instigated it?

Phillip dropped the papers he was holding. *I've got it. That's what I'll do.*

He grabbed a pen and a piece of paper, scribbled a short message, and sped outside. "Jorge," he called to a passing vaquero. "Get this to the telegraph office. Right now. *Apurate*."

The Mexican, tall and willowy as a reed, bobbed his head and swung a long leg over his horse. The two raced toward Goose Neck Ridge.

Phillip would not trust a positive answer to his telegram or place all his marbles in Jack's basket. To shore up the Triple P foreclosure, he needed to pay Higgins a visit and make sure he was holding up his end of the deal.

Hoping to calm his nerves, Phillip stepped through the gate leading into the flower garden. Despite the drought, the beds flourished due to the hard work of the gardener who carted water from the nearby creek. Phillip breathed in the scent of the honeysuckles hugging the trellises on the hacienda's south wing. Hummingbirds, butterflies, and bees competed for the nectar from the white, pink, and orange flowers. To compensate for their lesser scent, scarlet and deep-yellow hibiscus presented wide-open, sunny faces in greeting. Phillip trailed his fingers over lacy-white alyssum as made his way to the gazebo in the center of the garden.

The sweet scent of the flowers conjured up idyllic images of reading books with Cassandra under the lattice-work pavilion. He longed for those innocent days when anything seemed possible. How had the events of his life spiraled so far out of control? And was there any hope of turning them around?

Juanita startled Phillip when she popped out from behind a buttress supporting one of the hacienda's chimneys. She approached him with wide eyes. "Señor Brigham, what has happened? You do not look happy."

"You are right, my little Juanita. Running a ranch this size is not easy. There are times when I get upset."

"But you do a fine job of running Lazy Acres. There is no better ranch in all of Texas."

"And how would you know?" he teased. "Have you seen every other ranch in this big state?"

"I do not need to. I know in my heart this one is best. And there is no better *el patrón* than you."

The girl's simple faith in him and his ranch chased away Phillip's melancholy. He patted her head. "Thank you, *muchacha*. What do you have there?" He pointed to the two dolls she was clutching.

Juanita held up the doll wearing a dress stitched from scraps of fabric. "This is Lolita. Mamacita made her this morning. Isn't she beautiful? She has real hair."

Phillip ran a finger down the doll's long, black tresses. Rosa must have cut her own hair to use for her daughter's new toy.

"She is very pretty. Your mother did a fine job. Have you been playing with Lolita all morning?"

"Sí. But it is not so fun to play all alone. Would you play with me?"

Phillip wanted to return to his study, but Juanita's bright expression changed his mind. His gaze swept past the garden gate and onto the grounds. Good. The compound was empty.

"All right, my little one, but only for a short while. I must get back to running the best ranch in all of Texas."

Juanita captured his hand and led him through the garden gate and up to the porch. After settling on the bottom step, she handed Phillip the other doll. It was made of sticks and tied with string.

"This is Pedro. He is Lolita's *novio*. You can play with him." She batted her eyes. "Pedro, you have not bought me a present in a long, long time. As my *novio,* you must bring me many gifts."

"But we are in a drought, and rustlers have stolen all our cattle. We have no money."

Juanita giggled. "If you love me, you will buy me a new dress and a pair of slippers."

Phillip rolled his eyes and said in an exaggerated voice, "My sweet Lolita. Is my love not enough to make you happy?"

"Now, ain't that sweet?" Jack Dalton's voice reached over to the pair. He dallied through the wrought iron gate and into the courtyard, rolling a cigarette.

Phillip leapt to his feet. "I told you to—"

"And miss the boss of Lazy Acres playing dolls with a servant girl?" Jack smirked at Juanita. "And a Mexican at that."

Phillip rushed Jack and landed a fist on the ugly man's jaw. The impact of the blow sent Jack stumbling backward. In a flash, he regained his footing and drew his gun. Instinctively, Phillip shielded Juanita with his body. The two men glowered at each other.

Jack dabbed his bleeding nose with his shirtsleeve. "Can't say I wouldn't mind shootin' you, but I never shot no girl before."

"If you hurt her, I'll hunt you down and kill you." Juanita cringed against Phillip's side. He gently squeezed her arm.

Jack holstered his gun. "I was only funnin' with ya."

"If you want the rest of your money, you better ride out and earn it."

Jack tipped his hat. "Good day, Señorita. Mr. Brigham." He mounted his horse, jerked on the reins, and kicked the animal with his spurs. The horse bolted out of the compound.

Juanita peeked out from behind Phillip with frightened eyes. "I do not like him. He is a very bad man."

"Don't worry. I won't let him hurt you." He picked up the dolls and handed them to her. "Here. Take these and go back to your mamacita, *por favor*."

Juanita raised on her tiptoes, and Phillip leaned down so she could kiss his cheek. As she ran off, Phillip fingered the spot her lips had touched. He almost called after her, but the vision of Jack's leering face stopped him. That man didn't deserve another day on God's green earth. Like Judas betraying Christ, Jack deserved punishment in—

Phillip halted mid-thought. He hadn't considered the Lord since his mother and sister had passed away, and then it was to blame the Creator, who exercised power in determining those who lived and those who died. Phillip disregarded his religious musings and tried to concentrate on the task at hand. But all he thought about the remainder of the afternoon was his hands around Jack Dalton's neck.

☆☆☆

While Cassandra and Matt waited for George Thompson's answer to the telegram, they worked hard on the Triple P. Matt discussed his every idea with Cassandra first, while she in turn, at least listened before she laughingly overrode it. The two also took long rides around the ranch, teased each other often, and talked late into the night. At mealtimes they shared stories, both true and embellished, and Cassandra found herself thinking about what it would be like if Matt stayed on.

One afternoon she noticed the weariness in Maria's face and asked if she and Matt could prepare supper. Maria surprised her by agreeing but said if the meal did not meet up to her standards, she expected the two of them to weed her garden the next day.

The resulting beef stew, cornbread, and chocolate pudding received high praises, even from Maria, though she fussed when Cassandra served the stew in the iron kettle instead of a serving dish.

"There is one other thing," Maria said. All eyes fixed on her while she wiped her mouth and then set the napkin down beside her plate.

Cassandra's shoulders collapsed. "I knew the stew needed more salt."

"The stew is very good. But now Rafael and Roberto must weed my garden tomorrow."

Roberto put on a brave smile and asked his mother for another helping of pudding. Cassandra was glad to see the boy's appetite had returned. He must have gotten over his jealousy, although he still kept a watchful eye on Matt when he thought no one was looking.

Rafael was spooning the last bit of pudding out of his bowl when Cassandra and Matt started clearing the table.

"You two have done enough," Maria said. "Roberto and I will take care of cleanup."

"Mama," Cassandra said, "Please tell Maria she is to take the night off. I know she won't listen to me."

Maria opened her mouth to protest, but Helen hustled her and Roberto into the parlor to play a game of three-handed cribbage.

Cassandra prepared the dish basin while Matt finished clearing the table. He nudged her aside when she donned an apron to wash the dishes.

"I'll wash and rinse, and you dry," he instructed. "Gotta save those purty hands of yours." He plunged his hands into the basin, sending soap suds into the air.

Cassandra wiggled the third finger of her left hand behind Matt's back and imagined him sliding a wedding band onto it. *Don't get the wagon before the horse, Cassandra.* She glanced up at him from underneath her lashes. *Maybe I can help him along.*

"Matt, have you ever been in love?" she asked.

"You sure don't mince words, do you? Is there a reason ya wanna know?"

"Not particularly." She turned away to keep him from reading her intention. She didn't fool him for a moment.

"I gotta feelin' you're not tellin' me the truth," he said, handing over a plate to dry.

How did that man keep seeing right through her? Was she so transparent? "I just asked a simple question. It's not a big deal."

"You're the one makin' a big deal out of it."

"Matt Atkins, I don't know how you do it, but you have a knack for turning my words against me when I ask you anything personal. Are you hiding something?"

The muscle in Matt's jaw ticked. "All right. Since you're all bent on pryin' into my life, I'll tell you. I was in love once. There. Are you happy?"

Pain gripped Cassandra's heart. She had asked. She had no right to complain.

"Well? Aren't you going to ask me about her?"

"You have made it perfectly clear I need to mind my own business." She hooked the dish towel over a peg near the sink. "Thank you for helping with supper. I'll let you finish up. Good night, Matt."

As Cassandra fled the kitchen, she barely heard his last words, "Women. And who do you think is gonna wash the rest of these dirty dishes?"

Seventeen

Cassandra woke up early the next morning from a restless night's sleep with a stiff neck. She massaged her sore muscles and replayed her dismal attempt to pry into Matt's love life. Should she laugh and brush it off? Or should she ask him to explain? The more her mind trampled the questions, the muddier they became.

How absurd. Anything I say will only make things worse.

She flipped back the quilt and sprang out of bed. "I might as well get up and start my day."

She tucked a freshly-pressed blouse edged with ruffles into her jeans and took more care than normal in brushing her hair. Her tresses shone in the mirror as she pulled them into a ponytail with a blue ribbon. Over breakfast, at which Matt was thankfully absent, Maria insisted the fancy blouse was not suited for ranch work. Cassandra ignored the housekeeper's opinion and downed a glass of milk and a slice of bread smothered in strawberry preserves.

After breakfast she skipped down the porch steps, determined to not let her worries about Matt dampen her day.

Besides, morning was her favorite time around the Triple P. She relished the hustle and bustle of the ranch as it shook itself awake from a deep night's sleep.

The sun had already lifted its drowsy head and was now stretching tentative fingers along the eastern border of the Triple P. Cassandra closed her eyes and breathed in the fresh air of a new day. Anything was possible.

Bullet trotted up with a welcoming woof and a wagging tail. He nudged Cassandra's hand with a wet nose. "Are we the first ones up this morning?" she asked. The dog's tail thumped her leg in reply, his long tongue lolling out of his mouth. "Looks like it's going to be another blistering day. Huh, boy?"

The ranch needed a good hard rain–and soon. The scant shower a couple of days ago had provided little relief for grass now drying up in brown splotches.

"Bullet, it's unfortunate the rain isn't as abundant as Mama's faith." The dog darted after a jackrabbit, leaving Cassandra to continue her trek to the barn alone. She heard a muffled voice coming from inside. When she peered around the barn door, she saw Matt ruffling the fur of one of the cats.

"How are you, Mister Cat?" he asked. The creature butted him with its head and purred so loudly, Cassandra heard the rumble from where she stood.

"That's not a mister cat. That's Samantha." She walked into the barn, failing to suppress a giggle.

Matt dropped the cat like a hot branding iron. Samantha meowed in protest. "You don't have to sneak up on me," he said, a red stain creeping up his cheeks.

Cassandra picked up the cat and pressed her face against its warm fur. "I'd hardly call coming in to feed the animals sneaking, and you've no cause to be embarrassed. Your show of affection was quite endearing."

"Can't a man have a moment to himself?"

"Are you still mad at me for asking if you'd ever been in love."

"Good heavens, girl. No."

"Then what's wrong? You're acting awfully jumpy this morning."

"I'm fine. You surprised me. That's all."

"If you say so."

Matt marched over and brought his face to within inches of hers. "What do you mean by that?"

Samantha unsheathed her claws and took a swipe at Matt. He jerked away and took a wide stance. "Darn cat. Just like a woman. Acts like she cares, then up and changes her mind."

Cassandra stepped back to separate him from the agitated feline. So, he *was* still upset about that woman he mentioned last night. What had she done to make him so angry?

Not caring for the possible answer or the dark expression on his face, she said, "Samantha's a new mama. Want to see her kittens?"

"No."

"Ah, come on. They're cute little fluffs of fur."

Matt shoved his hands into his pants pockets and mumbled, "All right. Where are they?"

She pointed to the hayloft. "They've only had their eyes open for a few days." She held up a finger. "Listen." Overhead, faint meows accompanied the rustling of hay. Samantha jumped down from Cassandra's arms and bounded up a rickety ladder propped in the corner of the barn. The meowing stopped.

"She's probably servin' up breakfast," Matt said. "Maybe we shouldn't bother her."

"Samantha won't mind. Come on." She paused on the first rung of the ladder. "You never told me the other day if you'd convinced any of the ranchers to breed their mares to King."

"I managed to work out a deal with a few of 'em."

"That's great. I bet Jim Sexton was interested. I doubt Mr. Fairfax was. He already thinks he's got the best horses around."

"Let's don't talk business. I want to see those kittens."

"First, you don't want to see them, and now you do. I can't for the life of me figure out men."

"I could say the same thing about you women."

Cassandra was thankful his voice had softened. She climbed the ladder and took a chance by shouting back down, "Are you coming? Or is a big, strong cowboy like you afraid of heights?"

"I'm not scared of anything, Cassandra Jane. Just wait until I get a hold of you."

"You'll have to find me first," she yelled and squeezed between the wall and a mountain of loose hay.

Matt bounded up the ladder and hollered, "Where are you?" He stamped through the loft as though making a big show of searching for her. After several minutes he said, "All right. If that's how you want it, you can stay up here the rest of the day." His footsteps faded away.

The moment Cassandra peeked out from behind her hideout, Matt's hand snaked in and caught her wrist.

"Matt Atkins, that's not fair. You tricked me."

"Did ya think you'd get away from me that easy?" His eyes turned the color of blue smoke.

Goosebumps tickled the back of Cassandra's neck. She wiggled her hand in a weak attempt to free herself.

"You're about the purtiest thing I've ever seen." His breath caressed her brow as he pulled her into his arms and then lowered his mouth toward hers.

Any romantic notions Cassandra had about Matt vanished like morning mist on a hot Texas day. His chaste kiss on her forehead after they waltzed had been one thing. But here in the barn, the old demons reminded her of what had happened with Phillip beneath this very spot. She jerked away from Matt and raised both hands to her mouth in alarm.

Sorrow and shame filled his eyes. "I'm sorry. I shouldn't have tried that."

Seeing his contrite expression, Cassandra feared she had once again overreacted. "I'm sorry. I–I..."

Matt refused to meet her eyes. He brushed the hay off his shirt and said, "This wasn't your fault. I promise it won't happen again." He spun on his heel and retreated down the ladder.

Cassandra stood shock-still. In utter frustration, she grabbed a fistful of hay and threw it into the air. "Who does he think he is, coming here and turning this entire ranch upside down?"

The hay floated back to the floor. Who was she kidding? The only thing upside down was her heart.

☆☆☆

Phillip, dressed in a dark-gray cutaway suit, strode past the two columns supporting the entrance of the Goose Neck Ridge Bank. The three-story structure with its hewn archway housed the Brigham fortune and the modest incomes of the surrounding farms, ranches, and Goose Neck Ridge residents. The interior, with its stately colonnades and mosaic floor, owed its Roman Revival-style to Phillip's grandfather.

Lyle Phillip Brigham had brought his enterprising ways from Boston to southwest Texas in the early 1800s. After receiving a Spanish land grant for a thousand acres, he purchased five hundred head of longhorns. The rapid expansion of his cattle ranch nudged out most of his neighbors until he amassed enough wealth to establish the bank in which Phillip now stood.

Though Phillip admired the interior design his grandfather had achieved, he deemed it too pretentious for the likes of Goose Neck Ridge. Now, for Boston? That was a different story.

He bypassed a female teller waiting on a shabbily-dressed farmer, who was clutching a straw hat in one hand and a few dollars in the other. The man pushed the meager bills over the marble counter into the teller's waiting fingers.

Poor bloke. That's not enough money to buy a decent meal at the Goose Neck Ridge Hotel.

Phillip stopped at the next teller station and stared through the bars at William Higgins. The banker swallowed and ran a finger under the collar of his starched shirt. Phillip motioned for him to come out from behind the counter.

"Yes, Mr. Brigham?"

"How are things progressing with the Triple P foreclosure?"

Higgins's eyes nervously shifted from one side of the bank to the other. "Uh, the paperwork is drawn up and approved, but the Pickett women still have two more weeks to come up with the money."

Phillip leaned close to the banker's ear, and with a voice as smooth as silk, whispered, "And we both don't want that to happen, now, do we?"

Higgins shrank into his suit. "Yes, sir. I mean–no, sir, Mr. Brigham."

Phillip swiped a finger along the countertop and frowned at the slight line left in the dust. He ignored the impossibility of keeping dirt at bay in a cowtown.

"It would behoove the bank to maintain an appearance. The Brighams may not own this establishment anymore, but I still hold the controlling interest."

The door of the bank swung open and intruded upon Phillip's words of self-importance. Higgins gave him a sideways glance and scurried over to greet an elderly couple.

"Mr. and Mrs. Baxter, it's good to see you. May I help you?" He shook the hand of a gray-haired man dressed in a once-stylish, linen suit. Mrs. Baxter, every bit as gray-headed as her husband but slightly more fashionable, murmured a subdued greeting.

Phillip marched to the door, stifling a scowl. With a hand on the brass doorknob, he glared at Higgins and mouthed, "I'll be back."

Phillip longed for the day he could withdraw all of his money from the bank and deposit it in a financial institution in Boston. He cared little that his withdrawal might be the death of the bank his grandfather had established fifty years ago.

Making his way up the boardwalk toward the mercantile, Phillip saw a woman with orange-colored hair and ruddy cheeks sweeping the front porch outside Winston Harvey's law office. Instead of outright ignoring her, he wished her a good day.

"And a good day to ye, sir," she said in a thick Irish brogue. She stopped sweeping and leaned against a broom, the size of which he'd never seen.

"A lovely day to be alive, wouldn't ye agree?"

"If you say so, ma'am."

"Aye, I do be sayin' so. There be nothin' like a sun-shiny day to chase away the cobwebs. Eh, Mr. Brigham?"

"I'm afraid you have me at a disadvantage. How do you know me?"

"Oh, don't ye go worryin' 'bout the likes of me. I'm Fiona. Uncle Winne's me uncle. I'm keepin' an eye on the place while he and Auntie Allison be gone over California-way. As for you, everyone 'round town talks about Mr. Brigham, the big cattle baron. And…" She winked a hazel eye. "After ye left the bank, those two gals over there said your name."

Phillip followed Fiona's gaze a short gap up the boardwalk. Two young women quickly hid their admiring glances behind lace-trimmed parasols. Thinking to take advantage of his chance meeting of Mr. Harvey's niece, Phillip turned back to Fiona.

"Miss," he said in his most charming voice. "Do you happen to know anything about a man named Matt Atkins? I heard he wanted to do business with your uncle the other day."

Fiona wrinkled her nose. "I don't know any Matt Atkins, but even if I did, I wouldn't be sharin' what he wants with Uncle Winnie. Me thinks ye need to come back and talk to him when he and Auntie Allison get back in a couple of weeks."

She muttered almost under her breath, "Why do the men of this town keep askin' me questions about the law?"

Phillip berated himself. He should have known he wouldn't get any information from the woman. He nodded and made his way to the ladies of whom she had referred. Their parasols parted to reveal two blushing faces.

"Good morning, Mr. Brigham," said the older of the two women, though Phillip assumed she was not a day over nineteen. Her companion's face turned crimson. Dressed in high-waisted gowns of pale pink and mint green, the two held promise for a couple of town blokes and not for him. Cassandra was much more to his liking. She was taller and filled out her dresses better.

"Ladies, I thought the sun was bright until the two of you lit up my path." The compliment sounded lame even to his ears, but he enjoyed the young ladies' admiration just the same. The pair giggled behind their gloved hands.

"If you will excuse me," he said, "I have business to attend. Good day." The ladies' tittering followed him the rest of the way to the mercantile.

Phillip ignored the assortment of smells permeating the store. He bypassed a couple of saddles, a row of hams hanging from the ceiling, an array of kitchen utensils, and the dry goods section until he reached a bookshelf in the back of the store. He rummaged through the books until he found a small one with a cover picture of a redbird trapped in a gilded cage. He thumbed to the last page where the bird sang merrily from the top of a tree.

"Ah, good. A happy ending. Juanita will be pleased."

After he paid for the book, he strode out of the mercantile, tipping his hat to two women who were entering the store.

The pair were more mature and comelier than the women he'd met on the boardwalk, but Phillip had neither the time nor the inclination for any more pleasantries with the fairer sex of Goose Neck Ridge.

He sprang onto his stallion's back and headed for home. Above the steady beat of the horse's hooves, his thoughts fixated on one woman. Cassandra. When the bank foreclosed on the Triple P, she'd have no other choice than to marry him.

Samuel Pickett, you may have beaten me in poker, but in two weeks' time, I'll hold the winning hand. Soon, both your daughter and your ranch will be mine.

EIGHTEEN

For the next several days, silence hung as heavy as a wet blanket on wash day over the Triple P. Confusion dogged Cassandra about what had happened with Matt in the hayloft. She'd been silly and overreacted and wanted to apologize, but he kept her at arm's length, even taking his meals to the bunkhouse and eating alone.

Helen questioned Matt's odd behavior, asking if he was well. He mumbled an incoherent reply, then rode off in search of a coyote he'd spotted the previous day. Cassandra's heart sank. He only wanted an excuse to get away from her.

After the third day, Cassandra took matters into her own hands. She saw Matt leading a pair of horses past the corral and thinking she could corner him in the barn, followed him inside. Her plan might have succeeded had she not accidentally kicked over an empty milk bucket. The noise spooked the horses, and one of them stepped on Matt's foot.

Cassandra rushed forward. "Oh, Matt. I'm sorry."

"Doggone you, Cassandra Jane." He hopped on the other foot while trying to calm down the horses.

Cassandra took one of the lead ropes and spoke in a low voice to the roan mare. The horse lowered her head and followed Cassandra into an empty stall.

Matt limped into the next stall and slipped off the other horse's halter. "What's the big idea of sneakin' up on me?"

"I didn't sneak. Well, maybe I did, but it's only because you're not talking to me."

"Don't you think I have a good reason?" He grabbed the halter she had taken off.

"No," she lied. She shadowed his heels as he hung up both halters on an empty peg next to a row of bridles.

He spun around and shooed her away. "Can't a man move without you bein' underfoot?"

She latched on to his arm. "Stop asking questions. It's answers I want. Why won't you talk about what happened in the hayloft? You can't keep ignoring me."

"Says who?"

Without warning, he hoisted Cassandra over his shoulder and ignoring her protest and flailing arms, crossed over to a pile of straw and dumped her on her backside. "I don't have time for your idle chit-chat."

"Idle chit-chat?" Cassandra jumped up and yanked the straw from her hair. "You're not getting away that easy."

With no thought of the consequences, she charged him at full force. The momentum carried them outside the barn to land in a tangled heap on the ground.

"We go to town and look what happens," Rafael said. He, Carlos, and Maria were looking down at Cassandra and Matt from the seat of the buckboard. "Maybe we should have stayed home and kept an eye on these two."

Why did those three have to return right now? Cassandra prayed they couldn't see her burning cheeks.

Rafael sprang from the buckboard and helped down a concerned-looking Maria. Matt leapt to his feet and grabbed the horse's reins. "This isn't what you think. Here. I'll get the horse."

"Señor Matt," Carlos protested. "We have not yet unloaded the supplies and dry goods."

Cassandra uttered a silent curse as the wagon clattered by. Why did things like this always happen to her? And why did they happen because of that man?

Maria snatched control of the situation. "Rafael, help Miss Cassie up right this minute."

Rafael jumped to attention. He helped Cassandra to her feet. "I am sorry, Señorita Cassie. I thought you two were playing."

Maria slapped him with her fan. "Foolish man. Anyone can see they were not playing." She bustled over and circled Cassandra's shoulders with her plump arms. "Wait until your mamá hears about this."

"No. Don't tell Mama. This is between me and Matt."

Doubt clouded Maria's eyes.

"Maria, promise."

"I do not know why you keep sticking up for that cowboy." She whirled on Rafael and Carlos and clapped her hands. "Get the things out of the wagon." The men jostled each other as they hastened to do her bidding. "And Señor Matt," she called into the barn, "after you are done unhitching the horse, go feed the pigs or something."

"Now. We are alone," Maria said in a confident tone. "You can tell me. What is going on?"

Cassandra raced to the house, knowing full well she left Maria sorely perplexed.

☆☆☆

Matt threw his saddle on King and tightened the cinch in a swift, hard movement. The horse snorted and backed away. Matt laid a reassuring hand on King's flank. "Sorry, boy. This is not your fault."

He jumped on the horse's back, and the two sprang from the barnyard. Matt had no idea where he was heading. He only knew he had to flee Cassandra's anger. If another man had made her that mad, he'd have pommeled him to the ground and not suffered a moment's regret.

An image of his parents flashed in Matt's mind. They would have disapproved of his behavior. They had reared him to treat women as priceless gems, and he'd prayed to marry a virtuous woman like the one found in the book of Proverbs. The night he met Victoria Garrett at a ball hosted by her parents, he thought God had answered his prayers.

Smitten by Victoria's charm and beauty, he'd sent her a calling card the next morning. He was thrilled when she agreed to a drive in the park. As one outing led to another, Matt entertained the idea of asking for her hand in marriage. It took several more outings for him to work up the courage, but Victoria rewarded his proposal with an enthusiastic yes.

But soon after their engagement, he discovered that underneath her fancy gowns beat the heart of an opportunist.

When a man of wealthier means swept her off her feet at a charity ball, Matt was devastated. He swore off women and lost faith in God. He fled Boston for the Wild West, deeming cows, horses, and wide-open skies better and safer company than a woman batting her beautiful eyes.

He'd stuck to his resolve until he received that letter from Boston. Then he met the flame-haired Cassandra Jane and had lost his heart all over again.

"King, I blew it, didn't I? Well, it's time to get back to business. After I see Mr. Harvey and help save the Triple P, I can leave Goose Neck Ridge and forget all about Cassandra Jane Pickett."

As he urged King into a gallop, his heart told his mind it could not do the impossible.

★★★

Every morning since Phillip had sent the telegram to Fort Worth, he made a trip to Goose Neck Ridge. He first checked with Higgins to make sure the Triple P foreclosure was still proceeding and then stopped by the telegraph office to see if George Thompson had accepted his offer. Phillip assumed the rancher was heading up a cattle drive, or he would have responded by now. Even in Fort Worth, almost two hundred miles away, the Brigham name carried respect and commanded immediate attention.

Phillip barged into the telegraph office and stepped ahead of two customers, an elderly man and a young woman. The woman gazed at Phillip in open admiration. *If my plate wasn't so full, my dear, I'd follow up on your lovely face.*

"Did it come yet?" he asked Arthur Skinner, who had started foraging through a stack of telegrams as soon as Phillip entered the building.

The wizened man freed a piece of paper from the rest and read, "No deal. Can't use your timber. G. Thompson."

"What?" The intensity of Phillip's voice sent the young woman fleeing for the door. Arthur dropped the telegram and stepped back from the counter. Phillip retrieved the slip of paper, read it, and then crumpled it up. "This one isn't mine."

Arthur shuddered in relief. He flipped through the telegrams again and handed another one to Phillip.

Phillip quickly read the paper. *I accept your offer. Will contact soon. G. Thompson.* His lips curled into a smile. He'd beaten that Triple P cowboy at his own game.

"Sorry about the mix-up," Arthur said. "It won't happen again."

"Lucky for you, your mistake was to my benefit. Good day."

Phillip left the telegraph office in high spirits. Though the Triple P foreclosure was imminent, the possibility of the Pickett women gaining a timber contract had made him more than a little uneasy. The telegram from George Thompson served up the Triple P and Cassandra on a golden platter. Phillip had no intention of selling wood to the railroad, but by the time George Thompson figured that out, he and Cassandra would be on their honeymoon and then on their way to Boston.

Phillip hummed Mendelssohn's *Wedding March* as he made his way down the street. A young woman, wearing an ocher-colored dress with a lace jabot peeking out at the neckline, stopped and giggled at him. Her hair, the color of ripe wheat, clashed with her dress, but her azure eyes were appealing.

"Good morning, ma'am." Phillip doffed his hat and then ducked inside the mercantile before she could reply. Though he usually enjoyed a woman's attention, he had more pressing things on his mind.

Charlie Brewer was ringing up a customer's purchases. "Morning, Mr. Brigham. Be right with you." He finished boxing up the lady's canned goods and wished her a good day before retrieving a copy of *Aesop's Fables* from behind the counter. "You'll like this one. The words are more difficult, but the pictures are nice, and most of the stories have happy endings."

Phillip snatched the book from Mr. Brewer. "I make my own happy endings."

"Whatever you say." The merchant looked over at a cowboy admiring a saddle and said, "Take a look at the book and let me know what you think. I'll be right back." He hurried over to the cowboy and began extolling the merits of the saddle.

"I read that book as a child." A brunette woman plucked the book from Phillip's hand and flipped through its pages. "*The Ugly Duckling* was one of my favorite stories. I loved when the duckling turns into a graceful swan."

Phillip eyed the short, winsome woman dressed in a blue gown with a matching bonnet emblazoned with feathers. She granted him a gloved hand.

"My name is Elizabeth Anne Baxter. Over there is my friend Sarah Clemmons." She motioned to a woman wearing a rose-colored dress and a straw bonnet trimmed with ribbon. The woman took one look at Phillip and red-faced fled the mercantile.

"Never mind Sarah," Elizabeth told Phillip. "She doesn't know what to do in the presence of a man as distinguished as yourself."

"Distinguished? You make me sound like an old grandfather."

"I–I meant to say, you're more refined than the average man I've seen in town."

"Oh? Now, I am only above average?" Though he admired this woman's attention and mettle, Phillip wanted to purchase Juanita's book and head home. "Ma'am, it was nice to meet you, but I must be going."

Elizabeth fluttered her fan back and forth. "You can't leave. You've not properly introduced yourself yet. May I ask your name, sir?"

"It's Phillip Brigham, but you already know that, don't you?"

Elizabeth's face flushed crimson.

"Sarah's father works at my ranch," Phillip said. "I'm sure she told you who I was."

Elizabeth's mouth opened in defense, but Phillip held up a hand. "No need to apologize. I appreciate a woman with pluck."

She cleared her throat. "Sarah did tell me about you and your ranch. She said Lazy Acres is the biggest one around."

"A denial would be a lie, but I cannot take all the credit. My family has owned the ranch for years."

"Before I traveled here from Missouri, I thought living on a ranch would be so romantic."

"You've read more than your share of dime novels?"

"Oh, yes. I love to read. *Hurricane Nell, the Girl Dead-Shot* is my favorite, except for when she wears those dreadful pants.

Why would a woman want to do that? But she did get the handsome lawyer in the end."

Elizabeth batted her eyelashes so hard, Phillip was tempted to ask if she was all right. "I wouldn't put much faith in those books," he said, prying the book away from her. "They are fiction."

"They can be helpful. I was terrified of horses until I read about Nell riding a wild mustang. If she could ride, I can give it a try. I'm thinking about asking a handsome horseman to teach me." She blinked up at him and patted her dark tresses.

Phillip managed to keep from rolling his eyes. Could this young woman's interest be any more blatant?

Elizabeth pointed out the window to where Phillip had tied Sunny. "Is that your horse?"

"Sarah told you."

"Yes, but I've also learned to judge fine horseflesh from reading novels like *Hurricane Nell.* Compared to other horses, yours is the finest. Would you teach me to ride him?"

"I am afraid not. Sunny is—"

"Well, I'll be a prairie dog," Elizabeth exclaimed. She dashed over to the storefront window and waved at a horse and rider coming up the street. "There's Matt Atkins." When Matt passed by without noticing her, she said to Phillip in a high pitched voice, "If you would excuse me, Mr. Brigham. I must say hello to Mr. Atkins."

"How do you know him?"

The question went unanswered. Elizabeth ran for the door like a hungry wolf chasing a lone rabbit. Phillip's jaw tightened. *I can't believe she left me for that cowboy.* He peered out the window. How did Miss Baxter know Matt Atkins, and more importantly, why was he going into the bank?

Phillip brushed away the question. Matt Atkins's visit to the bank was of no consequence. Neither he nor the Pickett women had any money to put in it, and the bank certainly wasn't going to let them take any out. Higgins had ensured him of that.

Phillip paid for his book and left the mercantile. He patted the telegram in his pocket. Cassandra would not be happy when she found out the Triple P had lost the timber contract, and he was not about to let her know it'd been to him.

He galloped Sunny toward Lazy Acres. At least Juanita would be happy to see him. Especially when he placed the new book into her hands.

NINETEEN

After galloping King off the Triple P compound, Matt decided to ride to town and see if Big George had accepted the Picketts' timber offer. He dodged the saloon, having no desire to repeat the scene of his last visit. A man didn't need to court trouble when life dished up enough on its own. He rethought his position when he spied Phillip's palomino stallion outside the mercantile. But sanity prevailed. Matt would let fate deal his hand. If he ran into Phillip, he'd have his say, if he didn't, so be it.

He sprang up the steps of the telegraph office and flung the door open. Arthur's head jerked up from the telegram he was sending. "Mr. Atkins, you startled me."

"I'm sorry, Mr. Skinner. I'm in a hurry. Have I received any telegrams?"

"Yep. Sure did." He passed Matt a slip of paper. "It's from Walter Brigham in Boston. Said he's glad things are workin' out and to keep in touch. You sure he's no kin to Phillip Brigham?"

"No. Must be a coincidence. Was there another telegram?"

"That one will disappoint you." Arthur handed Matt a crumpled piece of paper. "George Thompson said he already got a low bid for timber."

Matt's stomach reeled as he read the message. His high hope that Big George would offer the Triple P a contract plummeted to earth. He stumbled out of the telegraph office without acknowledging Arthur's goodbye. How was he going to break the news to Cassandra and her mother?

Without a timber contract to use as a lien against the note, the Pickett women could not repay their loan–other than Phillip's promise to pay it off after he married Cassandra. And he'd never allow her to marry that lout. No matter how angry she was at him at the moment.

He wracked his brain for another solution. Maybe he could go to Fort Worth and change Big George's mind. But first he needed more information about the loan. He hadn't pried and asked Cassandra or Mrs. Pickett for the details, after all, he was a hired hand, but those details might give him a better idea of how he could help.

Matt crossed the street to the bank and stepped inside its ornate interior. He studied a framed painting of the bank's founder. The bearded man bore a striking resemblance to a picture he'd seen of his paternal grandfather. Matt took a second look. *At least that makes sense now.*

He removed his Stetson and jiggled the iron bars that separated him from a petite woman with graying hair. She glanced up from working on a ledger. "May I help you, sir?"

"I hope so, ma'am. I'm in charge of the financial affairs of the Triple P." Matt justified his lie as dull gray and not black. "I need to see the balance on their loan."

The woman sniffed and tugged the sleeve of her gray cotton dress. "That information is confidential. I can't give it to anyone other than Helen or Cassandra."

"I'm here on their behalf."

She dropped her pencil and edged back from the counter. "I can't help you, but if you wait here, I'll call my husband." The heels of her shoes clacked across the tiled floor as she hurried to the rear of the bank. She pulled open a carved door and hollered, "William, a customer needs your assistance. Now."

A minute later William Higgins appeared and conferred with his wife before crossing over to the counter where she'd been working. He squinted up at Matt but didn't offer to shake his hand.

"Mildred says you're interested in the Triple P account. Are you the new man they hired?"

"Yes, sir. The name's Matt Atkins. I need the balance on their loan."

"I'm sorry, but I can't reveal that without the direct consent of Mrs. Pickett or her daughter."

"I know, but I'm here on—"

"If you know, then this conversation is over."

Matt retrieved the last of his pay from his pocket and waved a fistful of bills in front of the banker. "Would this help?"

Higgins inched closer. "Mr. Atkins, this is highly unethical."

Matt peeled off three bills and worked them through the cold, iron bars into the man's outstretched fingers. "I don't see anything wrong with sharin' information. Do you?"

Higgins flipped through the ledger his wife had vacated moments before. He smacked his lips and pointed at a figure before feigning interest in a horse and rider heading up the street.

Matt's mind whirled. What had Cassandra's father been thinking? She and her mother could never come up with that kind of money. "That's a steep figure. I don't suppose you'd give Mrs. Pickett and Cassandra more time to repay it?"

"Sorry. I don't have a say in the matter, and they'd need at least half that amount by the end of next week. From what I hear, they don't have it." He peered over his spectacles, challenging Matt to contradict.

Choosing not to alienate the banker any further, Matt said with more optimism than he felt, "I think things are about to turn around for the Pickett women."

"I hope so for their sakes, but it won't matter in the long run. I already have a buyer for their—" Higgins bit his bottom lip.

"Would that person happen to be Phillip Brigham?"

"I–I can't say. I've already done enough. You need to leave." Higgins scurried out from behind the counter and showed Matt the door.

A thick cloud of rage settled over Matt. There'd be no mercy at the end of next week when the loan came due. He jammed his hat back on and charged out of the bank.

As he rushed across the street to his horse, he ran headlong into a woman approaching from the opposite direction. He reached out a hand to steady her. "Sorry, ma'am."

The woman straightened the feathered bonnet that had slipped over her eyes. "Well, sakes alive. Matt Atkins, how nice to run into you." She giggled behind a gloved hand. "Or should I say how nice you ran into me?"

Matt stifled a groan. There stood Elizabeth Anne Baxter, all five foot two inches of her, batting her lashes as if something was in her eyes. She wore a walking dress with bell sleeves and scalloped gathers that reminded him of the sitting room curtains back at White Oak Manor.

He removed his hat and forced a stiff smile. "Hello, Elizabeth."

"My, my, my. This must be providence. I was just thinking about you." She clasped her hands to her chest. "I need an escort. Are you available?"

"I can't. I'm on my way back to the ranch."

"Oh, for pity's sake. It's the least you can do after nearly running me over. I might have been hurt."

Fearing she'd make a scene, Matt allowed Elizabeth to hook her arm through his and tug him in the opposite direction from where he wanted to be. They idled down the boardwalk until they reached the mercantile. Elizabeth stopped and craned her neck to peer into one of the plate glass windows.

"He must have left," she murmured.

"Pardon me?"

"Oh, nothing." She pointed to a pair of ladies' bonnets displayed in the window. "Aren't those the sweetest little hats? I just adore feathers." She bobbed her head up and down.

"They're lovely." Matt's voice was flat as he swished a feather from her hat off his cheek.

"Do you think so?" Elizabeth's voice and eyes brightened. "I'll ask Grandfather to buy me one. Which do you prefer? The red or green one?"

Matt suppressed a groan. "I reckon the red one's nice."

Satisfied, Elizabeth threaded her hand into the crook of Matt's arm again and urged him back up the boardwalk. "There's nothing left to see the other way except for that awful place where men buy women's favor and the livery with those nasty, buzzing flies."

As they made their way up the street, Elizabeth peeked into each window and made a comment or two. Matt was finding it harder and harder to maintain interest and not hurry her along. When they finally arrived at the hitching post where King was tied, he shook Elizabeth's hand and was about to bid her goodbye.

She took an exaggerated sniff. "That delightful smell of roast beef must be coming from the hotel. Care to buy me dinner?"

"I'm sorry, but like I said, I was about to head back to the Triple P."

Elizabeth pouted. "But Matt, can't you spare a few more teensy-weensy minutes? After all, you did almost knock me down. Please, please, please."

Several people passing by eyed the young couple curiously.

"Oh, all right." Matt pulled Elizabeth inside and nudged her past four other diners eating the hotel fare. He seated her at a cloth-covered table in the back corner of the room.

"You're acting like a tomcat in a barn fire again," Elizabeth teased. She patted the chair next to her. "Sit here and tell me why you're always so nervous."

Matt ignored the request and straddled the chair across the table. Her hurt expression pricked his conscience. In his desire to ride back to the Triple P, his behavior toward Elizabeth had been anything but kind.

"I'm sorry, Elizabeth. I'm not the nervous type. You just keep catchin' me out of sorts."

"Oh, please. Don't insult me. There's more to it than that, but I've plenty of time to find out what goes on behind those marvelous blue eyes of yours."

A waiter with a mop of reddish-brown hair appeared at Elizabeth's elbow. Her face lit up when she looked at him. "I'm starving. What would you suggest?"

The young man rubbed the nape of his neck and stared at Elizabeth with wide eyes. She patted the side of her hair and returned the look of admiration with a giggle. Matt found their unspoken dialogue interesting. He sat up and seized the lifeline.

"Elizabeth. This is…" He grappled for the young man's name, having met him only in passing outside the mercantile.

"I'm Bill Sanders." The young man's voice jumped a register before settling back down. "I work here at the hotel. You're that cowboy at the Triple P Ranch, right?"

"Yes, I am. Bill, may I introduce Miss Elizabeth Anne Baxter?"

Bill dropped his hands to his sides as though unsure he should initiate a handshake. "Uh, the pleasure is mine, Miss Baxter."

Elizabeth held no such reservations. She offered her hand in greeting. "Mr. Sanders, you must save some of the pleasure for me. I am delighted to make your acquaintance." She batted her eyelashes, which sent color creeping up Bill's freckled cheeks.

"Bill," Matt said, as pleased as a mama cow with her first calf. "Maybe you and Miss Baxter can continue this conversation another time. I'd like to order."

Bill's cheeks changed from pink to beet-red. "Sorry, sir." He poised his pencil above a pad of paper. "What can I get for you and the lovely lady?"

☆☆☆

After a meal of roast beef, fried potatoes, and a green vegetable Matt couldn't identify, Elizabeth ordered two slices of peach pie–much to his chagrin. Under an ordinary circumstance, he might have enjoyed the pie and the bubbly brunette's company, but today her incessant chatter was wearing on his nerves. She did manage to capture his interest when she mentioned Phillip Brigham. He pushed his pie to the center of the table.

"I'm sorry. What did you say about Phillip Brigham?"

"I said he's dreamy except for that scowl of his, but I bet a good woman could wipe it right off." She dabbed the corners of her mouth with the edge of her napkin. "Sarah Clemmons and I saw him right before you ran into me outside the bank. Sarah's the first person I met after I came to Goose Neck Ridge three months ago. Since then, she's told me so many things about Mr. Brigham, I've been dying to meet him. And lo and behold, we both ended up in the mercantile at the same time."

She winked a blue-gray eye. "I do have a way of meeting the most interesting men at that store."

"What's your opinion of him?" Matt asked, keeping his voice level.

"He's handsome in a sardonic kind of way. Sarah says money practically falls out of his pockets. What more could a woman ask for? Present company excluded."

She looked in Bill's direction as if hoping he'd not overheard. The young man was scribbling the order of a couple three tables over. He glanced up from his pad of paper and gave Elizabeth a shy wave, which she returned.

"We were talkin' about Phillip Brigham." Matt reminded her.

Elizabeth nibbled a bite of pie. "He was distracted at first by business, but I captured his attention when we talked about literature and horses."

"Oh? What kind of business?'

"He didn't say."

Her comment failed to surprise Matt. Phillip Brigham kept his affairs close to his inside pocket. Especially his plan to take the Triple P away from the Pickett women.

"Oh," Elizabeth said, "And Sarah thinks Mr. Brigham's about to be married soon, but a girl can dream, can't she?" She fluffed a dark curl.

Matt was glad Elizabeth thought Phillip was spoken for. Nothing good could come from her pursuing that cad. Unfortunately, her good will came at Cassandra's expense.

He shoved a forkful of pie into his mouth, willing in vain for Elizabeth to eat more and talk less. His nerves stood on end by the time they bid farewell to Bill and left the hotel.

Matt grazed a finger over the brim of his hat. "Much as I've enjoyed your company, Elizabeth, I've gotta go. Please excuse me."

"Now that I know what ranch you're at, I'll tell my grandparents that Sarah and I are going for a buggy ride, and I'll drive out to see you the day after tomorrow."

Matt's mind had already returned to how he was going to tell Cassandra and her mother about the telegram. He swung up onto the saddle and asked King to trot. He called back over his shoulder, "Whatever you say. Bye, Elizabeth."

As he traveled back to the Triple P, Matt considered another idea that might save the ranch. It was crazy, and it scared him to death. And he was pretty sure Cassandra would never agree to it.

TWENTY

The last thing Cassandra wanted to do was sit still and work on a quilt with her mother. But Helen had insisted, and Cassandra found herself sitting by the window in the parlor, struggling to keep her stitches aligned and neat. Why had Matt tried to kiss her in the hayloft? Why hadn't he—

"Ouch," she cried. She had pricked her finger with the needle. A drop of blood threatened to drip onto the material she was sewing.

"Be careful," Helen said. She pulled a piece of scrap material from the sewing basket at her feet, tore a strip, and wrapped Cassandra's finger.

"See, Mama. I'll never stitch like you."

"That is because you have not practiced enough. I told your father you needed equal time working inside the house as well as out, but between the two of you, I faced a constant battle." She took the square from Cassandra's lap and whipped the last few stitches.

"Kind of like the battle we're facing with the ranch?"

"Not exactly. With God's help, we will win this one, but you know how stubborn your father was. His heart overruled his…"

"What do you mean?"

"It is nothing, dear."

"Mama, is there something you're not telling me?"

Helen laid the unfinished quilt over the arm of her chair. "What makes you say that?"

"You've never told me how we got so deep in debt. We had money at one time, or Papa couldn't have bought us all those nice things. And other ranches survived the drought without losing their homes."

"It is nothing for you to concern yourself."

"How can you say that? We're about to lose the Triple P, and you say I shouldn't worry?"

"I have told you to put your faith in the Lord." Helen poked her needle into a piece of felt and returned it and a pair of scissors to the sewing basket.

"The Bible says every good gift comes from God. Right?" Cassandra prodded.

"Yes, but he allows everything to work together for our good."

"I know, but there's nothing good about what's happening to us."

"Right now, it does not seem like there is, but the events of our lives are like the quilt we are sewing. Individual squares fit together to make a finished piece. Let me share a verse with you."

She went to the bookcase and pulled out a well-worn Bible. The book had belonged to Cassandra's father and had seen him through the joys and trials of running a ranch and rearing a family. Cassandra yearned for those childhood days when she'd crawled onto her father's lap and he'd read the Bible in a rich voice that tickled her ear. He hadn't talked about the deep things of God. Instead, he read her stories like Zacchaeus, David and Goliath, and Noah's Ark. Mama was the one who talked about prayer and trusting God.

Helen flipped to the eighth chapter of Romans. Cassandra chewed her knuckle. Why did Mama always read from there? But to her surprise, her mother didn't read verse twenty-eight.

"I want you to read verse twenty-nine," Helen said. "It explains why God works out everything for our good."

Cassandra hoped the verse might shed light on her spiritual confusion. "For whom he did foreknow, he also did predestinate to be conformed to the image of his son." She shook her head. "I don't understand. Does it mean I'll look like Jesus one day?"

"No, but God wants us to possess his son's characteristics. Do you remember the fruits of the spirit?"

"Let's see. There's love, joy, peace, long-suffering, gentleness, goodness..." Cassandra stopped. "I don't remember the other ones."

"You forgot faith, meekness, and temperance."

Cassandra fidgeted in her chair. Why did the word *faith* keep showing up every time she turned around?

"You see," Helen said, "if we accept what happens to us, our faith increases, and we become more like our Savior."

"Matt said something like that."

Maria entered the room and looked at the Bible on Helen's lap. "While you are at it, Señora Pickett, show Miss Cassie where Señor Matt is to treat a woman like a fragile vase."

Cassandra jumped up and nudged Maria back toward the door. "If you'll excuse us, Mama, I need to help Maria in the kitchen. We can talk more about this later."

As she whisked Maria out of the study, she heard her mother say, "It is a weaker vessel, Maria. Not a fragile vase."

Cassandra closed the kitchen door behind them and whispered, "You didn't tell Mama about me and Matt outside the barn, did you? You promised you wouldn't."

"I promised no such thing. I asked why you keep sticking up for him."

"I don't want Mama to find out, or she might make him leave."

"The way you have been acting, I think that is a good idea."

Tuning out Maria's voice, Cassandra collapsed onto a chair and dropped her chin onto her hands. Why was it taking Matt so long to return? Though she was less than happy he'd ridden rode off like he had, she still longed to make up and have things go back to the way they were before the incident in the hayloft.

Maria dished out a large slice of custard pie, then shoved the plate and a fork over to Cassandra. "Eat. We can talk."

"Like when I was young?"

Maria's eyes twinkled. "You shared everything with me. No?"

"Just about."

"And why do we not do that now?"

"We're too busy trying to save the ranch?"

"This is true. Each day is full to the top. Even with Señor Matt helping. He also has shook things up around here. Like your heart?"

"I don't know what to think. One moment I enjoy his company, the next..." Cassandra stabbed her pie, "I want to jab him with a pitchfork."

"That sounds like love to me."

"I'm not in love with him. Am I?"

Maria stuck her fork in Cassandra's pie and took a bite. "Only you can answer that."

"If I loved Matt, I could never marry Phillip and then what would happen to the Triple P?"

Maria set her fork on the table. "How could you marry Señor Brigham after what he did to you, little one?"

"Carlos. That man cannot keep a secret. He told you about the morning Matt arrived and chased off Phillip."

"My brother did not share that news with me. But if what you say is true, I can at least thank Señor Matt for that. I was afraid you would tell Señor Brigham yes to his marriage proposal."

Cassandra pushed the plate away. "If Mr. Thompson doesn't accept our timber bid, I still may have to marry Phillip."

"Even after what he did to you three years ago?"

The blood drained from Cassandra's face. "You know?"

Tears wet Maria's eyes as she hid Cassandra's hands in hers. "I am sorry. Rafael was outside the barn that day and saw what happened. I promised him I would not speak of it, but I must tell you my heart. Señor Brigham would not make a good husband. A man should not try what he did."

Though Matt's near kiss in the hayloft had frightened Cassandra, Phillip's behavior that day had been dark and evil.

The morning had begun like any other summer day, clear and bright and full of promise. Cassandra was helping Maria clear the breakfast table when she spied Phillip riding onto the Triple P compound. She ran out to meet him. He swung a long leg down from the saddle and put his hands behind his back.

"Phillip, what do you have there?"

He thrust a bouquet of wild phlox at her. She buried her nose in the sweet fragrance of the purple flowers. "They're beautiful."

"They pale in comparison to your beauty." He grabbed her wrist and led her to the barn. "Come with me. I want to ask you something."

He pulled her into the depths of the barn. "I love you, Cassandra. I think of you all the time. Let's move to Boston. Though I've not met my grandparents yet, I'm sure they would let us live with them."

"Are you asking me to marry you?"

He dropped onto one knee. "Would you say yes, if I did?"

"Phillip, I'm only seventeen years old, and although I'm fond of you, I don't love you. At least I don't think I do."

"You could learn to love me. Please say yes. We can leave for Boston tonight." His eyes darkened, and his face took on a look she did not understand. "I think about you day and night. And at times, it's more than I can bear." He pulled her toward a pile of straw under the hayloft with such urgency, she fell to her knees.

Apprehension formed in the pit of Cassandra's stomach. "Please, Phillip. Let go. You're scaring me."

He pushed her back onto the straw and started raining kisses on her face and neck. She tried to scramble away, but he grabbed her wrists with one hand and held her fast.

"You are so beautiful," he said, his voice low in his throat. He looked deep into her eyes before forcing his lips down on hers.

Cassandra's throat constricted as Phillip's mouth and the weight of his body drove the air from her lungs. She tried to push him off, but he pinned her arms against her sides and increased the pressure of his lips. Fear rose in Cassandra's breast like a wild thing. She screamed, but his mouth muffled her cry.

"I'll be with you in a minute, Rafael," Samuel's voice carried into the barn. "I need the yearling's halter." Phillip leapt up, leaving Cassandra to struggle to her feet by herself.

Samuel stopped short. His eyes traveled from Cassandra to Phillip and then back to Cassandra. "What's going on here? Cassie, are you all right?" His face mottled red as he strode toward the pair.

Phillip shoved his hands into his pockets. "Nothing's going on, sir. Absolutely nothing." He dusted off his hat and walked toward the barn door.

"Why you—"

Cassandra grabbed her father's arm. "No, Papa. I'm fine. Please. You'll only make things worse." She combed shaking fingers through her hair and prayed for the wild beating of her heart to subside.

Anguished filled Samuel's eyes. "Were you privy to Phillip's intentions?"

"How could you ask me that?"

"I didn't think so. Wait here."

"Papa, no!"

"I said, wait here."

Cassandra had never seen her father so angry. He raced to Phillip and snatched the reins of his horse before it could take off. Cassandra couldn't hear the exchange of words, but she saw the color drain from Phillip's face. He dug his spurs into his horse's sides and fled the Triple P.

Her father walked back to the barn with his fists clenched at his sides. Cassandra could tell he was trying to soften the angry contours of his face. He gathered her into his arms and hugged her tight. "This will upset your mother."

"Please. Don't say anything. It was horrible enough without Mama knowing about it."

He hesitated as though weighing her words.

"Please, Papa."

"I will honor your request, but that young man is no longer welcome at this ranch. What he tried was a sin against you and God and something not to be done before marriage."

"I never want to get married."

"You say that now, but one day God will lead the right man into your life."

"How will I know him?"

"Trust me, Cassie dear, you will." He hugged her again and kissed the top of her head.

She shuddered in his arms. "How will I ever forget this day?"

"The memory may not go away, but it will be easier to bear as new memories replace it. Hold on to hope because things do not stay the same. They always change."

"Oh, Maria," Cassandra cried. She jumped up from her chair and fell into Maria's waiting arms. "It was awful. I was so scared."

Maria stroked Cassandra's hair and murmured words of comfort. "Do you not think the time has come to tell your mamá what happened?"

"I can't. If George Thompson turns down our timber contract, I still may have to marry Phillip to save the Triple P, and Mama wouldn't let me if she knew."

"I do not want you to marry Señor Brigham. I will tell her." Maria rose from her chair.

Cassandra clasped Maria's hand. "Please don't. If marrying Phillip will save the ranch—"

"But he wants to sell the Triple P and live in Boston."

Cassandra moved over to the window. "I'm sure I can talk him out of it. And I cared for him at one time. Maybe I can again."

She squinted at a patch of dust rising on the horizon. Were her eyes playing a trick on her? They weren't. Matt and King were approaching at a slow jog.

"Matt's back. Maybe we can make up now."

Maria sighed. "My Cassandra Juanita, what will I ever do with you?"

Cassandra gave Maria a guilty smile and a peck on the cheek. "I'll talk to you later." She darted out the kitchen door and headed outside.

Matt gave her a nonchalant wave as he led King into the barn. Encouraged, Cassandra licked her lips and smoothed her hair with a trembling hand before trailing him inside. This time she cleared her throat. She'd give him no cause to accuse her of sneaking up on him again.

At her approach, he stopped uncinching his saddle. "Hello, Cassandra Jane. How are you?"

She kept her tone light. "You're the one I was wondering about."

"Why me?

"Carlos said you rode out of here like the devil himself was chasing you."

"King needed to stretch his legs."

She ignored his lie. "I'm not upset anymore. Are you?

"Me? Upset?"

"Matt Atkins, stop it."

"Stop what?"

"Answering my questions with ones of your own."

He turned his back toward her and ran a brush over King's back and sides. "I'm not mad. Can you just drop it?"

"That's another annoying habit you have?"

"What habit?"

"Not talking about things that make you uncomfortable. I wish you'd be honest for once and tell me how you—" She remembered the telegram they were expecting from Fort Worth. "Was there any news from Mr. Thompson?"

He stopped grooming his horse.

Disappointment struck Cassandra's soul. "He said no, didn't he?"

Matt closed the stall door. "I'm sorry. But I'm going to ride to Abilene tomorrow and catch the train to Fort Worth. Maybe I can talk to Big George man-to-man and convince him to change his mind."

"Oh, Matt. Do you think he will?"

He scooped up her hands. She managed a weak smile as the warmth and strength of his hands enveloped hers.

"I hope so, but there's another thing we can do, but only if it comes down to it. I know you think you can do anything a man can do, but it doesn't change the facts."

Cassandra opened her mouth to protest, but he touched her lips with a fingertip. "It may be different one day, but men are still the ones who earn respect in business." He jammed his hands into his pockets. "If we married, I can act on the Triple P's behalf and probably get an extension on the loan. That is... if my visit to Fort Worth turns up empty."

"You would marry me just to save the ranch?"

"Well, yeah. Don't you think it's a good idea?"

"You've not yet declared your affection for me."

"I care about you–and your mother–and the Triple P."

"I could never settle for a marriage of convenience." Cassandra lifted her chin and pushed her way past him.

Matt snagged her arm. "Now, wait one cotton pickin' minute. You were dead set on marryin' Phillip to save the ranch. Why can't you marry me?"

"That's different."

"How so?"

"It–It just is." She wrenched free from his grasp. "I know one thing, Matt Atkins. I won't be marrying you anytime soon."

"Even if it means losin' the Triple P? Come on, Cassandra Jane. You care about me. I've seen it in your eyes. We'd make a good match. I can help you in ways I can't tell you about right now."

"And what ways might that be?"

"I know some influential people."

"Those people can help after we're married but not beforehand?"

"Just agree to marry me," he pleaded. "We'll work out the details later."

"You up and ask my hand in marriage and think I'll fall all over myself and say yes? I told you. I do not want to marry you."

"Why not?" his voice pleaded.

"Because I–I just don't."

Cassandra burst from the barn and raced for the house. She sped past a surprised-looking Maria, took the stairs two at a time to her bedroom, and threw herself onto her bed.

Why had Matt said he would marry her only to save the ranch? Why hadn't he said—

Cassandra bolted upright as the truth hit her. She had lied to Matt. She did want to marry him, but not for the sake of the Triple P. She wanted to marry him because he loved her. Just like she loved him.

TWENTY-ONE

The next morning the sun was capping the horizon as Matt rode toward Abilene to catch the train to Fort Worth. He was thankful he hadn't encountered Cassandra before he left. His battered ego couldn't take another pounding. Yes, he'd presented his marriage proposal in less than a good light, but blast it, he'd make a heck of a lot better husband than Phillip. The thought plagued him the rest of the morning.

When he reached Abilene, Matt rode straight to the depot. He bought a ticket for the next train heading to Fort Worth, which pulled out early the following morning. With no other choice than to spend the night, he boarded King at a livery and checked into a hotel. After a quick meal in the hotel dining room, he retired for the evening. Although he feared thoughts of Cassandra would keep him awake, no sooner had his head touched the pillow than he fell into a deep, and thankfully dreamless, sleep.

☆☆☆

Matt woke with a start. *Great.* Of all the mornings to oversleep.

With only ten minutes to catch the seven o'clock train, he downed a cup of bitter coffee, then hightailed it to the depot. By the time he arrived, the coffee had burned a hole in his gut, and his traitorous thoughts had returned to Cassandra. His mood was anything but civil as he boarded the coach car.

He plopped into a seat mid-way back, his eyes daring anyone to sit in the empty seat next to him. A woman, squeezed in a dress a size too small, had the misfortune of not reading Matt's resolution.

"Is this seat taken?" she asked in a nasal voice.

"No," Matt's voice cut through the muggy air, "but you can't sit there."

"Why, I never," the woman said, her caramel-color eyes flaring. She bristled past him with a humph.

Guilt burned Matt's soul, but his anger squelched it. He thrust a scarred boot over the vacant seat and jammed his Stetson over his eyes to block out the view of the other passengers boarding the train. With any luck, they'd get the hint and pass by. He couldn't handle some friendly soul sitting next to him and chatting for the next three hours.

"All aboard," the conductor called out. The train's whistle split the air and with a jerk and a belch of steam, the Texas & Pacific train shoved northeast toward Fort Worth. Matt shut his eyes against the sting of smoke and soot drifting in through the windows of the car, but his pride burned even more.

Until the night he had begged Victoria not to leave, he'd prided himself on his ability to convince others to see things his way. He must be losing his touch, for Cassandra had not only refused his proposal, but he'd also made a fool of himself in the bargain.

The muscle in his jaw twitched. All women were the same. They only cared for themselves. They used men and then discarded them like dirty rags. Why had God created them? Wouldn't Adam have been better off without Eve?

But even as he nursed the sacrilege, a quiet voice spoke to his heart, and Matt could not escape its gentle call. His body and soul ached to find a woman to complete his life and help him believe that God still cared.

As the clickety-clack of the train's wheels lulled Matt into a troubled sleep, his mind's last picture was of Cassandra dressed in white, begging him to marry her.

☆☆☆

At the same time Matt was riding the rails to Fort Worth, Cassandra was attacking her chores and trying not to think about him.

Before the drought devastated the herd, the Triple P calves were branded in the spring after the vaqueros rounded up the cattle and separated those going to market. With the diminished herd, branding the calves and notching their ears was easier to do as time permitted, especially in the morning when it was a bit cooler.

"Will you tell Smokey to walk and lope like you do Ginny?" Rafael quipped as Cassandra saddled her horse. He and Carlos thought she and Matt were loco for telling their horses what to do.

"Hey, Rafael," Carlos said, "if you talk to your horse, will he obey you?"

"I will try." Rafael hollered at a coal-black horse tied to the corral, "Black Jack, come here and put on your saddle, *por favor.*"

The silly expression on Rafael's face made Cassandra giggle despite not wanting to encourage his fun at her expense. "That's not how we do it."

"Miss Cassie," Roberto said, "you have done a fine job of making Smokey understand English." He slipped a bridle on his buckskin pony and adjusted the headpiece behind its ears.

"Yes, but does he understand Spanish?" Rafael elbowed Carlos, who was throwing a saddle on his Paint horse.

"I do not know. Let me ask." Carlos cleared his throat. "Señor Smokey *¿cómo está usted*?"

"He's fine," Cassandra retorted. "You two stop that. You're almost as bad as Matt, trying to get my goat."

Carlos's voice turned serious. "Señor Matt gave a big sigh when you did not wish him Godspeed this morning."

"Are you sure it wasn't a sigh of relief?"

"I think you and Señor Matt need to work on being nicer to each other."

"Why me? He's the one giving me fits."

Rafael interjected, "Carlos, our Señorita Cassie has it bad for Señor Matt. Do you not agree?"

"Sí," came the reply, "but until they both say so at the same time, we shall see more fireworks."

"Carlos," Cassandra said, "you have never seen fireworks. How do you know what they look like?"

"Your papá once told me about them. He said they go up in the air with a big, scary boom and light the sky in much beauty. This is true of you and Señor Matt. Much noise hides what you two really feel."

Roberto stepped up into the saddle. "It is too bad he does not have Señor Brigham's money. He could ask you to marry him, and we all could live happily ever after." Sarcasm tinged his words.

Cassandra didn't reveal Matt had already proposed. The men would never understand. She wasn't even sure she did.

"Would you not like to marry Señor Matt?" Carlos prompted.

"Time to mount up and get those calves," Cassandra replied, forcing him and Rafael to hurry and finish tacking up their horses.

The four horses splashed across the creek toward the grazing herd. The cattle lifted their heads as the riders circled from opposite directions. The four went to work cutting out the calves, accompanied by the moos of distraught cows separated from their young.

When Carlos and Rafael turned the calves toward the ranch compound, Cassandra and Roberto kept the herd together. Cassandra was glad to forgo the branding process. Even after years of living on a cattle ranch, she still found it hard to bear the helpless bawling of the calves and the acrid odor of burned cowhide.

Roberto shooed a cow back into the herd and guided his horse to Cassandra's side. "Miss Cassie, may I ask you a question?"

"You can ask me anything."

"Do you love Mr. Matt?"

"Why would you ask that?

"Everyone on the ranch thinks I am still a child, but I can tell you and Mr. Matt have feelings for each other."

Cassandra covered her blushing cheeks with her hand. Roberto had the same knack as Maria in reading people.

"What I feel for Matt is complicated."

"If you love him, why do you consider Señor Brigham's marriage proposal?"

"Because I love the Triple P, and Mama, Carlos, your mother, and father… and you."

The young man's gaze fell to the saddle horn. "I love you too. Very much."

Cassandra had to clear things up. She couldn't allow Roberto to continue this line of thinking. "My love for you is that of a sister for her brother, not as a wife for her husband. And though you are almost a man, it will be some time before you fall in love with a pretty señorita and marry."

"Mr. Matt said the same thing. Though he said the Lord will help me pick her out."

"God does have a part, but you also need to fall in love with her."

Roberto whipped a thatch of black hair from his eyes. "I do not understand women. There are times Mamacita cries for no reason, and you tell me to marry for love when you would marry Señor Brigham, who you do not love. I think falling in love is not such a good thing after all."

"Your mamá cries because her body is different now. She carries your new little brother or sister. When the baby's born, she'll be back to the way she was before. And as for Señor Brigham… I would only marry him to save the Triple P."

"But what about Mr. Matt—"

"Saving the Triple P is more important."

"But Mr. Matt said you should want the best for the one you love." He sniffed and straightened his shoulders. "Because I love you I will step away and let him court you, so you can marry for love. But I will continue to watch and make sure he does not make you unhappy again. And," he looked toward heaven, "I will pray God sends big money to him, so you can keep the Triple P."

Cassandra laughed. *The Lord would definitely be a prayer-answering God if Matt Atkins ever came into any money.*

Roberto cast her a wistful eye before sending his horse to the other side of the herd. Cassandra knew his words had been brave. He was becoming a man with feelings and intuitions that would hold him in good stead. One day he would make a young lady a fine husband.

Pleased with how she had handled Roberto, Cassandra wished she could do the same with Matt. She had stopped kidding herself and admitted she'd fallen in love with him, but his proposal had been less than desirable. At least Phillip had been honest. He said he loved her and wanted to sell the Triple P. Matt wanted to save the ranch but wouldn't admit how he felt.

And Roberto thinks we women are complicated.

☆☆☆

With the calves branded and returned to the herd, Cassandra went inside the house to cool off. She splashed her face with water from the pump, causing gooseflesh to rise on her arms.

Maria came into the kitchen and said, "Your mamá is in her bedroom. She would like to talk to you."

"You didn't tell her about what Phillip tried in the barn, did you?

"No, I did not. That is for you to do. She wants to talk to you about Señor Matt."

Cassandra's shoulders heaved. Why in the world did everyone want to talk to her about Matt?

"Maria, I can't talk to Mama about him."

"And why not? She is your mother and a wise woman." Maria shoved Cassandra toward the door. "Go on. Maybe she can help."

"She'll just tell me to trust God," Cassandra muttered as she moped her way up the stairs. She knocked at the first door on the right and poked her head into the room. "Mama?"

Helen sat in a rocking chair, reading her Bible. "Yes, dear. Please, come in."

Cassandra entered her favorite room in the house. She loved her parents' bedroom with its soft blue walls, brocade chairs, and the four-poster bed with burl panels. An outsider would think the furnishings extravagant here on the Texas prairie, but they epitomized the wonderful things her father had bought for her and her mother.

Though it had been nine months since his death, her father's presence still filled the room. Cassandra closed her eyes and could see him standing by the fireplace with a smile on his whiskered face and could imagine the lingering smell of tobacco from his favorite pipe. She knew his clothes were still neatly folded in the oak dresser. Though her mother had given three or four work shirts to Carlos, she had not yet parted with the rest of his clothing.

"Cassandra," Helen's quiet voice reached out. "What is going on with you and Matt? You two have clashed off and on since I hired him, but things have gotten worse since the day Rafael, Carlos, and Maria came back from town."

Cassandra rushed across the room. "I asked Maria not to tell you about the mishap outside the barn."

A surprised look crossed her mother's face, Cassandra's stomach lurched. Maria hadn't said a word. *Lord, will I ever learn to keep quiet?*

"She told me no such thing. Would you care to elaborate?"

"It was all a misunderstanding." Cassandra bit her knuckle.

"Cassandra Jane, stop doing that and tell me what is going on. Your treatment of Matt has been anything but cordial."

Cassandra sagged to her knees beside the rocking chair. Helen cupped Cassandra's face in her hands. "I know you were more comfortable talking to your father, but he is gone now. Please tell me what is bothering you."

Cassandra needed no more than that gentle nudge. Her words rushed out as she told her mother everything about Matt except for his near kiss in the hayloft. Though her mother's body stiffened, her gray eyes remained calm.

"He offered to marry you to save the ranch? He is hardly in a position to help, but would you not rather marry him than Phillip?"

"I'd rather marry anyone other than Phillip, but I want Matt to marry me because..."

"Because he loves you?" Helen laid a hand on Cassandra's cheek. "Sometimes people marry in spite of not being in love. Your father and I were fortunate to have fallen in love so soon after we met."

"Papa loved you from the first moment he saw you."

"Your father told that tale so many times, he believed it himself. The truth is," pink touched her cheeks, "I pursued him."

"What?"

"It is true. When I first saw him in the general store, I thought he was the most handsome man I had ever seen. I determined to get his attention. A lady working in the mercantile had left her apron on the counter. I removed my bonnet, tied the apron around my waist, and proceeded to sell him a pound of black licorice."

Cassandra's hands flew to her mouth to stifle a giggle. "Papa didn't even like licorice."

A glint of mischief sparked Helen's eyes. "When your father found out I had tricked him, he asked for my hand in marriage right there on the spot. He said he liked a woman with spunk. I refused his immediate offer, but two months later we did marry, and I never regretted a minute of it, even when he..."

"Even when he what?"

"It is nothing for you to worry about. Now, what are you going to do about Matt?"

"He thinks he has a better chance of holding off the bank than we do, but I won't marry him unless I can make him admit his feelings. Do you think I could do that?"

Cassandra didn't need her mother's answer to the obvious. A man like Matt Atkins wouldn't do anything he didn't want to.

"That would not be wise," Helen replied. "A relationship between two people must be based on trust and love." Her gaze dropped to the Bible in her lap. "We need to pray about it. God is as interested in you and Matt as he is in saving our ranch."

"You may believe that, but I don't see God's hand in my life right now."

"In times of trials, you may think he is far away, but that is when he is the closest. Let me read a verse that sustained me when your father died."

She flipped through the pages of her Bible. Cassandra was surprised her mother stopped at the book of First Peter instead of the book of Romans.

Helen read a verse from chapter one with a clear, calm voice. "The trial of your faith, being much more precious than of gold that perisheth, though it be tried with fire, might be found unto praise and honour and glory at the appearing of Jesus Christ.

"Do you understand? The trial we are going through is more important than the money we need to save the Triple P. A day is coming…" her gesture took in the room, "when all of this will pass away, but our relationship with God will go on forever. When was the last time you got alone and sought his face?"

Hot guilt branded Cassandra's soul. At bedtime she read a few verses before throwing a short prayer to God, asking him to send rain and keep the ranch safe, but she couldn't remember the last time she felt his presence. She hung her head. "I don't know. It's been a long time."

Helen brushed back the hair that had fallen onto Cassandra's face "You need to ask his forgiveness. Then you can pray with confidence for the ranch and," her eyes twinkled, "for what to do about Matt."

"It's been so long since I've prayed in earnest. Would you pray with me?"

A hesitant knock sounded at the door. Maria stood in the hall with one hand on the doorknob and a perplexed expression on her face.

"Señora Pickett? Miss Cassie? I am sorry to bother you, but there is a young lady downstairs asking for Señor Matt. She says her name is Miss Elizabeth Anne Baxter."

TWENTY-TWO

After the train pulled into Fort Worth, Matt waited for the other passengers to disembark. The woman he'd shunned earlier turned her head away as she passed by his seat. Regretting his earlier display of anger, he hopped off the train and tapped her on the shoulder.

"Ma'am?"

When she saw who had spoken, she whirled around and swung her handbag at Matt. He ducked, and the purse completed its circuit and hit the woman square on the chin.

Matt gave a meek smile. "Ma'am, I wanted to apologize for how I acted when you boarded the train."

Her look shot right through him. "You don't say? All you cowboys are the same."

"Not all of us. I don't usually act that way. My morning hadn't started out on a good note."

"You didn't do much to help mine along either."

"Again, I'm sorry."

Without another word, she huffed off with her nose in the air and disappeared into the crowd. Matt rued his wasted effort. He located the stationmaster and asked where he might find the nearest livery. There he picked out a sturdy roan and declined the owner's offer to tack up the horse, preferring to do it himself. It was eleven o'clock by the time he arrived at the Circle T.

He took in the compound but didn't see his former boss at the numerous corrals or the stables housing his prized thoroughbreds, the blacksmith shop, the bunkhouses, or the commissary. Nor did he spy Big George in the yard that surrounded his sprawling *casa grande* with its separate wings containing a kitchen, a dining room, and a massive ballroom.

Matt frowned. A home with ten bedrooms and only four children was presumptuous, but the "mistress of the manor," as Big George lovingly called his Kentucky wife, took immense pleasure in flaunting her husband's wealth.

His search was appearing futile until he spied a dusty haze off in the distance. Matt caught up to Big George Thompson, barking orders over the noise of a thousand milling cattle.

"Shorty, make sure there's plenty of water in those barrels. Jim, you and Johnny ride out and relieve Wes and Hal. Bill Stuart, cut yourself out one of those ponies in the remuda. Not the big gray one. That's Hank's horse. And speaking of Hank, where'd he run off to? Joe, go tell 'im if he don't get back here this minute, he's fired."

George Thompson sat a big buckskin gelding in a saddle especially ordered to accommodate the man's generous girth. His pale blue eyes suggested weakness, but no one denied his physical and mental strength–at least not to his face. Big George wielded his authority like a club, but Matt knew him to be fair and capable of exercising an exaggerated sense of humor.

"Well, I'll be buffaloed," Big George said when he saw Matt. "Look who the coyotes dragged back."

Matt suppressed a wince at the bone-crushing handshake.

"You come crawlin' back for your old job?" Big George asked in his big, booming voice.

"I'm afraid not."

"That's too bad. We're headin' up the Chisholm Trail tomorrow. Some crazy English count in Oklahoma fancies himself a cattle baron. Says if I get these cows to him within the month, he'll pony up an extra five dollars a head. I got all hands and the cook cullin' out the herd and throwin' supplies together."

Matt thanked the Lord he'd caught Big George before he left on that drive. "I'm sorry to come all this way unannounced, but I have a business deal to discuss."

Big George threw back his head and laughed a bellow of a sound that carried over the din. The cowboys nearest him looked up and stopped working. Big George waved an impatient hand, and the men set back to their chores.

"You're kiddin', right? I'm in the middle of organizin' a cattle drive, and you want me to stop for a little chat?"

"I wouldn't ask if it wasn't important."

Big George settled his heavy frame in the saddle. "I reckon you wouldn't. What's up?"

"Remember the letter you gave me?"

"Yeah. The minute you laid eyes on it, you rode out of here faster than a barn cat chasin' a mouse. You never told me what it said."

"I'm sorry, I still can't. But I need help with what it set in motion."

"Well, I can only give ya a few minutes. Let's get to the house and have a go at it." He called out, "Hey, Shorty. I've got business to tend. Keep things runnin' 'til I get back."

After the two men entered the house, Big George directed Matt into a spacious study. The room matched Big George's size and personality, from the large stone fireplace and paneled walls to the over-stuffed chairs and mammoth set of longhorns behind a huge oak desk cluttered with paper. He sank into a cowhide sofa like he didn't have a care in the world instead of spearheading a cattle drive.

He motioned for Matt to sit on the chair opposite of him. "So, you're not here to beg me for your old job, huh? I can up my offer. I need a new trail boss. Ya interested?"

"That's mighty generous, but I'm happy where I'm at." Matt declined the imported cigar Big George offered from a carved, wooden box.

Big George snipped off the end of a cigar before lighting it with short puffs. "Never could figure why you didn't smoke these little beauties." He rolled the cigar between his fingers. "Come to think of it. I can't remember you imbibin' in anything, carousin' in town with the other hands, or stirrin' up a ruckus. No wonder I liked you so much."

"The Lord and my parents' upbringin' held me in good stead. Every time I was tempted, one or the other convicted me to do right."

"You ain't one of those Bible-thumpers, are ya? Whenever I go to town, one of 'em tries to convert me." Big George guffawed deep in his belly.

"I wouldn't go knockin' the Bible. It tells the beginnin' from the end and everything in between. It'd do you good to read it."

"Well, I might sometime." George blew a smoke ring that meandered across the room. "So, what brings you here?"

"The telegram I sent."

"Oh, that." George made a flippant gesture with his cigar. "The day after I got it, I received an offer from another ranch I couldn't refuse."

"You didn't hear ours. It might have been better."

"Naw. This man's practically giving away his timber."

Matt's mind raced back to the day he sent the telegram and the man who bumped into him outside the telegraph office. Did he work for Phillip? And if he did, it was probably Phillip who had undercut them. But why? He planned to sell Lazy Acres and the Triple P as soon as he got his hands on it. Unless his bid was bogus.

"Would that man happen to be Phillip Brigham of Lazy Acres?" he asked.

Surprise crossed George's face. "How'd you know?" His look turned sympathetic. "Sorry. I can't help ya unless he withdraws his bid. Besides, the real money comes after the rails are laid and the towns start a-growin'."

Big George's words gave Matt a couple of ideas that might help the Triple P. He'd have to wait until he saw Mr. Harvey before he could put the first one into play. But the other…

Anxious to set the second idea in motion, Matt bid Big George farewell and cantered his horse back to Fort Worth.

☆☆☆

Outside the parlor door, Cassandra gave a quick once-over to the petite brunette perched on the edge of the divan. Her dress was nice enough, but in all her days, Cassandra had never seen so many feathers on one hat. They stuck out every which way like a peacock who'd been in a fight with a tiger. And why had the woman chosen to wear a red hat with a pale-yellow dress? Cassandra might not be one of those fancy ladies from back East, but she knew a fashion faux pas when she saw it.

"Shall we greet our guest?" Helen asked, nudging Cassandra into the parlor. "Hello. I am Helen Pickett, and this is my daughter, Cassandra."

"My name is Elizabeth Anne Baxter, and I'm here to see..." The woman's blue-gray eyes fixed on Cassandra's hair. "You must be Matt's sister. He was right. Your hair is the color of a—" She clapped a gloved hand over her mouth. "But you can't be his sister. His last name is Atkins."

"I am *not* Matt's sister. He works here. Mama and I own this ranch."

Elizabeth eyed Cassandra up and down. "Oh, that would explain your pants."

Helen slid between Cassandra and Elizabeth. "Matt is not here. Are you a friend of his?"

"Much more than a friend. Especially after the romantic dinner we shared at the hotel a couple of days ago."

A flash of heat prickled Cassandra's cheeks. "What dinner?"

"We ran into each other, well, he ran into me, outside of the bank. I told him I was coming for a visit today. I thought he was expecting me."

“I am sorry, Miss Baxter,” Helen said. “I would invite you to stay and wait for him, but we are not sure when he will return.”

Elizabeth’s eyes flickered to Cassandra. “I think I’ve already worn out my welcome.” She rose to her feet, and Cassandra was glad to see she was nearly a head taller than the woman.

“Before you go, I must offer you refreshments,” Helen insisted. “Cassandra, please get our guest a glass of lemonade and a piece of Maria’s pie.”

Elizabeth held up a hand. “No thank you. My grandparents don’t live too far away. I’ll be home in time for the noon meal.”

Light dawned on Helen’s face. “Baxter? You must be Evelyn and Joseph’s granddaughter.”

“Yes. I came for a short visit, but I plan to stay. I like Goose Neck Ridge. And most of its inhabitants.” Her gaze flicked again at Cassandra.

“Isn’t that lovely?” Cassandra said in a dry voice.

Helen raised a brow at her before escorting Elizabeth to the door.

Ignoring Cassandra, Elizabeth asked Helen, “Will you please tell Matt I dropped by?”

“Of course. And give your grandparents our best. It was nice to meet you.”

“The pleasure was mine, Mrs. Pickett.” She placed a hand next her lips and whispered, “I’m sorry if I upset your daughter.”

Helen patted Elizabeth’s arm. “Everything will be fine. Good day, Miss Baxter.”

Giving a cheery wave to Helen and one last suspicious look at Cassandra, Elizabeth promised to come back and see Matt another day. Carlos beamed as he helped the young woman into a buggy drawn by a docile gray mare.

"Adiós, Señorita. Please be careful on your way home."

Helen escorted Cassandra back into the house. "Even though you may not like it, Matt is free to have a lady friend."

"I know that. He can have as many lady friends as he likes."

"Then why are you so upset?"

"Who said I'm upset? I don't hold any claim over him." She folded her arms across her chest. "But why did he ask me to marry him if he's interested in that–that woman."

"Maybe you need to hear his side of the story before you pass judgment. If you would allow it, the truth can set you free."

"Mama, please, not now."

Helen made Cassandra turn and face her. "Darling, you have been so busy trying to fix everything, you have neglected the Lord. And it shows in every area of your life, including Matt. You need to go to God with this problem."

"How come everyone thinks I'm the problem? Matt Atkins is, not me. And now Elizabeth Anne Baxter."

Helen's eyes followed the retreating buggy. "I am beginning to wonder if there is more to Matt than he has led us to believe."

"I said that the moment he rode onto the Triple P."

"I am not sure what to think. Please excuse me, I need to find a quiet place to pray." She left the study without another word of exhortation for Cassandra to seek the Lord.

Cassandra dashed upstairs to her bedroom and slammed the door behind her. "God," she prayed, though her voice was hardly reverent. "Was Elizabeth Baxter's arrival your answer to my prayers about Matt? If so, it wasn't what I wanted. And here I thought I loved him."

It only went to show. She couldn't trust prayer or her silly heart.

☆☆☆

The first thing Matt did when he arrived back in Fort Worth was to make a beeline for the train station. Again, he was met by disappointment. The stationmaster said the next train to Abilene wouldn't head out until eight o'clock the following morning. Matt had hoped to get back to the Triple P by nightfall.

He returned the horse to the livery stable and rented another room, but this time at a better hotel. Weary and dirty, he wanted a bath. A strapping young lad heaved a tin tub into the center of the room. Two maids giggled and gave Matt shy looks as they dumped buckets of steaming water into it. When they had finished, Matt shut and locked the door behind them before stripping off his clothes.

He lowered himself into the tub and stretched out as far as it allowed. With a sigh, he leaned his head back and let the hot water ease away the tension from his body.

The past month had changed the course of his life. Now, he bore not only the weight of his burdens but also those of the Triple P. Steam hovered above the surface of the water as he faced his dilemma.

When Mr. Harvey got back next week, he'd march in, get the documents he needed, and run Phillip Brigham off Lazy Acres.

Matt enjoyed the mental picture of Phillip when he was faced with the truth.

It wouldn't be as easy to save the Triple P and resolve his conflict with Cassandra. His mind replayed her delight when he gave her the ivory comb and the softness of her skin the night they waltzed. For the first time since he left Boston, Matt admitted he no longer wanted to run. What he wanted to do was take Cassandra in his arms and save the Triple P.

He had held the boyish expectation she reciprocated his affection and would gladly accept his marriage proposal. He'd not gotten the answer he wanted, but he knew she cared for him and not in the same conniving manner Victoria had. Maybe if he declared his feelings to Cassandra, she would admit how she felt about him.

He hopped out of the tub and dried off with a thin towel before dusting the dirt off his pants and throwing on a fresh shirt. He paced the floor and tried to figure a way to keep his house of lies from toppling until he made Phillip's timber bid null and void and told Cassandra everything.

The hour hand on the clock had moved from seven to eight before his ideas fell into place. The second one relied on the first, and he'd use the third one only as a last resort. Cassandra would probably not like it, but she'd have no other choice if she wanted to keep her ranch. But two of his ideas hinged upon sending another telegram to Walter Brigham before he caught the train to Abilene.

His stomach grumbled, forcing him to leave his room to search out a place to eat supper. He by-passed a nearby café, preferring a hot meal in a nicer restaurant.

Considering the dinner hour had already passed, the Saturday night crowds surprised Matt. The downtown streets were alive with gaily-dressed couples pouring into theaters and restaurants and people pushing their way into stores that had stayed open to entice late-night shoppers.

Matt worked his way through the crowds and said, "Excuse me," more times than he cared to count. He elbowed his way into the first restaurant he came to more to escape the throngs than for the food they served.

The plate of pork chops and creamed spinach proved favorable, though his thoughts kept drifting to meals shared with Cassandra at the Triple P. She and the others would have already eaten supper. Had she missed him?

Matt paid for his meal and left the restaurant. If his thoughts were to stay on that fiery-haired woman, he might as well allow them the privacy of his room.

As he headed back to the hotel, a familiar voice called out from the other side of the street. "Hey. Matt Atkins? Is that you?" A young cowboy zig-zagged in and out of a hack-driver, a streetcar, and a horse and buggy before catching up to Matt.

Matt exchanged a hearty handshake with Wes Cummins, a cowboy he'd enjoyed working with at the Circle T. Not yet old enough to grow a full beard, Wes's lined face showed the rough reality of drifting from ranch to ranch, staying on a cattle drive or two, and then moving on.

"Saw ya talkin' to Big George this afternoon," Wes said. "Ya comin' back to the Circle T?"

"Sorry. I was only there on business. I head out of here in the mornin'."

Disappointment stamped the cowboy's face. "Things ain't been the same since ya left. Why'd you up and leave in such a hurry anyhow? Big George cussed ya out for days afterward."

"It's a long and borin' story. What brings you to town? Don't you have a drive tomorrow?"

Wes patted his shirt pocket. "Just got my pay. Can't have this thirty bucks burnin' a hole in my pocket all the way to Oklahoma. How 'bout you? Where ya workin' now?"

"A small ranch outside of Goose Neck Ridge called the Triple P."

"Never heard of it. They payin' ya more than Big George?"

"I'm not workin' there for the money."

"You found a woman," Wes exclaimed.

Even though Matt had worked amicably with Wes for almost a year, he was not about to tell him about Cassandra. "Don't ya think a man's entitled to his secrets?"

"Before the night's through, I'll git 'em out of ya." Wes draped an arm over Matt's shoulder. "Since I got some money, why don't we go have us a little fun? I know the perfect place." He pointed toward Hell's Half Acre at the lower end of town.

When Matt had worked for Big George, he stayed away from the red-light district the locals dubbed "The Acre." The expanding area provided entertainment for the seedier inhabitants of Fort Worth and cowboys heading up the long Chisholm Trail. Indoor gaming halls, saloons, dance halls, and brothels spilled out into the streets and shared space with cockfights and horse racing. Matt didn't cotton to the idea of Wes rubbing shoulders with fast-talking men and loose, randy women, who'd not think twice about robbing him of his hard-earned wages.

"There's a café near my hotel," he said. "How 'bout I buy ya a cup of coffee and a bite to eat instead?"

"Not the fun I was aimin' for. But if you're payin', it's fine by me."

The men spanned the short distance back to the café, which was sandwiched between a five-and-dime drugstore and the Williams' Family Bakery. The bakery was closed for the night, but the aroma of bread still lingered in the air.

The two men took off their hats before they entered the café. A robust woman, who Matt assumed was the proprietress, issued a friendly greeting. "Find ya a seat, boys. I'll have someone get to ya in a minute."

Matt and Wes straddled two stools tucked underneath a gleaming counter that ran the length of the café. A pretty, young waitress smiled as she offered each of them a menu and took Matt's order for two cups of coffee. Wes sat up and tried to slick back his unruly hair before returning her smile and asking for a ham steak and three fried eggs.

The minute his meal arrived, Wes hunkered over his plate and shoveled the food in like he hadn't eaten for a week. A frown chased down his first swig of coffee. "Never did like this stuff. I prefer my brew with a little more kick."

"It wouldn't hurt ya to lay off the whiskey."

Wes shifted in his seat. "You gonna preach at me again?"

"I'm just tryin' to help. I've learned a few things over the years, and one of them is whiskey eats a man's pay and never does him any good. Let me ask you a question." Matt took a swallow of his coffee. "What do you plan on doin' after you quit cowboyin'?"

"Ah. I ain't never gonna quit."

"That's not true. After a cowboy hangs up his spurs, he hunts for a new way of life. You need to start savin' your pay. Then after you're tired of bustin' ponies and chasin' steers, you can buy a small spread, marry a good woman, and raise a bunch of kids. The Bible says a man needs to prepare his work in the field before he builds his house."

"Huh?"

Matt found it hard to believe that within the space of a few hours, he'd talked about God twice. First with Big George and now with Wes. What was coming over him?

"That means," he continued, "before we can do the big things, we have to handle the small ones."

"So, that's why you left the Circle T? Ya got some small things to take care of? Bet you're squirrelin' up some money so you can git your own place and a good woman to have all those kids with."

Matt chuckled. "Maybe. But I am lookin' for a place to settle down. Let me ask you another question. Pretend you had a choice between an estate back east or a ranch right here in Texas? Which would you choose?"

"Which one's worth more?"

"Probably the ranch."

"I'd take it."

Matt envied the young man's simple decision. Unlike Wes, his life was more complicated, and his choices were real. Should he go back to White Oak Manor or stay in Goose Neck Ridge? If Cassandra had agreed to marry him, he would have chosen to stay in Texas.

Wes stroked his stubbled chin. "Hmm... Is there a girl back east?"

"What?"

"This game we're playin'. There's gotta be a girl. Where's she at?"

"She's on the ranch."

Wes grimaced at his next gulp of coffee. "Then why ya askin' me these darn questions? The ranch is worth more, and it's got the girl. Don't take a lick of sense to figure out which one to pick."

Matt shook his head.

If it only were that easy, Wes. If it only were that easy.

Twenty-Three

Afternoon shadows were inching toward the porch when Matt arrived back at the Triple P. He trotted his horse to the barn and was thankful to see Rafael near the corral.

"Rafael, would you please take care of King? I have important business to discuss with Cassandra Jane."

"Sí, Señor Matt." Rafael tipped his hat and gathered the horse's reins.

Matt raced for the house, anxious to share his ideas with Cassandra. As he bounded up the porch steps, the front door swung open with such force, it halted him in his tracks.

Cassandra charged out of the house with fists balled at her sides. "Please, explain yourself. What exactly is your relationship to Elizabeth Anne Baxter?"

"Relationship?" Matt's mind stumbled at the implication. Hadn't Elizabeth mentioned something about coming to see him? Cassandra's hooded eyes and stiff posture proved Elizabeth had kept her word. He braced himself against the onslaught.

"You heard me. Explain yourself."

"Explain?" Matt groped for a plausible answer, which he knew would appear a lie. Though the time spent with Elizabeth had been innocent on his part, he doubted any words he said could persuade Cassandra in her present frame of mind.

"You said you checked into breeding King, but instead you were sharing a cozy little dinner with that prissy woman."

"We did have dinner, but it wasn't cozy. And Elizabeth isn't prissy. She's a bit of a flirt, but she wasn't flirting with me. Well… she was flirting with me, but it's not what you think." *Good job, Matt. Why don't you just ask her for a shovel and dig your own grave?*

When he realized the hard look in Cassandra's eyes wasn't budging, he jumped that sinking ship in hopes of staying afloat on another. "I've got a few more ideas on how we can save the Triple P."

"What do you mean *we*? I've told you time and time again, Mama and I don't need your help."

"Oh, come on. Don't you at least want to hear them? I can't tell you the details yet, but I can tell you—"

"Sure, you can't tell me." She brought her hand level with the top of her head. "And I'm up to here with all your secrets."

"I told you I had my reasons, but as soon as I—"

"The evidence has judged you already. I couldn't trust you to–to lead Smokey to water." She yanked the ivory comb from her hair and threw it at his feet. "You–You, trying to buy my affection. Take this. I don't want it."

Matt flinched but waited until Cassandra had stormed back inside before picking up the comb. Resigned, he tucked it inside his shirt pocket next to the letter that had started everything and trudged to the bunkhouse.

⭑⭑⭑

Cassandra bounded up the stairs, then ran into her bedroom and slammed the door. She flung herself onto the bed and let the angry tears fall. An hour later she was still upset but had regained enough composure to berate herself for at least not asking Matt what George Thompson had said.

A tap sounded on the door. "Cassandra, may I come in?" her mother's soft voice asked.

Cassandra quickly rubbed the tears from her eyes before saying, "Yes, Mama."

Helen crossed the room and sat on the bed next to Cassandra and reached for her hand. "The Bible says, 'Be ye angry and sin not.' Your treatment of Matt was anything but kind."

Cassandra jerked her hand away. "How can you defend him? That man has lied to us since the day he arrived here. And you talk about my sin?"

"For one thing, young lady, I was watching the two of you. You did not give him a chance to tell his side of the story, did you?"

Cassandra's gaze dropped to her quilt. She traced the outline of a pink petunia with her finger.

"That is what I thought. Whatever Matt did is between him and God, though I still believe he holds our best interests. And furthermore, Matt is not my child, you are. Remember you were about to pray and make things right with the Lord?"

"That was before that–that woman arrived. I don't have the heart to now."

"Satan's fiery darts can come from anywhere. I am not saying Miss Baxter is a fiery dart," Helen said with a smile, "but Satan may have used her to distract you. I will not push, but you must deal with this. The sooner you do, the happier you will be. True joy and peace come only from our Father in heaven no matter what the circumstances."

She smoothed back Cassandra's hair. "There is something else I need to discuss with you. Matt told me about his trip to Fort Worth."

Cassandra sat up in bed. "Oh, Mama, I was so upset, I forgot to ask him about it. What did Mr. Thompson say?"

"I am afraid the news is not good. He cannot use our timber."

Cassandra flopped back onto the pillow.

"But," Helen continued, "I have an idea that might give us more time to pay off the loan."

"What's that?" Cassandra propped up on an elbow.

"Tomorrow I am going to pay half of what we owe."

"You are? How? We didn't get that much money from the cattle we sold."

"I am also going to use my jewelry."

"You can't." She grasped her mother's hands. "Your jewelry is a precious reminder of Papa. I won't let you do it."

"The choice is not yours to make. The Triple P is more important than diamonds or rubies."

"But Papa bought the jewelry because he loved you. What would he say if he were still alive?"

"He would say he was a fool."

"What?"

A sigh escaped Helen's lips. "You know your father won Phillip's land, but what you do not know is how. Your father gambled for a living before we met. He went from town to town playing poker and most of the time winning. When he rode into Goose Neck Ridge, he was searching for a game, but he never found it. He found the Lord instead. The day I met him, I dragged him to a church social. Reverend Doyle led your father to the Lord, right next to the punch bowl."

"That's a wonderful story, Mama. Well, all except the part about Papa being a gambler, but how does that concern the ranch now?"

"Your father never learned to manage money. He always spent what he had won, then when it ran out, he looked for another card game. After he became a new creature in Christ, he still struggled with those old habits.

"When you turned fourteen, your father deemed you too old for the schoolhouse. He hired your tutor, bought the pianoforte, and showered both of us with expensive gifts. I told him we did not need all those things, but he would not listen. He ordered furniture from as far away as New Orleans and paid for it with money intended for the upkeep of the ranch. After the drought, our money was almost gone, so he took out the loan."

Cassandra's shoulders stiffened. What had Papa been thinking?

Helen wiped away the tear that had trailed down her cheek. "I wished he had not played that hand of cards with Phillip. It unleashed his old desires. He withdrew all the money we had in the bank with the resolve to win one more high-stakes poker game and pay back the loan. This time his luck ran out. He lost everything to a cardsharp who was passing through town."

She gave a helpless shrug. "And that is why we are in this situation."

A black hole filled Cassandra's soul. She stepped across the floor to her jewelry box, removed the necklace her father had given her, and dropped the circle of pearls on her mother's lap.

"Take it. Maybe Papa didn't care about the Triple P, but I do. Excuse me. I'm going for a ride. Maybe I can think of another way to pay back the rest of our loan."

Before she left the room, she turned back to her mother and said in a deadly calm voice, "If I can't, I *will* marry Phillip to save this ranch."

★★★

Cassandra tip-toed along the backside of the barn. If Matt was still in the bunkhouse, the last thing she wanted to do was see him. She pushed open the back door, which didn't see use on a normal day. Cobwebs hung from the doorframe as if blocking her entrance into the barn. She pulled down the clinging strands and then wiped them on her pants.

Smokey's high-pitched whinny greeted her, followed by King's low nicker. She marched over to Matt's horse. "Right now, I'm not very happy with your owner." The horse stepped back in his stall and showed the whites of his eyes.

"I'm sorry, boy." She stretched her hand through the rails. The horse took a tentative step forward. "It's all right," she coaxed. King took another step, and Cassandra patted his forehead.

Smokey shoved his nose through the railing of his stall.

"Jealous, boy? How about we go for a ride?" She slipped a bridle over her horse's head and jumped onto his bare back. "Smokey, Papa used to say, 'Hold on to hope because things always change.' At least he was right about that. Things do change, don't they?"

"And not always for the better," Matt said, catching Smokey's bridle as Cassandra passed under the barn door.

"Kindly unhand my horse."

"Don't you want to know what happened in Fort Worth?"

"Mama already told me."

"Please, Cassandra. Let me explain. And I have another idea that might save the ranch. The railroad may not want your timber, but an expanding town needs lumber. We could start—"

"We? There you go again, forgetting that Mama and I own this ranch. And how many times must I tell you, we don't need your help?"

Cassandra touched her heels to the sides of her horse, urging him into a gallop, and left Matt and his words of explanation far behind. When she and Smokey closed in on the chain of hills that formed the northern border of the Triple P, she reined her horse into a walk.

"I suppose I should have let Matt explain," she said. "But right now I'm so upset with him and Papa, I need to clear my thoughts."

Smokey bobbed his head as if in agreement. Cassandra petted his neck. "Smokey, you have always understood me."

She squinted against the barren peaks glistening white in the sun. As a child, the hills had seemed gigantic to her. She called them White Top Mountains, and the name had stuck.

At the base of the nearest summit, Cassandra ground tied Smokey and scaled a rock that blocked the lower half of the cave she and Phillip had played in as children. She disappeared into the cave's depth, shivering at the cool air inside. A sunbeam flitted in and gave just enough light for her to find a P and C carved into the far wall. She ran a finger along the rough grooves of the letters.

Phillip had wanted to carve *loves* between their initials, but at the tender age of fourteen, Cassandra insisted they become husband and wife first. She had assumed she and Phillip would marry when they grew up, combine their ranches, and live happily ever after, just like the fairytales they'd read together.

"How ironic," Cassandra's voice echoed in the empty cavern. "Now that I can marry Phillip, I don't want to, but since the timber deal fell through, I've no other choice."

Her mother's jewelry might stave off the bank a while longer, but there was no way the two of them could come up with the rest of the money. She imagined Phillip's great pleasure in marrying her and throwing Matt off the Triple P. Even in her anger, the thought of never seeing Matt again left her as empty as the cave in which she stood.

Her gaze traveled to the heart Phillip had tried to carve next to their initials. His knife blade had broken before he finished it, so they opted to ride to Cedar Ridge and skip rocks in the pond. There he taught her the art of flicking her wrist to send rocks skimming across the face of the water. Then they'd taken turns throwing rocks at the tall trees to see who could hit the highest branch.

"It's too bad Mr. Thompson can't use those trees for railroad ties."

Cassandra tapped her cheek trying to recall Matt's words. What did he say about an expanding town needing lumber?

"That's it," she shouted. She clambered out of the cave, sprang onto Smokey's back, and sent him home at a gallop.

Mama. I think I know how to save the Triple P.

TWENTY-FOUR

The next morning the heat of a southern wind gripped Cassandra as sure as the uncertainty of what lie ahead. Would Mr. Higgins accept Mama's jewelry as partial payment of the loan? And would Mr. Brewer agree with her idea? She worried the buggy reins with one hand and chewed a knuckle on the other to keep from asking questions she knew her mother could not answer.

She cast her mother a sidelong glance. Except for righting herself when the buggy hit a rough spot, Helen rode in serene contentment with gloved hands nestled in her lap. *Mama must be praying and still trusting God to somehow get us out of this mess.*

Fifteen minutes later, the two women arrived in Goose Neck Ridge, Cassandra eased Ben in front of the bank and drew him to a halt. The horse snorted but complied, and the buggy stopped with a creak. Her mother tightened her hold on a leather valise before accepting Cassandra's assistance down from the buggy.

"Miss Pickett. Miss Pickett." A young girl of ten bounded up the boardwalk, took a flying leap at Cassandra, and squeezed her neck. The girl's bonnet slipped off, uncovering shoulder-length hair the color of sunshine.

Cassandra returned the embrace of her former student with genuine pleasure. She straightened the girl's bonnet. "Leah Miller, how nice to see you."

Leah's reticent, younger sister, Rachel, approached with her head down and a thumb firmly planted in her mouth. The seven-year-old had taken up the habit after her mother died two years ago. Cassandra had encouraged Rachel to quit, but no words or enticements had tempted her to surrender her one bit of security.

"Hello, Rachel." Cassandra squatted to pat the girl's bare head. Her hair, a shade darker than her older sister's, touched the middle of her back, and while both girls' noses turned up, Rachel had freckles sprinkled across hers. She buried her face in the skirt of Cassandra's dress.

"Now, Rachel," Jonathan Miller, the girls' father, admonished as he strode up the boardwalk. "Don't go wrinkling Miss Pickett's pretty, green dress now." He removed his hat, freeing streaks of blonde hair that fell over clear, blue eyes.

He brushed back the wayward hair. "Mrs. Pickett, it's nice to see you. Miss Pickett, I haven't seen you in a long time." The color of his cheeks deepened.

Most of Cassandra's students had either ridden a horse or walked alone or in pairs to school, but after his wife died, Jonathan made a point of accompanying his daughters. Cassandra pretended not to notice Jonathan's interest when he brought the girls to the schoolhouse each morning and picked them up in the afternoon. She sensed he longed to court her, and though he was kind to a fault and nice-looking in his own right, her heart was not in agreement. To give him less would not be fair. She turned down his invitation to the Spring Festival as politely as she could. He'd not asked for her company since then, but when their paths crossed, his eyes were wistful.

"Miss Pickett," Leah said. "We miss you something awful."

"I miss you too, but I'm needed at the Triple P."

Jonathan twisted his hat in his hands. "I don't mean to pry, but will you keep the ranch?"

"Lord willing," Helen interjected.

"I wish I could help," he said. "I've saved a little money and plan to buy a few more acres." His eyes held hope.

Cassandra hooked a gloved hand in her mother's arm. "Don't worry about us, Jonathan. We'll be fine."

Rachel's tiny voice spoke up. "Miss Pickett, please come back to school."

Leah draped an arm around her sister's shoulder. "She can't do that. They already got a new teacher lined up."

"Oh? Do you know who she is?" Cassandra was curious about her replacement.

"Her name is Elizabeth Anne Baxter," Jonathan said. "She moved in with her grandparents not too long ago."

Cassandra's smile turned crisp. "Miss Baxter? How nice."

"I am sure Miss Baxter will do a fine job." Helen squeezed Cassandra's hand. "We are here to see Mr. Higgins. Remember? Good day, Mr. Miller. Girls."

"That woman," Cassandra fumed when Jonathan and his girls were out of earshot.

"She has a right to be gainfully employed."

"Oh, yes. To employ her feminine charms on Matt."

Cassandra stomped up the marble steps of the Goose Neck Ridge Bank but turned back around and waited for her mother to catch up. "Sorry, Mama," she apologized. The two women passed under the bank's two-story archway where Cassandra opened one of the double doors and allowed her mother to enter first.

Every time Cassandra entered the bank, her stomach tightened in knots. The towering columns and stiff, leather chairs did little to welcome her or any of its other patrons. A shiny, round vault embedded in the back wall protected stacks of money–none of which belonged to Cassandra or her mother. Even the air smelled of money and the possibility of losing the Triple P. The heels of the women's shoes ticked a staccato sound across the inlaid tile floor.

"Mildred," Helen cried, rushing forward to greet the wife of William Higgins. Though the banker had lost favor with Cassandra, Helen had chosen not to hold a grudge against her long-time friend.

Both women enjoyed quilting and baking, though Mildred swore Helen's dainty stitches were a gift from God. Helen, in turn, admired Mildred's baking skills. Her peach cobbler had won the first prize over Maria's apple pie at the Spring Festival that past April. Maria had tweaked her recipe and vowed she would take home the blue-ribbon the following year.

Mildred returned Helen's embrace with an extra squeeze. "Sakes alive, what a wonderful surprise. I missed you the last time you came to the bank, and it's been ages since we've seen you and Cassandra at church."

"We have not left the ranch in a good while. The vaqueros run most of our errands."

"Them and that new hand of yours?"

"Yes, I did hire a new man. He is helping care for the livestock and trying like the rest of us to figure a way to repay Samuel's loan."

Mildred's face softened. "Let me get William." She stepped across the floor and disappeared into the room at the far end of the bank. A minute later Higgins appeared, pushing his glasses up his nose with Mildred shadowing his heels.

"Ladies," he said, "I hope you're here to repay your loan. If you can't, you'll have to vacate the property in eight days. There are at least two ranchers who'd like to buy the Triple P, but frankly," he lowered his voice, "there's nothing I'd like better than handing the deed back to you free and clear."

Cassandra's eyes narrowed. "Would one of those ranchers happen to be Phillip Brigham?"

Higgins gaze shifted to Mildred, who did not look pleased. "Y–Yes, but if you pay off the loan, he can't do a thing about it." He retrieved a ledger from under the counter and peered down his nose at the figures. "Let's see. You still owe this much." He pushed the ledger closer to the two women and jabbed a number with a stubby finger.

Cassandra gasped. Mama had never revealed how much money they owed the bank. The amount was incredible. Her face burned. She had enjoyed, even encouraged Papa's gifts, not realizing the consequence of his buying them.

She handed Higgins the valise. "This is partial payment."

He eyed the satchel. "I can't accept whatever's in there unless it's cash and for the full amount. Otherwise—"

"William Sturgell Higgins," Mildred cut in, rising to her full height, which still left her four inches shorter than her husband. "You and Samuel were friends. You owe it to him to help Helen and Cassandra."

Higgins mumbled an apology and opened the valise.

"There's jewelry and enough money from the sale of our cattle to cover a good part of our loan," Cassandra said. "We figured at least half of it. Give us thirty more days, and we'll pay back the rest." She lifted her head high, daring Higgins to contradict. After glancing at his wife, he didn't.

He pulled an emerald necklace out of the bag. A ray of sunlight caught the jewelry and cast a prism on the wall behind Cassandra. She turned her head to keep from seeing the pain on her mother's face. When Higgins fingered her pearl necklace, Cassandra squeezed her eyes shut. She could still see her father's laughing face the day he gave it to her.

"These are beautiful, ladies, truly they are, but—"

"That is all we have," Helen's voice pleaded. "We will pay back every last penny. I promise."

Higgins snapped the valise shut. "All right. I can cover for you, but this is between the four of us." He leaned closer. "If certain parties found out, it would not be good for my health."

Mildred took a threatening step toward her husband. "They won't say anything."

"I can assure you, your secret is safe." Cassandra shook Higgins's hand harder than was necessary and followed her mother to the door. "We'll be back in thirty days."

The banker muttered behind them, "I sure hope Mr. Brigham doesn't find out about this."

Once outside, Helen collapsed against the building. "We just lied to Mr. Higgins. If Mr. Brewer does not agree with your idea, we cannot pay back the rest of the money. Oh, Lord. Please forgive us."

"I'm not sure the Lord's interested in our problems these days."

Her words penetrated her mother's melancholy. "Cassandra, that is not true. It breaks my heart to hear you speak like that."

"Well, I can understand why God isn't answering my prayers, but he should be answering yours. I can't think of anyone more righteous than you."

"I am righteous only because of his son. Though I confess my faith has lagged the past few days, and lack of faith does hinder prayer. Would you drive me to the church? I must speak to the Lord and ask his forgiveness."

Cassandra spoke nary another word but helped her mother back into the buggy. Five minutes later she pulled up to a white stucco building with stained glass windows. A simple, white steeple graced the roof of the church as though pointing the very way to heaven. From her perch on the buggy, Cassandra smelled the heady scent of gardenias that hugged the church's walkway.

Before her father had died, she and her family had driven the six miles to the outskirts of Goose Neck Ridge every Sunday and attended services at this church. Her mother listened with rapt attention to Reverend Doyle's sermons while her father often fell asleep and did not arouse until the final "Amen."

For the most part, Cassandra ignored the reverend's convicting words. Instead, she admired the beautiful, stained glass windows and recalled the Bible stories her father told her and the ones she and Phillip acted out. She also watched the other worshippers to see if anyone other than her father would fall asleep. Since his funeral, she'd not attended a single service.

"Are you coming in?" Helen asked.

The hope in her mother's voice caused Cassandra pain. "Go on, Mama. I need to talk to Mr. Brewer. While you're inside, pray God lets him find my idea acceptable."

The springs of the buggy creaked as Helen stepped down. "You do not have to be in church to pray."

Cassandra's pride held her fast to the buggy seat and kept her from running inside the church to beg God for mercy and forgiveness. She tightened her fingers on the reins and as soon as her mother passed through the carved front door, she whipped up Ben and drove straight toward Mr. Brewer's mercantile. As the most prominent and influential businessman in Goose Neck Ridge, any ideas for the wellbeing and improvement of the town would filter through him first.

Cassandra reined Ben to a walk as they reentered town. The horse snorted at a white dog with a black splotch over its eye that trotted in front of the buggy.

"Miss Pickett, are you trying to run over my dog?" Carl Aldridge teased from the door of his barbershop where he was sharpening a blade against a leather strop. The barber, with his kind eyes and gentle smile, had been a long-standing friend of her father.

"If he doesn't stay off the street, I might," she returned his banter.

"Come here, Butch," Carl hollered. The dog bounded over to his master and licked his hand.

The buggy passed E. J. Fairfax, dressed in a three-piece suit that failed to match his high opinion of himself. He returned Cassandra's nod with a brief one of his own, but his expression held not a trace of friendliness. Cassandra suspected he, like Phillip, wanted to buy the Triple P when the bank foreclosed on it.

She felt his eyes follow her as she pulled the buggy to a stop outside the mercantile. *Think what you want, Mr. Fairfax. There's a good chance me and Mama might still save the Triple P.* She marched into the store with her head held high and her eyes fixed straight ahead.

The whiff of tobacco was a painful reminder of her father. To mask the scent, Cassandra wiggled the cork free from one of the bottles of perfume Mr. Brewer had placed near the register. He kept the perfume there to entice his female customers as he rang up their purchases.

The cloying scent made Cassandra's nose wrinkle. Matt was right. She and Mama should sell their rose perfume.

Mrs. Brewer stepped over to greet her. "Hello, Cassandra. I haven't seen you in a long time. Is everything all right?"

"I need to speak with Mr. Brewer. Is he available?"

"He's helping Mr. O'Connor pick out a suit."

Cassandra followed Mrs. Brewer's gaze to where Mr. Brewer struggled to find clothing small enough to fit Thomas

O'Connor, the manager, editor, and the sole reporter of the *Goose Neck Ridge Gazette*. The news found in the weekly paper was as short as the man responsible for it, but Mr. O'Connor's optimism believed the town would expand, and he'd be there to report it. With the approaching railroad, his foresight might one day reap him big rewards.

"I'll wait," Cassandra said. She browsed through the items littering the aisles and shelves. How many times had she convinced Papa to buy her something in this store? If she'd only known.

She tried on a bonnet with a cluster of peacock feathers and preened in front of an oval mirror before realizing the hat was a blue copy of the one Elizabeth Baxter had worn when she came to the Triple P looking for Matt. She yanked it off and placed it back on the rack.

Meandering through the store, she came to a glass case that was holding jewelry and hair ornaments. Her heart lurched. There on the top shelf lay an ivory comb similar to the one Matt had given her. Smaller in size, it bore the same delicate birds and flowers. Her hand strayed to where he had tenderly touched her comb the night they had waltzed.

How could he propose to her when his affections leaned toward Elizabeth Anne Baxter? She wiped the sting of tears from her eyes.

A scruffy cowboy curiously eyed Cassandra from behind a rack of saddles. As she walked past, he turned his head. *He must think I'm silly getting emotional over a case full of jewelry.*

"Miss Pickett," Mr. Brewer's voice boomed out. "Mabel said you wanted to see me."

"I need to talk to you. Privately."

The storekeeper motioned her to the back of the store. He leaned an elbow against a bookshelf. "We can talk here."

Cassandra set her chin high and pushed back her shoulders, hoping her voice would match her confidant stance. "It's no secret the Triple P is in trouble."

Mr. Brewer gave an understanding nod.

She rushed on before she lost her courage "Papa is to blame, but you already know that. He bought many items from this store and ordered fine things from your mail order catalogs."

"I'll be the first to admit your father had excellent taste."

"Why did you let him do it?"

"Hold on a minute. Your father paid cash for everything he bought. I didn't find out until later he mortgaged your ranch to cover his expenses."

"Am I the only one who didn't know?"

"I'm sure your father didn't mean to get in such a fix. He just wanted to buy nice things for you and your mother."

"That's why I'm here. I need your help."

"What can I do?"

"You know about the railroad that's coming to Goose Neck Ridge?"

"Yes."

"Mama and I wanted to sell our timber for the railroad ties."

"That's an excellent idea."

"We thought so too, but someone offered the railroad a lower bid than us."

"I'm sorry, but how does that concern me?"

"How would you like to become partners with me and Mama?"

Mr. Brewer stroked his mustache as Cassandra outlined her plan. "Hmm... sounds interesting. I'll think about it. If it's something we can work out, I'll have Mr. Harvey draft a proposal when he gets back in town."

Cassandra thanked Mr. Brewer and shook his hand. She skipped down the mercantile steps with a glimmer of hope in her heart. Maybe God was going to answer her and Mama's prayers to save the Triple P after all.

TWENTY-FIVE

"Whoa," Cassandra called out and brought Ben to a halt in front of the church. Her mother stood by the door with a pleasant expression, and her hands folded as though she was still in prayer.

"Did you and God have a nice talk, Mama?"

"Yes, we did. Among other things, I talked to him about you."

Cassandra helped her mother into the buggy. "I appreciate it, especially since there's a better chance he'll listen to you than me."

"Did Mr. Brewer turn you down?"

"No. He liked the idea, but he wants to think about it first."

Helen bowed her head, and Cassandra knew the news was going straight to God. She let her mother finish praying.

Helen opened her eyes. "It still bothers me that I lied to Mr. Higgins."

"Did you ask God to forgive you?"

"I did, but I should go back and apologize to Mr. Higgins as well."

"So, he'd take the ranch away from us today instead of a month from now?"

She clicked her tongue, and the horse started for home. The buggy wheels slipped into the familiar tracks made by numerous trips to and from Goose Neck Ridge.

Cassandra glanced over at her mother and asked, "Mama, were you angry at Papa for what he did?"

"Why do you ask?"

"I can't figure out how to deal with his betrayal."

"Cassandra."

"It's true. He deceived us into thinking everything was fine."

"You are not being fair."

"It was Papa who wasn't fair, and why did you wait so long to tell me? I had a right to know."

"Stop the buggy." Helen's voice was sharp and demanding.

"What?"

"You heard me."

Cassandra reined in Ben. She'd never heard her mother raise her voice like that. "Mama, what's wrong?"

"Cassandra Jane, I loved your father with all my heart and love bears all things. I did not tell you what he did for fear of tainting your memories of him, and I was right."

Cassandra opened her mouth to speak, but her mother would not be interrupted.

"Do you remember when you were nine-years-old, and that cow chased you for getting too close to her calf?"

"What does that have to do with anything?"

"Your father yelled for you to run and not look back. He spurred his horse between you and the cow."

Cassandra's heart quickened at remembering how close she'd come to being gored. Papa had saved her life, but his horse took the full impact of the cow's horn and had to be put down.

"Do you know why your father told you to not look back?"

"No, Mama, I don't."

"He wanted you to see where you were going. Had you looked back, you might have stumbled and fallen."

"I still don't understand." Cassandra fidgeted in the buggy seat. Where was her mother going with this?

"Paul told the Philippians to forget those things which were behind and to press onward, or they might miss the prize. We cannot do a thing about what your father did, but we can keep trusting the Lord and go toward what lies ahead."

"That's not much from where I sit."

"God has not left his throne. He is still in control."

"What about Matt and what he did?"

"The same holds true for him. Do you love him?"

"Are you kidding?"

"I will ask again. Do you love him?" Her mother's voice brooked no argument.

"Yes, Mama. I love him. Are you happy?"

"Only from the standpoint that now you are telling the truth. Your love for Matt will allow you to forgive him. Like I forgave your father."

"I'm not the Christian you are. I don't know if I can do it."

Cassandra collected the reins and asked Ben to move forward again. The rhythmic striking of his hooves and the crunch of the buggy wheels broke the uncomfortable silence that hovered between the two women. Cassandra didn't want her mother to be upset, but she wasn't ready to forgive Papa or Matt.

Helen pointed a gloved finger toward the horizon. "Is that Phillip?"

Cassandra squinted against the sun at a fast approaching rider. It *was* Phillip. His horse cantered toward them on the path that separated his ranch from the Triple P.

There was nothing she could do. With the extra weight of the buggy, and even on a good day, Ben couldn't outrun Phillip's stallion. She had no other choice than to face her neighbor.

Phillip reined Sunny to an abrupt stop. The horse's hooves dug into the ground, scattering dust and loose rocks in all directions. Phillip settled back in his saddle, looking calm and tailored in a black suit and a contrasting white shirt. How did he always manage to look neat and clean no matter what the time of day, the weather, or the circumstance? Right now, Cassandra was hot and sweaty and felt anything but attractive.

Phillip tipped his hat. "Mrs. Pickett. Cassandra. What a pleasant surprise."

"Hello," Cassandra said. "Are you heading to town to gloat over our foreclosure papers?"

He raised a hand to his chest. "Your words cut me. Think how much easier it would be if we married. We could forget all about ranches and money problems."

"I have news for you. You won't be getting the Triple P anytime soon. I'm working on a deal with—"

"Cassandra." Helen held a finger to her lips.

Phillip's eyes narrowed. "And what have you and your dear mother been up to?"

"You'll find out soon enough, so don't go making any plans to sell our ranch. Good day, Phillip."

Cassandra snapped the reins and sent Ben into a brisk trot. She didn't slow the horse down until the buggy passed under the sign announcing they were on Triple P property.

Helen finally spoke up. "Cassandra, do you think it was wise to provoke Phillip?"

"He always seems to know our business anyway. Let him stew a while before he finds out about my deal with Mr. Brewer."

⭑⭑⭑

Phillip raced back to Lazy Acres. He had to find Jack Dalton. Sunny was lathered by the time he galloped onto the main compound. Lorenzo grabbed the stallion's reins and told Phillip that Jack had gone to town but was expected back any time. Phillip bounded up the porch steps and stomped into his office, slamming doors along the way.

An hour later he was still pacing the floor and waiting for Jack. He refused the tray of food Rosa brought him. She murmured an apology and left the study as quickly and as quietly as she had entered it. A few minutes later, Phillip heard the sound of approaching footsteps in the hallway. He assumed Jack Dalton had finally decided to show up, but instead, Juanita popped her head around the door.

"I was worried about you," she said. "You came home riding Sunny too hard again. And you yelled at Lorenzo when he took the poor horse to the barn. What did I say about that?"

"Some things are beyond your understanding," Phillip snapped back in reply.

Juanita's dark eyes widened in alarm. "*Lo siento,* Señor Brigham. I did not mean to make you more unhappy."

Phillip willed his frustration to recede. "I am the one who is sorry. Please forgive me."

"God does not like his people to be angry."

Phillip resisted the urge to say he did not belong to God. "I could work on my temper. How do you stay so happy all the time?"

"Jesus lives inside me. He makes me *muy alegre*."

Phillip pretended to play the girl's game. "He makes you very happy, huh? And how does this Jesus fit inside one so small?"

Juanita placed her brown hands on her hips. "It is not nice to make fun of the Lord. Jesus does not live inside me, but his spirit does."

Her sincerity touched Phillip. He recalled the word Emmanuel meant *God within us*. Or was it *God is with us*? His inept reasoning could not grasp the answer.

Juanita tapped his chest. "Jesus does not live in your heart, or you would not be so angry all the time." Her face brightened. "I will pray God will do something to make you become his child too." With the matter settled, she waved and called, "*Hasta luego.*"

"I will see you later as well, my little one."

How did one so young know so much about God? Had her parents taught her? Anyone as meek and quiet as Rosa possessed a faith he lacked. He wasn't sure Manuel, her husband, had held the same religious convictions, but he didn't doubt the vaquero's optimistic spirit. As he worked around Lazy Acres, Phillip had often heard him say, "Everything will work out for the best."

"It's been so long since Manuel voiced those words," he said to the empty room, "I had all but forgotten them."

But he'd not forgotten the absence of Jack Dalton. Where was that man? Phillip tried to read a book, but the words faded in and out as his anger increased. He admitted he was also angry with himself. Angry for being at the mercy of a man as despicable as Dalton.

Thirty minutes later Jack strolled into the study as though he was escorting a lady friend at the park. "Mornin', boss."

"Where have you been?"

Jack plopped down on the velvet chair, which now bore stains from his frequent visits. "You gotta stop gettin' yourself all lathered up. If ya keep actin' like that, I can't tell ya what I dug up."

"It better be good. My patience is nearing an end."

"You'll never guess who I saw comin' out of the bank today with her purty little mama in tow." He paused as if expecting a reply. When none came, he said, "It was that fiery, red-haired friend of yours. You two still aimin' to get hitched?"

"That's no concern of yours."

"Well, if you've done somethin' to make her mad, I suggest you apologize. She's got the nicest—"

Phillip banged his fist on the desk, caring not about the inkwell. The glass bottle held its own.

"You don't have to take everything so serious. I was only funnin'."

"Why were the Pickett women at the bank?"

"Ya ain't gonna like this. Old Higgins turned Redcoat. He gave 'em another month to pay back their loan."

For a fleeting moment a vision of William Higgins lying in a pine box filled Phillip's mind.

"It doesn't matter," he replied. "They will never come up with the money no matter how much time they have."

"I don't know. After they left the bank, they drove to that church outside of town." He squirmed at the mere mention of the word church. "That little redhead left her ma there and headed to the mercantile. She strode in all manlike and talked with the owner a spell. He said he'd think about it and then shook her hand. I couldn't hear what else they was sayin' without givin' myself away."

Phillip leaned back in his chair and closed his eyes, trying to make sense of Jack's words. What kind of deal was Cassandra trying to make? And how did it concern Charlie Brewer? Was that what she had alluded to?

"That ain't the worst of it," Jack continued, "Remember ya told me to find out why Atkins was at that lawyer's office? Well, last night I broke in. You owe me big for that one. Some Irish wench almost caught me. Chased me off with a broom the size of a door." The corners of his mouth slipped into a leer. "I might go back and repay her lack of hospitality sometime.

"Anyhow, before that orange-haired screech owl ran me off, I found something interestin' in Mr. Harvey's desk. He had a folder with 'Brigham' written right across the top."

Phillip stiffened. His father had done business with Mr. Harvey, but he had no knowledge of any legal papers other than the ones transferred to him after his father's death. "What was in it?"

"A copy of your pa's will. Did ya know, you ain't the real heir of this place? Your old man left Lazy Acres to some kin of yours named Ethan."

Phillip sprang to his feet, causing his chair to crash to the floor. "What? Of course, I'm the heir. I have my father's will to prove it." He ransacked the top right-hand drawer of his desk and with a flourish, slapped a document on top of it.

Jack leaned over and glanced at the paper. "Nope. That one ain't worth shinin' your shoes with. The one I seen was dated a few weeks 'fore your pa passed over into Glory Land or whatever those religious people call it."

Phillip's heart caught in his chest. A Bible story he and Cassandra had acted out as children flashed in his mind. It was about a wicked man named Nabal, whose heart had stopped when God judged him. Was Phillip on the verge of dying for his sinful deeds?

Jack prattled on. "Who is this Ethan guy anyway?"

"The only Ethan I know is my Uncle Walter's son. You must be mistaken." Phillip commanded his mind to think clearly. Why had his father updated his will and made Ethan his heir? And why hadn't Ethan ridden up and claimed Lazy Acres as his own?

Jack unwittingly suggested an answer. "Your cousin probably don't know about the ranch. For the right price, I'll sneak back and get rid of that folder, and no one will be the wiser. I couldn't do it before. That Irish wench and all."

He spat a stream of tobacco juice into the center of the spittoon. "Whatever you decide, you better do it fast in case that cousin of yours shows up. You think that Triple P cowboy has somethin' do to with it? Seein' he sent a telegram to your uncle and went to Mr. Harvey's office after he came to the Triple P?"

"I have no idea. I'm paying you to find out those things."

Jack showed his tobacco-stained teeth. "It'd be a whole lot easier if you'd let me kill him. A man could just up and disappear on a big ranch like this one."

"I doubt that will be necessary."

"It'll cost ya if I do. And speakin' of money. You owe me big for all this dirt I digged up."

Phillip counted out five bills and pushed them over to Dalton. "I'll pay you the rest after you destroy that file."

Jack eyed the money. "This ain't what ya promised. You said you'd give me three times as much the next time."

"Take it or leave it. Now, get out."

"One way or another, I'll get what's comin' to me. And I don't make promises I don't keep."

Jack spat again, but this time a good foot away from the spittoon. The tobacco juice soaked into the ink stain Phillip had forgotten to cover up. He shoved up from his chair and then ambled out of the study with nary a backward glance.

Phillip brushed aside the cowboy's empty threats, but even in his stupidity, Jack had spoken a truth. Ethan must not know about Lazy Acres, or he'd already have claimed it, and with the will destroyed, his cousin wouldn't have a legal leg to stand on.

But Phillip also had to get his hands on the Triple P, so he could sell it and Lazy Acres and get out of Goose Neck Ridge in case Ethan did show up. He could sell the ranches immediately if he convinced Cassandra to marry him. Even in his agitated state, the thought of marrying her stoked a fire Phillip longed to burn.

He slipped his father's useless will back inside the desk drawer. *I've got to put more pressure on Higgins and demand he revoke the thirty-day grace period he so stupidly extended to the Pickett women. Then when Cassandra marries me, things will be back on track again.*

For the first time in days, Phillip laughed. Yes, this situation was far from hopeless. In fact, things were just starting to get interesting.

TWENTY-SIX

For the next couple of days, Matt tried to explain his relationship with Elizabeth to Cassandra, but every time he tried to corner her with the truth, she flounced away, saying she couldn't care less about him and Miss What's-her-name. Though she flaunted a tough exterior, he worried about the dark shadows under her eyes and the pallor that had replaced her tan complexion. At night he lay awake, balancing the weight of his lies with how much he missed her company.

Rafael and Carlos sadly shook their heads at the situation, but Roberto called Matt out on it.

"Mr. Matt, I do not know what you have done," he said as he and Matt repaired a couple of broken boards on the hog pen. "But I warned you not to make Miss Cassie unhappy again. You must fix this."

Matt shooed one of the pigs back from where he and Roberto worked. The shoat flopped back down next to his littermate with a grunt.

"I wish I could, but Cassandra Jane won't give me the time of day. I've got to find a way to make her listen. Do you have any ideas?" Matt acknowledged his desperation. Here he was asking Roberto what to do about Cassandra, when not too long ago he'd been the one offering him advice about women.

Roberto pondered the question. "Hmm… Ask Señora Pickett. I know my mamá will not help you. You are not her favorite person right now."

His words were true. Whenever Matt crossed Maria's path, she threatened him with her eyes and with whatever she was holding in her hand.

Matt considered Roberto's suggestion. Maybe Mrs. Pickett would help him. Her worried expression showed concern for Cassandra too.

The opportunity for Matt to plead his case to Mrs. Pickett came the next day. He was helping Rafael mend a hole in the bunkhouse roof when he saw Cassandra leading a colt into the corral. "Rafael, Cassandra Jane's gonna be tied up with that yearling for a bit. I need to speak with Mrs. Pickett about her. I'll be right back."

Rafael took a nail out of his mouth and pounded it into the roof. "Señor Matt, I hope your talk helps put light back into Señorita Cassie's eyes."

"I do too, *mi amigo.* I do too."

Matt admired the older man's loyalty. Since his arrival, he'd learned the Triple P occupants banded together in times of trouble. They might lose the ranch, but they would never lose their love for each other. Matt envied their bond. He longed for that kind of relationship. With a sigh he clambered down the ladder and headed to the house.

"Mrs. Pickett," he called as he set foot in the hallway.

"I am back here."

Matt made his way to the kitchen with rising hope, but it crashed right back down when he smelled fresh-baked bread. Mrs. Pickett must be helping Maria with the baking.

"Just my luck," he mumbled. "Maria would like nothing better than to serve my hide as cracklin's."

Matt couldn't blame her. Like the vaqueros, her fierce loyalty to Cassandra and Mrs. Pickett made her challenge anyone who meant them harm. Carlos had said whenever his sister saw Mr. Higgins in town, she gave him an earful. As the recipient of Maria's ire, Matt almost sympathized with the banker.

"It's now or never," he mumbled, trudging toward the kitchen like a man condemned to die. He poked his head around the door, but Maria's withering look made him want to tuck tail and run.

"What is it, Señor Matt? Have you come to make the bread fall flat?"

"Maria," Helen scolded. "Did you need something, Matt?"

"May I have a word with you?"

"You cannot speak around me, one of the servants?" Maria taunted. "We are all family here. At least we six were before you came."

"That is enough, Maria." Helen's voice held a sharp note. "We may all be family, but I am still the head of this household."

Maria's lips snapped shut and she punched the dough with such force, flour flew into the air. Thinking she wished to do the same to his head, Matt retreated a step and prayed for help–something he'd done a lot of the past week.

Helen wiped her hands on her apron and laid a hand on Matt's arm. "We can talk in the parlor."

Maria punched the dough again, but this time with less force. Matt relaxed. After he cleared things up with Cassandra, he'd make amends with Maria too.

When he entered the parlor, he closed his eyes against the sweet remembrance of the night Cassandra had waltzed here in his arms.

"Shall we have a seat?" Helen indicated the chairs across from the pianoforte. "Now, what do you want?"

"It's about Cassandra. I know I didn't mention Miss Baxter. Not that there was anything to tell," he quickly added. "I met her at the mercantile the first time I rode into town. She sorta butted in while I was searchin' for those gifts."

"She does seem the type."

Matt warmed to the response. "She's a nice enough young lady, but I didn't encourage her. I shouldn't have said Cassandra was my sister, but it slipped out at the time."

"What you did or did not tell Miss Baxter is between you, her, and the Lord. What concerns me is the lie you told us the second time you saw her."

"I wish I could tell you why, but I can't. I have personal business I need to untangle first. Then I'll tell you the whole story. I promise I'm not jeopardizing the ranch. I'm hopin' it might help. Would you please trust me for a few more days?"

Helen lifted her chin and studied him. "The day I met you, I believed you to be a good man. I am not happy about your secrets, but for now, I will accept your word. But if you lie to me again, I will not be so forgiving." Her eyes turned dark, and

Matt acknowledged the steely strength beneath her calm demeanor.

Before Mrs. Pickett changed her mind, he plunged on. "I care a great deal about Cassandra. I want to explain Miss Baxter to her, but she won't give me the time of day."

"I carry part of the blame for her reticence. After your confrontation, I shared something that complicated the situation. I was right to tell her, but my timing was not the best. She was also upset about the means I used to obtain an extension on the loan."

Mrs. Pickett, as soon as I see Mr. Harvey, I'll take care of all your problems. Then I'll propose to that lovely, headstrong daughter of yours. Not for convenience sake but because I love her.

Matt had finally admitted he loved Cassandra, but the revelation had filled him with misery and not joy. If he didn't square things out with her soon, she might demand he ride out of her life forever.

Helen's mouth turned up into a conspiratorial grin. "I have an idea. Here is what we will do..."

☆☆☆

The hem of Cassandra's gown swished the wooden floor of the hall. With considerable effort, Maria had restored the emerald dress to its original beauty. When she handed it back to Cassandra, she grumbled, "Why you needed to wrinkle this, I have no idea. Señor Brigham is not worth it."

Cassandra had hugged Maria's neck. "You're right. I was frustrated about his proposal. It was silly of me."

Now, Cassandra's frustration and broken heart lay under Matt and her father's feet. Why had the two men she loved betrayed her? She knew she held no claim to Matt in the first place. His interest in Elizabeth, or any other woman, was his business, but she fought the demons of jealousy, nonetheless.

She stopped in front of an expensive oil painting her father had bought at a Dallas auction. The peaceful cottage sat on a verdant sea of grass, surrounded by red, purple, and blue flowers. Cassandra ran a finger over the carved frame. Up until the time she discovered what her father had done, she had appreciated the painting's beauty, but now its brilliant hues and picturesque landscape mocked her. Life was not so idyllic.

The family awaited her for supper, but how could she sit through another meal with Matt? Each time he tried to speak to her, she was afraid she would either say something she shouldn't or break down and cry. Resigned, she pushed open the dining room doors. She might as well get this over with.

Her heart skipped a beat. Dozens of candles flickered around the dining room, and a crystal vase full of roses sat in the middle of the table. As she crossed over to the arrangement, she stepped on crimson rose petals that were littering the floor. Cassandra breathed in the sweet fragrance and caressed a bud that was just starting to open. Her hand fell to the table. Why were there only enough dishes and silverware for two people?

She recognized the tread of Matt's step before he entered the dining room. He walked up behind her and cupped her shoulders in his hands. With no regard for the cost, she turned and laid her head against his shoulder. Tears for all her broken dreams spilled onto his shirt. He held her until those tears were spent.

Sorrow filled Matt's eyes. "I'm sorry, Cassandra. I'm sorry for everything."

As she accepted the handkerchief he offered, she noticed the white shirt and pressed pants he was wearing. She slid her fingers over the shirt sleeve. The material was as soft as the rose bud.

"This is too nice for a—"

"A hired hand?"

Her cheeks burned. "That's not what I meant. Where did you get these clothes? Papa had a shirt like this one. And how did you get creases in your pants? Did Maria iron them?"

"These were your father's clothes. Your mother let me try them on. And yes, Maria altered and ironed them. She protested the entire time, but your mother's influence won her over."

"You must forgive Maria. She is like a mother bear where I'm concerned."

Matt's laughter tickled her brow. "I don't blame her. I want to protect you too."

"You don't have to. I can take care of myself."

He touched a finger to her lips. "Before you ruin the mood, there's somethin' important I want to tell you."

He offered her a seat and then stooped down on one knee in front of her. She was able to look right into his wonderful blue eyes.

Her heart danced. He was going to propose.

☆✯☆

Matt's heart beat in his throat. Cassandra looked stunning in a gown that so perfectly matched her beautiful eyes. A bow of the same color was keeping her wild tresses in place. He tucked a loose tendril behind her ear before clasping her hands to his lips. Her skin smelled sweet like the roses.

Come on, Matt ol' buddy. Keep your mind on what you want to share.

"For the last week, I've been tryin' to make peace with God. I admitted he's not to blame for my problems and thanked him for puttin' up with me even though there's still a few things I need to take care of."

Cassandra's smile stiffened.

"Aren't you happy for me?" Matt asked.

"No. I mean–yes–but I thought you were going to ask—"

"You thought I was going to ask what?"

"Nothing. What needs to be taken care of?"

You thought I was going to ask you to marry me, didn't you? Be patient a little while longer, my darlin'.

Matt rocked back on his heels. "I came to Goose Neck Ridge to claim something, and when I do, I plan to help you and your mother save the Triple P. Please, give me a couple more days. I promise I'll tell you everything."

"Matt," Cassandra's voice piqued in excitement as she sat up in her chair, "I might already have a way to save the ranch."

"Really? How?"

"Remember when you said a growing town needs lumber?"

"I didn't think you heard me. You and Smokey were takin' off like a tornado at the time."

"Well, I talked to Mr. Brewer about building a lumber mill near Cedar Ridge. He said he'd think about it and get back with me. So, though I don't know for sure yet, I'm holding a barrel of hope."

Well, Mr. Brewer, ya out-trumped me on that one.

"That's great news," Matt said, "It sounds like something we need to pray about."

"That's what Mama said, but I'm crossing my fingers too, just in case."

She cast him a wary eye. "I'll be patient a little while longer, but you do need to tell me what you're up to. You also need to explain your relationship with Elizabeth Baxter."

"There isn't one. I met her by chance at the mercantile. I shouldn't have said you were my sister, but there was nothing romantic about the dinner we shared. And more importantly, I'm not interested in her at all."

"Are you sure?"

"Positive. Please, Cassandra Jane. I want things to go back to the way they were."

"I do, too, but if Elizabeth Anne Baxter shows up again, you'll be looking for another job." She swatted him with a napkin.

Smiling, Matt removed the silver covers from their plates to expose roast beef and gravy with new potatoes, corn, and creamed onions. They bowed their heads, and Matt prayed grace. Cassandra echoed his *amen*.

"Speaking of the Lord," she said, poising her fork above a slice of roast beef. "May I confide in you?"

"Sure."

"Remember when I asked about your relationship with God, and you said I didn't need to tell you about mine?"

"Yes."

"Well, I did want to talk about it. You said a Christian needs to grow, but every time I take one step forward, the devil seems to shove me two steps back."

"That's the Christian battle. God says we need to put on his whole armor to fight. Maybe you're missin' a piece. I was missin' the sword of the Spirit. I hadn't read my Bible for a long time."

"I remember there are six pieces. There's the sword of the Spirit like you mentioned..." She set down her fork and counted the other pieces on her fingers, stopping at the sixth one. Her eyes widened.

"I'm missing the shield of faith, and without faith, it's impossible to please God. Is that why it doesn't seem like he's answering my prayers?"

"Could be. Maybe your faith needs a little nudge. I'm findin' the closer I get to God, the closer he gets to me."

"It's still confusing."

"For me too, but I'm sure the Lord will help if you ask."

Matt sent up a quick prayer asking God to strengthen Cassandra. "There's one more thing I need to tell you."

"Yes?"

"That day I asked you to marry me, you told me—"

"You did not ask me to marry you for the right reason. You said you'd marry me just to save the ranch. That's not the kind of a proposal a woman wants to hear."

"I'm sorry. But when the time comes, I promise to do it right."

Cassandra's eyes shone, and Matt wanted to shout. She loved him too. As soon as he saw Mr. Harvey, he'd ask her to marry him, and nothing was going to stand in his way.

While the two of them ate, neither mentioned the food had turned cold. But to Matt, the meal was the finest he'd ever tasted. Love must make everything better.

TWENTY-SEVEN

Two days after she and Matt had reconciled, Cassandra woke up at first light and started her morning. She beat the multi-colored rug that hung over the porch railing with all the energy she could muster. The dust scattered into what promised to be another arid day. Maria stepped onto the porch carrying two more braided rugs.

"You keep pretending that is Señor Matt's big fat head."

Cassandra giggled. "Maria, Matt and I have mended our fence. Everything between us is as right as pigs in mud. Not that there is any mud. It's still as dry as a bone around here."

Maria flipped the rugs over the railing and grabbed the rug beater. "That man has managed to fool both you and your mother. Now, get inside before I use this on your backside where it belongs."

Laughing, Cassandra fled inside the house. *A merry heart doeth good like a medicine.* And for the past few days, her heart had overflowed with happiness. Each time she and Matt crossed paths, their eyes spoke the thousand words they wanted to say.

Still chuckling over Maria's comment, Cassandra spread the rug back on the parlor floor. She sobered when she saw the photograph of her father on the pianoforte. Since learning about his gambling problem and how he sunk the Triple P in debt, Cassandra had avoided looking at his pictures.

She picked up the photograph and traced his face with her finger. She had teased him the day he'd brought the picture home as a surprise for her mother. "You don't look happy in this one, Papa. It doesn't look like you at all."

Samuel threw his arms around Cassandra and pulled her close. His beard tickled her cheek, and he smelled clean like the rosemary soap Mama made.

"Cassie dear, the photographer insisted I look serious. The master of the castle, so to speak. He said one day my grandchildren would look at this picture and think I was a great and wise patriarch."

"For you to have grandchildren, I must first marry. Have you seen any eligible young men knocking at our door?"

His face turned as somber as it had been in the photograph. "My dearest Cassie, the Lord has the right man waiting for you."

"But Papa, you told me that two years ago when Phillip..." She couldn't bear to speak of it.

Samuel tightened his arms around her. "When God finishes molding the man you're to marry, he'll show up. Then I can pass this ranch on to the two of you."

Cassandra turned the picture of her father face down on the pianoforte. "Why did you let this happen, Papa? Didn't you love the Triple P?"

Helen entered the room with a soft tread and crossed over to Cassandra. She reached out and righted the picture. "Your father was a good man, and he did love this ranch. After he admitted his mistake, he begged God's forgiveness and mine."

Sadness settled on her face. "I told him he did not need to ask my forgiveness. We married for better or worse and for almost twenty years, he forgave me for the things I did wrong."

"You've never done anything wrong, Mama, and until you told me what Papa did, I didn't think he had either."

Helen touched Cassandra's cheek. "We all have our faults. The Bible plainly teaches that."

"But if I'm a new creature in Christ, why do I still think and say wrong things?"

"Because we still carry a sinful nature. Each time we trespass, we close the windows of God's blessings. When we ask for forgiveness, he opens them back up and listens to our prayers."

Helen sat on the divan and patted the seat. "Sit here. I will try to explain."

Cassandra slumped down next to her mother. Was prayer ever going to make sense?

Helen clasped Cassandra's hand. "God does not give us everything we ask for, though there are times he does to show us how foolish our requests are."

"Like the children of Israel asking for a king?"

"Yes. God allowed King Saul to rule over them, though he was not the Lord's perfect will."

"But praying for our ranch isn't the same as asking for a king. So, why hasn't God answered our prayers?"

"He has answered them."

"He has? Oh, Mama. Where did you get the money?"

"I do not have the money."

"But you said—"

"God's answer is for us to wait until he works everything out. Until then, we must put our faith in him and be patient."

The light of realization broke through Cassandra's deep confusion. "And faith cometh by hearing—"

"And hearing by the word of God," Helen finished. "When we read the Bible and pray in faith, we draw closer to him and he in turn, draws closer to us."

"Matt said the same thing."

"God is always there, Cassandra. We are the ones who move away."

"I'm ready to pray and ask God to forgive me and increase my faith."

She bowed her head, but for several minutes she struggled with the words. The sounds of lowing cattle slipped through the window, and the rich smell of chocolate cake drifted into the room–both reminders of God's blessings. Peace settled in her soul.

God, please forgive me for doubting you. I should have trusted you all along. I'm sorry I was bitter toward Papa. He loved the Triple P and didn't mean to jeopardize it. Please help my faith to grow, so I can draw closer to you, and while you're at it, could you help me control my pride? I have plenty enough of it to spare. Thank you for allowing me and Matt to make up. I don't know your will for my life, but I pray he is in it. And Lord, we still need rain. Could you send some our way? Amen.

Cassandra opened her eyes and looked into her mother's joyous face. She hugged Cassandra's neck. "I am so happy, darling. God has just answered one of my prayers. Let us share the news with Maria. The poor dear has been worried sick about you, and maybe at the same time we can convince her to forgive Matt."

"That might be easier said than done, but with God's help, we can. If we brag about the chocolate cake she baked, maybe she'll be more inclined to listen."

The two women laughed as they joined arms and went to find Maria.

☆☆☆

A chocolate cake was indeed cooling in the kitchen, but Maria was outside with Roberto watering the garden. Roberto was hauling bucket after bucket from the creek while Maria pointed to the plants she wanted watered. With a garden covering the entire backyard, Cassandra knew they would be occupied for some time. She suggested to her mother that they polish the silver. The two women worked side-by-side, talking about Matt, the ranch, and what God had in store for all of them.

"Maria would not be happy is she saw us doing her chores," Helen said as she replaced the lid on the silver polish.

Cassandra laid the last fork in the sideboard drawer. "We're done now. She'll never know." She kissed her mother's cheek. "Thanks for all your prayers. Things already seem so much brighter and sweeter."

"That comes from being right with the Lord. May I share something else at the risk of dampening your new-found joy?"

"Of course, Mama."

"Remember, God, and not your circumstances, should govern your happiness. If you trust him, you can remain joyful even when things around you are not."

"I know, but right now, I'm happy inside and out."

"I am glad, and I am also happy that you and Matt have made up."

"Me, too. And since we're done polishing the silver, I'm going to see what he's up to."

The back door opened and banged shut, followed by Maria's heavy tread approaching the dining room. Helen motioned to the sideboard drawer. Cassandra shoved it shut with her hip and started whistling before Maria cracked open the dining room door and peered inside. A frown marred her face.

"Did I hear you say Señor Matt's name? What has that man done this time?"

"Matt hasn't done anything wrong," Cassandra said. "Thanks to him, things are running as smooth as Samantha's fur. He even helped Carlos fix the sucker rod on the windmill. So, the horses are happy with him too. They were mighty thirsty."

"It is too bad Señor Matt did not fall into the well when they pulled up the broken plunger." The corners of Maria's mouth twitched as if she wanted to smile.

"Maria, admit it," Cassandra said, "Deep down, you like Matt."

"You are the one I care about." She squeezed Cassandra's neck in affection. "If you say you are happy, I will try to be."

"You have nothing to fear. I've never been happier." She patted Maria's round belly. "And how are you and baby Martinez doing?"

"We are both fine. So you can stop doing my work." She tilted her head toward the sideboard. "I know you two were in here polishing the silver. And Señora Pickett, you cleaned the parlor yesterday after you told me I must sit down and get off my feet."

Helen blushed a pretty pink. Cassandra laughed and said, "Maria, Mama and I should know nothing gets by you."

"And I will not let you forget it." The stern look on her face turned into a smile. "Now, scat. You have done enough of my work today. I am sure there is a horse to ride or a pig to slop."

Cassandra embraced both women and left them discussing a new recipe for rice pudding. She pinched her cheeks to give them color and went to find Matt. She spied him sitting on the bunkhouse porch, cleaning and oiling his pistol.

As she headed toward the bunkhouse, she passed by Roberto who was done watering the garden and was now practicing his roping skills. He twirled his lariat overhead and let the loop sail. It dropped neatly over her head and fell to the ground.

"Are you glad you are not a steer, Miss Cassie?" he asked as she stepped out of the rope's circle. With a few flips of the wrist, he recoiled his lariat.

Cassandra took the rope from him. She executed a flat loop and twirled the lariat above her head. She skipped in and out of the loop before zipping it up and down her torso.

"Hey, boss," Matt hollered, clapping his hands. "That's pretty good."

Cassandra thanked Roberto for the use of his rope. "And," she kept her voice low, "thank you for suggesting Matt talk to Mama. Things are much better between us."

Roberto nodded, albeit grudgingly.

Matt sauntered over. "Could you teach me those rope tricks? I'd like to impress the cows."

"You mean there's something I can do better than you? Imagine that."

"There are a lot of things you can do better than me. Churn butter, sew on a button–well, maybe not that–wear a fancy gown."

"Did I ever tell you how exasperating you are?"

"Time and time again, my dear."

"Well, there's another thing I can do better than you." She pointed to his gun. "Bet I can hit more targets."

"Think so?"

"Yes, I do. Papa—"

"Taught you how to shoot."

"He did."

"All right, Annie Oakley. You're on, but how about we make a little bet? If I win, you clean my tack. And if you win, I'll take you to dinner at the Goose Neck Ridge Hotel. The food there's pretty good." He winced. "Sorry about that. Bad idea."

"Just because you took Miss Baxter there, doesn't mean I'm going to stay clear of it." She shook his hand. "You're on."

Matt slipped into the bunkhouse and returned with five empty cans. Dinged and full of holes, Cassandra assumed they'd already seen their fair share of target practice. Matt marked off fifteen paces and set the cans a foot apart. He marched back and handed over his Colt. "Ladies, first."

The gun had a longer barrel and was a bit heavier than the one her father had taught her to shoot. Cassandra switched the weapon from her right hand to her left, so she could wipe the sweat off her brow.

"Nervous?" he asked.

"No," she lied.

She steadied her right arm and sighted in the first can. The sun was reflecting off the lid, so she tilted her head to get a better view. Confident, she squeezed the trigger. The bullet sent dust flying just to the right of the can.

"You missed," Matt teased. "Now you have only one bullet left for each can."

"Would you please be quiet?"

He held a finger to his lips. "Not another word, ma'am."

Cassandra steadied her hand and fired again. This time the can flew into the air. She turned her nose up at Matt, who raised a palm to display the other targets. After she finished off the last four cans in succession, she smugly handed the gun back to him.

"I'm impressed," he said. "This means I have to hit all five cans the first time. Right?"

"Matt Atkins, you are the most arrogant man I have ever known."

He flashed her a smile and reloaded the gun, took aim, and then fired five times. He not only mowed down all five cans, but he also hit the first can again with the sixth bullet.

"My saddle's in the barn."

Cassandra stuck her tongue out at him.

He trailed a finger down the tip of her nose. "You sure are purty with all that fire in your eyes." As she huffed past him toward the barn, he snagged her wrist. "Why don't you do the tack later? We've got a free afternoon. Let's do something fun. How about goin' fishin'?"

"What makes you think I want to do anything else with you?"

He nudged her chin with his fist. "Ah, come on. Admit it. You like spendin' time with me."

"No more competing?"

"Afraid you'll lose?"

"Would you stop teasing me?"

"Maybe, but I do so enjoy it."

"If I didn't like you so much, I'd tell you to pack your saddlebag and move on."

"Like? Afraid to say that other word that begins with the letter L?"

"Hmm. Let me think. Lemons? Licorice? Lollipops?"

"Now, who's teasin' who? But the last two sound as sweet as you–most of the time."

Cassandra chased him all the way to the house.

Matt waited on the porch while she hurried inside and found a jar of pins and a spool of string. She also grabbed a couple pieces of bread to use as bait.

The pair trekked to a deep section of the creek where they found two straight sticks and started assembling their poles. Matt offered Cassandra instruction, and she took great delight in refusing it. After her pole was finished, she removed her boots and socks and rolled up her pants legs before working her way down the slope of the bank. At the edge of the water, her toes squiggled deep into the cool mud.

Matt pointed to an area of the creek farther downstream. "Don't you think we ought to go over there where it's shady?"

"This spot's good. I catch fish here all the time."

"That place looks better."

"How about I stay here, and you go down there? Whoever catches the least amount of fish cleans all the rest."

"You said you didn't want to compete."

"Are you game or not?"

"Sure, but I'd hate to beat you twice in one day."

"We'll see."

Cassandra had wanted Matt to fish beside her so they could talk, but her stubborn pride planted her feet in the mud and sealed her lips shut. She'd show him she could catch more fish.

She threaded a piece of bread on her hook, but when she threw in the line, the bait flew off. A fish zipped to the surface, snapped up the bread, and disappeared. She carefully pinched the next piece of bread onto the hook and within a few seconds, pulled in a squiggling trout. Matt had just thrown his line into the water.

"Excuse me." Cassandra held up her pole for him to see. The fish flipped its tail, sending sparkling drops of water into the air. "How many have you caught?" she asked.

"Very funny."

A few minutes later, she caught another trout, though it was a good deal smaller than the first. "Oh, Matt…"

He turned his back to her.

Fifteen minutes later, Cassandra had caught six more fish to Matt's two. He threw his pole into the water and marched over to her side. "All right. You're a better fisherman, or should I say fisherwoman, than I am."

Cassandra did her best not to gloat. "I'd say between my fishing and your shooting, we'll never go hungry." Her cheeks stung at the implication of her words.

"What exactly are you trying to say, Cassandra Jane? Hmm...?"

She shimmied away and bent over to pick up her string of fish. "We better get back if you want to clean all these fish before supper."

"How about we switch jobs? I clean my tack, and you clean the fish?"

"A deal's a deal."

"All right, but while I'm cleanin' those trout, I'm gonna sing, 'Scalin' the highest mountaintop for you, Cassandra Jane'."

Cassandra shook her head.

You're impossible, Matt Atkins. Truly impossible.

TWENTY-EIGHT

The morning Winston Harvey was slated to return from his sabbatical, Matt paced the boardwalk outside the lawyer's office. "You'd think after bein' gone for almost a month," he grumbled, "he'd open up his office first thing." A matronly woman, who was walking up the boardwalk, raised a brow at Matt before gathering the sides of her dress and quickly passing by him.

Matt continued his pacing, but it was almost noon before the door finally clicked open. He barged into the office and, after introducing himself, showed Mr. Harvey the paper he'd kept concealed under his mattress. The lawyer gave him a document that surpassed it in legality and another one signed by a judge in Boston. As Mr. Harvey explained the right to primogeniture, Matt leaned forward and listened with rapt attention. A half hour later, and with a nod of satisfaction, he shook Mr. Harvey's hand.

Before leaving the office, Matt whisked back the damask curtains and searched the boardwalk and street for Elizabeth Baxter. He sure didn't want to run into her again.

The street was empty except for a handful of horses tied to hitching posts and a scattering of people outside the mercantile, so he hustled next door to the bank. Inside, he tapped his foot and waited for William Higgins to complete his transaction with another customer. When Matt finally stepped up to the counter, Higgins took one look at him and took two steps back.

"M–Mr. Atkins, how nice to see you. What can I do for you today?"

"I've come to take care of the Pickett loan."

"It–It's too late. The bank has already drawn up the foreclosure papers."

"You had an agreement with Helen and Cassandra. You promised them more time."

"It couldn't be helped. Mr. Brig—" Fear sprang into Higgins's eyes. "It–It was the shareholders' decision, not mine." Perspiration formed on his upper lip. "Sometimes things just..." He waved his hands. "They just happen."

Matt withdrew a thick envelope from inside his shirt and riffled the money he had wired to him from Boston. "Let's make some of those things unhappen. Shall we?"

☆☆☆

Before Matt left the bank, Higgins shoved a bulky package at him. He pumped Matt's hand with enthusiasm and promised he wouldn't tell Cassandra about their deal. Matt carefully strapped the package inside his saddlebag. "It's not exactly what I'd hoped for, King, but it's a start."

"What's a start?" A woman's voice behind him asked.

Matt sighed a deep breath. He should have known. It was Elizabeth Baxter.

"Hello, Elizabeth."

"Now, Matt, where are your manners? You're supposed to remove your hat in the presence of a lady." She played with the collar of her dress and fluffed a dark curl that was peeking out from underneath another bonnet trimmed in feathers.

When Matt yanked off his Stetson, a lock of hair fell over his eyes. Elizabeth raised a gloved hand as if to brush the hair into place. Matt jumped away from her and smoothed it back himself.

"Why, Matt Atkins, I do declare. You are the most nervous man I've ever met. Would it have anything to do with that pretty little sister of yours?"

"I'm sorry I lied to you, Elizabeth. To tell you the truth, I plan to ask Cassandra Jane to marry me. Today."

"You didn't have to string me along. I felt such a fool." She touched the back of her hand to her forehead.

"I didn't mean to hurt you. I don't always have the best way with women."

"Judging by Miss Pickett's jealousy and in light of your declaration, I'd say you're not giving yourself enough credit."

"I'm sorry. Really I am." Matt hoped his voice conveyed his sincerity.

Elizabeth stroked one of the feathers sticking out of her bonnet. "You're not the only man in town, you know. Bill Sanders invited me to supper last week. Since he works at the hotel, he got a special rate on the meal. He's taking me to church this Sunday, and afterward, I've been invited to his parents' home for dinner."

Matt sent silent praise Bill's way for occupying Elizabeth's mind elsewhere. "Bill is a nice enough young man."

"He's handsome in his own way with that mop of reddish-color hair. Not the color of a chestnut's coat, mind you." Elizabeth covered a giggle with her hand.

Matt's cheeks burned at being reminded of how he had described Cassandra's hair the day he met Elizabeth.

"Never you fear. I didn't breathe a word to your lady friend that you compared her to a horse."

Matt smiled at Elizabeth. She sure was something. Bill *was* a lucky man. "I heard you're the new schoolmarm."

"I'm glad for the opportunity to help develop young minds. School starts in two weeks, but I've already met many of the students." Her forehead wrinkled. "I'll be happy though when they stop saying, 'Miss Cassie did things like this,' or 'Miss Cassie, did things like that'."

"I'm sure in no time, the children will be singin' your praises as well." Matt waved a hand. "I need to go, Elizabeth. It was nice seein' ya." This time he meant it.

"Good-bye, Matt, and good luck."

With a final wave, Matt headed out of town. At the sound of an approaching stagecoach, he glanced back. Curiosity had already tempted the townsfolk into the street to see who might disembark.

"Another time, boy." Matt touched King with his heels, and the horse broke into a gallop. "Let the townsfolk have their fun," he hollered above his horse's thundering hooves, "I've got a woman to propose to."

★★★

The stagecoach had barely rolled to a halt when the driver called out, "If you're gettin' out at Goose Neck Ridge, move it along."

Victoria Garrett gratefully pushed open the door but pulled it shut right before the driver heaved down a bulging mailbag. She glared up at him, but all he said was, "Ya want out or not?"

A small crowd surged forward, hoping for news from their loved ones. Arthur Skinner pushed his way through. "Come on, folks. Move back. You'll get your letters when I'm done sortin' 'em." He grabbed the mail sack and headed across the street to the telegraph office. The people turned as one and trotted after him like young pups chasing a bone.

Victoria rubbed her aching lower back and thanked heaven she had finally arrived from Boston. The springs on the stagecoach sadly needed repair, and she could not have endured another minute of the dust kicked up by the coach's wheels. On the long trip to Goose Neck Ridge, she'd questioned her decision to journey so far from home, but the possibility of convincing Ethan to marry her and restoring her reputation had strengthened her resolve.

It had been impossible to keep her hair styled in the stagecoach, so she'd opted for a loose chignon. But several miles out of town, she crimped a few wisps of hair to frame her face. The results must have been satisfactory, for when she reopened the stagecoach door, three men stood in a row, staring at her with unabashed admiration. They rushed forward to help her step down. Victoria chose the hand of the more handsome of the three.

Though heading toward afternoon, she planned to freshen up and search for Ethan immediately. Common sense told her to wait until morning, but she'd already frittered away the last two years. She didn't want to waste another day.

Victoria presented the handsome man with a winsome smile and asked, "Would you be so kind as to tell me which hotel provides the best accommodations?"

"That would be the Goose Neck Ridge Hotel."

Victoria batted her sooty eyelashes at the other two hapless men. "Would you please see that my two trunks and valise arrive at the hotel?" The men bumped into each other in their effort to procure her matching luggage.

Placing a gloved hand through the crook of the first man's arm, she said, "If you're not busy, I need an escort."

The man blushed and stammered but managed to lead her across the street and up the boardwalk toward a two-story building with porches on both levels. The porch on the second floor sagged in the middle.

I hope the ranch Ethan's cousin is helping him buy will far surpass the buildings of this ramshackle town, Victoria thought. *If not, I'll change that in a hurry.* Thankfully the man bypassed the structure and stepped up to the next one.

Other than the bank, the Goose Neck Ridge Hotel was the grandest building in town. Rows of shiny windows lined its two stories, and a green canopy stretched out from the first floor to shade the hotel's occupants.

"Would you please have a buggy with a gentle horse outside the hotel in fifteen minutes?" Victoria asked the man by her side.

He hustled to do her bidding with such haste, he tripped down the hotel stairs. He would have stumbled into the street had a gentleman passing by not caught him. His cheeks reddened as he looked back at Victoria and said, "Sorry."

Victoria's pert lips turned down into a frown. Men. They were all the same no matter what part of the country they were from–predictable and easy to manipulate.

Despite her disapproval, she thanked the young man for his escort, then turned and crossed the threshold of the hotel. A tiled floor pointed the way to the front desk where Victoria rang the bell and then rapped her knuckles on the counter. A freckled-face clerk came up the hall and introduced himself as Bill, then pushed the register over for her to sign.

Victoria gave a haughty sniff. Why did the young man go by the simple name of Bill instead of William? Another sign of this town's utter lack of sophistication.

She followed him up the hallway to room 107. He motioned for her to enter and asked in a voice a half-octave above tenor, "Will this do?"

"If this is all you have to offer," she said, stepping inside the room. "I'm expecting the arrival of my luggage. Will you oversee its delivery?"

"Sure thing, ma'am. As soon as it gets here."

Bill made a grab for the silver dollar Victoria flipped to him, but he missed. The coin rolled underneath a dresser, so he got on his hands and knees to retrieve it. With a wide-toothed grin he thanked her and closed the door behind him.

Victoria gave the room a critical eye. Two rugs lay end-to-end on the floor, and a Windsor chair sat at an angle from a low-lying table. When she tested the brass bed, the springs squeaked, reminding her of mice. With trepidation, she peeled back the quilted bedspread. Thank goodness, the sheets at least appeared to be clean.

She poured water from a ceramic ewer into the basin sitting on a washstand. Ignoring the folded towel next to it, she dipped her handkerchief into the water and dragged the wet cloth over her hot skin.

"Wouldn't a bath be heavenly?" she asked her reflection. "But there's no time for that luxury now. It's time to find Ethan and have him fall in love with me all over again."

Her mind drifted to the reason she'd broken off her engagement with Ethan in the first place–Warren Wythe. She'd met Warren, a successful industrialist, at a charity ball her parents had sponsored. She had left Ethan's side and gravitated toward the short, older man with a decent face and pockets dripping with money. His bold chatter about his prosperous business, sizeable bank accounts, and two country estates intrigued Victoria. Before the month was over, she married Warren in her parents' garden under the very gazebo Ethan had proposed to her.

But after they returned from a European honeymoon, Victoria discovered her new husband had only one true love. Business. A year of late nights at the office paved the way for Bryce Ealdwode, an English Count who was visiting Boston.

A mutual friend introduced Victoria to Bryce at the opera. He was fifteen years older but still as handsome and charming as only an Englishman could be. At first, she slighted his alluring accent and smooth flattery, but Warren's lack of attention galled her and demanded retribution.

Each rendezvous with Bryce proved more brazen than the last until Victoria slipped the confines of her loveless marriage. But the moment she succumbed to Count Ealdwode's bedroom, he discarded her like an unwanted, dirty rag. To heighten her humiliation, he bragged of his conquest all over Boston. When the news reached Warren, he practically threw her out of the manor. If Victoria's parents hadn't allowed her to crawl back home, she would have ended up in the streets.

Victoria shook her head to erase the image. Count Ealdwode was a mere footnote in her past. Her future now depended upon Ethan. She was certain she could get him back. What competition would she find from any woman living in a town called Goose Neck Ridge?

After wiping away the dust from her travel, Victoria retrieved a bottle of perfume from her valise. The fragrance did its best to chase away the stuffiness from the room. She dabbed the perfume behind her ears and on her wrists before donning her lavender day dress with its matching velvet jacket. Then she ran a brush through her thick hair and with one last glance in the mirror, hurried to the lobby, anxious to see if the handsome man had fulfilled her bidding.

When she stepped outside, Victoria squinted at the sun and wished for a parasol. She hadn't taken the Texas weather into account and had packed clothing suitable for the cooler temperatures of Boston.

Her escort stood outside the hotel with a placid mare and a serviceable, but old-fashioned buggy. He rushed to her side and assisted her into the conveyance.

She pried her fingers from his hand. "I am grateful for your help, but I need something else."

"Anything."

"I need directions to the Lazy Acres Ranch. Isn't that where Phillip Brigham lives?"

Though clearly disappointed, the man braved a smile and said, "Yes, it is. Head west for five miles toward a range of hills, then turn north at a stand of scraggly mesquite trees, travel another mile, and you can't miss it."

Victoria thanked him, released the buggy brake, and slapped the lines on the horse's back. The bay jumped forward into a surprisingly brisk jog. Though Victoria deplored horses, she was thankful she had learned to drive a buggy.

She repositioned her fingers through the reins and with great anticipation headed toward Lazy Acres. Phillip Brigham would know where she could find his cousin Ethan.

☆☆☆

That morning, before Matt left for Goose Neck Ridge, he'd playfully tugged Cassandra's braid and said, "I'll explain everything as soon as I get back."

His blue eyes held promise as wide as the Texas sky, and Cassandra had given him a hearty wave as he and King left the ranch at a ground-eating gallop. She hoped when he returned, a marriage proposal would follow his promised explanation of what he'd been up to.

Eager to finish her chores, Cassandra asked Carlos to help her fix a section of broken fence line. While the vaquero saddled his Paint, she gathered the needed equipment.

"Carlos," Cassandra said as Smokey fell in line with Carlos's horse. "What was the most special day of your life?"

"Every day is wonderful in the Lord."

"But doesn't one stick out in your mind?"

"Let me see." He scratched his head. "Ah, the day your father gave me my first horse was very nice."

When Carlos had left Mexico and arrived at the Triple P, Cassandra's father had taken pity on the homesick young man staring at a pinto pony. He handed over the reins and told Carlos the animal was his. Since that day and in fond remembrance, the vaquero had chosen to ride only horses with large white patches over a dark coat.

"Papa enjoyed making people happy," Cassandra said. "He would do anything for someone he loved. Is there another day you remember as being special?"

"My first birthday at the Triple P. I had never celebrated the day of my birth."

"I don't remember that."

"You were but a small girl. Maria made me a nice dinner with a big chocolate cake. Señora Pickett wrote 'Happy Birthday, Carlos' on a piece of paper and tacked it to the wall. It was a most happy day."

He dismounted at a break in the barbed wire fence, and Cassandra handed him the pouch of supplies.

"Why do you ask?" He slipped on his leather gloves and started stretching the broken barbed wire across the post. Cassandra followed behind and stapled the wire back into place.

"No reason," she replied.

"Señorita Cassie, I do not think you speak the truth."

Cassandra could not keep silent any longer. She had to tell someone. "Carlos, today might be the special day I have dreamed about."

"And why is that?"

"When Matt gets back, I think he's going to ask me to marry him."

A smile split Carlos's face. "This is very good."

"I think so, too."

"For a long time, I have believed you and Señor Matt would make a fine pair. He will also be a good boss for the Triple P."

"I will still be in charge of the ranch."

Carlos's eyes shone brightly. "Señor Matt will have his hands full. But with the two of you, the Triple P will soon be on its feet again."

"If Mr. Brewer agrees to my idea, Mama and I won't have to worry about the loan."

"If Señor Brewer becomes your partner, may I keep working here at the ranch? I would not like to work at a mill with all those people and equipment."

"Mama and I plan to rebuild the Triple P. We might make you the foreman."

"Do you think Señor Matt will mind?"

"Señor Matt will have his hands full with me, remember?"

When she and Carlos finished the fence, Cassandra tied the pouch of supplies behind her saddle and mounted Smokey. "I'll race you back, Carlos. Lope, Smokey."

The horse broke into a canter, and Cassandra raced home to her dreams.

☆☆☆

Victoria screamed at the sky. That fool of a man had given her poor directions. She refused to admit, she didn't know the difference between a mesquite tree and an oak tree, and her ignorance was responsible for her current predicament.

The afternoon sun showed little mercy as it beat down, adding to her misery. Her dress clung to her skin and foam dripped from the horse's mouth. Victoria feared the beast would drop dead and leave her stranded.

"God," she gasped, "if you do exist, I need a miracle." She clucked to the tired animal and continued to wander aimlessly.

A half-hour later Victoria squinted at the horizon. Was that some type of a building? Tears of joy blurred her eyes. As though sensing water and a place to rest, the weary horse broke into a trot even before Victoria could slap the reins on his back.

As she drew closer, Victoria exclaimed, "This can't be Lazy Acres. The man in town said Phillip owned a sprawling, one-story adobe. That house is two-story and certainly not spacious."

The horse passed under a wooden sign declaring Victoria's assumption correct. She'd not arrived at Lazy Acres. She had arrived at a ranch called the Triple P.

Twenty-Nine

Cassandra had just finished helping Roberto pick the horse stalls clean when Matt and King cantered onto the Triple P compound. She dashed out to greet them.

"Did you get what you needed from Mr. Harvey?"

"You bet I did, darlin'." He swung a long leg over the saddle horn and slid down beside her. "Let me take care of King, and I'll tell you everything."

Cassandra was about to reply, "It's about time," when Carlos ran toward them from the vicinity of the creek.

"Señor Matt, Old Bull pushed his way through that new section of fence. Rafael is trying to keep him separated from the lady friends he should not visit. Can you and Roberto help us, please?"

Matt handed the reins to Cassandra. "Would you mind?" He tapped the tip of her nose. "I'll be right back."

"Well, hurry up. I can't wait much longer."

Matt motioned to Roberto, and the two followed Carlos over the creek to the broken fence.

When Cassandra led King into his stall, he touched noses with Smokey. After she unsaddled and groomed the horse, she gave him water and an armful of hay. Smokey shoved his nose over the railing of his stall and whinnied in protest.

"Are you jealous, boy?"

She threw hay in the corner of Smokey's stall and leaned against the stall door to watch the horses eat. The sound of their chewing and the scent of leather and hay filled the barn.

From where she stood, she could see Matt and the other men off in the distance still working on the fence. With a sigh, she picked up the saddle soap and a soft rag and started to clean the tack. Visions of her and Matt as husband and wife kept the chore from becoming tedious.

She was finishing the last bridle when Samantha sauntered up and wrapped her body around Cassandra's leg. Five kittens scampered after their mother, tripping over each other in an effort to greet Cassandra first. She picked up a smudgy-gray kitten and snuggled its warm body against her neck. The kitten purred and licked Cassandra's cheek with its raspy tongue.

"Guess what, Shadow? I think Matt's going to ask me to marry him." She hugged the fluff of fur. "And I'm going to say—"

The neigh of an approaching horse interrupted her affirmation. Cassandra set the kitten down and stepped outside. She brushed off the front of her shirt and shielded her eyes against the glare of the sun.

An open buggy, driven by a woman with white hair, entered the compound. She yanked the horse to halt within a few yards of the barn. The animal's head sagged to the ground, and Cassandra's heart went out to the hot, tired beast.

Exasperation marked the woman's voice. "Oh, thank goodness I've found someone. I'm quite lost, and this stupid animal is about to keel over and die. I'm looking for the Lazy Acres Ranch. Can you give me directions?"

Cassandra gaped at the stunning woman with the musical eastern accent. She'd been mistaken about the stranger's hair. It wasn't white. It was silvery-blonde. She ran fingers through her own hair and wished for a brush.

The woman wore a lavender dress with an embroidered jacket that matched the purple color of her eyes. Though the dress was exquisite, Cassandra judged the jacket as impractical. No one around here wore velvet in August, and for heaven's sake, why hadn't she taken it off in this heat?

"My name is Victoria Garrett," the woman stated, "and I've come all the way from Boston to see Ethan Brigham. I understand he's at the Lazy Acres Ranch."

The woman's words puzzled Cassandra. Hadn't Matt said a violet-eyed woman with silver-colored hair had jilted his friend Ethan? Was he related to Phillip? Matt had gotten nervous when she asked if he knew the Brighams of Boston. Did he know them? And was that one of the things he planned to tell her?

"I don't know any Ethan Brigham," Cassandra replied. "Are you sure you don't mean Phillip Brigham? He's the owner of Lazy Acres." Her curiosity got the better of her. "Would you happen to be the woman who was engaged to Matt Atkin's friend?"

Victoria arched dark blonde brows. "Ethan is Phillip's cousin, and he's here in Goose Neck Ridge. And though his middle name is Matthew, he'd never go by the common name of Matt. Now, if you would kindly give this beast water and point me in the right direction, I'll be on my way."

She turned at the sound of approaching footsteps. "Ethan," her voice rose in breathy recognition. "Whatever are you doing here?" She jumped off the rig, flipped the reins to Cassandra, and darted straight for Matt.

"Victoria?"

"Darling, how could you run off and leave me to do this silly cowboy-thing? You broke my heart. Your parents' hearts too."

Cassandra's dreams crashed to her feet in a thousand pieces. The man standing in front of her, looking all the world like he wanted to run and hide, was related to Phillip, and worse yet, the woman devouring him with her eyes was the beautiful blonde who'd rejected him. Matt Atkins was Ethan Brigham.

Betrayal pushed aside Cassandra's shattered heart. "I thought your parents were dead–Ethan."

Victoria slipped a hand into the bend of Matt's arm. "Don't be ridiculous. Ethan's parents are very much alive." She batted her lashes at Matt. "Your father showed me the telegram you sent and told me about the ranch you planned to buy. Though I didn't envision one so small. But don't worry. We'll tear down that old house and build a much larger one. The two of us can make this little old place the biggest ranch in all of Texas."

☆☆☆

Matt disengaged himself from Victoria's arms. What in blue blazes was she doing here? His eyes flew to Cassandra. "Cassandra, this is not what you think."

"Ethan," Victoria said, "you shouldn't call a servant by her first name. You've been out west far too long. I will have to reteach you everything."

She arched her brows at Cassandra. "Where I'm from, women don't work in the barn. Shouldn't you be in the house baking or something?"

Matt lunged between the two women. "Victoria, you're wrong. This young lady is not a servant, though she works as hard as one." He gulped. Cassandra did not appear the least bit pleased he had defended her. "Cassandra Jane and her mother own this ranch."

"Cassandra Jane?" Victoria's lilting voice rose. "You call her by her middle name as well? And please explain yourself. I surmised this ranch to be yours, though I am relieved to find out it isn't."

Matt gave a nervous laugh, frantically trying to think of a way to calm down both women. "The Triple P belongs to Miss Pickett and her mother. I work here."

Cassandra finally spoke up. "Now, I'm Miss Pickett? Before long, you won't acknowledge me at all. Maybe I should leave the two of you alone."

Victoria laid a hand on Cassandra's sleeve. "Would you mind?" She pulled back and studied her glove as though touching Cassandra had dirtied it.

Matt pleaded with Cassandra. "Please. I can explain."

"So, you've told me time and time again."

"She's a feisty little thing–this boss of yours." Victoria turned her attention to Cassandra. "Cassandra, Cassandra Jane, or whatever name you go by, since you seem to like working outside, would you please run along and take care of the horse? Ethan and I have so much to talk about."

The screen door of the house squeaked open, and Helen stepped out onto the porch. Matt didn't know if he should beg for Mrs. Pickett's help or insist she go back inside until he sorted the whole mess out.

She decided the matter for him. She crossed the yard and extended a hand to Victoria. The young woman hesitated before shaking it. Helen lifted a brow at the rebuff. Her gaze shifted from Cassandra to Matt and then returned to Cassandra.

"Mrs. Pickett," Matt blurted. "This is Victoria Garrett, I mean, Victoria Wythe from Boston. She's a friend of the family." The word *friend* sounded weak even to his ears. "She's come all this way to see me."

"How nice." Helen stepped closer to her daughter. "Isn't it, Cassandra?"

Even though Matt could tell Mrs. Pickett was far from pleased, he thanked God for her intervention. Surely, Cassandra wouldn't make a scene in front of her mother. If he could get her to take Victoria inside, he'd clear all this up with Cassandra.

"Mrs. Pickett, I'm sure Victoria's thirsty from her trip. Could you offer her a glass of tea or lemonade?" Guilt filled Matt at his contrivance. Mrs. Pickett would show hospitality no matter what the circumstance. Hadn't she done as much for him?

Helen's face showed immediate concern. "Please, come inside. I will have Maria pour you a glass of lemonade and give you a slice of the molasses pie she baked this morning."

Victoria glanced up at Matt. "Are you coming?"

"I'll join you in a bit. I'm going to help Cassandra tend to the horse."

"Well, don't be long. It's only a hired hack." She gave Helen a sugary smile. "I'm all yours."

After the two women entered the house, Matt tried to pry the reins from Cassandra's fingers. She pushed past him, her eyes glittering a brilliant emerald. "Your Miss Garrett told me to take care of the horse."

"She's not *my* Miss Garrett, and Victoria is a missus, not a miss. Well, she was the last time I heard."

"You must have heard wrong. She's come all this way for her long-lost love, Ethan Brigham, who just happens to be looking to buy a ranch. I bet it's the Triple P the moment the bank forecloses on it."

"I did not come here with the intention of buying your ranch. My interest was in Lazy Acres."

"Sure. I bet it was." Cassandra stormed into the barn, pulling the horse behind her. Smokey laid back his ears at the mare. A cynical laugh escaped Cassandra's lips. "Horses have more sense than some people."

"This is not the horse's fault."

"You're right. It's yours."

"I'll explain everything as soon as you let me take care of her."

"Oh, this will be rich." She dropped the reins in Matt's hand and leaned against the door of Smokey's stall.

Matt unhitched and led the tired animal into an empty stall. He threw an armful of hay and sloshed a small amount of water into a bucket before closing the stall door and facing Cassandra.

"My real name is Ethan Brigham." Matt replaced his cowboy twang with the easier eastern accent. "And Victoria was right. My middle name is Matthew. My adopted mother's maiden name was Atkins, so Matt Atkins isn't too much of a stretch. And my parents are alive–that is my adopted parents are. My birth parents aren't."

"That didn't make a bit of sense. Whatever are you talking about?"

"The parents who reared me, Walter and Mary Helen Brigham of White Oak Manor, are alive. And they do breed Morgan horses. Just like I said."

"Mary *Helen*? You can do better than that."

"Her name *is* Mary Helen."

"Oh, please. Go on."

"My real parents are Harold and Margaret Brigham. I'm Phillip's older brother."

"Phillip is an only child. And that woman said you were his cousin."

"Even she doesn't know the whole story." He commanded his mind to keep every fact straight. "Remember the night you told me about Margaret's first child? The one she had out of wedlock?'

Cassandra acknowledged the question with the briefest of nods.

"That baby was me."

"I don't believe you."

"I'm telling you the truth. I promise," Matt willed his voice to remain calm. "To save the McAllister name and still keep me in the Brigham family, Margaret's parents gave me to Walter and Mary Helen and made them promise to never reveal my parentage."

Matt didn't blame Cassandra's incredulous look. He'd had a hard time believing Walter's letter the first time he read it.

"He and Mary Helen had tried for years to have a child and were in the process of adoption. My arrival at the Brigham residence seemed a natural conclusion of that process. When I was old enough to question Walter about my birth parents, he said the adoption agency had lost the papers in a fire and he had no record of them."

"And you never wanted to find your parents?"

"No. I figured if they didn't want me, I didn't want or need them."

"And I suppose Harold didn't know he had another son?"

"He didn't until last year when he and Phillip went to Boston for a visit. I guess the burden of Walter's secret became too much for him to bear and he finally told Harold."

"I'm sure Harold wasn't pleased."

"You're right. He wrote a new will and named me his rightful heir with the proviso of Phillip's compensation if I chose Lazy Acres over White Oak Manor."

"Phillip would have preferred that. All he cares about is money."

Matt took Cassandra's agreement on this one small point as a good sign. He rushed on. "Harold hired a private investigator. He wanted to meet me and see if I had any interest in Lazy Acres, but he died before the man had a chance to find me."

Cassandra's eyes narrowed. "Assuming this is true, and I'm not saying it is, how'd it all come to light?"

"When Harold died, Walter's conscience must have gotten the better of him. He wanted me to have what was legally and rightfully mine. He mailed me a letter explaining everything along with a copy of Harold's revised will. He sent the original to Mr. Harvey with a letter from a judge, stating everything was legitimate."

"Then why'd you lie about needing a job? Why didn't you just march onto Lazy Acres and take it?" Cassandra tore a piece of hay apart bit-by-bit.

"I didn't aim to kick a younger brother I didn't know, off a ranch he thought was his. I wanted to find out more about him first. Since your ranch was right next to Lazy Acres, it was a perfect place to check things out. I was looking for a job the day I rode onto the Triple P. I just didn't tell you why."

"And your plans to breed that–that horse of yours? Did you lie about that too?"

Matt's slumped back against the stall door. "Yes. I needed an excuse to come and go without anyone questioning me."

"Like me? And Mama?"

"I should have been honest with you and your mother right from the start. But when I saw Phillip trying to kiss you the day I rode up and found out who he was, I decided to take Lazy Acres from him anyway. Can you understand?"

"No. I cannot. And even if I believed your ridiculous story, how do you explain that Victoria woman?"

"We were engaged several years ago, but she broke off our engagement and married another man. That's why I left Boston."

"Well, she's obviously not married now. And what about your father owing money to the bank and you not having any?"

Matt grimaced. She wasn't about to make this any easier. "I said that so you and your mother might be more sympathetic toward me. But I told you the truth about my financial situation at the time. The only money I had on me was my last pay from Big George."

"And now? As the owner of the biggest ranch in Texas and the heir of a Bostonian estate, I'd say money is no longer a problem."

"You're right. I've got plenty. When I got back from Fort Worth, I planned to tell you everything and see if you and your mother would like to start a lumber mill. But you'd already asked Mr. Brewer to partner you in one, and then that mess happened with Elizabeth Baxter." He lifted his hands helplessly in the air.

"Miss Baxter and now Miss Garrett. You have quite the dance card, don't you? Well, you can erase me and the Triple P off of it. Neither of us needs you."

"Come on, Cassandra," Matt pleaded. "If the deal with Mr. Brewer doesn't come through, I can still help. I could pay off your loan."

"Oh, really? There you go again, thinking you can waltz right in and solve everything. I told you, we don't need your help."

"I didn't mean pay off your loan," he lied. "I meant I could loan you the rest of the money. You can pay me back when you get the chance. Or maybe I could buy—"

"You're the last person on earth I'd be indebted to. You spin a fine tale, Ethan Matthew Atkins Brigham, or whoever you are, but I didn't trust you the first day you stepped onto my ranch, and I certainly don't trust you now. Enjoy your last supper at the Triple P. First thing tomorrow, I want you to leave my ranch and never set foot on it again." She threw a bridle on Smokey, jumped on his back, and the pair tore out of the barn.

Matt rubbed his sleeve over his burning eyes. He'd only cried one other time in his adult life, a month ago when he read about the deaths of his birth parents, Margaret and Harold Brigham.

He didn't blame Cassandra. His story was outrageous. He'd comply with her wishes. First thing tomorrow, he'd leave. He owed her that.

THIRTY

Cassandra dug her heels into her horse's sides, and the gray gelding shot across the prairie. When they neared Cedar Ridge, she guided Smokey through rock formations and scrub brush until they reached the mouth of the canyon where her father had died. She slid off Smokey's back, collapsed at the water's edge, and cast her tear-brimmed eyes toward heaven.

"Why, Lord? Why did you bring Matt Atkins into my life? You were wrong. He wasn't the answer to my prayers."

You are wrong, the Holy Spirit convicted. *My will is perfect, and I promise to work out all things for those who love me.*

"I don't see how anything good can come from this."

She chucked a rock into the waterhole. The stone sunk with a plop, sending ripples across the surface of the pond.

How like life. Matt's arrival at the Triple P had started a chain of events that reached out and touched everything in its path.

She pitched another rock into the water. "So, what do I do now, Lord?" A screeching hawk riding the wind was her only reply.

★★★

An hour later, Cassandra had cleared the entire bank of stones, and long shadows were creeping over the ground. A chilly breeze blew across the face of the canyon. She better get home before her mother worried.

"I hope that wind's bringing rain," she told Smokey as he scrambled over the rocky ground leading away from the canyon. "We could use it. Maybe some good might come out of this day after all."

When Cassandra arrived back at the ranch, the compound was empty, but Miss Garrett's buggy was still there. Where was everyone?

She unsaddled Smokey, then rushed inside to see why that woman from Boston hadn't left yet. When she heard voices coming from the dining room, she tiptoed up the hallway to listen in and have a peek.

"It sounds like your passage to Goose Neck Ridge was eventful," Helen commented.

"The train ride was fine," Victoria replied. "I've ridden a train dozens of times, but I've never traveled by stagecoach."

"You haven't?" Roberto asked. He sat at the table with his chin propped up in his hands, his eyes shining at Victoria.

Cassandra tapped her fingers on the doorframe. *So much for his childish infatuation with me.*

"Oh, no," Victoria replied. "Father's carriages are nothing like that one. It was big and smelly, and dust kept blowing inside the windows, but the worst part was the man who drove it. His teeth were stained, and he spat awful tobacco juice everywhere. And his language. Why, I'd never heard such words before."

"Maybe," Maria said in sarcastic tone of voice, "the man wanted to impress you. You being from Boston and all."

"If that were true, he did a horrible job of it. And imagine my shock when another equally awful man hopped up beside him wielding a gun the length of this table."

"As long as this table?" Maria quizzed.

"Well, maybe not that long, but it did scare me half to death."

Rafael joined the conversation. "He was a shotgun messenger. His job is to guard the money box from robbers."

"I found that out later, but I also didn't realize we'd change horses every twenty miles. The driver said I could get a meal at the second stop, but the place was little more than a shack, and the food wasn't fit for our dogs back home."

"And what do your dogs eat?" Maria asked. "Steak and lobster?"

"Maria," Helen's voice lifted.

Victoria glanced around the table and said, "I've overstayed my welcome. I should go."

"But Señorita Victoria," Carlos argued. "If you leave at this late hour, you might get lost again."

"This is true," Rafael's booming voice agreed.

Cassandra longed to march in and call the men out. Didn't they have enough problems already without inviting another?

"They are right," Helen said. "You must spend the night and leave in the morning."

Though she didn't care for the idea, Cassandra conceded the men's comments and her mother's invitation were wise.

Out here, one didn't turn visitors away, especially at this hour. The prairie, while alluring and serene during the day, could turn cold and hostile at night.

"Will Ethan mind if I stay?" Victoria asked.

So, Matt hasn't left yet? He's probably back at the bunkhouse packing. Good. He and that woman can leave tomorrow–together.

Carlos spoke again. "Señor Matt–uh–Señor Ethan, would not want anyone, and certainly not a lady, to travel at—"

"Carlos," Maria interrupted her brother, "is it not time to feed the livestock?"

"We already fed the animals."

Maria's barrage of Spanish was so quick, Cassandra understood only *fool*, *hurry up*, and *barn*, but Carlos understood. He almost knocked Cassandra over as he fled the room. Rafael and Roberto tailed Carlos's heels as if fearing a reprimand as well.

Helen looked across the dining room and noticed Cassandra. She excused herself from the table, took Cassandra by the elbow, and escorted her down the hall.

Cassandra freed her arm. "Mama, what are you doing?"

"I am keeping you from saying something we will both regret."

"This may surprise you, and as much as I hate to admit it, you're right. It's too late to send Miss Garrett back to town, but don't expect me to be a gracious hostess."

"I only ask you to be a civil hostess."

"I'll try, Mama. I'll really try."

☆☆☆

At dinner, Carlos delivered a message from Matt. "Señor Ethan will not be joining us. He says he is not feeling himself this evening."

"Of course, he's not feeling himself," Cassandra said. "He's not even sure who he is."

She held back a smug smile at the meal Maria had prepared for their guest. It rivaled anything she assumed a fine restaurant in Boston would serve: thick juicy steaks, roasted potatoes, string beans, and velvety vanilla pudding for dessert. Victoria raved on and on about Texas cooking—far too brightly, in Cassandra's opinion—until she wanted to throw that cooking right onto the blonde woman's lap. As the meal wore on, Cassandra counted the minutes until Maria rose from her seat and started stacking the dirty plates at the end of the table.

Cassandra was carrying an armful of dishes toward the kitchen when Matt's frame filled the doorway of the dining room. All heads turned toward him. "I'm sorry to disturb you. I wanted to—"

"Ah, Señor Matt." Maria grabbed his arm and gave Cassandra a sly wink. "You are just in time. Here. Sit. A big man like you can finish what is left of the food."

Matt's gaze fell to the food that had now grown cold. "*Gracias*, but I'll pass on your kind offer."

Maria pushed him down onto an empty chair and set a plate in front of him with a clatter. "Nonsense. Be a good boy and eat."

Cassandra refused to make eye contact with Matt while she finished clearing the table. Finally, all the dishes but Matt's untouched plate were stacked in the kitchen. "Mama, if you'll excuse me, I want to check on Smokey."

Her mother hesitated. "I'd rather you not. I think the Lord is going to send rain this evening."

"I'll be fine. I need some fresh air. It's stuffy in here."

Her words had the desired effect. Matt's face blanched. The quiet voice of the Holy Spirit convicted Cassandra for throwing fiery darts at Matt's heart, but she pushed away the conviction. Matt had no heart.

Bullet trotted up when she stepped onto the porch. She ruffled the dog's ears. "Bullet, you're the only friend I have right now."

"I'm your friend, Cassandra." Matt's low voice behind her made her jump.

She whirled on him. "How can you say that? Friends don't lie to each other."

"I said I'm sorry. What more do you want?"

"I want you to leave."

"I plan to, but before I do, I want to make one thing clear. What I did was wrong. I'm not perfect. I never claimed to be. But you've taken it upon yourself to be judge and jury with no chance of forgiveness. You're on such a high pedestal, no man could reach you. I'm glad I realized that before I asked you again to mar—."

Cassandra slapped Matt so hard, her palm stung. Other than a twitch of his jaw, he didn't even flinch.

"Are you happy now?" he asked.

"I am. And I'll be happier when I wake up tomorrow morning and find you gone."

"As you wish. Good night, Miss Pickett." Matt clicked his heels together and headed toward the bunkhouse.

Cassandra ran to the barn, slipped a bridle over Smokey's head, and for the second time that day, vaulted onto his bare back. She failed to heed the black expanse of clouds brooding on the horizon. "Come on, Smokey. Let's get out of here." She urged the horse onward, not caring which direction they headed as long it was away from Matt Atkins. Smokey grabbed the bit and galloped into the prairie.

Cassandra upbraided herself for not making Matt leave the moment he had ridden onto the Triple P. Instead, she had allowed him to enter her home and her heart, and he'd repaid that devotion with one lie on top of another.

She reined Smokey to a trot. For the first time, she noticed the absence of the chirping and humming of nocturnal creatures. The chill wind of a fast-approaching storm made her shiver. As the sky darkened, she couldn't get her bearings. A few minutes later, jagged bolts of lightning ripped the sky and blinding sheets of rain soaked her to the skin. The sound of rumbling thunder spooked Smokey.

"What have I gotten us into, boy?" Cassandra yelled over the tumult. She urged Smokey toward a distant smattering of lights. They could seek shelter there until the storm broke. But when she drew closer, Cassandra groaned. How could she have been so foolish? Of course they were on Lazy Acres property. Where else could they be?

She nudged Smokey's sides with her heels. "We've got to get out of this storm, and right now I'd prefer Phillip's company over Matt's."

Smokey splashed through puddles on the way to the barn. Cassandra jumped off his back and looped his reins over the rail of an empty stall. She rubbed him down with a gunny sack before making a dash for the house. At the door, she paused and questioned her decision to seek shelter here rather than take a chance and ride back home. Maybe a thunderstorm was safer than a lion's den. She was turning to flee back to the barn when the door groaned open.

"Cassandra?" Phillip's voice reached out to her. "Is that you?"

"It–It's me."

"What are you doing out on a night like this? Come in. You'll catch your death of cold."

Cassandra stepped inside the hacienda and untangled her wet hair. Her rain-soaked body trembled. She followed Phillip into the study where a fire crackled in the hearth. The comforting heat and smell of cedar lured her toward the flames and away from Phillip and the dark shadows of the room.

She forced her voice to remain light. "On an impulse, I took Smokey for a ride. He must have gotten lost, and here we are."

Phillip surprised her by not contradicting her words. "I'm glad you came. It's been a long time since you've stopped by. I've missed you." He closed the space between them. "Cassandra, can things ever return to the way they once were?"

"I–I don't think that's possible."

"It was possible enough for you to consider my marriage proposal."

"I only wanted to save the Triple P."

"I can pay off your loan as a wedding present, and I'll even consider staying here and not moving to Boston." He ran a finger down her cheek. "I can make you happy in ways of which you could only dream."

Fear crept up Cassandra's spine just like it had three years ago in the barn. She licked her lips, which had suddenly gone dry. "I–I'm sorry, Phillip. I should never have come here. I need to go."

"You can't. It's pouring rain, and we have so much to talk about."

"Talk? Yes, we can talk. About Ethan–Ethan Brigham."

A muscle rippled in Phillip's jaw. "What do you know about my cousin?"

"Ethan isn't your cousin. He's your older brother. And you're never going to believe who he is."

Tongues of firelight flickered on the side of Phillip's face. Cassandra blinked. How had she missed it? He and Matt *did* look like brothers.

"It's Matt Atkins," she blurted. "He's Harold and Margaret's firstborn son. The one they thought had died. Your Uncle Walter and Aunt Mary Helen adopted him before you were born. You never met him because he'd left Boston before you and your father went there for a visit."

Comprehension dawned on Phillip's face. "I thought he looked familiar the day he ran me off your ranch. There was a portrait of him in Uncle Walter's study. Only he was shaven and dressed like a gentleman."

His voice dropped to a whisper. "It makes perfect sense now. That's why he wanted a job at the Triple P. To spy on me.

And why you wouldn't accept my proposal. You two have been plotting all along to steal Lazy Acres out from under me."

A log cracked in the hearth, making Cassandra jump. Cold sweat trickled down the back of her neck. *I made a huge mistake. I've got to get out of here.* She started inching toward the door, but Phillip stepped in front of her and blocked the way.

"I don't want your ranch," she insisted. "I'm telling you the truth. I promise." She closed her eyes against the very words Matt had used that afternoon. She hadn't believed him. Could she expect anything more from Phillip?

She babbled on. "I'm sure you and Matt, I mean, Ethan, can work things out. Maybe he'll let you stay."

"Oh, yes. And maybe if I'm lucky, he'll let me clean his horse's stall." Phillip stepped closer and grabbed her by the shoulders.

Panic tightened like a noose around Cassandra's neck. With strength born of fear, she shoved Phillip with all her might. He stumbled backward with his mouth open in surprise and his hands clutching at air. His head hit the mantel with a cracking sound. The impact pitched him to the floor. Blood began pouring from the back of his head.

A scream died on Cassandra's lips. She tore from the house and ran for the barn. Smokey shied at his mistress's fright. She put a reassuring hand on his neck before yanking the reins loose and leaping onto his back. The horse needed no urging but galloped into the violent night.

Cassandra shut her eyes against the pelting rain and the horrible picture of Phillip's head hitting the mantelpiece. *Oh, God. I've killed him.*

She raced for what seemed like miles, trying to outrun the vision. Suddenly, Smokey's hooves gave way beneath them. Cassandra jerked on the reins, but it was too late. They tumbled into a large ravine. She heard a snapping sound before her head hit the ground. Then blackness rushed to meet her. Followed by total silence.

THIRTY-ONE

Matt paced the small enclosure of the bunkhouse. His cheek still stung from where Cassandra had slapped him. His heart ached from the anger in her eyes and voice as she ordered him off the ranch. Outside, the thunder rattled the windows and jagged bolts of lightning slashed the night sky.

He dropped to his knees. "God, I've been wrong. I've blamed you for my troubles and lied to people I cared about. Please forgive me. And while you're at it, please help Cassandra forget the hurt I've caused her. Otherwise, she may never trust another man—" He choked on his words. "And–And never trust her heart to love again."

The picture of Cassandra as another man's wife broke through Matt's last defense. Hot tears coursed down his face. Tears for his deception and tears for breaking the heart of the only woman he had ever truly loved.

A frantic banging on the bunkhouse door roused him to his feet. "Matt," Mrs. Pickett's voice rose above the pounding rain. "Cassandra is gone."

Matt sprinted across the floor, rubbing his hand across his eyes. When he opened the door, Mrs. Pickett stood there, her face lined with worry. "She must have taken Smokey for a ride. Carlos and Rafael are saddling the horses. Please. We must find her."

He groped for his boots and hat, strapped on his gun belt, and threw on a rain slicker. The vaqueros were waiting for him. He grabbed King's reins from Carlos and shouted directions. "Rafael, you head south toward the Diamond D. Carlos, you go east. Roberto, get over to the Fairfax ranch. I'll head toward Lazy Acres in case she headed that way."

Fear clutched Matt's heart as he jumped onto King's back. He clicked his tongue, and the big horse shot off into the night.

☆☆☆

The pain of a thousand needles pierced Cassandra's head. She raised a hand to an egg-sized lump on her forehead. She wasn't sure, but she thought she was bleeding. Shivering, she tried to clear her muddled mind. She remembered riding to Lazy Acres and following Phillip into the study—

The study. Bile rose in her mouth as she remembered the sound of Phillip's head striking the mantel, his blood, her flight from Lazy Acres, and the fall into—

"Smokey," she screamed. She fought the blackness that longed to draw her back into unconsciousness and crawled through the mud and the rain to her horse.

Smokey lifted his head a few inches off the ground. A grunt emanated from deep within his chest. Cassandra's fingers traveled over his body. When they touched his near front leg, a cry broke from her lips. His leg was broken.

"Oh, Smokey. What have I done to you?"

Great sobs wracked her body as she laid her horse's head in her lap. He sighed in pain, his breath warm against the skin of her arm. She couldn't let him suffer alone. She wept into his mane, her tears joining the pouring rain.

☆☆☆

Panic threatened Matt's sensibilities. Where in the world was Cassandra? "Lord, please help me find her." He used the jagged flashes of lightning to illuminate his way.

Was that a dark shape in the gully straight ahead?

He shouted into the night. "Cassandra, is that you?" King let out a high-pitched whinny, and Matt allowed his horse to lead the way.

At the head of the gully, another bolt of lightning sparked the sky and revealed the still forms of Cassandra and Smokey. Matt sprang from King's back, slipping twice before he reached her. He ripped off his slicker and used it to cover her shaking body before circling her with his arms and willing her his warmth and strength.

"Sm–Smokey. His front leg is broken. I–I couldn't leave him."

Matt ran his hand down Smokey's leg. *Oh, Lord. No.*

He picked up Cassandra and made his way back to King. He set her down beside his horse. "Take care of her, King. I'll be right back."

Matt freed his gun and trudged back through the rain and mud. He stooped down to pat Smokey one last time. "I'm sorry, old boy. I have to do this."

He took careful aim. A shot ripped the night. Smokey's suffering was over.

It seemed a hundred miles back to his horse. Matt lifted Cassandra onto the saddle and swung up behind her. Her head lolled back against his chest. He tightened his hold around her waist and gathered the reins. "Let's go home, King."

☆☆☆

Matt reined King to a halt in front of the Picketts' house. He slid off the horse's back and pulled Cassandra into his arms.

As he carried her up the porch steps, her groggy voice asked, "Are we home yet?"

"Yes, darlin'. We're home."

"Good." She closed her eyes and snuggled back against him. The shock of the night had taken its toll.

Matt smacked King's hindquarter, and the big horse trotted off to the barn. *Thank you, Lord, for a good horse and for letting me find Cassandra.*

The front door burst open. A worried-looking Mrs. Pickett and Maria rushed out. "Thank God you've found her." Helen stroked Cassandra's wet hair. "Is she all right?"

"She injured her head. I don't know how bad it is. Where should I put her?"

Helen led the way to Cassandra's bedroom with Maria close behind, murmuring grateful prayers in Spanish. After Matt carefully laid Cassandra on the bed, Maria nudged him aside.

"I will take over, Señor Matt. Please. Go find the men. They will be happy to know you found Miss Cassie." She removed Cassandra's boots and covered her with the quilt.

As Matt hurried down the porch steps, he tightened his rain slicker around his neck. He was heading to the barn when Carlos cantered up on his horse. "Señor Matt. I have not found Señorita Cassie. Has she come back?"

After assuring Carlos that Cassandra was in the house and in good hands, Matt instructed him to find Rafael and Roberto. With a wave, Carlos galloped back into the night. Matt made his way to the barn and found King nosing Smokey's stall. "I'm sorry, boy. He won't be back."

Matt pulled the saddle and pad off King's back and bowed his head against the horse. "Lord, please be with Cassandra," he prayed. King turned his neck and nuzzled Matt's arm.

By the time Matt finished grooming King, the vaqueros had returned, and the storm had exhausted itself to a drizzle, leaving behind a fuzzy crescent moon and crisp-smelling air. Matt went back into the house to check on Cassandra. Maria greeted him with a soft voice. "Miss Cassie has asked for you. Señora Pickett said her head is not so bad. But she needs her rest. You may not stay long."

Matt knocked on Cassandra's bedroom door and waited for Mrs. Pickett to grant him entrance. She looked up from her vigil. "Cassandra is fine. The cut is long but not deep."

Relief flooded Matt's soul.

Cassandra stirred. "Matt?"

He crossed over to the bed. "What is it, Cassandra?"

Her voice was weak. "I love you."

He slid a finger down her cheek. "I love you, too."

With a sigh, Cassandra drifted back to sleep.

☆☆☆

Dawn broke the next morning to reveal puddles of water, downed tree limbs, and a fallen rail off the corral. The sun made a feeble attempt to chase away the heap of gloomy clouds still covering the sky.

Cassandra's head throbbed with pain. She touched her forehead and moaned. Her mother's cool hand restrained her attempt to sit up. "Cassandra, please. Lie still."

As the force of last night's events returned, Cassandra buried her face in her hands. "I went for a ride and ended up at Lazy Acres. I told Phillip about Matt being his brother. He was furious. I was afraid he was going to hurt me, so I–I pushed him. His head hit the fireplace. Oh, Mama, I think I killed him."

Helen laid a damp cloth on Cassandra's forehead. "Hush. I doubt you killed him, or we would have heard something by now. But if it will set your mind at ease, I will send Carlos to Lazy Acres to find out." She crossed to the bedroom door and called out, "Maria. Come here, please, and hurry."

Maria's heavy tread ascended the stairs and stopped outside the door. Cassandra's hazy mind could not understand her mother's soft words, but it did make out Maria's louder and anxious ones. "Oh, no, Señora Pickett. I will tell Carlos immediately." Her footsteps retreated down the hall.

"Mama," Cassandra sat up and cried, "Matt had to shoot Smokey. It was my fault."

"Blaming yourself will not bring back your horse."

"Where's Smokey now?"

"The men took care of him."

"Is Matt still here?"

"He is downstairs. He has been worried about you. We all have been."

"Did he tell you the truth about who he is?"

Helen removed the cloth from Cassandra's forehead. "Yes."

"And?"

"I tend to believe him. I am not pleased with the way he went about it, but he did what he thought was necessary at the time."

"But how can I ever trust him again? Our whole relationship is based on lies."

"He lied about his background. I do not believe he lied about his feelings for you."

Cassandra's eyelids fluttered. Healing sleep beckoned. She sank back onto her pillow. Helen kissed Cassandra's cheek. "Sleep well, my darling. God will work everything out."

★★★

Matt paced the parlor, waiting for word about Cassandra. He rushed to Mrs. Pickett's side as soon as she entered the room. "How is she?"

"She will be fine in a day or two."

Matt's shoulders sagged in relief. "Thank the Lord."

Helen laid a hand on his arm. "Matt, we are all so grateful. Even Maria." Her concerned expression softened. "If you will excuse me, I am going to help her make a pot of soup. When Cassandra awakens, she will be hungry."

"May I see her?"

"It would be best to wait until later this afternoon."

Matt swallowed his disappointment but bowed to Mrs. Pickett's wishes. "All right. Maria told me about Phillip. Do you think he's dead?"

"Word travels fast out here. If he was, we would have heard about it, but I sent Carlos to check on him."

"I can't say I care for Phillip any more than the first day I met him, but he is my brother. I'd rather yank Lazy Acres out from under him than win the ranch by default."

Helen gave a sad shake of her head and left the parlor. Matt angled over to the window and watched Carlos gallop his horse toward Lazy Acres.

"Ethan?" Victoria hesitated before she entered the room. "How's Cassandra?"

"Mrs. Pickett assured me she will be fine within a few days."

"I'm glad." A moment of silence passed. "I'm to blame. I never should have come here."

Matt asked the questions that had nagged him since Victoria's arrival. "Whatever possessed you to come to Goose Neck Ridge in the first place? And how did you find me?"

Victoria's cheeks colored. "I lied about your father showing me the telegram. I'd gone to the manor to ask him of your whereabouts and saw it lying on his desk. It said you planned to get a ranch, so I assumed you were staying with your cousin, and he was helping you find a place of your own. I wanted you back and didn't care how I did it. I'm sorry I muddied the waters. It wasn't enough I ruined my life. Now, I've ruined yours too."

She dabbed her eyes with a lace-edged handkerchief. "The only thing I can do is return to Boston and rebuild my life. What's left of it."

"You're a beautiful woman, Victoria, and can be gracious when you want to be. Though Boston society has a long memory, they'll eventually find someone else to judge and forget about what you've done."

"You're a gentleman to the end, Ethan Brigham."

"When will you leave?"

"Mrs. Pickett invited me to stay for the noon meal. I think the housekeeper's pride initiated the invitation. To send me back on an empty stomach might ruin her reputation."

Matt returned Victoria's smile. "Will you excuse me? In my concern for Cassandra, I've neglected the chores."

"Can I watch?" Victoria asked in girlish excitement. "I've never seen a real cowboy in action."

Matt wanted to give a negative reply, but he figured he'd be finished before Cassandra woke up, and then he could see her. "All right, but you can't get in the way."

"I won't. I promise." Victoria hooked her hand in the crook of his arm. "Now, what shall we do first?"

☆☆☆

A woman' laughter awakened Cassandra. She swung her legs out of bed and struggled to stand. She had to wait for the room to stop spinning before she could toddle across the room and investigate.

Her heart lurched. Victoria shadowed Matt like an orphan calf. She giggled and commented while he nailed the loose rail back on the coral and then trimmed the sorrel gelding's hooves. Cassandra gritted her teeth when Matt led the horse back into the barn with Victoria following at his heels.

"Ooh, that man." Cassandra stomped over to the bed. A tap on the door kept her from throwing her pillow at the window. Helen cracked open the door and stuck her head inside the room. "May I come in?"

"Yes, Mama."

"I have good news. Phillip was hurt, but the doctor said he should be fine after a week's rest."

Cassandra's body sagged, and she closed her eyes in relief. Although she never wanted to see Phillip again, she was more than thankful he would recover. For his sake as well as her own.

"Do you think Matt will make Phillip leave Lazy Acres?" she asked.

"I do not know. Matt would run the ranch better than Phillip. He has a real love and feel for the land."

"He also has a way with the ladies. First, Elizabeth and now Victoria."

"I do not believe Matt fancies either of them. It is you he has been worried about."

"Ha. Worried I might make it, and then he'd have to juggle all three of us."

Helen patted the pillow. "You need to get more rest. After a nice nap, you will see things in a different light."

After Cassandra collapsed onto her pillow, Helen set Cassandra's Bible on the stand next to the bed. "You might want to read this before you fall asleep." She shut the door behind her with a soft click.

Cassandra flipped away from the stand. She closed her eyes and made a half-hearted promise to read the Bible after she woke up.

☆☆☆

Cassandra woke with a start. How long had she been asleep? A neigh and the crunch of wagon wheels drew her back to the now open window. Her mother or Maria must have come in while she was sleeping and opened it. She peeked out from behind the curtain and saw Matt leading Victoria's horse and buggy into the yard.

Rafael, Carlos, and Roberto removed their hats while Victoria hugged Helen's neck. Carlos mugged his best expression, and Roberto shook Victoria's hand, releasing it with apparent reluctance. The three vaqueros said good-bye and resumed their chores, leaving Victoria alone with Matt.

Cassandra struggled to hear Victoria's words. Did she say something about Boston and the stagecoach? Why didn't she speak up?

Victoria raised on her toes, laced her fingers around Matt's neck, and kissed him full on the mouth. Cassandra staggered from the window. Mama was wrong. Matt didn't care for her. He loved Victoria instead.

She struggled into her dressing gown and faltered down the stairs, squelching the nausea that threatened her. By the time she stumbled down the porch steps, Victoria was more than shouting distance away. Matt, unfortunately, was not.

He raced to Cassandra's side. "You should be in bed."

"And miss your little farewell scene?"

"Victoria told me to tell you goodbye."

"Are you sure she didn't say, 'I hope she dies'? I saw the two of you kissing while you thought I was tucked away in my bed."

Confusion carved a path on Matt's face. His eyes traveled to Cassandra's window. "You saw that? Then you must have seen me stop her as soon as she kissed me."

"That's not what it looked like to me." Cassandra was not about to admit that she might be mistaken.

"Please, Cassandra Jane. Last night you said you loved me. Why don't we talk about that instead?"

"If I said I loved you, I must have hit my head harder than I thought. I told you to leave yesterday, and I've not changed my mind."

"You don't mean that. You're still not feeling yourself."

"Not feeling myself? You're the one who passed yourself off as someone else."

"I tried to explain it to you."

"I'm not interested in any more of your lies."

"But what about the Triple P? I can help you save it."

"I'd rather marry Phillip than ask for your help." Cassandra's foggy mind grappled for an insult. "You– You, hired hand."

Her strength gone, Cassandra's knees buckled. Matt's arms shot out to catch her. She righted herself, then pushed away from him. "Don't touch me. Save that for your lady friend. If you hurry, the two of you can travel back to Boston together. You don't belong here, Ethan Matthew Brigham."

Matt blew out a breath. "As you wish." He turned around and for the second time in as many days, headed toward the bunkhouse and away from her.

Cassandra silently nursed her pride. *Good. The sooner he gets out of my life and off my ranch the better.*

⭑⭑⭑

Matt slammed the bunkhouse door. He threw his clothes into his bedroll and started jamming his few belongings into his saddlebag. *What now, Lord? What should I do, and where am I supposed to go?*

He mulled over the possibilities. Before he'd received Walter's letter, he had planned to go back to White Oak Manor, but now, he had no desire to return to Boston.

He scratched his head. Should he accept Big George's job offer? And if he did, what should he do with Lazy Acres?

The last two items he shoved in his saddlebag were a pocket knife and a small Bible, gifts from his parents before he'd left Boston. The knife had proved invaluable. Matt used it every day, but the Bible had seen little use until his arrival at the Triple P. Then Helen's strong faith and the Holy Spirit had urged him to reread its pages.

For the past month, he had wrestled with a verse in Romans chapter eight. The one Mrs. Pickett was so fond of sharing. *And we know that all things work together for good to them that love God.*

Fragments of his life drifted through his mind–a baby given a better life with Walter and Mary Helen, a man jilted by Victoria, the life of a cowhand, and the day he'd met Cassandra. As he pieced the fragments together, the veil lifted from his spiritual eyes.

"God, if your path led me here, I've gotta trust you to work everything out. Even with me and Cassandra Jane."

Matt picked up his bedroll, threw his saddlebag over his shoulder, and marched to the barn. He would honor Cassandra's demand to leave, but before he did, there was something he had to do.

Thirty-Two

Four days after Cassandra's accident, a solitary figure used the cloak of night to dismount a short distance from the Lazy Acres hacienda. He hid his horse behind a clump of mesquite trees and made sure the compound was empty before sneaking over to the house. He was glad the night was cloudy and blocked the moon. No one would see him.

He tiptoed up the porch stairs and paused to listen. Except for the chirp of crickets and the lowing of nearby cattle, all was silent. He fished a knife out from his pocket and used it to pry open the lock. The door creaked open. The man froze. He listened for a moment before creeping inside to the lingering scent of cinnamon.

That dog probably had dessert after supper. Hope he enjoyed it. It'll be his last.

With determined grit, the man inched up the hallway to the study, keeping the tread of his boots light as he crossed over to the desk. He forced open the top drawer on the right and scooped out its contents, which contained several legal documents and a stack of money. He shoved the money inside his shirt and retrieved a match from his back pocket. After striking the match on the fireplace, he touched the flame to the documents and used them to set the curtains ablaze. The flames leapt up the fabric and reached for the ceiling. The man circled the room, torching anything that would burn. Satisfied, he tossed the remnant of the documents on the floor and fled the house.

He vaulted onto the back of his horse and wheeled the animal around to admire his handiwork. Smoke snaked out from under the front door and joined the eerie orange glow emanating from the window of the study.

"I could have killed ya in your sleep, but that'd been too easy. Now, you can suffer before goin' to the devil where you belong."

The man collected the reins of his horse and galloped away from Lazy Acres into the dark of the night.

☆☆☆

Phillip woke from a nightmare. Satan had hurled him into the dark pits of hell. Crackling flames filled his ears, and the acrid smell of smoke burned his eyes and stung his nostrils.

I must be dreaming.

He blinked to rid the vision, but his eyes still burned. He sprang from his bed. It was no dream. The house was on fire. Thick smoke enveloped the room, and flames curled around the doorframe. Phillip covered his mouth with his nightshirt and struggled to keep from succumbing to the fire and his fear.

The smoke was not as thick near the floor, so he dropped to his hands and knees and crawled toward the window. He skirted a nightstand and found, to his great relief, that the window was open. Clutching the sill, he pulled himself up and over. With a groan he landed in a heap on the other side.

"Señor Brigham," Antonio called out. The vaquero ran to Phillip and dragged him away from the burning house.

The Lazy Acres vaqueros yelled in Spanish and scurried like ants as they lined shoulder-to-shoulder and passed buckets of water pumped from the well.

But it was a battle they could not win. Phillip watched in horror as one section of the house after another burst into flames. Within minutes, the entire hacienda was engulfed, and the heat forced the men to retreat. The roof caved in with a mournful groan before the woodwork of the walls succumbed, leaving a huge, crumbled shell where the house once stood. After the vaqueros made sure none of the surrounding buildings were in danger, they each expressed their sympathy to Phillip and returned to their homes.

Antonio was the last to approach Phillip. "Señor Brigham, I am sorry. Me and Camelia do not own a fine home, but you are welcome to stay with us tonight. In the morning, you can decide what to do."

Dazed, Phillip stared at the house in which he'd been born and reared. It was gone.

"Please, Señor Brigham. Come with me." Antonio circled his arm around Phillip's waist and slowly led him away.

☆☆☆

As though God showed him mercy, Phillip slept a dreamless sleep the remainder of the night. He awoke the next morning with a raw throat and a raspy voice. He gratefully accepted the cold cup of water Camelia offered and a change of clothes from Antonio. The vaquero volunteered to see what remained of the house, but Phillip waved him off. "I must do this myself."

With a broken heart, Phillip staggered to the ruins of his home–black and stark against the clear, blue sky. Here and there, fingers of smoke curled skyward contributing to the caustic smell, while pieces of charred wood crunched under his feet.

Phillip rummaged through the ashes and searched for anything of value, but everything he owned, other than a smattering of kitchen implements and other metal objects, was either gone or lay twisted or distorted. He found his way to where his bedroom once stood.

"Señor Brigham, I am so sorry." Juanita's soft voice interrupted Phillip's search.

She stood on the outskirts of the ruined house, clutching the two dolls they had played with on the porch. Tears traced down her cheeks as she ran into Phillip's outstretched arms. He hugged the girl to his chest and stroked her hair. His eyes stung and for the first time since his sister had died, Phillip wept.

Juanita sniffed and patted his cheek. "Do not cry. We will build a new house. Much bigger and better than this one. I can help. I am very strong." She displayed the small muscle of her upper arm.

Phillip tested the bicep with a finger. "Yes, my little Juanita. You are. Much stronger than I am."

"Oh, no. That is not true. You are the strongest man I know. One day, when I am a grown-up lady, I wish to marry a man as strong and handsome as you."

Pain seared Phillip's heart. If a man such as himself even approached Juanita, he would kill him with his bare hands.

Juanita freed herself from Phillip's arms and kicked through the ashes. Soot rose in the air, making her sneeze. She watched him sift the rubble before veering off to a skeletal place between the walls.

"Señor Brigham," she called. "I have found something."

Phillip pried out a charred metal box that had escaped the fire's destruction. Inside lay a diary written in his mother's hand. He turned to the first page, being careful not to destroy the brittle paper that was singed on its edges.

August 13, 1863
I love Manuel, but why is God so cruel as to have us both married to another? I know he cares for Rosa, but I own his heart.

Phillip's mind floundered. His mother had been in love with Juanita's father? His gaze followed the young girl, who was busy searching through the debris. He read on.

I am with Manuel's child. I know it is his as my marriage to Harold has been in name only for many months.

His mother had not only loved Manuel but had also been pregnant with his child? Phillip rechecked the date of the entry. It had been written eight months before his birth. Could it be? With a sinking heart he continued reading.

I will go to Harold in the way of a woman tonight. He will consider this child his and the heir to the Brigham name and wealth of Lazy Acres. I pray Manuel will forgive this betrayal, but he knows we can never be together as man and wife. I hope it will bring him comfort that if I bear a son, I will name him Phillip after his beloved grandfather.

Phillip groaned. He was the baby. Now he understood why his mother had claimed he was premature. He riffled through the next pages, caring not if they crumbled. He came to an entry written a year later.

August 21, 1864
Though God has given me another son, I cannot forget the one who died two years ago in Boston. I love Phillip, but every time I see his face, it makes me long for the child I lost.

Tears blurred Phillip's vision as the diary fell from his hands. He dropped to his knees, gripping his sides. Cassandra had been right. The baby his mother thought had died was Matt Atkins, the son of Harold Brigham, the true heir of Lazy Acres and his half-brother. Phillip had lost everything. His home, his birthright, and even his identity. Everything was gone.

"I asked you not to cry." Juanita's voice was determined. "If that little book makes you so unhappy, and you have thrown it on the ground, I will help you get rid of it."

She picked up the diary and tore the pages to bits. Tiny scraps of paper fluttered to the blackened ground. "There, you do not have to be sad anymore." Her voice remained self-assured. "Things may not look good, but Mamacita says if we have each other and the God of heaven, we are very rich."

Phillip contemplated his half-sister's innocent words. He groaned under the weight of the wicked things he'd done. All of his motives had been selfish and his will only his own. Words spoken to him as a child about a God of love and mercy returned. Were those words still true? Could he ever be forgiven?

There amidst the ruins of his life, Phillip bowed his head and asked God to forgive him and make him worthy of his new sister's love. When he opened his eyes, a thousand rays of sunshine lit Juanita's face. "It is good you prayed. God is happy when his children talk to him. We are all part of God's family. But since you no longer have one, you can be part of mine."

Phillip scooped the girl into his arms. "Yes, my darling Juanita. What if I become your big brother, and you, my little sister?"

She hugged his neck. "That would be *muy bueno*. Let us go tell Mamacita. She will be most pleased."

"I'll return you to your home, but we will tell Mamacita the good news later. Right now, I must take Sunny for a ride. I have not ridden him since I was hurt. Both of us need some exercise."

Juanita touched the bandage on the back of Phillip's head. "You should not ride so soon after you slipped and fell," she admonished. "As your new sister, my job is to take care of you."

He squeezed her to his chest. "I appreciate your concern, but I will ride Sunny at a walk and come find you the moment I return."

"I still do not like it. But since you have promised to come see me when you get back, you may go."

Phillip held Juanita's hand as he led her to one of the tiny cabins dotting the Lazy Acres property. He waved off Rosa's concern and made his way to the stables. His head pounded, and he knew he should find a bed and lie down, but no rest would come until he rode to the Triple P and confronted Cassandra.

THIRTY-THREE

Since the day Matt had ridden out of her life, remorse had replaced the cold spaces in Cassandra's heart. And even though she'd asked God to forgive her anger and the consequences of it, she doubted she'd ever find happiness again. Other than doing her chores and taking a quick trip into town to see Mr. Brewer and Mr. Harvey, she had stayed in her bedroom, read her Bible, and prayed.

On the fifth day of her seclusion, Helen entered Cassandra's bedroom to find her staring out the window. "Darling, you have got to stop this. You must get on with your life." She nudged Cassandra away from the window.

"Oh, Mama, I never should have let Matt go."

"You did tell him to leave. Despite what you think, Matt Atkins is an honorable man."

Cassandra chewed her knuckle. "Why didn't you ask him to stay?"

"You are the one who overstepped your boundaries, but I chose not to interfere. The two of you had played with fire since the day he set foot on this ranch. Though I still believe God had a purpose for allowing him to come here."

"He did give me the idea to build a sawmill." A quiver of excitement edged Cassandra's voice in spite of her melancholy. "Mr. Brewer said the B & P sawmill will be operational by fall, and Mr. Harvey's finalized the contract with the S & R Railroad for us to supply beef to the crewmen laying the new track. When Mr. Higgins found out, he bent over backward to cancel our foreclosure and extend the loan. But you had a part in that, didn't you, Mama?"

"I am grateful for my friendship with Mildred. She demanded William beseech the board of directors on our behalf."

"I'm sure Mrs. Higgins didn't mind. I think she enjoys telling her husband what to do."

"You are probably right."

"Poor Mr. Higgins. To think I wished a pox upon his house."

"Cassandra Jane, whatever am I going to do with you?" Helen's voice was teasing. "Since the ranch is no longer in danger, I will spend the extra time praying for you."

"I appreciate that, but lately I've been doing a lot of praying on my own." Her face sobered. "You're right. It's my fault Matt left, but I've asked God to forgive me. I wish I could ask Matt's forgiveness as well."

"You could send a letter to him at White Oak Manor."

"I'm sure Miss Garrett would be none too thrilled about that."

"Matt might not have left with her. Alicia Lawson has been wrong before."

"Nothing gets by Alicia. She said a handsome cowboy joined a silver-haired woman on the eastbound stagecoach and tied a big, brown horse behind the coach. Who else but Matt?"

"I pray he will find happiness."

Tears tinged Cassandra's lashes. Matt did deserve a happy life, even if that life included Victoria Garrett instead of her. She crossed the room and resumed staring out of the window. A movement on the horizon caught her eye. She squinted to get a better look.

"Mama," her voice quickened. "Someone's coming. Oh, Lord. Please, let it be Matt."

With her heart in her throat, she rushed downstairs and out the front door. She shielded her eyes against the morning sun. If the rider was Matt, why was he astride a light-colored horse? What happened to King?

As the horse and rider drew closer, fear tightened Cassandra's chest. The rider wasn't Matt. It was Phillip. "Mama. Quick. Get the rifle."

Helen fled inside and returned with the Winchester. Cassandra lifted the rifle to her shoulder, willing her knees not to buckle. Relief flooded her at the sound of galloping hooves. Carlos and Rafael must have seen Phillip's approach as well. Two separate clicks proved the men had cocked their guns and must be aiming them at Phillip.

Time idled as the four awaited the palomino's leisure approach. Cassandra wiped a trickle of sweat from her nose but kept the rifle trained on Phillip. *He can see we're armed. Why doesn't he turn tail and leave while he has a chance?*

Phillip reined his horse to a stop in front of the group. He crossed his hands over the saddle horn and said in a surprisingly calm voice. "Greetings. Hasn't God made a lovely day?"

Cassandra's mind reeled. Had Phillip just spoken pleasantries, and about the Lord, no less?

Her mother broke the awkward silence. "I am sorry we appear less than hospitable, Phillip, but you must recognize our concern."

"Oh, I do, Mrs. Pickett."

Cassandra exchanged glances with her mother. "Wh–What do you want?"

"I've come to make amends, especially with you, Cassandra. I've been a fool. I don't know why the Lord spared my life last night, but I deserve both your anger and his. He's forgiven me. Now, I'm asking your forgiveness as well."

"Spared your life? My forgiveness?"

He flipped up the edges of his coat. "I'm unarmed. May I dismount?"

Helen used a hand to lower Cassandra's rifle and called off Carlos and Rafael. The two men holstered their weapons. "Yes, you can," she said. "I am sorry for our lack of hospitality."

"But Mama," Cassandra protested.

"You can see he is unarmed."

When Phillip swung down from the saddle, Cassandra retreated a step.

"It's all right, Cassandra. I won't hurt you. I deserved what you did." He touched the back of his bandaged head. "And now my house is gone. A fire destroyed it last night. It's only by the grace of God that I escaped."

Despite her misgivings, pity washed over Cassandra. "I'm sorry. Were you able to save anything?"

This time, Phillip's smile reached his eyes, and the transformation was miraculous. The hard edges that had marred the corners of his eyes and mouth vanished along with the scowl that had dipped his brows.

"Just one thing," he replied. "A long-forgotten diary, but now even that's gone. But God saved a far more important thing–my everlasting soul. That's why I'm here. I wanted to tell you and your mother how sorry I am for trying to get my hands on the Triple P. I also need to speak with Ethan. Is he around?"

Cassandra bit her bottom lip before replying. "Matt's gone."

"Gone? Where to?"

"We think he went back to Boston," Helen interjected.

"Splendid. After I move there with my new little sister and her mother, I can visit him at White Oak Manor and make things right between us."

"You and Matt, I mean, Ethan, have a sister?" Cassandra asked.

"No. Juanita is my half-sister by my father, Manuel López. I found a diary my mother had written in the remains of my house. It revealed Ethan as my half-brother through her. I am not Harold Brigham's son, so I no longer hold claim to Lazy Acres. Ethan is the true heir."

His eyes begged absolution from Cassandra. "I had hoped to move to Boston with you as my bride. Can you ever forgive my behavior?"

"I'm–I'm not sure."

"Maybe one day you will." He eased a foot in the stirrup. "I wish Ethan had stayed. I don't know what will happen to the vaqueros when I move to Boston. They will be out of work and lose their homes. If Ethan had stayed, I would have asked him to let them keep their jobs."

Rafael cleared his throat. "Uh, Señor Brigham. Señor Matt did not go back to Boston."

"What?" Cassandra shoved the rifle into her mother's hands and rushed over to Rafael. "Where is he?"

"He made me promise not to tell."

Cassandra grabbed Rafael by his collar. "If you don't tell me this instant, you'll be seeking work with Phillip's vaqueros." She ignored her mother's gasp. "Tell me."

"Señor Matt is staying at the cabin on Cedar Ridge. He said he could not leave until he knew you would be all right."

"The cabin?"

"Sí."

"I'm taking Black Jack." Cassandra vaulted onto the black horse's back, slapped him with the reins, and galloped straight for Cedar Ridge.

⋆⋆⋆

Over her shoulder, Cassandra saw Phillip's horse gaining ground. Black Jack could never outrun Sunny. She reined the horse to a trot, and Phillip easily caught up to her side.

Though Phillip did seem different, Cassandra fought the inclination to trust him. She knew she should forgive others as Christ had forgiven her, but how could she pardon Phillip after all he had done?

"I hope you don't mind my coming," he said. "I need to sort things out with Ethan. Do you think he'll understand?"

Cassandra doubted Matt would. She didn't understand everything herself. She breathed in the tangy scent of cedar. "I love Cedar Ridge. Before Papa won this land—"

Why did I go and say that? The last thing I need is for Phillip to get angry about his bet with Papa.

"Don't worry," Phillip reassured her. "It was my fault I lost it. My father, I mean, Harold, did the right thing by willing the ranch to Matt. I don't deserve it."

"Don't talk like that. You're the reason Lazy Acres prospered after your father died. He loved you," she said. "And he bragged about you to Papa and voiced regret he'd never sent you to an eastern university."

"He did?"

"Yes, though Papa didn't talk much about you after what happened in the b—" Cassandra bit her bottom lip. Would she ever learn to control her tongue?

Phillip grabbed Black Jack's bridle and reined Sunny to an abrupt halt. Fear sent tremors up Cassandra's spine. "I'm sorry. I shouldn't have brought that up."

"I'm glad you did." Phillip released his grip on the bridle. "It gives me a chance to ask your forgiveness for that as well. I'm sorry, Cassandra. I'll go to my grave with many regrets, but what happened that day will be the worst."

Leather creaked as Cassandra shifted in the saddle. She silently quoted a verse she'd memorized since Matt left. *Forgetting those things, which are behind, and reaching forth unto those things which are before.*

It was time to forget the past and concentrate on her future. Her future with Matt. If he'd forgive her. But first, she needed to forgive Phillip.

"Well," Cassandra replied, "if God can forgive the foolish things I've done, I'm sure I can do the same for you."

Phillip flashed a smile, and she wondered how different their lives might have been.

Pine needles muted the horses' hooves as they picked their way up the canyon. When they neared the top, Cassandra saw smoke drifting from the chimney and King eating hay in a small corral next to the cabin. Her heartbeat quickened. Matt must be there. She urged Black Jack to pick up his pace.

Cassandra and Phillip were reining in their horses when the cabin door burst open. Matt rushed out in bare feet with his gun aimed at Phillip. "Cassandra. Are you all right? Hurry up. Come over here."

Cassandra jumped down from her horse and dashed over to him. "I'm fine. Phillip just wants to talk to you."

The muscle in Matt's jaw twitched as he slipped a hand through his unkempt hair. Even wearing wrinkled clothing and a nearly week-old beard, Cassandra thought he was the most handsome man on earth.

Matt kept his gun pointed at Phillip. "What do you want?"

Phillip revealed he was unarmed before he dismounted.

"Get back on your horse," Matt demanded. "You can say whatever you have to from up there.

"It's all right," Cassandra said. "He's perfectly safe."

Matt's eyes questioned hers, but he relaxed the grip on his pistol. Phillip looped the two horses' reins over a crossbar of the corral. King pinned back his ears and bared his teeth at the newcomers but then resumed eating.

"Who told you I was here?" Matt directed his question at Phillip.

Cassandra butted in. "I made Rafael tell me."

"Why am I not surprised, boss lady?"

"I deserve that. I let pride and jealousy cloud my reasoning. I'm sorry."

"So, you believe me now?"

"Yes. Especially in light of what Phillip told me."

"And what is that?"

She pointed to his gun. "If you'd be so kind as to put that thing away and ask us in, we'll tell you."

Matt motioned for them to enter the cabin but held up a hand to stop Cassandra before she passed by. "How's your head?" His voice held concern.

"It's fine. The wound has scarred over." She gave him a nudge. "I'm glad you dropped the cowboy twang. I like your eastern accent better."

Cassandra had not stepped foot inside the cabin since her father had died. Not much had changed other than King's saddle sitting in the middle of the floor and two flannel shirts strewn on the unmade bed. Water from the hand pump dripped into a metal bucket, and a simmering pot of beans filled the cabin with a warm, spicy smell.

Matt grabbed his saddlebag and gun belt off the back of two chairs so Cassandra and Phillip could sit down. He straddled a chair across from Phillip. "All right," he said as he holstered his gun. "Out with it."

While Phillip retold his story, Cassandra studied Matt's face. He occasionally quirked an eyebrow but otherwise remained silent. After Phillip told him about the fire, Matt finally spoke up. "Do you know how it happened?"

"No. It was too warm to light the fireplaces that night."

"Did someone deliberately set it?"

"I don't know. Though, at first, I thought you might have. Dumb idea, huh? You wouldn't burn down your own house."

Matt returned Phillip's smile, and Cassandra sent up a quick prayer, asking the Lord to reconcile the two brothers.

When Phillip recounted the entries in his mother's diary, Matt expressed regret. "I'm sorry. I had no idea. I guess both of our birth parents surprised us."

"It turned out to be a blessing," Phillip said. "I never wanted to be a cattle baron and run Lazy Acres. Even as a child I preferred raiding Father's, I mean, Harold's library over branding cattle and visiting feedlots in search of more cattle. I guess it wasn't in my blood." He gave a wry smile. "But I have gained a little sister. Her name is Juanita. Plus, now you get the ranch without having to chase me out of town."

The two men exchanged laughter, and Cassandra nervously giggled. *So far, so good.*

"And there I stood," Phillip said, "lamenting my loss, and my sweet, new sister said if I had God and people who loved me, I was a rich man."

"Phillip made things right with the Lord," Cassandra exclaimed. She covered her mouth at her outspoken revelation.

Matt shook his head in amusement "What should we do about her?"

"Does this mean you forgive me?" Phillip's eyes lightened with hope.

"You never did anything to hurt me. I didn't like your treatment of Cassandra, but I've done a mess of things I'm ashamed of too." His look was bashful as he put a warm hand over hers. "If Cassandra Jane can forgive you, so can I."

Phillip sprang from his chair and shook the hand Matt offered.

"Thank you, Lord," Cassandra whispered.

Matt beckoned for her. Tears of joy sprang into her eyes as she leapt up and raced into his and Phillip's embrace.

"So," Matt said to Phillip, "looks like we both have decisions to make. Do you know what you're going to do?"

"I plan to move to Boston with Juanita and her—"

Outside the cabin, the sharp report of a pistol split the air. A bullet ripped through the window, shattering the glass and missing the trio by inches. Matt shielded Cassandra with his body, then pushed her to the floor.

"Get under the bed," he yelled, grabbing his sidearm. When she hesitated, he shouted, "Do as I say."

Cassandra dropped onto her hands and knees and crawled across the floor. She squeezed under the bed but poked her head back out. Matt crouched on his heels and crab-walked to the window. Phillip followed suit but flanked the window's other side.

"Can you see anyone?" Matt yelled to Phillip.

"No, but there's a horse tied by that grove of trees."

A man's voice called out. "Hey, Atkins. I recognized that hoss of yours. Well, ain't this just dandy? Now I can get the two of ya for the price of one."

Phillip's face blanched. "It's Jack Dalton."

THIRTY-FOUR

"Who in the heck is Jack Dalton?" Matt demanded, his mind grappling for a way to save all three of them.

Phillip's eyes flicked shut. "I hired him to dig up information after you showed up at the Triple P. He threatened retribution when he felt I didn't pay him enough. I'm sorry."

"There's been enough apologizing for one day. Let's find out why he's here." Matt hollered out the window, "Hey, Dalton, what do you want?"

"I'm here to finish off Brigham since the fire I set didn't get him. What a nice surprise to find you here too. Now I can kill both of ya."

"You don't stand a chance." Phillip hollered back. "There's three of us and only one of you."

"Makes no never mind to me. I know you and that redhead ain't packin'. I trailed the two of you up here from the Pickett place."

"Mama!" A scream tore from Cassandra's lips. She crawled out from under the bed on her elbows.

Matt waved her back. "Mrs. Pickett better be all right." His finger twitched on the trigger of his pistol. If Dalton would clear cover, he'd shoot him and be done with it.

"Don't hold no grudge with her. But I'll enjoy that pretty little daughter of hers after I'm through killin' the two of you."

Matt squinted at a movement in the bushes. He could just make out the dark outline of a hat. He took aim and fired. Dalton's body jerked up and fell backward before the bushes reclaimed him.

Phillip collapsed against the wall. "I think you got him."

"Can't be sure. Stay here. I'll go check."

Cassandra wiggled out from under the bed and rushed to Matt's side. "No. I won't let you."

He gripped her shoulders. "I'll be all right. Phillip, take care of her."

But before Phillip could reply, Jack Dalton burst through the cabin door with blood dripping from his left shoulder. He fired his gun at Matt.

Cassandra screamed. She charged Jack and flailed his chest with her fists. Phillip shoved her away as a second shot exploded from Jack's gun. A stunned look crossed Phillip's face before he crumpled to the floor.

Another gunshot ripped the air. Jack reeled backward. Matt had shot him dead-square in the chest.

☆☆☆

Cassandra's prayer was desperate. *God, let them be all right. Please, God. Let them be all right.* She rushed over to Matt, who was struggling to balance himself on his elbow, his smoking gun still aimed at Jack. "Your leg," she cried. Blood trickled from a wound in Matt's upper thigh.

"It just grazed me." He waved her away. "Check on Phillip."

A scarlet pool was spreading underneath Phillip. Sobbing, Cassandra struggled to turn him onto his back. She cradled his head in her lap as blood began to bubble from the side of his mouth.

Matt hobbled over and knelt beside her. "Hang on," he said, stroking Phillip's hair. "We'll get help."

Phillip coughed, spraying blood on the front of Cassandra's blouse. She held him and rocked back and forth. "Please, Phillip, please. Please don't die."

Phillip's eyes fluttered as he tried to focus on Matt. "It's–It's too late," he wheezed. "Ethan… promise me…"

Matt's voice pleaded. "It's not too late. Don't give up."

"I'm not afraid." Phillip's hand trembled as he weakly grabbed the front of Matt's shirt. "Promise me… Please take care of Juanita. Promise."

Through his tears, Matt said, "From this day forward, she is my sister."

Phillip's hand fell to his side. With his last breath, he whispered, "I am glad… I–I found out you are my brother." His head lolled back on Cassandra's lap, and his sightless eyes stared at the ceiling.

Matt closed Phillip's eyelids with trembling fingers. "I am, too, my brother. I am, too."

☆☆☆

Matt and Cassandra returned Phillip's body to Lazy Acres. Juanita clung to her mother as Matt explained to Rosa what had happened and promised to care for them for the rest of their lives.

The following morning under a gray, leaden sky the Pickett household, along with the Lazy Acres vaqueros and their families, attended Phillip's funeral. They buried him on a knoll overlooking Goose Neck Creek next to Harold and Margaret Brigham and his infant sister.

Dark storm clouds heaped the sky as Matt delivered a touching eulogy. He extolled Phillip's love for his family and his desire to do what was right in the end. Matt's voice choked with emotion as he offered a final prayer and thanked God for Phillip's entrance into the Kingdom. The black thunderheads opened up, and the heavens wept with the mourners, drenching them and the land they all loved.

☆☆☆

A week later Cassandra returned with Matt and Juanita to Phillip's gravesite. After Matt placed a wooden cross at the head of the grave, Juanita read the words he'd carved with trembling lips. "Ph–Phillip Nathaniel Brigham–Died August 1887–Beloved brother of Ethan and Juanita."

Matt scooped the young girl up to his chest. She sniffed back her tears and wrapped her thin brown arms around his neck. "It will be all right, little one," he assured, giving her a hug.

Cassandra watched the exchange with a heart full of love. Matt would make a wonderful big brother, and Juanita already adored him.

She patted the mound of Phillip's grave. "Adiós, my dear, old friend," she whispered. "May you find peace with God."

As she and Matt returned Juanita to her home, Cassandra considered the girl's future. Between Matt's resourcefulness and the Brigham fortune, she would lack for nothing. She would grow up to be a fine young lady. Phillip would have been pleased.

Back at the barn, they settled the horses in their stalls. "I keep forgetting to call you Ethan instead of Matt," Cassandra said.

"You can still call me Matt. Any name you say will sound sweet to my ears."

"I like the name Ethan. It's a new name for a new beginning. And I'm glad you're taking over Lazy Acres instead of returning to Boston." She gave him a shy look. "Mainly because we're going to be neighbors, but also because the vaqueros can now keep their jobs."

"The ranch has been in my family for generations. I could do no less." His face glowed with pride. "And after I canceled the timber contract with Big George, he convinced the railroad to offer one to you and your mother. B & P Mill will have more business than it can handle." He reached for her hand. "Come on. Let's go inside."

Cassandra allowed Matt to guide her by the elbow into the parlor. "Ethan Brigham, whatever are you doing?"

"Don't go asking a lot of questions. For once in your life, please be quiet."

"I can keep quiet. Well... Every now and again."

He touched her lips with a fingertip. "Shh. Now, be a good girl and close your eyes."

She squeezed her eyes shut, but it took great restraint not to peek.

"All right," he said. "You can open them."

Her pearl necklace dangled from his fingers.

"Oh, Matt," she cried, forgetting to call him Ethan. She snatched the necklace from him. "How did you get it? Mr. Higgins said he sold our jewelry to a—" She searched his face. "That wealthy gentleman was you, wasn't it?"

Matt's face colored. "He promised not to tell you about it, but he was only too eager to sell the jewelry back to me at above market value. That man needs to work on his scruples."

"He means well."

"That remains to be seen. I bought the jewelry with part of the money Walter wired to me. I had wanted you and your mother to use it to start a lumber mill, but since you'd already talked to Mr. Brewer, I decided to let that play out." He gave her a mischievous grin. "Especially since I know how much you like being in charge. If it hadn't worked out though, I planned to either pay off your loan or buy the Triple P when it went on auction and give it back to you and your mother."

"That's a mighty grand gesture, but you know I wouldn't have let you."

He tweaked the end of her nose. "I know, you stubborn Irish wench, but one way or another, I was not going to let you lose the Triple P." He captured her hands in his. "I am proud of you though for coming up with the idea for a lumber mill."

"I did get it from you." She jabbed his chest with her finger. "How would you like to run Lazy Acres *and* be the foreman of a lumber mill?"

"Would you still be my boss?"

"Of course. I have to keep my eye on you, hired hand."

His twinkling eyes belied his frown. "If that's the case, you've got yourself a foreman."

"Good. Let's go tell Mama about the jewelry. She'll be thrilled."

"She was." Matt sat on the divan and pulled Cassandra down beside him. "And she was happy to run everyone out of the house at my request."

"I was wondering why Maria hadn't bustled in and pretended to dust the furniture or open a window. Why did you want everyone to leave?" Her heart beat faster in her chest.

"Remember I said I'd search until I found the right place to call home?"

"Y–Yes."

"And the next time I proposed to you I would do it right?"

Cassandra's second affirmation caught in her throat.

Matt reached behind the divan, dropped to one knee, and presented her a bouquet of yellow roses tipped in pink. Cassandra breathed in the scent of the roses before looking into the sky-blue eyes of the man she loved with all of her heart.

"After I left Boston," Matt said. "I didn't think I'd find another place to call home. But God showed me home isn't the place you live. It's the place within your heart. From the first moment I saw you, I was home. You own my heart, Cassandra. Every part of it."

He stroked the inside of her wrist with his thumb, just as he had the day they'd met. And just as it had then, a quiver danced up Cassandra's back.

Matt's voice was husky. "Will you marry me? Not for the sake of the Triple P, but because I love you." He rushed on. "We can build a house on the border of our two properties and start all over. Please, Cassandra. Say yes."

"Oh, Matt. Yes. Yes. A thousand times. Yes."

Cassandra's heart took wing as Matt drew her into his arms. His lips sought hers, and this time her thoughts were safe and only of him. Papa had been right. God did lead the man she was to marry. Right to her doorstep.

Several long moments later, Matt pulled away from her and said, "I have something else for you."

"I don't need anything else. I have everything I want."

"Come on. One more thing. Close your eyes."

Cassandra complied. What else could he possibly give her?

"You can look now."

Her eyes fluttered open. In his palm lay her ivory comb.

"Oh, Matt. I wasn't sure what happened to it. Why didn't you return it sooner?"

"I wanted to wait until the perfect time. That time is now."

She reached for the comb, but he halted her hand.

"Please. Let me."

She shivered as he gently swept back the sides of her hair and secured them with the comb. He pushed a wisp of hair behind her ear. "I've dreamed of doing that since the day I bought it."

Cassandra's fingers trembled as she touched the comb. "Thank you," she whispered.

"You know what? You did show me you could run a ranch and still be a lady. And you, Cassandra Jane," his warm breath caressed her brow, "are all lady."

As Matt gathered her back into his arms, his lips found hers once again. Cassandra's heart overflowed with love and the promise his kiss held. A promise of a new beginning and a love to last a lifetime.

THE END

ABOUT THE AUTHOR

As far back as she can remember, Janine Mick Wills has loved the Lord and the written word. A former pastor's wife, she now resides in South Carolina, where she heads the ladies' ministry at her church and fills every spare minute writing for the glory of God. Janine considers a Child of the King to be her most important title, but she also enjoys being called a wife, a mom, and a mamaw to seven grandchildren. Janine would love to connect with her readers. You can find her at any of these locations:

Visit her Web site at
www.janinemickwills.com

Like and follow her on Facebook at
Janine Mick Wills - Writing for the Glory of God

Follow her on Pinterest at
https://www.pinterest.com/janinemickwills/boards/

Follow her on Twitter at
https://twitter.com/MickJanine

Here's a sneak peek at ***Juanita and the Outlaw****,*
the second book in the ***Texas Treasures*** *series,*
coming Fall 2019 from Journey Fiction.

"Do you think we could start over?" She held out her hand. "My name is Carmen Juanita López, but I am called Juanita. I am most delighted to meet you."

Pete enveloped her hand in his large one. Juanita could feel the warmth of it through her glove.

"My name's Peter Daniel Murphy, and it is I who am honored to meet you."

"Peter? May I ask why you go by the name of Pete?"

His back straightened, as though her question had upset him. She was quick with her apology. "I am sorry. I can see that is a personal question. I will call you Pete if you like."

"Juanita, where are you?" Reginald's voice carried over the distance to where Pete and Juanita stood. "Are you out here?"

Juanita ducked into the grape arbor. "Oh, no. It is Reginald."

"I thought you were to marry Mr. Davenport."

"That was—" Juanita was about to say, *until I met you*, but caught the words before they escaped her lips. Pete Murphy probably thought her brazen enough already.

"You don't want his company?" Pete asked.

"No. I do not."

He grabbed her hand. "Then come with me." He pulled her farther into the night and in the direction of the stables.

TAKE A TRIP THROUGH TIME WITH JOURNEY FICTION

A Worthy Suitor

by Jennifer AlLee

Reluctant socialite Gwendolyn Banks is happier in the woods surrounding Tuxedo Park than attending the vibrant parties hosted there. But after stumbling upon accomplished archer Albert Taylor, she reconsiders her life of solitude.

The Counterfeit Clue

by Lisa Karon Richardson

When Gemma Gaines sees her friend killed in a hit-and-run, all her instincts tell her it was no accident. With the doggedness of the great Girl Detective herself, and the help of a handsome new neighbor – who may be more than he seems – she's soon on the trail of a counterfeiting ring that would like nothing more than to put her out of circulation for good.

The Case of the Clobbered Cad

by Debra E. Marvin

Heather Munro is determined to excel at the University of Edinburgh but finding the corpse of a visiting professor in the Archives room is more than just a distraction. As clues come to light, it's clear someone wants to frame Heather. With the help of her quirky landlady and a quiet, Scottish historian she hopes she can trust, Heather sets out to prove her innocence and find the murderer.

22458030R00225

Printed in Great Britain
by Amazon